SNAFU

...• DEAD OR ALIVE • •.

Edited by Amanda J Spedding & Geoff Brown

COHESION PRESS

Mayday Hills Asylum
Beechworth, Australia
2022

SNAFU: DEAD OR ALIVE
Amanda J Spedding & Geoff Brown (eds)

* ••*

Cohesion Press
Mayday Hills Asylum
Beechworth, Australia
www.cohesionpress.com

Also From Cohesion Press

SNAFU: An Anthology of Military Horror
– eds Geoff Brown & Amanda J Spedding

SNAFU: Wolves at the Door
– eds Geoff Brown & Amanda J Spedding

SNAFU: Survival of the Fittest
– eds Geoff Brown & Amanda J Spedding

SNAFU: Hunters
– eds Amanda J Spedding & Geoff Brown

SNAFU: Future Warfare
– eds Amanda J Spedding & Geoff Brown

SNAFU: Unnatural Selection
– eds Amanda J Spedding & Geoff Brown

SNAFU: Black Ops
– eds Amanda J Spedding & Geoff Brown

SNAFU: Resurrection
– eds Amanda J Spedding, Matthew Summers & Geoff Brown

SNAFU: Last Stand
– eds Amanda J Spedding, Matthew Summers & Geoff Brown

SNAFU: Medivac
– eds Amanda J Spedding & Geoff Brown

Love, Death and Robots: The Official Anthology Vol 1
– eds Amanda J Spedding & Geoff Brown

SNAFU: Holy War
– eds Amanda J Spedding & Geoff Brown

Love, Death and Robots: The Official Anthology Vol 2/3
– eds Amanda J Spedding & Geoff Brown

WANTED
DEAD OR ALIVE

AIN'T NO GRAVE

Justin Coates

The Hangman's wolves came for the posse when it was a mile shy of Rifle Road. Jeb McKannon, the town cunning, riding near the head of the dozen-strong patrol, was the first to notice them. His veins turned dark blue, witchfire lighting his eyes as he pointed a trembling finger to the boulder-strewn quarry to the north.

"Ware!"

It was the only warning the posse received, and one that came far too late. The wolves broke from cover, rising from all fours to lope forward on their hind legs. Their howls drowned out the hasty shouts of men drawing their rifles and pistols.

Sheriff Stanton Creed unsheathed his old cavalry saber as he galloped up to ride beside McKannon. "Hit 'em, McKannon! Don't wait for a goddamn invitation!"

The cunning took a deep breath, then screamed. Creed shielded his face as witchfire poured from McKannon's eyes and mouth and down the length of his arm. A bolt of multicolored light hit one of the werewolves mid-charge, peeling fur and flesh from the towering monstrosity, leaving it a writhing, yelping mass of skinned gristle and pulsing black organs.

Creed whooped a congratulations to the skittish little sorcerer. McKannon grinned at him, then swelled, mouth opening soundlessly, eyes bulging before disappearing in rolls of skin that sloughed from his forehead. Dark magic burst him like a dropped watermelon, showering Creed in blood and loops of intestines. Creed's horse, Blackjack, screamed and reared. A lifetime of riding kept the sheriff in the saddle. The black death mandalas on his saber spun and vibrated, the red smears of blood on the blade waking the hateful enchantments.

In his days as a dragoon, riding out from the walled town of Gunhollow to hunt the monstrous things that lurked in the Rocky Mountains, such an ambush would've been swiftly countered. The cavalry would've disengaged, and the infantry would've seen off their attackers with disciplined volleys of warded .30-.30 fire until the mounted men could charge back in. As it was, the posse dispatched from the small settlement of Sweetwater to apprehend the Hangman had no infantry, and of the twelve brave men deputized just for this occasion, only Creed had any combat experience.

The wolves tore through them.

Their wyrdcaster, a goliath cloaked in human skins, swung a bone staff in one hand and a rusted meat cleaver in the other. The cleaver took a horse's head off at the neck, and the unlight blazing from the staff popped another rider like it had McKannon. Creed kicked in his spurs, and Blackjack took off, eyes rolling, flecks of foam splashing back onto the sheriff's arms.

"Hai, Blackjack!" Creed shouted. "Gunhollow! Gunhollow, and the Wasteland Gods!"

His blade took the wyrdcaster on the wrist. The death mandalas shrieked. The saber carved through unnatural flesh and bone with a burst of crackling red light. Blackjack screamed as one of the wolves sank its claws into his flanks. The war horse kicked, staggering the abomination, giving Creed time to twist in the saddle and ram his blade up into the wyrdcaster's throat. Steaming gore ran down his arm, scalding his flesh.

Creed didn't see the wolf that gutted Blackjack. His mount went out from under him, tackled at shoulder height. The old creature managed to stay upright just long enough for Creed to roll free. He came to his feet as a wall of red fur and snapping jaws came at him. His sturdy .40 caliber dragoon pistol thundered as he lurched away from the charging werewolf. The thing collapsed a foot away from him, but there was another bearing down, and then he was out of ammunition, his saber flashing in the hot Colorado sun.

He saw Doc Merriweather pulled from his saddle and ripped

apart. Two wolves fought over the half-eaten corpse of Matthew DeLeon, the town postman. Violent smears of bone and gore covered the mountain soil; it was impossible to tell who they were, if they were once men or horse or something worse.

The sheriff took another wolf with his blade, slicing off its muzzle, then plunging the saber through its putrid heart in a spray of blood before the wyrdcaster finally caught up to him. Its cleaver took Creed on the right shoulder, nearly carving off his limb and driving down into his lungs. It kicked him to his knees, forcing him to look up into its rabid black eyes. Its breath was the blast of a furnace, stinking like spoiled meat.

"You smell like piss and fear, boy," it said. "I'll tear out your heart, and bring it to the Hangman's altar."

Creed spat bloody gobbets on its apron of human flesh. "Hope he chokes on it."

The werewolf laughed, gripped the cleaver, then froze. It cocked its head to the side, looking for all the world like a hound trying to make out some strange noise in the wood line.

Its head exploded as thunder barreled down the canyon. Freezing winds cast rimes of frost in Creed's spilled blood. Storm clouds rolled across the sun, and, from the south side, a black rider came upon a fire-belching horse the color of bleached bone. The flames from its nostrils consumed the lycanthropes, and the massive wheelguns in the rider's hands put down any that tried to flee.

Creed collapsed, his will and his body finally spent. He saw the rider gallop over to him, its gigantic revolvers billowing black smoke and whispering terrible secrets. The thing that stared down at him was not human, or at least hadn't been for a long, long time. It holstered one pistol, and withdrew a rusted handbell from inside its worn leather duster. As the blackness claimed Creed, he remembered the words his grandmother had sung for him as a child.

Oh, Death... won't you spare me over for another year?

* * *

He was back at the cabin on the outskirts of the Denver ruins. Kneeling, this time, with chains around his neck and wrists. He'd been mounted before; riding high on Blackjack, saber in one hand and wheelgun in the other. Powerful, young, free. How long ago had that been? *Decades, seems like.*

Something terrible loomed over him. He could feel it watching, for all it did was watch, with ten thousand eyes staring from ten thousand wings. He did not meet its gaze. Its voice alone made him weep tears of blood.

"It's merely a request for parole, Your Honor." The black rider, the dead man who rode a dead horse, stood beside him. One bony hand rested on Creed's shoulder as he spoke to the nightmare all around them. *"This one here has intimate knowledge of the land, and was killed attempting to apprehend the outlaw soul in question."*

Inside the cabin, a woman screamed. A man pled for his life. For both their lives.

"Please, we had nowhere else to go, please, don't—" Creed's whisper barely passed cracked lips. It was so hot, and he was dying of thirst. He was bone dry, a husk of gristle on the trail, a bleached buffalo skull gleaming in the sun.

"I will take personal responsibility for his time topside, Your Honor."

Two shots, point blank range inside the cabin, followed by a feverish whisper.

"...shouldn't have been here, we told you to leave, we—"

He was so hot, and so thirsty, because he was burning. All of him, his flesh and his eyes and his tongue and teeth, burning, alight with flames that had waited an eternity for his company. He tried to scream, but his mouth filled with ash and gravedirt.

"I'm much obliged, and humbled by your trust. We'll have the Hangman back in custody soon." The bony hand on his shoulder squeezed, and Creed heard the sound of a rusting bell. *"Hang on tight, compadre. It's a bumpy ride back."*

• ••

The giant buzzard perched on Creed's chest fluttered free the moment the dead sheriff sat up. He wheezed for air he no longer needed, the dead meat of his heart already too necrotic to pump in panic. He scrambled to his feet, but the black rider was already there, hauling him up and dusting him off.

"Right as rain, Sheriff." The dead man's voice was the rasp of a coffin lid, pushed open from within. "Here. This'll put the sting of life back in you." He pressed a jug into Creed's hand, then helped it to his lips. "Corn liquor. Cure for all our ailments. Go on."

The firewater burned down his gullet, settling heavy somewhere lower in his abdomen than it should have. He gasped from it, eyes watering. He wiped away tears with a swollen, blue-black hand. "You... you raised me, specter."

The dead man took a pull of his own. "That was more the Warden's work, compadre, but I won't mind taking credit for arguing your case." He tapped a rusted badge on his rotting duster. "Name's Hellmarshal Jubal Anderson. Sent forth by the Warden of the 666th Gate, to apprehend the wayward soul of the Reverend Ezekiel Keene. I suppose you wouldn't much mind helping me in that task."

Creed put a hand to his head. It was close to night, the sun setting fast in the west. They were still on the battlefield where he'd died, and the corpses of men and horses lay rotting around them. "You suppose right, Hellmarshal." Creed gestured at the killing fields around them. "But that's what they dispatched my posse to do. Look what came of it. His wolves are far stronger and more numerous than we expected."

The huge vulture landed on Creed's shoulder. It turned its scabbed, bald head to the side, peering at him with milky white eyes. "Their mouths are full of lies and deceit," the buzzard rasped. "I shall also choose their delusions, and bring their fears upon them."

Creed shuddered. Talking beasts were common in the Wastes, but they were almost always malevolent witches or their familiars. If the thing noticed his discomfort, it gave no sign, instead immediately setting up preening its rotting black wings. *Vast wings, full of eyes and swords, staring at him, seeing him, knowing and judging his every failure...*

Creed stumbled. Anderson caught him by the arms. The dead sheriff coughed out a cloud of dust and ashes.

"Don't think about it," Anderson rasped. "Perdition, or the Warden.

Eventually, parole is up, and the fire calls us home. It ain't meant for mortal minds to ken."

Creed regained his composure. Anderson's cadaverous smile was not without sympathy, though a fat black beetle did crawl out from one of the rotting pits where a tooth had been.

"I'll help you bring in the Hangman," Creed said. "As part of my... parole."

"Vengeance is mine," the bird said. "Their doom cometh swiftly."

Anderson clapped Creed on the shoulder. "First things first, compadre." He walked to the corpse of Blackjack, and held out his bone bell. "We need to get you your mount."

• •●

They rode through the night, out into the deeper Wastes. The bird, whom Anderson called Hades, kept pace with them, backlit by the scarred face of the moons. Creed never once saw the buzzard flap its tattered wings. Blackjack seemed not to notice his undead state, or, if he did, seemed to take it all in stride despite the loops of intestine dangling from his split belly. Creed tried to emulate his destrier's nonchalant attitude.

Hades lit on a lightning-struck tree trunk overlooking the lowlands. Anderson pulled hard on the reins of his mount, a massive zombie brute that exhaled cinders through its mouth. "Whoa, Abaddon. Easy." Plastic tubing plunged in and out of its bloated body, connected to glass boxes full of bubbling green liquid on its haunches. The monster pawed at the grass, which seemed to wither and die beneath its bleeding hooves.

"I can smell him, somewhere down there," Anderson said. "But can't place a trail."

6

"He's been plaguing these lands since before I was born," Creed said. "You've had all this time and you still haven't found him?"

"We weren't actually sure where or when he'd turned up. I spent a whole five years looking for him, a decade from now on the wrong side of the world."

Creed raised his looking glass to one eye, scanning the creek beds and trails between the thick copses of aspen trees. There was a thin trickle of blue smoke rising from one of the trailheads leading deeper into the Rocky Mountains. "Our scouts reported he'd moved to the town of Khard Bower at the foot of Godfall Pass," he said. "We'd hoped to draw him out rather than confront him in the town itself. The folk there are wicked."

Hades spread his wings, claws tapping on the scorched tree. "They hath built high places in Tophet, and burned their sons and daughters in flames to Moloch: which I commanded them not, neither hath it come into my heart."

"Something like that," Creed said. "They buy slaves from one of the confederate freeholds to the north of the Wastelands. None are ever seen again."

"If we know where he is, we can bring him in." The black rider clicked his teeth. Abaddon snorted, a blast of ashes and cinders spilling past the maggots wriggling in its snout.

"You got a plan, Hellmarshal?"

"'Course," Anderson replied. "Go in shooting."

* * *

The trail down to Khard Bower took them to the very mouth of Godfall Pass. Something had fallen from Heaven long ago, in the war that broke the world: a devil or a god machine, whose glistening bones still rose higher than the black peaks around them. Khard Bower stood at the foot of the great wound in the mountainside. Dark and smoke-filled, its scrap walls were lined with barbed wire and the corpses of the ritually sacrificed. The sound of industry, metal against metal and the shriek of steam engines, came from within.

Creed spat, and made a warding gesture. "A town of lost souls."

"So are most towns," Anderson said, swaying back and forth on his mount. "And most souls."

"Not like Khard Bower."

The Hellmarshal shrugged. "Maybe not. Still, hard times make weak men. In fear, we turn to anything that offers us power, no matter the price."

"What about that thing in Perdition? The Warden?"

Anderson's laugh turned to a coughing fit. He spat a gobbet of maggot-choked phlegm to the earth. "Salvation is the Warden's business, compadre, not power. For souls like Keene, there's no greater punishment."

The gate to Khard Bower stood open. Men and women daubed in garish war paint clutched ancient firearms and fire-hardened spears. Creed kept his eyes forward, following Anderson's casual lead. Hades squawked from its perch on Abaddon's shoulder, and preened its feathers. There was only one real road in the town, dusty and dry beneath the high noon sun. Men and women adorned in jewels and precious silks watched from balconies, attended by slaves who shuffled about in silver and brass chains. Gallows stood in the town square, strewn with body parts before a terrible scrap effigy that hurt Creed's eyes to look upon. He remembered the wyrdcaster werewolf that had killed him.

I'll tear out your heart, and bring it to the Hangman's altar.

Anderson stopped at a saloon with the words 'Dripping Bucket' painted on its side. Creed went to tie his horse, but the Hellmarshal stopped him. "He won't go nowhere. He's tied to me for calling him back, and can't wander far. Besides..." He winked, eye sticky with filth. "We'll need their help later."

Creed looked at Blackjack, then down at his skeletal hands. Bone was beginning to show through the bruised, purple tissue. Soon he'd be as cadaverous as Anderson. He wondered if he, too, was tied to the Hellmarshal, strung along at the end of an invisible rope.

AIN'T NO GRAVE

From his perch on Abaddon's neck, Hades looked down at him, and squawked in a language Creed didn't know. "Eloi, Eloi, lama sabachthani?"

The inside of the saloon was given over to a dance floor on one side and tables on the other. Trail breakers and teamsters laughed and ate and drank. Whores moved among them, their faces painted, the bells on their slave collars tinkling with each fake laugh. Two boys, their own collars bright and clean against filthy, unwashed flesh, swept the floor. Creed's gut twisted in disgust. The Wastelands were a harsh place, but the gods who ruled it weren't without pity. There was no place for slaves and masters, even in such a broken world.

Anderson leaned over the bar. Creed kept watch from the corner of his eye, aware that more than a few patrons had taken notice of them from behind their card games and drinking jugs.

"One shot of whiskey for myself," Anderson wheezed. "And one for my friend."

The bartender, a stout man with vivid scars running down the center of his forehead, started at the dead man's voice. He looked them both over, then reached for a jug of whisky and two clean glasses.

Anderson filled them both, and offered one to Creed. "For the living," Anderson said, tossing the shot back.

The barman's eyes flickered from the sheriff back to the Hellmarshal as they set their cups on the bar.

"I'm here on business, compadre," Anderson said conspiratorially. "Mayhap you can help me find what I'm looking for."

"I'm eager to have you gone, specter," the bartender said. Sweat ran down his pale, puffy cheeks. "But I confess, I fear to give offense."

"You've already given plenty of offense, slaver," Creed said, louder and angrier than he'd intended.

Anderson chuckled low in his throat. The bartender paled. "We're here for the Hangman."

Silence fell. Then a dozen chairs scraped against hardwood floors as men ended their card games and stood. Anderson turned, smiling, lazing back against the bar. Creed's hand drifted toward his holster. His saber, sensing violence, warmed in its sheath across his thigh. The slaves quickly scattered.

"You gentlemen look like the sort who knows where we can find him," Anderson said. "Why don't you tell us where he is?"

"What business do you have with the Lord?" The speaker was a towering brute, easily six and a half feet tall, with lank blonde hair that fell over his face. "If you wish to meet him, I can take you to his altar myself."

Anderson laughed. "It'd be better if he just came on out."

"The Hangman is at work for his people. His thoughts are turned toward us, always, as he seeks to remake the world destroyed by our degenerate forebears. What are your intentions toward him, stranger?"

"Oh," the Hellmarshal said. "We aim to kill him today."

Then his guns were up and firing, each bullet screaming like souls in torment. The brute's head vaporized in a shower of blood and bone shards. What came next was a blur of claws and teeth and shaggy fur. Six of the men burst out of their skin and clothes, shifting into towering lycanthropes, their shed flesh falling like steaming cloaks behind them.

Creed cleared leather before they'd taken a single step forward. His dragoon pistol roared in the enclosed space. The runes on each cylinder hissed curses as they rotated through the chamber. One of the wolves went down, three smoking holes in its chest spreading a web of necrotized tissue. Another lunged for him, but Anderson caught it in crossfire, his brutal hand cannons hollowing out its torso and blasting its foul organs over fleeing patrons.

Creed drew his sword. There was something different about the death mandalas on the blade; something crueler, more vicious. Black arcs of lightning danced on the killing edge as he slashed it against a lycanthrope trying to come to grips with the Hellmarshal. Smoke and ashes poured from the wound rather than clotted blood. The wolf shrieked and ran, clutching its wounded arm and diving out of the window.

Claws plunged deep into Creed's torso. There was a moment

of weightlessness, and then he crashed down onto the tables. He rolled back to his feet, the wound painless, his undead body oozing green ichor from the punctures. The wolf that had caught him howled, lowering its head to rush him like a bull. The impact hurled Creed through the wall, the wolf's arms wrapping around him and bearing him down to the ground outside. He hammered its eye with the pommel of his saber. The monster yowled, rearing back, clutching at the blood that squirted in a foul, stinking river.

Blackjack was there a moment later. The horse opened its mouth impossibly wide, blunt teeth meant for hay and grass growing sharp like fangs. Those terrible jaws closed around the wolf's head, savaging it, pulling the beast off Creed and dragging it back out into the street. The sheriff stumbled to his feet, grasping for a speedloader and snapping six .40 caliber rounds back into place. The wolf's screams were cut off by the wet snap of severed bone. Its head and neck hung out of Blackjack's mouth. The horse's eyes rolled back white, and it reared, front legs pawing the air.

Rifle and scattergun fire snapped and boomed around him. Creed took cover on the saloon porch, heedless of the ongoing conflict inside as cultists took potshots at him from across the street. He returned fire. Two men, with strange, jeweled piercings were punched off their feet. Hades swooped at one of them, black talons and yellow beak shredding eyes and lips.

"He that stealeth a man, or selleth him, shall surely be put to death!" A second head, and then a third, burst from Hades' neck. The demon bird grew, swelling in size, its taloned feet growing in length until it towered, raptor like, as tall as the buildings around it. "I am the Lord your God!" Lightning burst from its beaks, incinerating panicked slave owners as they desperately tried to flee.

Anderson stomped out of the bar, eyes alight with fervor. "Come on," he grunted, jerking his head toward the town square. "He's close. I can feel it."

Creed followed. The souls of the dead, still lingering near their Earthly bodies, screamed and cowered at the whirling mandalas on his blade. Pistol high, he watched the alleys and corners, calmly putting down the handful of vagrants lunatic enough to charge at them. Hades continued his rampage, tearing down the slavehouse with great, raking sweeps of his massive wings.

"Quite the bird," Creed said.

Anderson grinned over his shoulder. "He's actually a Hittite prince. Damn handsome, too, before the Warden turned him into a shit-eating vulture on account of his sins."

Creed had no idea what a Hittite was, and the sudden burst of fire from the gallows didn't give him time to ask. Desperate to protect their altar and effigy, more cultists and slavers had clambered up onto the platform. A hail of poorly-aimed bullets, spears, and lead darts filled the air. Anderson took a spear to the chest, ripped it out, and kept going. Creed felt a bullet zip out the back of his skull, taking most of his scalp with it. It tingled. Nothing more. In response, the two undead gunmen raised their pistols, firing as they advanced, methodical and cold and unstoppable as the grave.

The return fire stopped as the last cultist died. Blood and gore dripped from the rotting boards of the gallows. Strange imps grew from the congealing vitae beneath the platform, scuttling about on all fours, tittering and glaring out at Creed and Anderson with fathomless black eyes.

"Keene!" the Hellmarshal shouted.

Behind them, still busy destroying the slaver dwellings, Hades mimicked the cry.

"Keene! Ezekiel Keene!"

"I call you to account, Keene! By the innocent blood you've shed, and by the authority of the Warden of the 666th Gate, the Watcher Kasrial, Who Purifies By The Sword!"

The effigy burst into flames.

Something moved inside it; vast and terrible, coalescing down into a shadow shaped like a man. The stale, sluggish blood in Creed's veins ran colder.

"Hello, Jubal," the shadow said, stepping out of the fire. The corpses on the platform jerked at the sound of its voice.

AIN'T NO GRAVE

The things beneath the platform shrieked in fear, scampering out into the light of day before seeking shelter in nearby alleys. "Took you long enough."

Anderson raised his pistol. Creed followed suit. The monster his people called the Hangman, who was worshipped as the Reverend Ezekiel Keene by the cultists and werewolves of Khard Bower, stared back, unimpressed. He was nude, save for a silver circlet on his brow that glistened in the sunlight. His muscles looked powerful enough to tear one of his own werewolves apart. He was, Creed realized, incredibly beautiful; bewitching, almost, in confidence, in power, in sheer animal charisma.

"I am about important business, Jubal." The corpses around the Hangman began to contort. Their bones bent and twisted, snapping, breaking, bursting from their flesh to form hooks and talons. "And it's a long ride from Perdition."

"Your business has tacked on eons to your sentence," Anderson said. "Though if you come willingly, the Warden may have mercy."

"And leave my flock?" He raised his arms. For a moment, he was no longer beautiful: just another bloated corpse in a whitewashed tomb, a thousand petty fears hidden behind grandiose lies meant to give purpose and keep the darkness at bay. The beauty and power were a lie, but a damn convincing one. "You've come to the end of the river road. Now's the time; lay down your load."

The twisted corpses sprang from the platform. Creed fired, but the devilry animating them was of hardier stuff than the werewolves. One of them clambered up to him, shrieking, its ribcage forming a gaping maw that snapped inches away from his face. He lunged back, then slashed his saber from shoulder to groin, bisecting it in a steaming spray of reeking shit and gore. Two more came for him, their claws rising and falling, punching through the rotted flesh of his chest, grappling with his arms, forcing him back, gnawing with blunt teeth on his sword hand.

Blackjack and Abaddon thundered into the melee. The undead horses whinnied and screamed, the flames bursting from their nostrils reducing the Hangman's puppets to stinking meat. Creed swung himself up into the saddle, his booted foot kicking the head of a flaming corpse clean off.

Anderson was atop Abaddon a moment later, the great black war horse roaring rather than neighing. "It makes no difference, Ezekiel. Run and hide or stand and fight. Salvation comes all the same."

The Keene-thing grinned so wide the flesh of its face burst, revealing three rows of teeth lining a maw that stretched from ear to ear. "You should've stayed in Hell, Jubal."

And then he was running, swelling like Hades had, into a nightmarish miasma of swirling bones and screaming faces. Anderson shouted and kicked in his spurs. Creed followed, Blackjack snorting and trampling the charred remnants of the corpses beneath them to ash.

Lightning fell, and the sun turned red. Keene's spiritual form cursed the souls it passed as it swarmed away from the Hellmarshal and the sheriff. Worshippers fell down before it, screaming praise. It flayed the flesh from their bodies all the same, hurling them back at the pursuing riders like cannon shot. Creed pulled hard on Blackjack's reins, ducking low to avoid being knocked from the saddle.

Keene's face resolved in the miasmatic cloud, leering at them. "I won't be judged by anyone, Jubal. Not by the Warden, and certainly not by you."

That leer turned to a snarl as Hades crashed through a nearby building, wading into the unliving storm. The bird demon screamed, lightning arcing from its beaks. The cloud scattered, reformed, then enveloped the towering entity. The sound of armies clashing in the desert, armed with bronze spears and shields, mingled with the shouts of men-at-arms standing in a gun line, their volleys tearing through flesh and bone.

Hades fell first. The strange creature was suddenly a vulture again, hurtling to the ground and into a nearby building, out of sight. Even as it fell, the miasma returned to a human shape: a man, clothed in bandages that dangled from his sutured skin, staring at them from soulless pits where his eyes should've been. It raised its hands. A wall of dust rose from the cursed soil of Khard Bower. Creed threw up his arm to shield his face. Blackjack reared, shuddering, and no training in the world was enough to keep Creed in the saddle.

• •*

He's back at the cabin on the outskirts of the Denver ruins. Kneeling, this time. He'd been mounted before; riding high on Blackjack, saber in one hand and wheelgun in the other. Powerful, young, free. How long ago had that been? Decades, seems like.

Something terrible loomed over him. The Reverend Ezekiel Keene, the Hangman, watched Creed's own memory alongside him. "You were a mercenary, yes?" the demon god asked. "In your youth. Employed to run out ranch squatters and water thieves."

Inside the cabin, a woman screams. A man pleads for their lives.

Creed's cracked lips parted. "Don't do it." His past-self did not listen.

Keene looked down at him. "Why not? You were paid to kill them, for the crime of stealing water. More importantly, they weren't powerful enough to stop you."

"They were thirsty." *He's in the cabin, standing over them. Nothing more than vagrants; a man and a woman, half-alive beneath rags. The Wastelands are a terrible place to live.* "They only wanted to live."

"All animals want to live." Keene knelt beside Creed. "And that's what the weak are: animals, for us to use and consume."

He raises the pistol, watching the man cover the woman with his body, hand stretched out as if to ward off the evil that was coming.

"The Warden wants to enslave us. Anderson thinks being its dog will help him atone for Wounded Knee. He doesn't understand that we don't *need* to atone. Gods like us shouldn't suffer in Purgatory until our tears drown our pride." He put a hand made of shadow on Creed's shoulder. "Khard Bower is mine. Its people are my slaves. Worship me. Embrace the power within you, and rise above a slave's notion of good and evil."

Creed closed his eyes. The cries of the water thieves fell silent as he turned, the weapon aimed at Keene as he squeezed the trigger.

The vision burst around him. The gunshot wound in Keene's chest burned with oily smoke. The liche snarled, lunging forward, but Anderson was already there, ramming his pistols into Keene's chest and emptying the cylinders. Wings sprouted from Keene's back as the dead thing tried to flee, but Hades was there, descending from the sky, claws outstretched to rake its face and eyes. Anderson reloaded, but Keene was growing again, his limbs stretching and swelling even as flecks of red sand danced around him like motes of dust.

Creed's saber was in his hand. He raised it high, letting the death mandalas glare in the light of the sun, then brought it down across Keene's neck. The blade bit deep. Creed ripped it free in a spray of coagulated gore, then drove forward, skewering Keene to the hilt.

Anderson gripped the convulsing dead man by the shoulders and hurled him to the ground. His spurs jangled as he planted one boot firmly on Keene's ribs. A cigar dangled from his lips. He lit it with a wisp of hellfire on his thumb, then reached into his pocket and withdrew the bone bell. "Quite the run, Ezekiel. You'd have gone farther if you weren't such a damned prideful fool."

The instrument rang loud as a church bell. Chains burst from the cursed soil of Khard Bower. Each link glowed white hot, and each echoed with the voices of Keene's victims. They twisted around him, binding him tight, crawling and singeing his necrotic flesh.

"Close your eyes, compadre," Anderson advised. "This part ain't pleasant."

The Warden came up through the earth, holding the chains in fists made of scorched brass. Creed fell forward, pressing his face into the dust.

Keene screamed. "I'm sorry! I can't go back! Please, give me more time, I can't—!"

The Warden spoke.

Even with his eyes screwed shut, and his hands to his ears, the fury of its words battered and tore at Creed. It was the sound of a bonesaw carving off a gangrenous limb, of merciless redemption that could not be bargained with or escaped.

"Saved," Anderson said, his voice not untouched with awe. "As through fire."

• •

The destruction of Khard Bower didn't go unnoticed. It was only a day or so before minutemen and rangers came up from Gunhollow, following the billowing black smoke of the ruined city. The fire spread swiftly, consuming the petty manses of the slavers. Whatever treasures their former slaves hadn't carried off were reduced to molten slag.

Creed watched them from atop Blackjack. The horse needlessly grazed on grass stalks growing up through the rocks of Godfall Pass. Below him, the men and women he once considered compatriots combed through the smoldering ruins, attempting to make sense of what had happened. Above and behind him was the Pass, the canyon walls smooth and polished as glass from the heat of the ancient titan's descent.

Anderson was there as well, though his gaze was fixed on Creed. "Getting late," the revenant said. "We best leave them to it."

"Is that what's waiting for me?" Creed asked, still looking back. "Chains, and fire?"

Anderson nodded. "Waiting for most of us, compadre. One way or the other, we drink the shot we poured in life."

He offered Creed the jug of corn liquor. The dead sheriff clutched it with skeletal fingers, staring down into its murky depths. "The cure for what ails you," he muttered before taking a long pull.

Anderson laughed, then clicked his tongue. Abaddon turned, and Blackjack followed, snorting softly.

Creed took one last look east, then followed the Hellmarshal toward the next bounty.

HIDEBEHIND

Josh Reynolds

Kemper woke instantly. His hand emerged from his coat, the Colt single action cocked and his index finger on the trigger. Quillen froze, a tight grin splitting the thicket of black beard that covered everything below his nose. "Easy, Pink," the bounty hunter said, with a nervous chuckle. "Ain't fixing to rob you. Just wanted to wake you up, is all."

"I'm awake," Kemper said, slowly, still half lost to sleep. He'd dreamt of pursuit, of something out of the corner of his eye, darting after him like a fish through the shadows of his mind's eye. He couldn't get away, no matter how fast he ran. Whatever it was, it never revealed itself, but it was always there.

"My mistake. Guess they was right, Pinkertons never sleep." Quillen retreated, hands raised. New risen sunlight painted tiger stripes across the clearing where they'd made camp. But the night still held fast beneath the trees. It never went very far, up in these hills. Kemper remembered his momma talking about how the night was always waiting for you to dawdle, then it would swoop in and swallow you up when you least expected it.

Kemper lowered the Colt's hammer and took his finger off the trigger. "You can lower your hands. If I wanted to shoot you, I would've done it already." He looked around the camp, taking it all in at a glance. Scattered bedrolls and blankets. Davis, red-faced and sweaty despite the cool, perched on a log, cleaning his rifle. Eugene cutting a swat of chaw and plumping it in his cheek. McMeekin pissing in the bushes near the river. Locke, the oldest of them, had stoked the fire, and there was coffee brewing.

The air was cool and mild, but felt wet to the touch. Red spruce clustered thick about them, and Kemper felt a familiar chill as he came to his feet. He'd left the mountains as a boy, but they'd never left him, not way down deep in the pit of his soul. Much as he'd hoped otherwise, the Appalachians held tight to those born in their shadow.

"An' if we wanted to cut your throat, we'd have sure as hell done it before we come up into the hills," Quillen said with a laugh. He looked at Locke and the others. "Ain't that right, boys?"

"Leave us out of it, Quillen," Locke said. He was older and weathered, with the lean look of a man used to hard riding through bad country. Grisly scar-tissue from an interrupted scalping covered part of his head – a memento of his time out west, he claimed. Locke had fought Indians before he'd decided hunting white men was more profitable. Easier too, from the way he told it.

"We got to be hospitable, Locke. Can't have the Pink thinking we don't care for his company, can we?" Quillen grinned at Kemper as he said it.

Kemper wasn't sure whether Quillen meant what he said, or whether he was trying to cause trouble. Maybe Quillen didn't know himself. It didn't much matter, in any event. Once the job was done, he never had to see the man again. He didn't have to see anyone, if he didn't want to. Part of him thought that might be for the best. He looked around. The trees seemed as unfriendly as ever.

According to his momma, God rest her soul, there was a haint for every five feet of dirt in the hills, and worse besides. He'd seen enough bad since coming down out of the holler to know that haints were the least of a man's worries, but even so, he didn't like being back in the mountains. When this was done, he intended to request a transfer to one of the new offices in Illinois, maybe Chicago or Peoria. Somewhere with no mountains or trees to intrude on his dreams. A spell in some flat emptiness would be balm for his soul.

Kemper holstered his pistol and went to pour himself a cup of coffee. The bounty hunters were the best the agency could afford, or so he'd been told. Locke seemed competent enough, and had worked for the agency before, but Quillen and the others were little better than the saddle trash they were hired to bring in. Eugene was all hat and no trousers; Davis was a drunk, and McMeekin had a reputation for backshooting. Quillen was the worst, because word was, he was on a few wanted posters himself, out west.

All of them were armed to the teeth; knives, pistols, rifles and God alone knew what else. Whatever his opinion of them, they all seemed to know their way around a shooting iron and have no qualms about gunplay, which was the only real benefit to their presence.

Kemper crouched in front of the fire beside Locke. The older man gave him a lazy look and offered him a scrap of jerky. "What do you think?" Kemper asked. He was ostensibly in charge, being the agent in question. But mostly he deferred to Locke. It was Locke who kept the others in line, and kept the posse moving.

"We should be there this afternoon, depending," Locke said. Kemper nodded, took a bite of jerky and washed it down with a swallow of scalding coffee. Locke continued. "They ain't going to give this fellow up easy. You know that, right?"

"I know." Kemper gnawed on the jerky. The agency had been hired by Ackroyd Timber to handle a labor dispute at a logging camp way up in the high timber of the Appalachians. Some firebrand named Parks had come slinking up from Clarksville into the hollers and hills, and started talking strikes. The company couldn't have that, so they'd turned to the agency, and the agency had sent Kemper.

It turned out Parks, for all that he was popular with the men in camp, wasn't so popular with the county or the state. He had enough warrants to paper a shack, and had likely headed up into the hills to get away from the bounty hunters that swarmed the low country looking for him. It had been a simple matter to put together a posse of willing and able bodies, for the promise of the reward on Parks' head.

But nothing was ever that simple. These mountains ate men. Even folks who'd lived on them all their lives were wary of the dangers they held. They were hostile territory, and no one with any sense or without a good goddamn reason went up into them. You left the mountains. You didn't come back. But here he was, back again. Because he was the only poor son of a bitch to hand who knew the area. He hadn't wanted to go, but there was no arguing with the agency, not about this.

"They're going to fight us tooth and nail," Locke went on. He didn't sound particularly bothered by the prospect. He took a swallow of coffee and spat a stream of dark liquid into the fire. "Tastes like shit."

"You make it next time," Quillen said in an aggrieved tone from where he sat on the other side of the fire. He pulled his coat tight. "Rough country. Barely got any sleep last night, between Davis' snoring and something prowling around out in them trees. They got bears up here, Pink?"

Locke ignored him, but Kemper thought about his dream and wondered if maybe he'd heard something, even in his sleep. "If Parks is smart, he'll have people watching for us," Locke said. He squinted at the trees. "Mountains are full of good places to ambush someone."

"You scared, Locke?" Eugene asked. The other two – Davis and McMeekin – sniggered at this. None of them liked each other, but they all hated Locke for some reason. Maybe because he was older; maybe because he looked at them like they were something he'd scraped off the bottom of his boot.

Locke gave Eugene a steady look. "Not particularly. Though you might should be. Fragile as you are." His eyes slid away, as if Eugene were of no more importance than a gnat. Eugene flushed. Blonde, with a wispy moustache and an unshaven chin, he looked younger than he was. He acted it too, in Kemper's opinion.

Eugene put down his tin cup and made as if to stand, but McMeekin, a lanky sort with a scarred face and mouthful of bad teeth, put a restraining hand on his arm. "Leave it. He's looking for an excuse."

"Best listen to McMeekin, Eugene," Quillen said. "Old Locke here ain't the squeamish sort. I hear tell he once ate a fella's liver." He looked at Kemper. "Besides, I want to hear what the Pink thinks. Bet he's got some stories about these here mountains."

"Nope," Kemper said flatly. He poured out the remainder of his coffee and went to the river to wash his face and shave. He carried a compact mirror – his mother's. The only thing she'd left him when the fever had taken her. That and his eyes. He'd pawned the silver backing and replaced it with brass. He met her eyes in the mirror and rubbed his chin. He looked like rough weather and hard going, but that was to be expected.

"Putting on your paint, Pink?" Kemper angled the compact, and studied Quillen, who was standing behind him, one finger tap-tapping the pommel of the big Arkansas toothpick thrust sideways through his gun-belt. "That the secret of them good looks?"

Kemper snapped the compact closed and washed his face. Shaving could wait. He stood and gestured lightly at Quillen. "You know, there are a lot of holes in these here hills. Lot of places a man can get lost. Especially if nobody gives a shit about him."

Quillen's smile vanished as surely as if he'd been slapped. "That a threat, Pink?"

"I should have thought that was obvious, even to you," Kemper said. He made a show of looking up. "The sun rises late up here and sets swiftly." He looked at the others. "We should get moving. Sooner we get there, and get Parks, sooner we can leave."

Locke and the others didn't argue, though there was some grumbling from Eugene and Quillen as they gathered up their gear. Most bounty hunters got into the trade because they were good with violence and not much else. Effort was a dirty word as far as they were concerned. Ones like Locke were different; they had a coldness that came of hard times, and they'd climb any mountain or ford any river to get whoever they were after.

Some of Kemper's fellow agents were like that. They'd

convinced themselves they'd been given a higher calling. That they weren't just railroad bulls and company gun thugs. Kemper knew better; he'd always known better. He had no illusions as to what he was. Mostly, he was just tired. He wanted to go somewhere where nobody knew his name and do nothing in particular. That'd be a good life.

Once he'd finished here, once Parks was in custody, he'd go. He'd turn in his badge and derby and forget about the look on the faces of the miners as he turfed them out of company housing, or the way that mill striker had screamed as they'd shoved his hand in the press. He'd pretend it had all been someone else all along.

The camp wasn't hard to find, situated as it was on an isolated tributary of the Cumberland River. You just moved upriver from the log boom, and followed the signs of clearcutting up onto the ridgeland to the camp. Even so, it was an arduous climb, and took the better part of the day. The rutted path wasn't made for a leisurely hike. Despite the coolness of the day, and the chill mist that seeped up from the broken earth, Kemper was soon sweating under his woolen suit. The others weren't faring much better, except for Locke, who didn't seem bothered at all.

The older man led the way, though Kemper was the guide. Locke had more experience in rough country, or so he said, and Kemper was happy to let him take the lead. The farther up the ridge they went the more the skin between his shoulder-blades itched. Locke was right. It was good country for an ambush. And Parks was just the sort to have set one, or so he'd heard. Truth was, he didn't know much about the man that wasn't hearsay. Some of it was likely true, but most of it probably wasn't.

Either way, not the sort of man you wanted to chase after through hills and hollers. Not this time of year, when the cold was hiding around the corner, the air tasted like metal and the deep dark forest all around. Black branches dripped morning dew, and the sound of it reminded Kemper of a clock, ticking away the hours. Or maybe counting down.

Once or twice, he thought he heard something dogging their trail. A lowdown, slinking sort of sound, like something creeping along just out of sight. But there was never anything there. Just the trees rising wild, hemming them in. Just the mountains, whispering their welcome to a prodigal son. He tried not to think about his dreams, or his momma's stories, or anything at all, save doing what he'd come to do, and getting himself to the Midwest.

The higher they wound up and along, the worse the rutted track got and the worse the ridgeland looked, with bald patches among the spruce, and deep, irregular furrows cut into the slope where the timbered logs were dragged to the river or loaded up on wagons. The sight of it reminded Kemper of something, but he wasn't sure what. Quillen figured it out, though. "Looks like your head, Locke," he called out, gesturing to his own scalp for emphasis. Eugene and the others laughed.

Locke paused in the lee of a slab jutting from the slope of the ground, its outline rough with lichen and moss. For a moment, Kemper thought Locke was going to turn and put a bullet from his rifle in Quillen, just to shut him up. Instead, he held up a hand, bringing the group to a halt. "Hear that?" he said, looking at Kemper.

Kemper heard nothing.

Quillen frowned. "I don't hear shit."

"That's what he means," Kemper said, softly, his eyes on the trees that rose and fell like slow waves around them. "We're close to the camp. It's just at the top of the ridge there. We should hear something, even if Parks has convinced them all to down tools and strike."

"Not even any damn birds," Locke said, his gaze sweeping the trail. He hefted his rifle as if to shoot, but there was nothing to aim. They might as well have been the only living things in the forest. Kemper had the unsettling thought the mountain was holding its breath, as if in anticipation.

A branch snapped. Far off and away, but close enough that the sound carried. Kemper had his pistol out before he realized it. He wasn't alone. Quillen and the others began to look around, weapons raised.

"Shitfire," Davis muttered. He was a heavyset man, which was handy in a fight, but made him too big for this sort of trek. His face splotched up alarmingly whenever he had to move too quickly. "Somebody is watching us, ain't they?"

"Hell, if they was, they'd have shot us by now," Quillen protested. His eyes were wide, but he wasn't frightened. Just bewildered.

They all were, except Locke. The old man stood stock still under the slab, head cocked – listening.

Kemper sidled towards him, keeping his eyes on the trees, and the spaces between. "Quillen is right," he said, in a low voice. "I expect they'd have started shooting by now if that was their intent. We made enough noise coming up the trail, after all."

"Wasn't me making a racket," Locke grunted, not looking at him.

"No. But it was made all the same." Kemper glanced back at the others. Davis especially had sounded like a dying buffalo as he climbed the trail. More than once, Kemper had feared the big bounty hunter might simply keel over from the strain. If that happened, the mountain could keep Davis' bones, as far as he was concerned – and be welcome to them.

The silence stretched for miles. The forest stood still and mute. The mountain held a darkness, even in the morning light. A heavy dark, like a shroud weighted down with stones. Kemper was tempted to let off a shot, just to break that dreadful stillness.

Locke lowered his rifle and sighed softly. "Whoever it was, they're gone now."

"If they were even there in the first place," Eugene said. "If you weren't just hearing shit, old man." Locke looked at him, and Eugene fell silent.

Kemper holstered his Colt and took a step up the trail, out into the open. No bullet came, nor any hue and cry. He shaded his eyes against the morning sun and took in the ridgeline. No trees up there, not now. Just the scar of the peaks in the distance, and the sun riding low over them. Night never fled far in the mountains, and it always came back fast.

HIDEBEHIND

Kemper could just make out the edge of the camp in the dim. It was small, as camps went, he knew that. Fitting, given that Ackroyd Timber was barely big enough to be a company. But it had money, enough at least to hire the agency. Kemper looked back at the posse – a bulk of black shapes in the failing light. For a moment, he imagined he saw six where there should only have been five, but it passed between one blink and the next. "Enough lollygagging," he said, fighting a sudden chill. "Let's get up there and say hello."

"Now we're talking," Eugene said, with a whoop. "Let's go get us that bounty, boys!" The others howled in agreement. Only Locke remained silent, his eyes on the forest. Part of Kemper wanted to ask what the other man thought he'd seen or heard, but the other, more sensible part of him knew better. Whatever was out there could stay out there, and welcome to it. He'd come to get Parks, and nothing else.

When they reached the camp, it was as quiet as the forest. The stoves were cold, and there was not a sound to be heard. Not even the braying of mules, or the scuttle of rats. The crude, square-cut buildings sat just above a crooked tributary of the Cumberland, so close you could just roll the logs down the slope into the water, if you were of a mind. Not that many logs had been rolled since Parks had turned up, looking for work.

The bunkhouse sat silent and, to all appearances, empty. Cookhouse too. Kemper and the others spread out, moving quick and quiet. Just because buildings looked empty, didn't mean they were. You learned that right quick with the agency. There were the outlying shacks to be searched as well, and the small, blunt square of the camp store.

Kemper and Locke took the bunkhouse. It was much like every other bunkhouse Kemper had seen – a large open room, with narrow beds and no privacy to speak of. He'd slept in a similar building as a boy, during his turn down the mines. Before he'd gotten some sense and seen that digging coal was just slow way of digging your own grave.

Locke prowled up the line of beds, eyes shifting. "Stove's

stone cold," he said, after a moment. His words fell on Kemper's ears like weights. Kemper nodded absently. His eyes traced a stain high up in the far corner, behind the stove. A patch of damp, maybe. But something looked off about it, though he couldn't say what.

Instead, he turned his attentions to the beds. "Beds ain't been made," he said, lifting a rumpled blanket and tossing it aside. There were shirts and braces. Hats. Straight razors and socks. Not cleaned up and put away, but left out, as if they'd meant to come back. "Personal effects. Lock-boxes. Boots on the floor. What kind of logger leaves his boots behind?"

"Might have been in a hurry," Locke said. He was staring at the wall opposite the door, a curious expression on his face. Kemper joined him.

"What is it?"

Locke used the barrel of his rifle to tap the wall, where several parallel gouges marked the boards. High up off the floor.

"Looks like somebody was marking time with an axe," Kemper opined, but he knew better.

So did Locke.

"Ever seen what a tree looks like after a bear uses it for a scratching post?" the old man asked. It was a rhetorical question. The marks were too small for a bear.

Kemper grunted and turned. There were more marks along the wall, and some on the floor he hadn't noticed earlier. He pointed them out to Locke, and the bounty hunter made a sound deep in his throat, like a hiss. He sniffed the air, like a hound dog, but there was nothing to smell. At least nothing Kemper noticed. Just the stale stink of abandonment. Even so, something about it made Kemper nervous.

That was why, when something thumped on the roof, Kemper had his gun out and cocked. Locke raised his rifle. There was a quick rattle, like a herd of squirrels running across the rooftop, and then – nothing. Kemper followed the sound across the bunkhouse, darting the occasional glance at the windows, but saw nothing. And when the sound stopped, he found that he was holding his breath, waiting for whatever it was to come rushing in the door. But it didn't. He looked at Locke, and for the first time he could recall, the old man looked unsettled. Downright worried, even.

From outside came a yell. Quillen was shouting to beat the band. Kemper and Locke hustled outside and found Quillen and the others standing around. Not all of the others though.

"Where's Davis?" Locke growled.

"He's gone. Last I saw, he was checking the damn outhouse, and when I turned back around – he was gone."

"What do you mean gone?" Kemper asked, thinking about the rustling on the roof. It had been moving quick, and light. Faster than a man; faster even than a child. Rats, maybe. Or squirrels. Logging camps attracted vermin. Attracted other things too, according to his momma. He quickly pushed the thought aside.

Quillen looked at him as if he was an idiot. "I mean gone. Not there no more. Snatched out of the world."

"Hear anything?" Kemper pressed, his eyes roaming the camp.

"If I had, I'd have said. None of us heard nothing." Quillen looked around at the others.

Eugene shook his head. "I was in the cookhouse."

"I was in the filer shack," McMeekin piped up. He licked his lips nervously. "I could see the outhouse from where I was. I didn't see nothing. Davis went around the back and – and he was gone." He rubbed his face. "Nothing back there when I went to check, just…"

"Just what?" Kemper asked, softly.

"His boot," Quillen said. "Whoever it was, they snatched him right out of his damn boot." He looked around nervously. "Must be Parks. Got to be, right?"

"Parks would have started shooting," Kemper said. "He ain't one for games." That was what he'd heard, at any rate. Maybe Parks had gotten smarter. Or maybe he'd gone the way the others had, with nary a trace left behind. The thought sent a chill through him.

"Maybe, but somebody was shooting," Eugene said, hesitantly. "Found a couple of bullet holes over in the cookhouse. And something else..." He trailed off and shook his head. He rubbed his mouth. "Can't make head nor tails of it, if I'm being honest."

"Show me," Kemper said. He looked at Locke. "See if you can find some sign of Davis. Or anyone. Something funny is going on here."

"Understatement," Locke grunted, but he started for the outhouse, McMeekin trailing in his wake. Quillen followed Kemper and Eugene, still muttering to himself. Kemper ignored the other man, and focused on what Eugene was saying as they entered the mess hall.

"It's like they forted up or something, but I can't figure why, or where the hell they went after," he said, sounding puzzled.

"What do you mean?"

"See for yourself," Eugene said. The cookhouse proper was a small shack that weighed down the far end of the structure, separated from the mess hall by a rough-cut door. The hall was a mess – tables had been overturned and dragged into the center of the hall, away from the door and windows. The benches had been broken up and scattered around the impromptu fort like bulwarks.

Kemper stopped and stared, trying to make sense of what he was seeing. "What the hell is all this?"

Eugene nodded. "That's what I said." The younger man shook his head. He indicated the far wall. "They was shooting at somebody, though. You can see the holes. Must have missed whoever it was, cause there ain't no blood that I can see."

"Maybe they was moving too fast," Quillen muttered as he hauled a bench aside and made his way into the ring of tables.

"Or maybe they were just bad shots," Kemper said, following him. He kept one hand on his pistol as he moved.

Quillen hugged his rifle like it was a bosom chum. He crouched amid the mess at the center of the makeshift fort. "Look at all this," he said. There were torn open boxes of ammunition, cans of beans, a jug of something that smelled like a slow death – and a knife, embedded in the flat surface of a table. As Quillen picked through the ammunition and the beans, Kemper stared at the knife. It seemed out of place.

It was only when he bent low to wrench it loose from the wood that he realized it had been used to carve something in the table. Kemper squinted, trying to make it out. He traced the letters with his fingers. The first word was entirely illegible, but the rest of it was easy enough to make out. "Behind you," he said, sounding it out. And a mark under it… a big P, and the date. P for Parks? Had Parks left the message? If so, for who? Not him, that much he was certain of.

"What the hell does that mean?" Eugene asked, leaning over the table.

Kemper shook his head. The phrase nudged something, a long-buried memory. One of his momma's stories, maybe. But he couldn't call it to mind just now. All he knew was that he wanted to be somewhere else – Chicago. He'd heard it was nice.

"Don't know," Kemper said. He stabbed the knife into the top edge of the table. If Parks had left the message, then that meant he'd definitely been here. They might still be able to find him, if they were lucky. "Don't much care. See any sign of Parks?"

"No sign of anybody," Quillen said. "They all vanished."

"Like Davis," Eugene said, softly. He turned as Locke stepped into the cookhouse, a strange look on his face.

"You need to see this," the old man said, in a ragged voice. "Out here."

"Did you find Davis?" Kemper called after him, as he and the others followed.

Locke didn't reply. He hurried towards the far end of the bunkhouse, where he stopped. There was a stain on the wood, dark like sap. Only it wasn't sap or anything like it. And it stank to high heaven. Kemper waved a hand in front of his face. There were flies everywhere, bobbing up and down on the stain like children at play.

"Look at that," Locke said, indicating the stain. "Coming from up on the roof."

Eugene pressed the back of his hand to his mouth. "What the hell is that smell?"

"Blood," Kemper said. He looked at Locke. "Did you find Davis?"

Locke shook his head. "It's up there. I found it."

"Found what?" Eugene asked.

"Thought I smelled it earlier," Locke went on, in a hushed voice. The old man seemed even more subdued than usual. "Just a whiff of it. It was smart, left it downwind, where the stink wouldn't carry down the trail."

"That don't sound like no animal I ever heard of," Quillen said, a tremor in his voice.

"I didn't say nothing about no animal," Locke hissed, shoving Quillen against the side of the bunkhouse. "Ain't no animal did this. Leastways not no animal ever walked the clean earth." He darted a nervous look around. Kemper could feel the agitation bleeding off of him. Locke was on edge. Maybe for good reason.

He looked around, and noticed another missing face. "Where's McMeekin, Locke?" he asked, slowly. There was no sign of the other man. Quillen and Eugene looked around, just now noticing that the other bounty hunter was missing.

Locke fixed him with a wild glare. "That's what I'm trying to tell you. There ain't no McMeekin. Nor no Davis. Not no more. It snatched them up." He pointed up to the roof, where the flies buzzed. "I got up on the outhouse, that's how I spotted it. Wouldn't have noticed it otherwise."

"Noticed what?" Kemper asked.

"Forget that, what do you mean McMeekin is gone?" Quillen demanded. He got in Locke's face. "First Davis, now McMeekin – where the hell is he?"

"Same place Davis is, I expect," Locke said in a flat tone. Quillen stepped back, eyes darting left and right. Locke looked at Kemper. "They're all up there. All of them. Every damn one of them – or what's left of them, at least." Locke sagged, running a hand over his scarred-up scalp.

Kemper stared at him for a moment, trying to process what Locke was saying. He looked at the others. Quillen shook his head and looked away. Eugene hitched up his gun-belt. "I'm game if you are, Pink," he said, pugnaciously.

Kemper nodded and looked around. "Must be a ladder somewhere."

Eugene snorted and clapped his gloved hands together. "We don't need a ladder. Just give me a damn boost. I climbed trees taller than this back home."

Kemper gestured to Quillen. "Help me." Together, the two of them boosted Eugene up onto the roof of the bunkhouse. They heard the creak of him getting to his feet, then a sudden inhalation. Kemper looked up. "What is it?"

Eugene came to the edge of the roof, face pale, eyes like hollow pits. He pressed a hand to his mouth, his throat working. "It's blood," he gulped out. "Other stuff. They was – they was torn apart." He hung his head over the edge and loosed a torrent of bile. Kemper and Quillen moved hastily aside, avoiding the resultant splash. Eugene's body shook so fiercely as he emptied his stomach that Kemper thought he might topple from his perch.

Locke watched the display in silence. When Eugene had finished, the old man straightened and said, "We need to leave. Before it gets us the way it got McMeekin and Davis. Be safer on the trail than here."

Kemper fixed him with a look. "You sound like you know what it is." Cougar, maybe. There were supposed to be some high up in the mountains, prowling the fastnesses where man rarely went. Could a cougar take a man that quick? Maybe. But something told him that the crew hadn't forted up because of any damn cougar.

Locke shook his head. "I know what it ain't, and it ain't no Indian, or no bushwhacker. No bear either. That tells me we should get while we can."

Kemper turned away. The old man was right, but something told him that there was no getting away, not now. It'd had two of them already, and easy as pie. It'd come for the rest of them, no two ways about it. It'd taken a whole logging camp, after all. What was four more men, next to that?

He thought about the message in the cookhouse, the way Davis had gone, and McMeekin. He thought about his momma's stories, and finally, that nagging memory surfaced, sluggish and resentful. "Hidebehind," he murmured.

Locke looked at him. "What was that?"

"Story my momma told me, when I was in knee-britches," Kemper said, slowly, as it came back to him. "About something in these here woods that'd sneak up on a fellow and drag him off, lickety-split, before he could even cry out. No one ever saw it, on account of it always hiding behind something – sometimes even the folks it was stalking. So they called it the Hidebehind."

"What kind of name is that for a thing?" Quillen asked.

"I didn't name it," Kemper said. He looked up. The sun was riding low over the trees, and long shadows crept across the camp like the bars on some great cage. He shook his head. "We need to fort up. We'll leave at first light."

"We should go now," Locke said, but he didn't sound as certain as he had before. Maybe his mother had told him similar stories. Or maybe he, like Kemper, understood that whatever they'd walked into, it couldn't be outrun – only endured.

"Go if'n you want," Quillen said, "But me, I think the Pink has the right idea. We hole up and skedaddle when the birdies start to chirp." He looked up. "Come on down here, Eugene... Eugene?"

Kemper looked up. Eugene wasn't there. Somehow, he wasn't surprised – he was too far past that now, tramping off the edge of the map: Here Be Monsters. He'd always known there was some truth to the stories, though he'd never admitted it. He wanted to run back down the trail, to leave and forget. Let the mountains keep their secrets, let them keep Parks and Eugene and all the rest.

Instead, he drew his pistol. "Give me a boost. Now." Quillen frowned but did as he bade, and a moment later, Kemper was hauling himself up onto the edge of the roof. The wood shifted beneath him, and he heard the thick hum of flies at their business. There was red all over the roof, a slop of it, spreading in all directions. There was a heap of something – meat, maybe – in the lee of the smokestack. He spied the white of bone, and the curdled yellow of fat. Tatters of clothing. A boot. A hat. The refuse of a dozen messy meals, all piled up downwind, facing the trees.

No Eugene, though. No McMeekin, no Davis. It was too smart for that, a cold, analytical part of him thought. It had dragged them elsewhere, to eat in peace. Or maybe just to store them, the way a farmer might hang a hog's carcass for salting.

As he turned, searching the trees, the roof of the cookhouse, the camp, he wondered how long it had been here. Had it come slinking in when they'd built the camp – like a coyote, looking for an easy meal? Or had they built the camp in its territory? Maybe this was less about food than about protecting its patch. Maybe, maybe, maybe. Questions rattled around in his head as he strained to hear something, anything but the flies.

"You still up there, Pink?" Quillen called, nervously. His voice had an edge of hysteria to it that Kemper didn't like.

"Still up here," Kemper said. There was something – what was that? Behind the smokestack. Nothing could hide behind it, for it wasn't all that wide. Just a thin tube of metal, really. But he was sure he'd seen something, just out of the corner of his eye. A quick tremble of movement. And he was certain he could hear something, under the susurrus of the flies. A sharp noise, like something digging into the wood, and an undercurrent of eager breath – like the panting of a dog.

His momma's voice came to him again. *It can hide behind anything,* she'd said. *Behind a tree or a rock or even a blade of grass. It's clever like that. It's always where you ain't looking, just out of sight.* There was something else, as well, but he couldn't bring it mind. Not at the moment.

Kemper cocked his pistol. The faint scraping ceased. No movement, either. The tableaux held for one minute, then two. He heard something behind him, a shuffling creak. He whirled, nearly losing his balance on the sloped roof.

Quillen froze, hands up. "Whoa, whoa, I just – *shitfire!*"

His eyes widened in an almost comical fashion, and Kemper heard a quick shuffling scrape coming from the direction he'd been looking and he whipped back around and saw it coming at him, saw the glint of fangs, smelled its carrion-breath, felt the heat of its body as it came at him – *Lordy, how can anything that big be that fast?* – and fired wild, emptying the cylinder in a convulsive squeeze of the trigger.

There was a sound like parting sheet metal, and it whipped away and over the side. He heard Locke cry out, and the boom of the old man's rifle. Quillen dropped to the ground, and Kemper followed with such haste that he nearly fell off the roof.

Locke was reloading, his eyes on the outhouse. "It went back around there," he said, not looking at them. "Quicker than greased lightning."

"What was that damn thing?" Quillen nearly shrieked. "Looked like a bear, only it was – it was thin. Ungodly thin."

"Looked more like a weasel to me," Locke said. "Only it was bigger than any weasel I've ever seen." He raised his rifle and sighted down the length. "Faster, too."

Kemper spilled empty brass on the ground and began to reload. "It was hiding behind the smokestack," he said, trying to keep his hands from shaking.

"That ain't possible," Quillen scoffed uncertainly. "Is it?"

"Whether it is or ain't, that's what it was doing. Minute I took my eyes off of it, it came for me. That must be how it got the others so quiet. It waited until they weren't looking, and then…" Kemper swallowed and shook his head. "We need to get into the cookhouse. We can hold it off there. Not a lot of places for it to hide."

"Didn't look like it did them others no good," Quillen protested.

Kemper didn't look at him. "You want to run for it, be my guest. Me, I'm putting some cover between me and whatever this thing is." He looked at Locke. "You coming?"

Locke hawked and spat. "Guess so." He hefted the rifle but didn't take his eyes off the outhouse. "Lead the way."

HIDEBEHIND

Kemper snapped his revolver shut. "Stay close. Don't let no daylight get between us."

The three of them hurried back towards the cookhouse in an awkward huddle. Kemper knew the thing – the Hidebehind – was following. Could hear it slinking along, just out of sight. He thought of the marks they'd found in the bunkhouse, and knew them now for claw-marks. It was fast; agile. Then, it would have to be, wouldn't it?

They'd almost reached the cookhouse when Quillen cried out. He fired his rifle into the air and broke away from Kemper and Locke. "It's above us," he yelped, and fired again. Kemper took a step towards him, and knew, even as he did it, that it was exactly what their pursuer had been waiting for. He spun, but too late. Locke was on the ground, clawing for his rifle as the Hidebehind tried to drag him under the cookhouse.

Instinctively, Kemper lunged and grabbed the old man's hand, hauling back with all his strength. Locke was cussing and clawing at the turf, trying to pull himself free, but his leg was already under the cookhouse up to the knee, and there was an awful sound – like an angry dog, worrying a bone. Locke began to scream, his face white, eyes wide. His scars were flushed red, and Kemper realized that the old man was praying in between obscenities.

Taking a chance, Kemper fired into the dark beneath the bunkhouse. Locke slumped as the tension on his leg went slack. Kemper dragged the old man out with one hand, even as he fired again and again. "Help me out here, Quillen," he snarled, glancing over his shoulder at the other bounty hunter.

Quillen stood stock still behind him, a curious look on his face. He had his hand on his knife, and made as if to speak, but no sound emerged. As Kemper watched in incomprehension, slowly, almost gently, his head tipped backwards as if he were looking up at the darkening sky. Then back farther still, and there came a sharp sound, like the crack of wet branches beneath a man's boot. The knife slipped from his hand and fell to the ground.

Quillen jittered in place, hands twitching uselessly, as his head went back and back, dragged down by some inexorable, unseen force. Another, final crack, and Quillen folded up and sank down with nary a sound, revealing his killer. *It can hide behind anything,* his momma had said. *Behind a tree or a rock or even a blade of grass*

Kemper stared at the hunched shape that crouched there, its claws sunk deep into the back of Quillen's skull. It resembled nothing so much as an overgrown weasel, but only in the sense that it resembled nothing else that had ever walked the earth. It was gone in a flash, lolloping along in the way that made it look less like a living thing than a piece of black string caught in a strong wind.

Kemper tried to track it, but it was moving too fast. He quickly grabbed a handful of the old man's coat and kept moving, dragging the injured man in his wake. Locke was moaning, barely conscious. A slick, red trail marked their path.

He could hear a soft panting coming from somewhere above as he headed for the cookhouse. There was an awful eagerness to the sound. Abruptly, it fell silent. He allowed himself to hope that it had gone back for Quillen. Perhaps it would spend some time dragging him to wherever it had stashed the others, and leave them in peace.

Locke mumbled something and fumbled for the pistol in his belt. Kemper risked a glance behind them, but saw nothing. Maybe it truly was gone. Locke clawed the weapon free as they got to the cookhouse door and cocked it. His gaze was vague, bleary. He'd lost too much blood, Kemper thought. That'd get him, if the Hidebehind didn't. A part of him wondered if the agency would send anyone after them. For their sakes, he hoped not.

"Up you get," Kemper grunted, trying to get the other man to his feet. Locke mumbled again, and pushed away, stumbling into the open. Kemper ducked as Locke popped off a shot at the doorway of the cookhouse. There was a screech. Kemper looked up and saw a flash of sable pelt as the Hidebehind skedaddled. It had been waiting for them inside. It had known where they were going, and beaten them there.

He turned. Locke had fallen to his knees, head bowed. The old man's face was drawn and white as snow. The pistol slipped from his fingers as Kemper reached him. Locke tried to say something – failed. With a last sigh, he toppled over and lay still.

Kemper was alone.

He straightened and looked around, heart thudding. He wanted to run, but where was there to go? It was faster and sneakier. Smarter too, maybe. It had taken out a whole logging camp, after all. What was six more men, next to that?

Sweat stung his eyes, but he didn't dare blink. If he did, it would be on him, sure as sin. He swallowed and looked around, trying to spot any sign of it. But there was nothing. He knew it was there, somewhere, but he couldn't see it.

He tried to push past the rising panic, to think. His mother's words came to him again: *It's always where you ain't looking, just out of sight.* He grimaced. The pistol was getting heavy in his hand, and the urge to flee was overpowering – even if it meant being run down and devoured. There had to be something, some way to—

Oh.

It was such a simple thing, that he dismissed it at first.

Carefully, he reached into his coat and found the shape of his mother's compact. He pulled it out and flipped it open. The light was fast fading, but there was just enough left to see his reflection – haggard, frightened. He dropped to one knee beside Locke's body and lowered his pistol. And he waited, but not for long.

It might have been smarter and faster than a man, but it was a damn sight less patient. He caught a hint of movement in the mirror, and saw it slinking towards him. It had flattened its bulk nearly parallel to the ground and was coming in fast.

At the last moment, as the sun set and no shadow would be cast, it rose up over him. He caught a flash of its eyes in the mirror, the gleam of fangs and he threw himself forward, rolling onto his back and firing in one motion. He didn't hold back, emptying his weapon a second and final time – and this time, striking true.

The Hidebehind made a sound like a drowning cat and fell back, writhing in an ungodly fashion. Something like tar or oil spurted from its wounds, hissing in the cool air. A rear limb clipped him, knocking him sprawling, but the beast didn't notice, busy as it was with dying. It squalled piteously, shivered and finally, went still.

Kemper stared at it for long moments, not quite believing it. Not quite certain he'd managed it. But the thing was still, and the ground was soaked with whatever passed for its blood. Slowly, he rose, empty pistol in hand, and retrieved the compact.

He looked down at the thing, wondering what he ought to do with it. Burn it, maybe. Or just roll it into the river and pretend none of this had happened. He looked up. The sun was all but gone, just a ribbon of light above the peaks.

The cookhouse roof creaked. Kemper froze. Maybe it was the wind. He tried to use the compact to see, but there wasn't enough light – and the glass was broken besides. He glanced at his empty pistol. Another creak, and a soft sound, as of something panting.

The last of his momma's warning came to him, then. *It's always where you ain't looking, just out of sight. And if you do see one,* she'd added, *be sure there's another one creeping right up on you.*

He laughed softly, humorlessly as he dropped his empty pistol and the compact both. He thought he knew now what the rest of Parks' message had been.

He heard the sound of something dropping down from the roof behind him. The soft panting grew louder. And not just from behind him. He heard the bunkhouse door scrape, as if something were easing out into the open. Flickers of movement, too quick to follow, tugged at his attention.

He'd been wondering how one creature, even one so fast, could kill so many men so quickly. And it hadn't. Because there was more than one. A whole posse, in fact. He shook his head and thought about Chicago. It'd have been nice to have seen it, at least once.

His eyes flicked down to Locke's pistol, laying by its owner's hand. He knew he'd never reach it. There were too many of them, too close. He went for it anyway.

It might as well have been in Illinois, for all the good it did him.

PATCHWORK REAPERS

Pamela Jeffs

In the desert, against the common smells of sun-blistered sand and rock, the scent of blood stands out. That's how I first find his horse. The Appaloosa, with its head missing, rests laid out in the dust. Bosco, my boss, lies fifty yards farther on. He's face-up by the edge of the dried creek that runs the length of Skullcap Canyon. His boots, tips worn, point awkwardly to the vast midday sky. Blood seeps from the hole that's been punched clean through his heart.

Damned stubborn idiot.

He knew what we were up against. We went out to find missing longhorns and men, and he saw the same as I did—a gore-soaked plain littered with slaughtered cattle and the bodies of our boys, Billy, Ike and Jonah, alongside them.

Bosco saw how whoever killed them, stole their heads.

But he was anxious. Went ahead alone to warn that new wife of his, even though everyone knows she's more than capable of looking after herself.

My horse, Isha, shifts uneasily. Not sure if it's being so near to the body or her response to my own fretfulness. I glance up at the rugged crags that line the ravine. Are Bosco's murderers waiting for me in the cliffs? Lots of places to hide up there. Places easy to set up an ambush.

I spit to clear the fear-taste from my mouth. Shit. I didn't ask for any of this. Just came west to drive longhorns for coin.

A rock clatters, breaking the canyon's silence and I twist in the saddle, my heart a knot. Around me the dry red cliffs bare their teeth.

My trigger finger twitches. Got to keep moving. Won't leave my boss behind though. I slide off Isha. The blood on Bosco's shirt is dark and clotted. I reach in under his arms and lift him to a sitting position, noting how his body has started to stiffen. My mare holds steady as I ease him up to rest belly down across the saddle. Then I lead us away, following the creek bed.

My plan is a simple one. Get back to the ranch, drop Bosco to his widow, pack my bedroll and hightail it the hell out of here. They're good folk I work for, but I'm not getting paid enough to stick around.

Ahead a tall, lean shape detaches from an outcrop of rocks. Two others join it.

Bandits?

I suck a breath through gritted teeth. Something about the way they walk isn't right.

These things don't move like men.

The light play changes and their features solidify. Hell and damnation. They look to be some kind of machines, rusted iron arms and hands hanging lax and ready by their sides. Metal legs and torsos too, but they…

Gods. Each one wears a dead man's face – Billy's, Ike's and Jonah's – lips all jerking, eyes blinking unnatural-like.

Bile claws up my throat.

The monsters move in perfect unison. Their heavy feet break stones as they approach, an awful crunching like the snapping of bones. Isha screams and rears. Her reins slither free from my grasp, and I snatch for the flying ends but miss.

The last machine-man in the line – the one with Billy's face – lifts its hand, palm facing out and glowing. A terrible whine fills the air followed by a knife of blue-white light from the creature's hand. Isha falls to it, her skull lost in a rain of blood and brains. Her momentum carries her on for two more strides then, along with Bosco, she topples sideways to the ground.

"Isha! NO!"

Heart pounding, I draw. Bullets spark uselessly off the metal chest plates until my cylinder clicks over empty.

The machines halt ten paces from me, and blink stickily. The one wearing Ike raises its hand, again with palm facing forwards and glowing. The high-pitched whine builds again.

PATCHWORK REAPERS

I run.

A blast of heat and light sears past me.

My boots catch in depressions of stone and sink through softer patches of red-yellow sand. I know I'm already dead, but a man in his last moments wants to know he gave his all.

I reach the rock arch that marks the end of the canyon. The cliffs past it veer away, bleeding into empty desert. I glance across my shoulder.

Another whine and another shot scores past my ear. I swerve left. Their uncanny footsteps grow louder.

I reckon I can smell the oil in their joints.

Saltbush clutches me as I barrel past. Ahead, an errant gust of wind twists up into a column of dust and then dances away. The vast emptiness calls me on.

Before long, my legs and lungs betray me and I collapse to the sand with a grunt. Gravel grazes my palms. I taste sweat on my lips. These are the last, small details of my life.

Will I know it when they take my head?

A gunshot shatters the plain. Good, human-sounding gunfire. The noise ricochets off into the distance and is replaced with the drumming cadence of galloping hooves.

Two horsemen approach huddled low over their mounts. Where the hell did they come from? I cover my head as one of them leaps over me. Amidst dust and falling grass, I see the rider swing a tomahawk. Billy's head sails free, trailing a bunch of cables out from the severed neck.

Decapitated, the mechanical body stops dead.

Two more cuts and two more heads roll to the grass. Sparks spit from the ends of the severed wires as Ike's and Jonah's mouths open and close for a few moments. A wash of black liquid floods past their lips and then they stop moving.

The lead rider loops back to me, the tomahawk held wide of the mount and the edge dripping black. He lifts his chin and the stark light catches his features.

Except *he* is a *she*. A forty-something-aged woman, eyes and hair dark as pitch, and her skin the colour of warm dusk.

45

Bosco's wife, Orenda. The half-Cherokee woman he gambled and lost his life for.

"You all right, Clayton?" she asks.

I nod, too exhausted to speak.

"The others?"

I shake my head.

"Bosco?"

"Gone," I croak. "He's back there in the canyon, still tied to what's left of my horse."

No emotion registers at the news of her dead husband. Orenda tips her chin to her offsider – her lean brother, Ahuli, the cowboy who arrived only last week to help with work on the ranch.

Glances pass between them. Ahuli then nods and gallops off in a cloud of dust. Seems he'll be the one to bring the boss home.

Orenda, dressed like a man in trousers, blue neckerchief and a button-up shirt, slithers off her horse. She wipes her axe's edge clean on a tussock of wiry grass and re-holsters it to her saddle. She offers me a waterskin.

The liquid is warm and tastes slightly oily but I'm thankful for her kindness.

"We found..." I begin, but then words fail me.

"I know," says Orenda, saving me from finishing. Ghosts dance in the depths of her eyes. "The house was attacked this morning. We two are all that made it out."

I bite my lip. There was twenty other staff stationed at the ranch.

Ahuli returns, his bay gelding huffing out urgent breaths as he's reined to a stop. "I found the mount but the boss is gone," he says, his voice as deep as the drum he was named for. His horse sidles and Ahuli pulls him straight. "Their tracks head back down the canyon."

"We will follow them," says Orenda.

"You can't be serious!" I clench my hands to fists. "You've seen what those *things* will do to us."

"I'll not leave my husband with them."

"But he's dead!"

Orenda frowns. The lines running from her nose to her mouth deepen. "To believe that means you don't know *all* they are capable of."

"And how would you know?" I ask.

She cocks her head for a moment. Her lips twitch. "Because I listened to the stories my mother told me. I know the truth of what dwells out here."

"And what's that?"

"Unnatural deaths."

• ••

The shots start as soon as we pass back under the rock arch. The cliffs ignite into a hailstorm of the machine-men's blue-white firepower. There are at least a hundred of them, hiding like rats in the rocks. The sizzle of their weapons and the creak of their metal limbs sets my teeth on edge.

Ahuli's horse is the first to fall, the gelding's scream cut short as he's mown down. Orenda's buckskin dies next. As her mare drops, we leap clear of the shared saddle and tumble to the sand. I scuttle for shelter behind the closest boulder.

Dodging blasts, Orenda skids over to Ahuli. Grasping the back of his shirt, she drags him to safety. Her brother falls in beside me with a thump, hat missing, hair awry and his Winchester rifle held close to his chest. He rolls over and levels the gun against the top of the boulder and begins to fire. Orenda covers him from the opposite side.

With my own pistol useless, I grab the one tucked into Ahuli's belt. He nods his approval. Together we fire into the approaching enemy, hoping to score the lucky shots that will send them all packing to hell.

The gunfight lasts all of two minutes.

The machines circle us without losing even one of their number—an unholy army gleaming dull in the drifting dust of battle and the dying light. Half of them wear human heads, and others wear human limbs—an arm here, a leg there—a profane blend of flesh and machine. For a moment, the creatures remain motionless, then they swivel and step back, creating a corridor.

"Why have they stopped?" I whisper.

"Watch," says Orenda. "Their didanawisgi approaches."

I recognise the Cherokee word. *Medicine man.*

A shuffling shape moves from the back of the assembled warriors. A wizened old man appears, bent over a walking stick of gnarled brown wood. At his throat is a thin red welt – a horizontal, knotted scar. I see the same at the exposed flesh on his wrists. His hands are different colours. On one, the skin is black and the other is white. His face is different again, an olive tone.

"Put down your weapons," says the Patchwork Man, his voice holding a curious clicking quality. He lifts his head, revealing two different-coloured eyes—one blue, one brown.

I aim my pistol at his heart. "We've come for the body of our friend. Hand it over and we'll be leavin' without further conflict."

"There is no conflict here. Only survival," says the man, tipping his chin toward the closest machine.

It turns.

The creature wears Bosco's face.

* *•*

With hands tied behind our backs, we are taken south and into the night. Skullcap Canyon lies far behind us while ahead a mesa rises – a great black shadow against the clear, night desert sky.

Jonah, Billy and Ike, heads now restored to their mechanical bodies, guard us as we march. I try and ignore the Bosco-machine that also keeps pace. It keeps turning to glance at Orenda and mutters unintelligible words. The clouded eyes of my dead friend seem to beseech his bride, asking her to love him still. But she pays him no heed. Back straight, chin up and eyes forward, Orenda walks on.

PATCHWORK REAPERS

The mesa's steep sides soon tower overhead. At ground level, the rock face is split by a large vertical crack. A faint humming emits from the crevice.

The Patchwork Man slows. He taps his walking stick against the ground and utters a series of clicks. The humming stops and the rock splits to reveal a corridor lit by a distant spill of light. We are led across the threshold, and I draw one last breath of clean air before the dreadful door slides closed behind us.

The pathway beyond is short and opens out into a large cavern. Within, the ceiling is concealed by shadow and distance, lost as it is to the heart of the mesa. The area is flooded with an unfamiliar white light. It holds none of the warmth of a lamp or an open fire. Tarnished silver tables lined up in neat rows fill the floor, each with a square metal box connected to the far end. Some hold machine-men lying prone, the rest are filled with half-mutilated human corpses – the staff from the ranch house. I clench my teeth. None of those good people deserved an end like this.

I turn from the gruesome display, searching for an escape. The place is a fortress, heavy and well-fortified. Everything's metal and wires and machines painted over with a ramshackle patina of dust and ancient rust.

There is no way out.

Next to me, Ahuli takes a sharp breath. His usually dusky face is pale. I follow his gaze to a pile of weathered sticks stacked up high against the far cavern wall.

No. Not sticks…

Bones. Both animal and human.

I reckon my face turns the colour of Ahuli's. "We gotta get out of here," I whisper.

He nods.

The Patchwork Man pauses at the centre of the cavern. He turns and the harsh light of the room reveals his skin to be blotched in shades of palest blue and green.

"Welcome," he says.

Welcome? I bunch my fists tighter. "Killin' our folk and haulin' us to this crazy-ass tomb ain't no kind of welcome!"

The old man looks confused for a moment. His mismatched gaze turns to Orenda. "You haven't told them?"

She shrugs. "They would not have come if I had."

"What are you talking about, sister?" asks Ahuli, disbelief etching his tone.

"The old stories," Orenda replies. "The Reapers are real."

Ahuli's eyes widen. "It can't be," he whispers.

"It is," she says.

"What in damnation are Reapers?" I ask, not really sure I want the answer.

"Myths. Monsters," says Ahuli, eyes still fixed to his sister. "Desert dwellers who came before men were even a seed of a thought on this land."

"I don't care how long they've been here," I say. "Why do they wanna kill us?"

"Not kill," says Orenda. "We only wish to survive."

"We?" I ask.

She undoes her neckerchief and drops it to the ground. A thin white scar circles the base of her neck and another runs down to disappear between her breasts.

Ahuli steps back, disgusted.

"Why are you not pleased, brother?"

"Pleased? Sister, you are a monster!"

The Patchwork Man shakes his head. "No. She is a gift. She has saved us."

"Your kind should not be saved," whispers Ahuli.

I've had enough of this. I don't like feeling afraid. "What are you, and what the hell do you want from us?"

The Patchwork Man blinks. "We are worker droids left here thousands of years ago by masters who, when finished seeding life on this planet, abandoned us." He points to the other machines standing behind us. "Our original parts are failing," he continues. "We have been forced to survive on blended metal and flesh – flesh that always rots away."

The Bosco machine gurgles a quiet cry.

"You don't look like you've got any issues," I say.

The Patchwork Man holds up his different-coloured hands. "I have only perfected my new body recently," he says, "with a new modification process I resolved on this female human."

Orenda remains eerily still.

The old man catches me staring at her.

"You are wondering for how long she has deceived you?" he asks, voice sly.

"Thought did cross my mind," I say.

"We captured her two months ago." The old man smiles and I glimpse copper teeth behind his greenish lips. "I successfully transplanted her skin casing and various critical organs onto one of my own people's exoskeletons. Then we sent her out to gather others that could be used for our purpose."

"My sister has been dead for two months?" Ahuli's voice cracks like a bullet through glass.

"Dead? No," says the Patchwork Man. "The machine at her core has control of the body and its programming dominates the flesh-mind processes, but she still maintains her awareness behind that. That is our gift for the sacrifice of her body to our cause."

Gift? Orenda is still alive in there somewhere?

A butterfly trapped in a spider's web.

Suddenly, the pain I saw in her eyes earlier takes on new meaning.

"You have violated my sister!" Ahuli launches, locking his broad hands around the old man's throat.

With a swing that seems all too easy, the Patchwork Man sends Orenda's brother flying. He lands heavily against a table. Bone crunches and he howls, clutching his chest. Bright blood soon dribbles down his chin.

The Patchwork Man's eyes glow white for a moment as a thin beam of light runs from them to scan over Ahuli's body. The old man's features ripple into anger.

"Your critical organs are damaged. You are of no value now!"

He nods to Orenda and the tall woman-made-machine stalks over to her brother.

"Orenda," pleads Ahuli.

Without hesitation she tears his head free from his shoulders.

The machine within made her do it. The tears streaking her cheeks betray the truth of that fact, even as her mouth remains cold and resolute.

A different machine-man, one whose rusted limbs screech with every step, strides over and takes possession of the grisly prize.

"Take its arms and legs for yourself too," says the Patchwork Man irritably.

The creature nods and complies. It carries Ahuli's parts to a table and lays them out. Clear tubes, with a life of their own, snake out of the box at the table's end and imbed themselves into what remains of Ahuli's neck and severed limbs. A black liquid is pumped through them. The head reanimates, lax lips beginning to move and eyes blinking in rapid succession. Ahuli's disconnected limbs shudder also, fingers and toes twitching.

The machine-man detaches its degenerated parts. More cables snake from within its body's open connective points and slither through the raw, bloodied ends to link with fleshy tendons. The last part replaced is Ahuli's head, fitted to the metal neck socket, his eyes mirror abject horror.

My stomach surges. Palms turn sweaty.

Orenda grabs me by the shoulder. "This way."

Her grip is iron.

I have no choice but to go where she leads.

We pass what's left of Ahuli's body. The spreading pool of his blood is too scarlet against the red rock floor. If what the Patchwork Man says is right, eventually, fitted to that machine, Ahuli will die. Right now, all-the-way-dead is better sounding than becoming trapped as a machine's skin overcoat.

We stop at an empty table. When encouraged to lie down I twist and drop my shoulder into Orenda's chest. Her skin gives but beneath I meet a wall of iron. I grunt and fall back against the table.

Orenda lifts her hand, balled into a fist but the old man stops her.

"Do not damage it," he says. "We need the body whole."

Orenda complies. She steps back and to one side.

"Get on the table, " says the Patchwork Man.

"No."

"It was not a request."

"I didn't take it as one."

"I am gifting you immortality."

I shake my head. "It's slavery."

The old man frowns. He lifts his walking stick and for the first time I notice the back length of it is honed and sharpened to a knife's keen edge. "We will do what we must to survive."

"Go to hell," I snarl.

The Patchwork Man leans in.

I don't feel the slice across my neck as his blade passes.

But I do taste the blood in my mouth.

PENDULUM OF ASH

John Coming

Arthur's rearview mirror was filled with smoke and flame. The sky gleamed a sickly orange. He reached down to fiddle with the cracked dashboard display, but the radio signal from Lockwood had gone to static half an hour earlier. The only other sound was the cooling fan above the engine's slowly dying battery. The car was using more power than its solar panels could generate from the smoke-covered sun. The faint green display behind the wheel read fifty-four miles left on the car's range. He hoped it would be enough.

It was the heaps of rusted cars spread out from the distant buildings like untended weeds that slowed Arthur's approach. He weaved forward through the jagged rows, staying towards the outskirts, and parked facing away from the town.

When he pressed his thumb to the display screen, a green line circled it twice, before blinking: *Shut Power Off?* Arthur tapped yes. The cooling fan turned off with a sigh of relief, and he stepped out onto the cracked ground and looked out over the graveyard of cars. *What the hell is going on here?*

There was a faint pattern in the strange parking lot he had missed at first. The cars were split into two sides. The half Arthur parked in was filled with cars tagged with angel wings, painted on in a uniform design. *The Rangers.*

Arthur resisted the pull to grab the gun on his hip. The Rangers would play nice if he kept his cool. In Arthur's experience though, they often had the same solution to every problem. *Hammers often see nails.*

He squinted towards the other side of the cars, and walked into the small clearing between the two factions. *If the Rangers are on this side...*

Drawn haphazardly, and unevenly onto the edge of each vehicle opposite him was a red, seven-pointed star. As a child, his brother once told him that each member of Babalon's Children drew the symbol in blood. Superstition, nothing more.

Arthur popped open the cracked leather holster on his hip anyway.

Hundreds of BC and Rangers all clustered together. This place is a time bomb.

He glanced back at his car. Leaving now, without finding the tapes would mean no payday. No irons to pay for a new battery, or purchase food. It was well over two hundred miles to Surge City, and how welcome would he be if he didn't finish the job?

Arthur pressed forward.

Half a mile down the lot, he passed a metal sign with black lettering that read: *Welcome to Sugar Run, Home of the Re—*

The end of the sign was painted over in black with a new message. *Leave all weapons at Sheriff Carrington's Office.* Arthur wondered how many of the new guests would comply with the local rule.

The smell of the town hit him before anything else. Rot. Sweat. Rust. Nothing pleasant. The soft wind stirred the scent and mixed it with the ashy air.

A rusted-out silver semi-trailer blocked what Arthur figured was the main street of the small town. While he squeezed around the small gap between the edge of the trailer, he heard two gunshots in rapid succession, then distant laughter.

The street beyond the rusted trailer was covered with broken glass and ash. Dozens of dirty forms stumbled or crawled through the road. Some bodies didn't move at all. Storefronts were shattered open, and doors were tagged with messages in alternating white and red. A short bald man to Arthur's left leaned against the side of an old rotted front porch and pissed onto a welcome mat.

On his right, Arthur spied a small pair of eyes peer over a tipped wheelbarrow. A child. He gave the young girl a little wave, which caused her to jump and scurry deeper into the alley where an old man scooped her up. Arthur took a step towards them, but when he saw the old man's frightened face, thought better of it.

Arthur put his palms together, and gently twisted them before spreading his hands apart with the palms facing down. Sign language for *Peace.*

The old man squinted at the motion before turning with the child and darting deeper into the shadows. Once, the symbol may have been recognized, along with Arthur's long gray coat, but that time had long since passed. Now, he was just another wanderer. Most people only saw him as dangerous. *And maybe they're right.*

Ahead, brown smoke billowed from an exposed building. Arthur moved towards it, hand partially covering his eyes when he saw the frayed rope swinging with a burnt corpse at its end. He clenched his stomach to stop the rising bile. Behind the hanged body, faded blue lettering was visible on the smokey building – *Sugar Run Police Station.*

"Shame, truthfully," a voice yelled out.

Arthur turned, casually placing his hand on his gun. Across the road, a wiry man in an old leather jacket hobbled across the ruined pavement. The man held his hands up to reveal no weapons, and Arthur begrudgingly took his hand off his hip to return the motion.

The wiry man held out a hand that had been tattooed with black angel wings. Arthur took it and gave a quick shake.

"Finally, a new face that ain't BC," the man said. "Platoon calls me Runner."

"And what should I call you?"

Runner gave an uncomfortable laugh. "Runner will do. Anything I was known as before that wasn't worth much. What's your name?"

Arthur had used a thousand fake names since he'd been on the road. It was the safe thing to do. A name gave someone power over you. It created a connection. Safer to ignore the question. "What's going on here, Ranger?"

"You aren't coming from Forest Camp?" Runner asked. Arthur shook his head. "Wildfire moved in quicker than their scouts predicted. Whole place is up in smoke now. Pushed out our entire platoon, and the red neighborhood where the BC were holed up."

"And you all fled the fires and landed here."

"Not by choice," Runner said, motioning Arthur to follow. "I know some folks went west, but anyone who started south... this is one of the only towns between Forest Camp and Surge City."

Arthur glanced back at the hanging form of Sheriff Carrington. "A shame for everyone living here."

"That was the work of the BC," Runner said, spitting. "Devils, all of them."

Arthur nodded, but as he looked around at the broken town, he only saw Rangers. Drinking, looting, fighting. Whatever order the group once possessed had vanished in their exodus south. All that pent-up anger and hunger made them just as destructive as the fire they ran from. *And just as likely to wipe Sugar run off the map.*

The Rangers functioned like an amalgam of law enforcement, private security, and old-world biker gang. Above all, every Ranger Arthur had ever met shared a smug self-righteousness. Out here where things were getting desperate, that surety made them as dangerous as the BC.

"I need to speak to someone who actually lives here," Arthur said.

"Sure, sure," Runner said, continuing forward. "There's a place that's still open if you can believe it. Friendly lady's been serving drinks to anyone with Irons since the day before last. She's a Vestige. Never thought I'd see one of them out here."

Runner stopped them outside of a bustling building with a wide archway. "Here we are, the Cobra Tavern."

"I appreciate the help, Ranger," Arthur said, nodding towards him. Runner grabbed his arm, and on instinct, Arthur slammed the smaller man's wrist with his fist, forcing him to let go.

"Shit, didn't mean to startle you," Runner said, rubbing his arm, "It's just... well, the robe and all... You're one of them, aren't you? From the Strongholds?"

"I am," Arthur said slowly.

"I thought you were all dead."

"Not yet."

"Right, obviously, stupid thing to..." Runner started. "What were you then? Marine, Collector...?"

Arthur lowered his still raised fist, feeling somewhat foolish for his reaction. It had been the first human contact he'd had in weeks and... *and the last one hadn't gone so well.* He remembered grappling for the man's knife out in the cold desert night. Arthur had been careless and had started a fire to eat something warm. "I was a historian."

"Right, of course," Runner said, nodding as they entered the tavern. Then a moment later, "A what?"

"Thank you for helping me. I hope your platoon makes it to Surge City soon, for everyone's sake." Arthur paused then noticed the expectation on Runner's face. "*Salus in arduis,*" he said, repeating the motion for peace.

Runner smiled widely and tried to return the motion. "Same to you."

Arthur stepped up to the dark wooden bar of the Cobra Tavern. The bartender was an older woman, nearly seven feet tall. Her gray hair was pulled back into a long braid, and she looked down at Arthur with unnervingly pale eyes.

Though she looked sixty, Arthur was sure she was at least twice that. Vestiges were a rare sight these days, rarer still out here in a small town like Sugar Run. They were genetically modified from birth, with a technology that surpassed anything Arthur had seen, even in the Stronghold. Vestiges aged more slowly, their bodies attacked diseases and cancers more efficiently. They were stronger, taller, *better*, than regular humans. The Professor had once told Arthur that some people revered them like Gods. Sometimes, that reverence led to sickening ends. There were groups who believed that consuming a Vestige would grant the eater their gifts.

The woman before Arthur had been alive longer than this new world had been. She was from before The Fall.

"What do you want?" the woman asked bluntly.

"Information," Arthur said. "I'll buy a whiskey to go along with it." He threw three Irons down on the bar top, double what the drink would go for.

The Vestige rubbed the old bars for a moment, considering. "Let me guess... you're here for the tapes, aren't you?"

Arthur frowned. "How...?"

The Vestige dried off an upside-down glass, then poured a dark liquid into it. When she set it down, she motioned Arthur forward. "There's a man dressed in black sitting in the corner. He asked after them about an hour ago. I'll tell you the same thing I told him. Finish your drink and get the hell out of my town." The older woman slid an Iron beside Arthur's drink.

He pocketed the Iron, and held up the glass in a mock salute, before drinking. Arthur turned and saw the man the Vestige had described sitting alone in the shadows, watching him. The man walked forward to the bar, gently nudging an unconscious man off the stool beside Arthur.

"Pleased to meet you, friend," the man in black said. "*Salus in Arduis.*" Stronghold in difficult times. The man motioned the sign for peace.

Arthur returned the motion. "*Per unitatem vis.*" Through unity, strength.

"Boy, do I feel safer with one of your esteemed Order here. I thought you were all dead."

"So, I keep hearing."

The man smiled, his cheeks a wind-burnt red and his head covered in messy black hair. His words and face seemed friendly enough, though the man's eyes were fixed and predatory. He never kept his hand far from his hip, where Arthur guessed a gun was hidden beneath his dusty black jacket.

Behind them, a small crowd had gathered around a table in the center of the room. Two women sat alone, surrounded by a dozen Rangers and a smaller group of newcomers. Members of

Babalon's Children had arrived. The two women sat at the table, one Ranger, one BC. The Ranger placed a small silver gun down on its side and spun it.

"Heartwarming, isn't it? Seeing two historically hateful groups get along?" the man in black said.

"What is it you wanted?"

"Who hired you for this? Someone from Four Rivers? Jed? New Augusto?"

The gun stopped spinning, facing the woman in red. She picked it up reverently and smiled as she placed it to her temple. *Click.* A gasp went up from the crowd.

"My buyer is none of your concern," Arthur said.

"No, none of those fit. It must be Surge City... Diane's decided to get her perfect little hands dirty again then?"

Arthur frowned but said nothing. The truth was, he had never met the buyer. He was instructed to meet an intermediary when he arrived at Surge City. *If I ever make it there.*

The Ranger picked up the gun and tried to give a confident smile that looked more terrified than anything. She put the gun to her head, and hesitated before pulling the trigger. *Click.* She laughed, and set the gun back down, her hand shaking.

"My buyer died along with a quarter of Forest Camp," the man said, eying the strange roulette game behind them. "Which makes me amenable to... a short-term partnership, say."

"No thanks."

The woman in red picked up the gun in an automatic motion, put the barrel to her temple, and pulled the trigger without hesitation. *Click.*

"This town is a gonna blow, and you're out of time," the man in black said. "I happen to know where the tapes are. Without a buyer, I'm at a loss though."

The Ranger picked up the gun, and slowly raised it up to her head. She held it there, contemplating her next move. *Don't do it. Put the damn thing down.* The Ranger steeled herself, closed her eyes, pulled the trigger.

The gunshot was deafening in the small space. Arthur flinched, as a droplet of blood hit his cheek. The tavern went silent. The woman in red, her face splattered with dark blood smiled, and put her palms on the table as she gently pushed herself up. "Another soul for the Scarlet Woman."

The man in black slid off his stool. "Meet me at the old supermarket in an hour if you're interested. Otherwise, I advise you find a different place to rest your head tonight."

The man in black slinked towards a side door just as one of the other Rangers smashed his bottle on the side of the woman in red's jaw, and the two groups lunged at each other.

Arthur took a deep breath before downing his drink and setting the glass upside down on the bar. The Vestige walked out from around a corner, a black shotgun in her hands. Arthur slid the Iron forward. "You might need this more than me. I suggest you find a way to get out of here before long. Your town might not survive the night."

The Vestige frowned. "This is my home. There are people depending on me."

"Those people will wind up dead if you're too stubborn to leave."

"Word of advice," the Vestige called out, as Arthur walked towards the side door. "Stay away from that man, the one in black."

"You know him?"

The Vestige nodded. "That was CK Richards, I'm sure of it. These eyes won't let me forget a face."

Arthur clenched his jaw. "Thanks for the tip-off." He threw the side door open. *CK Richards.* One of the most well-known names in the south. An infamous bandit, an invisible thief, a hunted outlaw. The assassin who killed one of the most beloved men of the new world.

● ●[●]

Clouds rolled across the weak sun, casting the world into a sinister red. Hundreds of miles north, the forest was still ablaze along with any living creature trapped within. Arthur could almost imagine the dim heat on his neck through the chilled air.

The supermarket was the largest building in Sugar Run. An abandoned mecca sitting atop a small hill. The parking lot was littered with rusted-out cars, torn tents, and emptied crates.

CK Richards leaned against the edge of a pillar near the awning, brushing softly-falling ash off the shoulder of his black jacket. He gave Arthur a thin smile. "Hello again, friend."

Arthur stopped a dozen feet away, cautiously watching the abandoned store.

"No need to worry. If I wanted to kill you, you'd be dead," CK said.

"Not a very comforting thing to say to someone."

CK shrugged. "Not a very comforting time or place, is it friend?"

Friend. I'm not your friend. I'm not like you. I'm... Arthur suddenly saw himself back in the desert, grappling for a knife on that cold night with the half moon. Seeing the fear in his attacker's eyes when it was all over. Realizing how thin and weak the other man looked now the fight was over.

"Let's get on with it," Arthur said, banishing the memory.

"What should I call you?"

"Is that important right now?"

"I'm worried you have me at a disadvantage," CK said flatly.

Arthur met the man's eyes in silence while small black flakes of ash fell between them.

Finally, CK shrugged, breaking the tension. "Friend it is. A couple miles up the road, there's an old farmhouse. My, regretfully deceased buyer told me which one to look for."

Arthur frowned. "Why don't we take your car?"

"A couple of trigger-happy Rangers decided they'd try and requisition it."

"They stole it?"

"It was a lose-lose situation," CK replied.

"How the hell do you intend to make it to Surge City?"

"This is a partnership. I help you find the tapes; you get us to Surge City, we split the profits when we make it."

Arthur clenched his jaw. *Or I help you find this tape, you kill me when I turn my back, then steal my car and my buyer.*

Trust. It was the only thing that would still hurt you when you gave it to someone else. Arthur hadn't made that mistake in a long time. He sure as hell wouldn't make it now. "One step at a time," he said. "Tapes first."

CK gave a short laugh. "Fair deal. Follow along. And... don't try anything. Messy business, killing a new friend."

* * *

The massive farmhouse was set back on a long driveway lined with dead gnarled trees. Dark brown wooden panels rose high into an ash-covered roof. The structure was intact, save for the broken windows and sections of slumped roofing.

Arthur paused and stared up at the house. It was—

"Down," CK whispered, pulling Arthur to the ground behind a wide trunk. CK held a finger to his lips, then pointed to the edge of the driveway.

Arthur saw the front tire of a car sticking out from under a dirty tarp. *If there's one there's likely...* "Two more cars on the far-right side of the house, possibly some bikes too," Arthur whispered. "Think they saw us?"

"They would've taken a shot if they did."

"Could be there waiting for us to come up close."

CK nodded. "Maybe so. What say you, we creep into the back?"

Arthur frowned while the assassin craned his neck to the house. Why had CK taken him all the way out here? His fingers twitched, expectantly.

The paranoia fell apart when he thought it through. *Expect the worst, but don't make it.* Arthur had known more than one person who'd let a good thing go bad out of fear alone. Some people were so afraid of being double-crossed, they figured the only way to avoid it was to be the one that shot first. Arthur relaxed his hand.

If CK had noticed Arthur's fears, the man did an admirable job hiding it. "Well?"

"There could be twenty people in there. Doesn't leave us with great odds," Arthur said.

"No, it does not," CK admitted. "Suppose we just walk back to town then, say better luck next time?"

Arthur sighed. "Fast and silent. No killing if we can avoid it. Could be townsfolk holed up in there, avoiding the mess back in town."

"I knew it. You have an optimistic streak hidden under all that gruff. I wondered at first if you'd killed a member of Salus and stolen that coat, but you're the real thing, aren't you?"

Arthur's forehead furled. He was *not* optimistic. Optimistic people didn't worry about killing every person they met. "Does it matter?" He left unsaid the rest. *Does it matter who my family, city, people were if the rest of them are all dead?*

CK shrugged. "It does if you want it to."

Both men froze as they heard a door thrown open. Voices drifted over to one of the covered cars, and a moment later a battery cooling fan turned on. Arthur and CK pressed themselves against the tree-stump as the car rolled past, throwing gravel and ash into the air. On the car's side, Arthur noted a red star.

When the car was out of sight, CK turned to Arthur. "Onward?"

Arthur nodded, and followed softly behind.

The house seemed frozen in time. Dust hung in the air like a snapshot of a blizzard, so thick that Arthur covered his mouth with the sleeve of his dark gray coat. The backdoor had been left unguarded, and CK picked through the old-fashioned lock with ease. Red ambient light crept through the drawn windows and holes from the roof. The house was drenched in silence. CK tilted his head a moment, then motioned for Arthur to go left, while he went right.

Arthur crept as silently as he could. Each creak of the floor and beat of his heart felt like a siren disturbing the tomb.

A sickening smell wafted from the closed kitchen door. Arthur put his ear to it and counted. Thirty seconds. A minute. Two minutes. Finally, he pushed the door slowly open, the hinges screeching as if they served the enemy.

Empty, but fat bloat flies hovered behind the counter. Arthur steadied his long, silver gun, and when the grip touched his palm, a faint *click* sounded from within the barrel, and a dull white light blinked. The silver sun pattern of Salus pulsed once with faint warmth against his hand, confirming the gun was active.

He poked his head around the counter. A gory, unrecognizable form was stretched along the floor, surrounded by bloody symbols. The cult was famously secretive, though one tenet of their religion was whispered of in every corner of the new world. The BC left offerings to their Scarlet Woman wherever they went, and the only offering she accepted was blood.

Arthur found CK sitting by a wide staircase, the man nodded and motioned that the bottom floor was clear.

Tapes? Arthur mouthed.

CK shook his head, pointed up the stairs, and led the way.

The edge of the staircase showed remnants of a ripped-up carpet. *Maybe the house's original occupants, looking for additional warmth, or material for clothing.* Arthur wondered if it helped.

They arrived at a wide hallway with a door at either end. CK motioned to start on the left, but Arthur shook his head. A faint sound came from the far-right door. A muffled voice, but more distant, like it was playing from underwater, or behind a crackling radio signal.

"Someone is playing the tape," Arthur whispered.

They crept down the hallway, closer and closer to the muffled voice. Arthur glanced at CK. *I wasn't the only one contracted to find the tapes. And it doesn't seem like a coincidence that the BC are here either. What the hell does everyone want with them?*

At the end of the hallway, Arthur put his ear to the lit door. The tape recording was still playing, and he could make out faint words.

"It's strange... she never said that... I'm *changed* now that... the machine is gone, bu...."

Arthur leaned back. CK stood with his back to the wall, one hand holding his gun, the other a long black knife. He nodded towards the door. Arthur reached up, gently turned the blackened copper doorknob, and pushed the door ajar. Beyond, a long room with a table and two flickering candles at the end that cast dark shadows over the floors. A tall woman stood at the table with her back to the door, hunched over the tape recorder. Near the ceiling, a glassless window was open, bathing the floor in blood-red light.

I've got her, C.K. mouthed. He pushed the door open with the hilt of his knife.

Arthur saw a flicker of movement from the sides of the room. He grabbed CK's arm and pointed. Half a dozen forms lay sleeping under black blankets. The one closest to the door turned onto its side and let out a deep sigh.

CK gently pulled the door closed and turned to Arthur. "So, that—"

"What are you doing up?" A voice whispered harshly from down the hall. A middle-aged man in a dark red robe walked towards them. "We are to conserve our strength. The Scarlet Woman demands that..."

The man froze when he reached the staircase, his eyes studying their unfamiliar faces. He reached into his robe, but CK was quicker. Arthur heard a faint *twang* in the air, and a moment later CK's knife was buried hilt deep in the stranger's heart.

The man looked down, almost in surprise, and put his hand to his chest. He fumbled for the staircase railing with his bloodied hand, his grip slipping as he fell headfirst down the steps.

"The hell was..." A voice sounded from inside the end room.

"New plan," CK whispered, pushing Arthur against the wall. CK ran towards the staircase just as the door flew open, with Arthur pressed between it and the peeled yellow wallpaper.

"Wha—" a voice yelled.

A gunshot rang out through the hallway, and a body crumpled to the ground.

"Rangers fall back," CK yelled. "There's BC up here!"

Arthur listened as CK half ran, half fell down the stairs and the sleeping occultists stumbled out from the room to give chase. Downstairs, more shots rang out, before Arthur heard a crashing sound.

Get the tapes now, or it was all for nothing.

He glanced into the room. Empty. The tape was still playing softly on the table. He walked forward, eyes darting into each corner.

The tape recorder was an old-fashioned thing, flat and gray, with two small speakers on either end. Arthur reached out to turn it off but froze as he heard the voice continue.

"...went downhill fast, just like they said it would. Four Rivers went with more of a bang than a whimper, but we didn't hear about it for weeks. The Forest Camp went up in smoke next. Everyone kept their eyes on all the tension between the Rangers and the BC, and we missed the real man pulling the strings. Surge City fell less than a year after that. You told me to record this with as much detail as possible, but everything feels so... I just see so differently now. I can't believe I'm back before it began."

The tape played white noise for a moment before stopping. *How could the speaker know about the forest fire? Was there a fire earlier? And what was that about Surge City?*

"Amazing, isn't it?"

Arthur spun, gun pointed towards the voice. The tall woman stood in the doorway with a man either side, their guns trained on him.

"It shouldn't exist," the tall woman said. "It's... an apple of discord. Chaos concentrated. That's how the Scarlet Woman described it. I should have known it would draw others to it."

Arthur eyed the two guns pointed at him. *Bad odds.*

"Who sent you for it?" the tall woman asked. Arthur said nothing. "Where is the other set?" It was a demand, but her voice betrayed a panicked fervor Arthur hadn't noticed before.

"No matter," she said. A scream came from outside, and one of the men flicked his eyes towards the sound.

Arthur fired on the other man, hitting him squarely between the eyes, then turned to the distracted man. They fired simultaneously.

A searing impact drove into his shoulder, throwing him against the table, but the second man crumpled, hands pressed against his neck.

Arthur steadied himself against the table. *Now just the—*

The woman rammed into his stomach, sending him to the ground, his shoulder exploding in pain. He reached for his gun, when a knee drove into his shoulder, forcing his grip loose. Arthur blinked through sweat and tears as the tall woman grabbed his silver gun and pointed it at his forehead. Arthur's eyes darted to the gun's side. Near the barrel, a line of light pulsed a dull red. The tall woman smiled, then pulled the trigger.

Click. She flicked her eyes to the gun in confusion before her face contorted into sharp pain. She screamed, throwing the gun across the room, and held out a shaking hand. Faint lines of smoke swirled up from her burnt skin, seared with the swirling sun pattern from the hilt.

He lunged forward, and they rolled towards the corner. Arthur kicked the woman off him, sending her crashing into the wall. The flickering candles reflected off her eyes like pillars of lightning as she crouched, readying to attack. Arthur fumbled for the gun as the tall woman leapt.

Arthur swung the gun, hitting the side of her head with a *crack*. She collapsed onto him, and he tossed her aside, the back of her head smacking into the table. *She's still breathing. I should—*

No. He wouldn't. He couldn't. His hands were already bloody, but that didn't mean he was lost.

Arthur reached for his shoulder wound with shaking fingers. Could have been worse, but it was enough to leave trails of blood down the right side of his coat. He stumbled to his feet and grabbed the tape recorder.

A shock ran down his hand as soon as he touched the edge of the device, and for a moment, he was somewhere else. At the Stronghold again, as a boy. Then a teenager, reading beside the

Professor. He was a young man, weeping as he watched the city burn. Back in the desert, grappling with a starving man.

But the vision didn't end there. A thousand lines shot out from him, leading to infinitely more roads. In one of them, Arthur walked down the stairs, and was shot from the side by a hidden gunman. In another, the alarm went off on one of the occultists cars when he tried to break into it. The next, Arthur stood in the darkened parking lot outside of Sugar Run while a group of Rangers surrounded CK and killed him. He felt pieces of himself peeling away, getting lost, deeper and deeper into possibilities, chances, roads, deaths. Chaos.

Arthur snatched his hand back and gasped. He was back in the candlelit room. The tape recorder sat on the table before him. *Just a tape recorder...* Arthur reached out tentatively and touched the side of it.

Nothing.

He put it into his robe's pocket and paused at the doorway, remembering the gunman who had shot him in the back.

It was impossible. Had to be. But somehow, Arthur *knew* that it was true. He turned, climbed out the open window, and on to the slanted ash-covered roof. Arthur slid down to the edge, levered himself to the lower level of roofing before finally dropping to the ground. His ankle rolled over, and he hobbled into the darkness towards Sugar Run. Hopefully, CK had been able to escape, and had made it safely back to the supermarket. Hopefully—

A hand slipped over his mouth, and a gun pressed into his back.

"Is that you, friend?" CK whispered. Arthur nodded, and the hand released. CK looked out of breath and sported a fresh cut that dripped blood down his cheek. But he was alive, somehow. *Of course, he is. He'll make it to the parking lot, where...*

"Did you get it?" CK asked, both men standing ankle-deep in the gray weeds of a field that had once been good land.

"I did." Arthur tapped the recorder within his coat. He reached to reveal it when he noticed that CK's gun was still drawn. The man's eyes looked suddenly hungry in the purple dusk. "Everything all right, friend?" Arthur said quietly.

CK blinked, like he had been shaken from a dream. He holstered his gun, and took a deep breath, then trudged ahead of Arthur, back towards Sugar Run.

* • •

The town was engulfed in flames, echoing with constant gunfire amid screams. Fire devoured the air, roaring and spreading. Somewhere nearby, a child wept. Arthur turned and ran towards the sound.

"Friend, where are you... Oh come *on*," CK said, before trailing after.

Arthur and C.K. followed the sound to the back of the Cobra Tavern, which had so far avoided the worst of the carnage. Behind the bar, a group of townspeople huddled near the Vestige, who crouched beside a young boy.

"Do not cry, Charlie," she said softly. "You must be strong now."

Arthur and CK walked forward, and the group took an instinctive step back. None of them had guns, though one woman held a long wooden bat in both hands, and stepped between Arthur and the Vestige.

Arthur raised his hands then made the sign for peace.

The Vestige stood, towering over the group. "Peace, Maria."

The young woman reluctantly backed down. An explosion shook the ground, and a withered corner of the Cobra Tavern crumbled into the darkened alley.

"You all need to get out of here, now," Arthur said.

"There is a safe place where I am gathering those I can," the Vestige said. "I would welcome you, man of Salus, but I won't invite a viper into my nest." She turned her eyes on CK.

"I'm the least of your concerns, Vestige," CK replied icily.

"Is that what you told the Mayor of Surge City before you —"

"Are you sure it will be safe?" Arthur said, ignoring the exchange.

The Vestige nodded. "There is a bunker, not far from here."

"You'll be trapped until they leave, or kill each other," Arthur said.

"And what would you have us do? Run on foot into the night? Starve to death in the wastelands or become refugees in Surge City? No. We will stay here and wait for the storm to pass through our home."

Bullets ripped through a nearby window, forcing everyone to the ground. A licking flame danced on the ground floor of the Cobra Tavern.

"Friend," CK said, looking around the alley, "We've gotta move."

"I'm sorry," Arthur said, moving past the townspeople.

The Vestige reached out to him.

"*Salus in—*" the Vestige started before their hands made contact. Arthur felt a spark again, like he had when he first touched the tape recorder, though no vision followed. But the Vestige's eyes had gone white.

"This has all happened before," she whispered. "The fires, the ash, the town already burnt, and..." She gasped and gripped Arthur's arm, her nails digging into his skin.

"The bombs... they fall again, the wars start again. I thought... I thought... it *repeats*. It never ends, it..." The Vestige blinked, and her eyes cleared. She looked down at Arthur. "What...?"

Another explosion rocked the ground, this one far closer than the last. "Come on," CK yelled.

"Protect your people," Arthur said to her, then squeezed her arm. "And no matter what you saw, don't lose hope."

The Vestige released Arthur and scooped up the young boy while giving orders to the rest of the small group.

Arthur caught up to CK, who was already moving towards the parking lot.

"Where's your car?" CK said.

"Far left side," Arthur whispered, "but the battery is nearly shot."

"We'll need to borrow one—" They were forced to the ground by another explosion. "Not that they'll mind," CK muttered.

The fighting had spread into the parking lot where scattered bands shot at each other between cars. *They thought they escaped from the Forest Camp's fire, but they only brought it with them.*

CK angled them to the left as a group of Ranger's took a bat to the windshield of a car marked with the red star. "I'm gonna strip one of these trucks for the battery, be lookout for me," he said, then moved to crawl forward, but paused and turned back. "And this time, don't let me get shot at please."

CK winked, then slid underneath a large truck twenty feet ahead of Arthur. He pulled out a small multi-tool from his black coat and began working on the battery.

The wind whistled through the field of steel and rust, throwing ash into Arthur's eyes.

"You sure it was him?" a voice said from behind. Arthur ducked low, huddling behind a small, rusted car.

"I'm sure. Knew his face the minute I saw him in the bar," a second voice said. "Townie confirmed it for me, said he saw the bastard with the Salus man running this way."

CK was prone beneath the truck, perfectly still as the group passed Arthur's hiding spot. He counted five, maybe six Rangers, as they moved to where CK lay.

"The Salus man isn't a threat, no matter who he's with," said a third, familiar voice.

Runner.

"The fool probably doesn't know," the second voice said. "And if he does, he deserves the dirt too. There's not a person left alive as evil as CK Richards. If there's a hell, it's too good for a man like him. A man that could kill someone like the Mayor..." A spitting noise followed.

The group surrounded Arthur's car, only a dozen paces from where CK waited unseen in the quickly fading light. One man casually kicked at its worn tires. "You sure they'll even come back for this piece of garbage?"

"Maybe not," the first man said. "But I've got a feeling they're close." The man flipped a switch on a handheld device and began to wave it at nearby cars.

Some sort of bio, or thermal scanner.

The group moved quickly; they would be on CK in moments.

As CK slowly reached for the gun under his coat, Arthur recognized the familiar scene. *This is what I saw. This is how he dies.* CK would burst out, and take two, maybe three of them. But those men all had their guns drawn, and he would go down quickly. If Arthur did nothing, it was as good as done. Like it had already happened.

And maybe it should happen. I'm not choosing this, just... letting the timeline play out. Maybe CK Richards shouldn't be alive. How many people has he killed? How many more will he kill?

There was no excuse Arthur could hide behind, no questions of causality. He knew exactly what outcome his indecision would bring. Now, he had to choose.

"Runner," Arthur called out. "I'm standing up, don't shoot."

Arthur pushed to his feet, hands raised. Ahead, all six Rangers had their guns trained on him.

"Good lord," Runner said, flashing a light on him. "What the hell happened to you."

Arthur grimaced, and grabbed his shoulder. "That bastard, CK Richards, double-crossed me. Tried to kill me. If I knew it was him..."

A bald man stepped forward beside Runner. "Where did the assassin go?"

Arthur nodded to the far side of the parking lot. "Said he has a bike stashed east of town."

The bald Ranger frowned and looked up and down at Arthur. "You've helped a dangerous man. I think you owe the Rangers a penance." The bald man motioned to the men behind him. "Take his gun and anything you find inside the car worth keeping."

The men moved forward but Runner stepped between them and Arthur. "The bounty on CK Richards is a hundred thousand Irons, Erik. We'll need the whole group to catch him. Let's not waste time with this," Runner said, motioning to Arthur.

The bald man considered for a moment, before sighing, and

putting his gun away. He turned to where Arthur had pointed, and the group followed.

Runner looked back at Arthur and motioned the sign of peace at him. "Good luck out there."

Arthur returned the motion, but Runner had already caught up with the group.

CK rolled out from underneath the truck and set the wide battery against Arthur's car.

Arthur limped up beside the man and opened the trunk with a swipe of his hand.

"I'll fit the new battery when we're a bit farther from all this fun," CK said, jumping into the passenger seat. "How many miles have you got?"

Arthur turned on the engine with a thumbprint against the cracked display. Behind the wheel, the green numbering read 7.5. "Enough."

• ••

Arthur took a different road south so they wouldn't pass by the farmhouse again. He looked down at the tape recorder nestled on the backseat of the car and wondered who else out there knew about it and was tracking it. *Not just tracking it. They'll come for the one who has it.*

CK rested his head against the back of the passenger seat, staring out the window. Despite how calm the man may have looked, Arthur noticed his hand kept clenching, and unclenching at his side. How could he ever truly relax when he was the most infamous man every place he went? What would a life like that do to a person?

"I'm Arthur, by the way," he said, and CK turned to look at him. "Can't have you calling me friend the whole way to Surge City."

CK gave him a thin smile, then turned back to the window. "I'd tell you my name, but it looks like I was right. You already know it."

"I do."

They drove in silence for a while, and once the car's battery was replaced, the range read 165 miles. Judging by the smoke coverage, they'd need every one of them.

"I appreciate what you did back there," CK said.

Arthur nodded. "We're partners in this. Judging how it's gone so far... I'll need a friend from wherever I can get one. Regardless of how many men seem to want him dead."

CK smirked. "I'm ashamed of more things I've done than I can remember. But you know what I refuse to take blame on? The one thing everybody hates me for." CK looked out the window, grinding his jaw. "I was only fifteen years old when they had me pull that trigger. Old enough to know what I was doing, but young enough to be fooled into thinking it was the right thing. And all those friends, those people who were older, who knew better? They all pretended like they didn't know me after it was done."

"Nobody's hands are clean," Arthur said. "Least of all my own. I won't judge you for what you've done. The only thing we can do now is move forward." *Hope that the world lets us be.*

"Forward," CK repeated. "It's a good dream."

Arthur chanced a look in the rearview mirror, where the early morning sun rose like pink scar tissue over the withered land. His ears still rang with the sounds of gunfire and rushing air. He could still feel the heat from the flames devouring Sugar Run on his cheeks.

Above all, he could feel the lightning in his fingertips from where he'd touched the tapes.

How can we move forward when something like that exists? Something that comes from a place that already happened, and is still happening?

Arthur didn't know. And he was too tired to find any answers now. Instead, he focused on the road ahead. He flicked on the radio, but all that came through were waves of static. So, they drove on in silence.

Always forward.

THE SHADOW UNDER SAD HILL

Robert Lassen

Ma Pegram never did like me much, but she must have dug down deep into that gossip-filled pit she called her soul to find the extra level of contempt she now wore plastered over her wrinkled face. "What the hell happened to you, kid? You fall off your horse again?"

"Looks like," her husband chuckled, rubbing his hands on his apron. "Maybe got a whole cactus up his ass."

They both laughed, forty years of married mean spiritedness still in perfect holy union.

I stood in the doorway, trying to suck up enough of the stale hotel-lobby air to fuel a few words. Sweat ran in thin rivulets from beneath my hat, carving a path through the dust on my cheeks before tumbling to the even dustier floorboards. Behind me, across the street, the church bell began to ring. Not the gentle tinkling call to worship. Instead, the urgent clamour of warning, careening towards us on a carriage of afternoon heat. "Where's the sheriff?"

Ma Pegram frowned as she looked past me. "It's daylight out, ain't it? Where do you think he is?"

Dust caked my throat as surely as my face. My eyes flickered to the whisky behind Joe Pegram's bar, not that they would have sold me any. Old enough to be apprenticed to Deputy Jim Taylor, not old enough to drink. Not in this town. Sheriff Stanton had some odd ideas when it came to liquor and the morals of the young.

Not that his morals were the oddest thing about him.

"The Henderson boys," I croaked. "Riding into town. Be here in five minutes."

"The Hendersons?" Joe looked at his wife in confusion. "From Missouri?"

"Old man, you would forget your balls if they weren't in a bag." Ma shook her head. "Sheriff took care of those Godforsaken sons of jackals three summers back. This will be the Henderson boys from Iowa." She sniffed. "Amateurs. Sheriff said he thought they might head this way. I told him the reward for them brothers ain't hardly worth him getting out of bed. Still, old Jim is ringing the hell out of that bell. You brave enough to wake him, kid?"

I swallowed, looking up the stairs. Truth was, I'd hoped he might already be awake, which was dumb of me. Sheriff Stanton was never up during the day, especially during the summer. When I was a boy – well, a smaller boy – I'd seen him a few times before sunset, back when outlaws and smugglers thought they could use the road through the little town of Mount Auburn as a short cut to the border and maybe do a little thieving or murdering on the way. That was before word of Mount Auburn's new sheriff spread, first around the county, then across the state, until pretty soon any dishonest fellow knew to avoid our town.

No one had died by murder in Mount Auburn since the winter night nine years earlier when Jedediah Cross had mistaken my father for an old gambling rival and shot both him and my mother in front of my five-year old eyes. The Sheriff had avenged my parents before their bodies were even cold. Then he'd taken me aside and said one word to me. Sorry.

Even then, I knew he meant it. Really meant it. But still I shuddered now, both at the memory of that sepulchral whisper and the thought I had to ascend the stairs and hear it again.

Four minutes.

Four minutes until the Henderson boys got here and I found out whether I could truly draw my father's little old Colt 1849 on a living target.

My body still wanted to hesitate. I didn't let it. Taking the creaking steps two at a time, I plunged into the dim corridor above. A lone candle, half-shielded, flickered pathetically below the shuttered window. While the bar and lobby below smelt of desert dust trapped too long, the top floor of the Pegram Hotel stank of something worse. Like a possum had crawled under the floorboards of a house and died there, too deep to pull out.

I reached the door and knocked quickly, before I could change my mind and run.

No answer.

The metal of the handle felt oddly cold despite the stagnant summer heat that cloaked everything else. I turned it and opened the door. Just a crack, enough to peer into the tomblike dark within, just enough to let the miasma within escape. Its stink caressed my nostrils while thick ropes of the foulest stench seemed to close like grasping hands around my throat.

"Sheriff Stanton?" I forced the words out, tried to keep my voice low, like a man. I failed. It came out like the damned bleat of a new-born goat.

Silence. *Three minutes.* I opened my dry lips to try again. But then the reply came from the darkness, and I forget about trying anything except keeping my bladder from emptying itself across the hallway floor.

"I heard the bell," the voice said.

All of us at one time or another had tried to describe Sheriff Stanton's voice. It was almost a tradition in Mount Auburn, a parlour game for evenings when the liquor was flowing and the sheriff wasn't in earshot (or, at least, you hoped to God he wasn't). Some called it a twisted echo, a hateful curse hurled in the depths of a canyon maze. Ma Pegram always said it sounded like a growl, like your old family dog had found the words to tell you it was going to kill you in your sleep. To me, as a kid, it had been the sound of dead leaves gusting into the sky from the bottom of a bone-dry well.

Now, hearing it again, it sounded like any of those sounds and none. Like nothing any man, or child, should ever have to hear on God's clean Earth.

"It's the Henderson boys, Sheriff," I told him, then hastily added, "the ones from Iowa."

"I remember the ones from Missouri," he said.

I heard a wet sound. The licking of lips.

"Deputy Taylor is going to try to slow them down," I said.

"You should be by his side. You're *his* deputy, aren't you?" The sheriff laughed, a disembodied chuckle from within the darkness. If his voice was unsettling, his laugh… despite my best efforts, a little trickle of pee escaped. "You got your father's pistol there?"

"Yes, sir."

"Good. Never trust a gun from a man you don't know. Get out there, kid. I'll be there in two minutes."

"Yes, Sheriff." I closed the door and ran. Down the stairs. Past the knowing smiles on the faces of the Pegrams. Out into the afternoon heat, blinking at the sudden brutal assault of the sun on eyes that had stared too long into the darkness. Grey-haired Jim Taylor stood in the centre of the road with his Springfield Trapdoor rifle cradled in his hands. As always, he seemed calm, utterly relaxed except for the hawk-like focus of his eyes.

Then I saw the three approaching riders that were the subject of that focus and remembered there were things in this life more dangerous than a voice in the shadows.

"Well, I'll be damned," the tallest Henderson brother whistled, bringing his horse to a halt twenty feet from us. "You got children peddling the law in this town?"

The rider next to him laughed, his bearded and weathered face crinkling with mirth. Older than the first speaker, I guessed, but subservient to him. "Looks like, Beau," he said. "Or is this maybe the sheriff of Mount Auburn everyone seems so worked up about? Best this side of the Mississippi they said, didn't they?"

Beau Henderson stared at me. He was a good-looking man, with tousled blond locks poking out from under his hat. Like an overgrown choir boy, except for the ice-cold blue of his eyes. A killer's eyes. "How old are you, boy?"

"Old enough," I snapped, then suppressed a curse. There my voice went again with that kid bleating.

"Old enough to be shot in the face," the third rider muttered through thin lips.

"It isn't too late, gentlemen," Jim said. "You can still turn your horses around and ride back the way you came. It doesn't have to go down like this."

All three riders laughed. "I think I'm going to like this place," Beau said to his brothers. "What do you think? Once we've killed ourselves this here old fart and his grandson, maybe we should avail ourselves of this town's hospitality?" He looked around, at the windows of the neat, well-kept schoolhouse and library, the general store, the faces half-hidden behind twitching curtains. "There must be some pretty ladies somewhere."

Jim didn't look at me, but his grip tightened on the rifle. The pistol at my side felt suddenly heavy, and I knew with certainty that my sweaty hands were going to struggle to keep hold of it. That was problem enough when I went out to shoot bottles.

Wondering if they would be the ones to finish the killing Jedediah Cross had started nine years ago, I looked up at the three riders. But they weren't looking at me, or even at Jim. They were looking at the front steps of the hotel.

Like I was a gawking child again, I gasped at the sight of Sheriff Stanton.

Well, not at the sight of *him*, I suppose. Nothing of the man himself was visible, every inch of skin swaddled beneath layers of mismatched clothing. Workman's boots, Union cavalryman pants and tunic beneath a Confederate quartermaster's great-coat, a long rent in the back of it from a sword slash. He might have been six feet or more stood to full height, but he hunched over almost at a right angle, as if the sheer weight of clothing bore him down. The shadows beneath his broad-brimmed hat couldn't quite disguise the brown stains on the off-white cloth layered around his face, wrapped so thickly it seemed to make the front of his head protrude. Smoked welder's goggles hid his eyes. Even his hands were concealed beneath folds of lurid purple cloth, so voluminous that I wondered how he could possibly unsheathe the cavalry sword hanging at his side or draw and fire the trigger of the long-barrelled .36 Colt Texas Paterson five-shooter tucked loosely in the sword belt.

"That pistol is older than me," the bearded brother laughed. "And why are you dressed like that? You taking your grandmother's antiques to the County Fair or something?"

Only Beau Henderson didn't laugh. He knew, as surely as I did, that Stanton would find a way to draw that pistol, and that none of them would be laughing afterwards. His hand slowly crept towards his holster and his waiting Smith and Wesson Model Three.

"Beau Henderson. Tucker Henderson. George Henderson."

They flinched at the sound of the sheriff's voice. Of course, they did. Everyone did.

"I love this town," Sheriff Stanton said. "And men like you ain't welcome in it."

Beau recovered his composure first. "Well," he said, his fingers edging over closer to the pistol, "that's mighty rude of you. I'm figuring we might have to teach you and yours some manners."

"Warrant says dead or alive," the sheriff continued. "Guess you made your choice already."

"Hey, Beau," Tucker mumbled, "you think maybe we should head on back a few miles, take that left turn like I wanted to?"

"Too late for that," Beau murmured.

"A lifetime too late," the sheriff agreed.

George moved first, his hand a blur as he went for his gun.

My own hand moved a fraction later. Slower. Like I was pushing my fingers through molasses.

Somehow, despite George's blinding speed, Beau still got his own pistol free before his brother.

Which was why Sheriff Stanton shot him first.

The roar of the Texas split the afternoon air, startling the horses and drowning out the sodden thump of the .36 slug of metal punching into Beau Henderson's throat and tearing free amidst a bright spray of arterial blood and fragmented spinal column.

Unseen hands moving with demoniac speed beneath the purple cloth, the sheriff worked the action of his old pistol, his body twisting as he turned to George. He fired again, just as Tucker Henderson's terrified horse reared up on its hind legs and sent its equally terrified rider lolling back. The bullet meant for the inviting space between George Henderson's eyes instead took his brother between the ribs. Arms flailing for the reins, Tucker tumbled back and slammed onto the dusty street, a single wracking cough coating his beard with blood as he lay staring at the sky in shock.

George Henderson's Smith and Wesson belched a cloud of smoke.

The .44 slug, heavy and brutal, tore through the grey of the Confederate coat and sent its wearer stumbling back.

George Henderson smiled, as if the death of his two brothers was nothing compared to the joy of taking a life himself. Carefully, he drew a bead on the sheriff and prepared to fire again.

He was still smiling when Jim Taylor's bullet messily divorced the top of his head from the rest of it.

Silence returned, broken only by the whistle of Tucker's laboured wheezing and the rustle of wings as a single Turkey Vulture dropped to land on the roof of the General Store, where it squatted with unblinking eyes staring at the three bodies.

Smart creature. Most birds would flee at gunshots. Not this one. It knew what they signified. A gunshot to this one was like ringing a dinner bell.

Jim kept his rifle aimed for a few more seconds, waiting for Tucker's final rattling breaths to cease, then turned to the sheriff. "You okay, boss?"

"Yeah," Sheriff Stanton grunted after a few seconds. "Just slow." His gloved hand picked at the new hole in his filthy coat. Around it, one stain seemed newer and darker than the others.

Jim saw it too. "You're bleeding," he said. Quietly. A note of surprise in his voice.

"Wouldn't be the first blood spilled on this coat."

"Yeah, but—" The words died on Jim's lips. He pointed instead to the bodies. "What do you want to do with these? The usual?"

A nod. Jim called out, and the Pegrams emerged wordlessly from their hotel.

With an inquisitory croak, the vulture shifted its weight on its perch and stared hungrily at the bodies before tilting its head to look straight at the sheriff. He stared back, motionless.

Ma and Joe took the corpse of George Henderson by the ankles and dragged it into the shade of the hotel interior. It left a viscous sheen on the wood as the shattered cranium thudded on each porch step in turn.

I couldn't be sure, the movement almost imperceptible beneath the layers of bandaging, but it seemed to me the sheriff kept his gaze on the great bird and shook his head. With a disappointed shriek, the vulture exploded upwards, great wings beating as it clawed its way into the blue sky.

The sheriff watched it go.

Despite the clothes, his body stiffened. He sniffed the air, head jerking towards the horizon.

Jim frowned. "What is it, boss? What do you smell?"

Another sniff. Deeper. Exploratory.

"Death," the sheriff said simply. From beneath his clothing, I heard the muffled gurgling of his stomach.

Jim shrugged. "Well, you know, we did just shoot us three outlaws—"

"Not them. Not… fresh. Old death. Decay. Rot." His body gave a queer shudder, his feet edging forward in the sand, like a dog straining at a leash. Then he seemed to regain control and turned away, slipping his pistol back into his belt while he watched the Pegrams drag Beau's body into the hotel. "When did you last patrol Sad Hill, Jim?"

"Saturday, boss. Same as always, regular as clockwork."

"And what day is it today?"

Jim smiled. "It's Wednesday, Sheriff."

"Do me a favour. Take a look, will you?"

"Sure. Today?"

"Now."

I didn't need to have known Jim Taylor my whole life to know he was confused. "What am I looking for, boss?"

"Nothing," the sheriff said. "Anything. You'll know it if you see it. Just don't go underground, you hear me?"

"Underground?" Jim snorted. "You know me better than that. Besides, I ain't taking no spade with me."

The sheriff paused – just a beat – and then shrugged. "Take the kid. He can watch your back for me. Be home before dark." Without another word, he stepped over the body of Tucker Henderson, coattails scattering the flies already crawling over the dead man's open eyes, and disappeared inside.

"Come on, kid," Jim muttered. "Let's get it over with."

＊ ＊＊

It was a twenty-minute ride to Sad Hill, hot and sweaty and with the horses' hooves kicking up fresh clouds of suffocating dust with every step. No wonder Jim didn't want to go. His Saturday trips to the old cemetery were a standing joke in Mount Auburn – every one of them uneventful, their necessity another of the sheriff's weird quirks – but at least he normally got to head out after dawn before the sun got too hot. His sullen silence, though, so out of character for the normally garrulous deputy, seemed to be a product of more than just the heat. I'd spent two years as his notional apprentice – a role I figured the townsfolk had bestowed on me because they were fed up passing an undersized orphan from house to house – but I'd never seen him like this.

"Jim," I ventured once the town was lost from sight behind the scrubby trees and rocks. "Did you ever see the sheriff bleed before?"

Jim barked a laugh. Fake as the ivory in Brent Bean's

General Store window. "What kind of Sheriff would he be if he let people see him bleed?"

"Did you?"

Jim spat on the ground. "No, kid, I didn't. Neither did anyone else."

"And how many times you seen him get shot?"

"Too many. Even shot him myself once, back when he was new in town." Jim swallowed. "I reckon that makes me the only man to turn a gun on Sheriff Stanton and keep breathing afterwards."

"But you never saw him bleed?"

"Damn it, kid," Jim snapped, "you want me to write it down for you? No. I never saw that... *man*... bleed, and neither did anyone else. Now shut your yapping and let's get this over with."

We crested a slight rise, and there it was, laid out before us. Sad Hill Cemetery. I'd only seen it from a distance before, but like every kid in Mount Auburn I'd heard about it. The escarpment that towered over it. The concentric rows of wooden crosses, interspersed with the occasional headstone or shoulder-high monolith. The stunted trees. The central cobbled circle where three of the greatest outlaws in the West had once faced off against each other, if you believed the history books. Back in town, they said if you took a ride up here on a moonlit night, you might see the ghost of the gunfighter who never made it out of that circle, still going for his gun too slow, still desperate to avenge his slaying.

Not that anyone came up here after dark anymore. The sheriff had forbidden it. Rumour held that Tommy Barker had brought Dorothy Pleasance here three summers back to propose to her under the moonlight, but no one had ever seen either of them again to ask about it. The Pegrams had told anyone who would listen that Tommy and Dorothy had eloped and gone to Albuquerque.

The sheriff had said nothing, but for weeks afterward he had sent Jim Taylor to patrol the cemetery every day.

With Jim leading, we picked our way past the little grassy

hummocks between the grave markers. I'd once asked Jim why, after the odd stranger wiped out the entire murderous Forbes-Baker gang who had murdered the old sheriff and terrorised the town for months, Stanton's first decree as the newly-appointed sheriff had been to ban the use of Sad Hill and build a new cemetery on thick bedrock on the other side of town.

I still remembered Jim's reaction to my question. Angry. Evasive. Just like when I asked him about the bleeding.

You've known him from the start. What else aren't you telling me?

"You see anything, kid?"

I shook my head. "Looks normal. I mean, as normal as an abandoned cemetery gets."

"Yeah," Jim said. "Normal." His hand rested on the rifle hanging from his saddle. "Come on. Let's finish the job and get out of here. It'll be dark in a few hours." There was an odd tremor in his voice.

He was nervous. Jim Taylor, who hadn't so much as blinked when facing down the three Henderson boys, was anxious about something in an abandoned cemetery in the full glare of the afternoon sun. We reached the edge of the stone circle, lines of graves on the shallow slopes on all sides of us.

My horse suddenly reared. I almost fell, and my cheeks reddened with shame as I looked over at Jim, but he'd barely held on to his own mount.

Wordlessly, we dismounted and drew the horses back a few yards, tying them to the skeletal remains of a dead tree. I wanted to ask Jim what had spooked the horses, but then I saw him unclip his rifle and step over the low, half-broken wall to walk slowly across the stones.

He glanced at my pistol as I drew alongside him. "You loaded?"

I nodded, my attention too fixed on the sight ahead to wonder why he was asking. A few yards from the far edge of the stones, a grave seemed to have been freshly dug. Oddly, the marker was already in place above the empty plot. A thick, split wooden plank had been driven into the ground, with a sun-bleached oblong of wood nailed to it.

"Arch Stanton," I read. "3 February 1862." Near thirty years dead. "A relation, you think?"

"Be silent, kid," Jim snapped. "You hear that?"

I didn't. Not at first, anyway. Just the silence of the cemetery, and the gentle rustle of the breeze in dead grass. Not even a bird in the sky. But then...

"Is that a drum?"

He nodded. "Like a heartbeat in the ground," he murmured. "Do you hear the whispering, too?"

I did, now. Barely even a whisper, more like a single drawn-out sigh. But there were words there, even if I couldn't understand them, and they were calling for me. Beckoning me towards the open grave.

"Kid," Jim warned.

I ignored him.

The whispering continued, the syllables and the meaning tantalisingly close to my understanding. Stones and dirt crunched under my boots as I walked slowly forward. I just needed to be closer. Needed to hear them properly. To understand.

Come to us, they said. Getting louder with every step. *Join us in the feast*.

"Kid, not another step, you hear me?"

Now, only three feet away, I saw at last what Jim had spotted. It wasn't an open grave at all, but a tunnel, plunging away into the darkness below the grave marker. The steady drumbeat was loud enough to shake the earth loose. This time, I heard the words clear as day.

Live forever.

Sure sounded good to me.

I stepped forward. Jim's hand fastened like a manacle on my arm. "Goddamn it, kid, I said—"

Something lunged up out of the ground, showering my face with dirt, blinding me. Stumbling back, blinking furiously,

I caught only a glimpse of the pale abomination that wrapped long, thin arms around Jim Taylor and dragged him forward. Jim's fingernails tore the skin of my arm as his grip was ripped away, the thing dropping back out of sight into the hole, pulling him off-balance, bringing him tumbling headfirst into the darkness. I grabbed for him, but my fingers closed only on air before one flailing boot struck them.

Then he was gone.

And his screams began.

The whispering had stopped, and with it any compulsion to go closer. I knew I should try to save Jim; somehow, I knew that time had already passed. Feral snarls and whines echoed up from deep within the earth. The tearing of cloth and flesh. Jim's screams, rising to an awful falsetto before lapsing into the gurgling incoherence of a man drowning in his own blood. Something barked. No more a dog's bark than the accompanying childish chittering came from any human mouth.

I ran for my horse, heedless of the hooves it flashed near my face in its terror, not pausing to grab Jim's discarded rifle or to free his own screaming mount. I wrestled my way into the saddle and was galloping towards town even as my brain registered the way the sunlight seemed almost to die when it reached the mouth of the tunnel.

A voice echoed in my ears, louder than the frantic clatter of my horse's hooves. No longer a whisper. Now, it sounded like nothing less than the sound of dry leaves, crashing in the grip of a hurricane.

"Tell him we're free! Tell him we're coming for you all!"

* * *

Joe Pegram broke the silence first. "Ain't no way Jim could be alive, kid?"

I shook my head, looking at the gathered faces in the town hall with my throat too thick to answer. When Cross shot my parents, I hadn't cried, but damned if I hadn't come close when

I told them everything I'd seen and heard at Sad Hill. There was no judgement on those faces – not at the child holding back tears, not at the young deputy who had left Jim Taylor to die.

"No," the sheriff answered for me.

Heads turned. Now I saw judgement. Anger. Hostility. I knew then the truth in what Jim had always said. The town tolerated the sheriff because he kept them safe, but they had never accepted him. Not really. Even Jim sometimes couldn't see past the *thing* to the man beneath.

"Well, Sheriff, how about it?" Brent Bean stood, his bald head glistening with sweat after a long day counting his profits at the General Store. If there was one man in town who had never cared to disguise his loathing for Sheriff Stanton, it was Brent. "What the hell kind of demons you brought down upon us now?"

A chorus of grumbling signalled their support. Beyond the windows, the sun had dropped below the mountains, leaving their rocky peaks aflame with pink luminescence.

"You watch your mouth, Brent," Joe snapped. "You think you'd be rolling in those dollars of yours without the sheriff keeping you safe? And what about the rest of you? You remember what the schoolhouse was like before he came here? You remember how many good folks we had to take up to Sad Hill in the old days? Ain't more than a dozen folks buried in the new cemetery, with flowers and pretty headstones, and most all of them died peaceful in their sleep."

True enough. But not everyone who died in this town made it that far. No Henderson brother would ever sully the town cemetery. Right now, their bodies were rotting in a locked top-floor room in the Pegram Hotel.

The owner of that establishment stood tall in front of us now, hands on hips, his old frame placed protectively between the crowd and his hotel's only guest. "Charles Forbes and Sammy Baker would have burned your place to the ground with you in it, Brent, and them Henderson boys this very morning would have put a bullet in you, taken your money and taken that young wife of yours too if it weren't for Sheriff Stanton. So, you'd better show some goddamn respect before I whip your ass myself."

"Easy, my friend," the sheriff rasped. "They deserve the truth."

Ma swallowed. "Sheriff, maybe it's better you don't—"

"It's time, sweet Lily Pegram," he said. "I have been living this lie long enough." He took a deep, liquid breath, the sound muffled below the layers of clothing, and rose to his feet. Slowly, he drew his pistol. A few people flinched. Most didn't, just leaned forward on their seats as he placed the weapon on the council table and unbuckled his sword belt.

"I love this town," he said. "I loved it the first night I came here, even when my face scared Mrs Johnson and I had to spend the night hiding from old Sheriff Cardigan and his posse. I loved it when the children threw rocks at me, and even when Jim Turner put me on the dirt with three bullets in my chest." He leaned the sword against the side of the table and reached for his hat. "Maybe he could have finished me then, maybe not – Lord knows I was ready to let him – but he didn't try. He was a good man, and maybe he thought he saw something good in me too. I will miss him. Ma and Joe brought me into their home and took care of me. Good people. So many good people in this town. For the longest time I thought Jim was my only friend, but I was wrong. You're all my friends, even if some of you maybe don't know it."

With his hat off, the layers of bandages didn't quite cover his head. Gaps exposed pale skin. Rough enough that I could see the texture from five yards away. Tufts of black hair, coarse and matted.

Someone gave an audible gasp. Reverend Hardaker crossed himself.

The sheriff ignored them all. "Lots of you been wondering how I came to Mount Auburn. Maybe I once had a life like yours. Breathed fresh air, played in the sunshine. I guess I must have, but I don't remember it. I remember the day I was born, and I was as old as I am now." He shrugged the coat off his hunched shoulders and let it slide onto the floorboards.

I wasn't the only one staring. His shirt, old-fashioned with frilled cuffs and stretched thin over the cat-like curve of his spine, might once have been white. It was so encrusted with years of dirt, though, I would not have wagered a single cent on that proposition. I barely noticed the shirt anyway, other than to acknowledge the red stain on the shoulder, too fresh to have browned like the others. My gaze remained transfixed on the spot where the shirt ended and the skin of his long arms showed, a sickly grey and stretched paper thin over wiry muscles and protruding bone.

Reverend Hardaker muttered a prayer. I hoped it was for Jim Turner. I'd seen arms like those before. Dragging him into that hole.

With a sad but affectionate smile towards the sheriff, Ma Pegram picked up the discarded coat and folded it neatly before laying it on the back of a chair.

The sheriff unwrapped his hands. Impossibly long fingers with thick knuckles, tapered to jagged black nails. Claws, really. Carefully removing his goggles, he looked out over the room through sunken, yellowed eyes. "I was born in the shadow under Sad Hill. And I wasn't alone."

He reached for the material that concealed his face, and for the first time I realised what it was. Not bandages at all, nor strips of bed linen like I had naively assumed. No. A burial shroud, used and sliced neatly with those razor-sharp claws.

Joe struck a match and lit the lantern hanging from the wall.

I wanted to look away. Truth is, I wanted to empty my stomach and my bowels and my bladder over the town hall floor. But I didn't. None of us did. And none of us looked away.

With infinite care, Sheriff Stanton unwrapped his face and let the shroud flutter to his feet.

"My God," Brent Bean whispered. "What are you?"

"We go by many names," the sheriff said. Without the

coverings, his voice sounded clearer and yet more guttural, though I was amazed it could even produce human sounds at all. It was not, after all, a human face. In the shadows it might have passed for one, but in the last light of the sunset and the growing confidence of the lantern, we all saw it for what it was. "You know us best as ghouls."

What I had assumed to be layers of bandaging distorting the shape of his head was nothing of the sort. The skull was huge, elongated, wrinkled cheeks narrowing to a doglike muzzle with flat, flared nostrils. The massive bone structure of his sockets left the eyes seeming like two glowing rocks at the base of a rattlesnake's den. The ears stuck up, each the size of my hand and sharply pointed, their rubbery skin crowned with fine and oddly childlike fuzz. The mouth stretched almost from ear to ear, as if the whole head might flap back and forth. The teeth inside, yellow and chipped, stood proud like needles. Too many to count, but for the big triangular incisors.

We'd always known there was something about the sheriff. How could we not? Still, I found it amazing that not one person ran for the door. I saw the way surprise mingled with fascination and not a little disgust. No fear. Sheriff Stanton had kept us safe for a decade. How could we fear him?

"Not every cemetery has a ghoul," he said, "but enough do. Normally, it's one or two. Living underground. Hiding from the sun. Burrowing with our hands, breaking into the coffins from below, eating what we find rotting there. Sometimes a body comes down to us that isn't quite dead, not really. Those we don't eat. We feed them back to health. We watch them change. That's what happened with me. I don't remember the man I once was, or what kind of bastard I must have been that the Good Lord left me out of Heaven and gave me this life instead." He poked a claw towards his foul visage, mouth twisting in self-loathing. "There were only three of us, but then came the Civil War, and the most bountiful feast any of us could have imagined. They couldn't dig holes quick enough for all the new bodies. And given enough corpses to feed on and enough time, we multiply."

I shut my ears to the imagined sound of those whispering voices. "How many like you are there, Sheriff?"

"There were twelve others when I left," the sheriff said. His body sagged, exhausted by the sheer effort of telling the truth.

Twelve. All like him. Lord, help us.

"You should sit down, honey," Ma Pegram told him gently.

Sheriff Stanton ignored her. "One day some gunslingers cracked open a grave. Looking for gold, I heard. I was hungry and looking for scraps and broke into the casket. Fortunately, it was nightfall, else the sun would have burned the flesh straight off my face. Instead, I saw the moon and the stars, and I'd never seen anything so beautiful. I climbed straight out, and it seemed the whole world was stretched out there for me. I got dizzy. You can't appreciate how vast the night sky is until you've lived your whole life without it. Maybe the fresh air triggered some memory of my life before, or maybe something just snapped in my brain, but I knew then I could never go back. And I knew they would never let me leave. So, I sealed up the hole. Filled it in with my bare hands. Took a name from the grave I'd climbed out of, and ran into the night, running like I'd never been able to do before. I knew the sun would come up soon and end me, but I didn't care. I figured one night of living was better than an eternity dying."

"I'll never forget Ida Johnson's face when she found you hiding in her barn," Ma said. "Mind you, she deserved the fright you gave her. Never could stand that woman."

"You gave me a home, Lily," the sheriff growled. "I have never thanked you enough for that."

"Oh, hush," Ma chided. "That this town is still standing is all the thanks any of us need."

Sarah Blackwood, the schoolmistress, raised her hand like she was one of her own pupils. "These... *others*," she began, "they will come here tonight?"

"Yes," the sheriff said. "The sun scares them, but it's all but asleep now. They could be here within the hour."

"But we haven't any dead bodies for them to eat."

"We got them Henderson boys," Brent said brightly. "I mean, I know you were saving them for yourself, Sheriff, but maybe if we left them out..."

"It won't be enough," I heard myself say. "And they don't just eat dead flesh." I felt an acrid burn in my throat, bile rising in waves.

Brent swallowed. "You mean... Jim?"

I nodded.

"I brought this upon you all," the sheriff said. "I will face them alone."

"Like Hell you will." Joe said the words, but from the murmurs around me, I knew he wasn't the only one thinking it. "This town stands with its own, Sheriff, and ain't no man or woman here going to refuse to call you one of us. Ain't that right, Brent?"

Brent sighed. "Well, it does seem to me I have a little too many cases of ammunition cluttering up my store, and a few pistols I might see going for a special low price."

"You might want to pick up that sword and pistol of yours, Sheriff," Ma Pegram said. "It seems the good folks of Mount Auburn aren't ready to let you go anywhere just yet."

"God bless you, Sheriff," Miss Blackwood said.

The sheriff stood in the centre of the room, listening to the echoed blessings and the sounds of people running to get their weapons and prepare to stand with him. I flinched as he sniffed loudly, wondering what it was he smelt now, but I needn't have worried. Not yet.

A single tear rolled down his cheek, and damned if it wasn't the clearest, brightest water I ever saw.

* * *

"What now?"

"Now we wait, kid," the sheriff told me, staring out into the darkness. At his request we'd lit every light in every window, placed oil lamps and candles out in the scrub outside the town limits, lit a big fire in the middle of Main Street. Ghouls could see in the dark, and we were afraid of it. The lights would blind them and give our people courage. We'd need it.

I touched the grip of my father's pistol and wondered if my hands, sweating despite the chill of the night air, would even be able to hold it.

Six hours had passed already. Six hours of waiting. Early enthusiasm had given way to a gnawing dread, the kind that makes you want to run. No one had, though. Like the sheriff had told us when he gathered us together to set our defences, the ghouls could run faster than any man, and even the strongest horse would tire long before they did.

The sheriff cleared his throat. "Remember," he shouted, voice carrying deep into the night, "ghouls take a lot of killing because they ain't really living to start with. Aim for the legs and put it down. Shoot it twice as many times as you think you could ever need to. Then shoot it again in the head to be sure." He lowered his voice again. "You stick close to me, kid, you understand?"

"Yes, sir." I glanced at him. His clawed hand rested lightly on the pommel of his heavy cavalry sword. He had put his hat and coat back on, leaving his face exposed but hiding the bullet wound in his shoulder. "Sheriff?"

"Hmm?"

"How come you bled this morning? I thought... that is, Jim said..."

"I've been here too long," the sheriff said. "I used to be human before I became... this. I guess it works both ways."

"You're becoming human again?"

"The worst parts of it, at least."

"Like the dying?"

"Yeah. Like the dying." The sheriff drew in a great draught of air. His snout twitched. "Enough questions," he said, drawing his pistol.

Out in the darkness, a candle winked out, then another. One of the oil lamps seemed to rise into the air, then slammed into the ground with a crash of shattering glass. Burning oil flared on the desert sand, briefly silhouetting three loping figures before it faded to nothing.

"I saw one," someone called, their voice teetering on the edge of panic.

"Steady," the sheriff called. "They are close."

Closer than we knew.

With a keening snarl, something ran out of the darkness forty feet in front of us, bipedal but tearing at the ground with its long hands, leering as it rushed into the light. I fumbled for my pistol, but four others beat me to it. Shots rang out in a staccato rhythm, deafening in the silence of the night. The ghoul stumbled, writhing as two rounds struck it in the chest and another ripped a bloody furrow through its naked thigh. Howling, it kept coming, hands reaching for my eyes, only to jerk back as the sheriff's Texas Paterson bullet destroyed its nose and burrowed deep into the skull. It fell squealing, legs still churning and spinning it around on the sand like a dog chasing its tail.

The sheriff tucked his pistol into his belt and drew the sword. Striding forward, he pinned the ghoul with a heavy boot on its throat, then drove the point of the sword down into the left eye socket. I heard the distinct sound of metal grinding on bone and a fainter wet popping. The creature writhed a full ten seconds before it finally lay limp.

"Sorry," the sheriff murmured. He looked up, saw me watching, then wiped the blade clean. He nodded toward the pistol still holstered at my waist. "You ever going to use that thing, kid?"

An animal snarled in the desert. No, not an animal. It took me a second to pick out the words, but I knew that voice, almost lost beneath the guttural growls. I'd heard it whispering to me, drawing me closer to the pit at Sad Hill. I'd heard it echo in my ears as I galloped away.

"It is true, then," the voice said. "You have turned your back on your kind."

"You should have stayed in the ground," the sheriff said, sheathing his sword.

"As should you, *brother.*"

"Let's have us a family reunion. Just step into the light."

"Soon," the voice said. "When we have eaten our fill. We will kill them all, brother. You will be last. I want you to watch."

"Sunrise is in an hour. You might want to get a move on."

"The daylight will not save you."

The sheriff spat on the ground, yellow eyes glinting in the glow of nearby fires. "But it will end you."

"Not before my teeth meet in your throat."

With banshee howls, several dark shapes raced from the shadows. Frozen, I watched as two of them leapt across a watch fire and bore a hapless figure to the ground. Young Aaron Longfellow, the junior bank teller. Newly married, soft hands, too soft to even bring his pistol up before two-inch fangs sank into his forearm. One creature dragged him screaming to the ground, the other squatting on his chest before sinking its head and tearing a chunk of cheek flesh from his face.

The sheriff cursed and ran towards the young man, but then another creature bounded across the sand, heading for the schoolhouse. Sheriff Stanton turned, raising his pistol, but the ghoul had miscalculated and passed across the front of the porch of the Pegram Hotel. Two shotguns roared in unison, one caving the side of the thing's head and ripping away an ear and eye, the other knocking it off balance. Whining as it stumbled, it tripped and plunged headfirst into the biggest fire. Despite the shattering horror of the head wound and the half-dozen pistols slamming round after round into it, it remained alive and conscious enough to shriek as the flames consumed it.

From the far end of Main Street, a woman screamed.

"Some of them must have circled around," the sheriff growled. "Go. I'll take care of these."

I stared at him, dumbfounded. I knew where he wanted me to go. My legs simply weren't interested in taking me there.

"Go," he roared, putting a bullet into the back of the nearest ghoul's head.

I ran, more afraid of him in that moment than of the things in the shadows. Ragged gunfire rang out on all sides of town. I almost tripped on the twitching legs of the dead ghoul in the fire, and narrowly avoided following it into the flames. The thing had stopped screaming, mercifully, the only sound coming from it now a gentle pop and crackle of boiling fluids.

Above me, on a rooftop, someone shouted a warning and fired their rifle. In the darkness I heard another pained yelp, but with the pulse pounding in my ears I couldn't tell if it was human or ghoul. Sounds flowed and merged in a uniform howl of terror and pain.

The unseen woman was still screaming. A man crawled across blood-soaked sand, dragging himself forward with his powerful arms, eyes pleading as he saw me. Thomas Lowell, the farrier. But he looked odd – too short. I finally lost my battle with my stomach when I saw why. In a single violent convulsion, my last meal sprayed its urgent protest across the dirt.

Ten feet from where Lowell collapsed, unnaturally white and still, two ghouls looked up from the meal they were making of his disembodied legs and stared at me. One gave me a contemptuous glare and returned to worrying at the muscle of Lowell's calf. The mouth of the other twitched in a grotesque mockery of a smile as it rose and stalked towards me.

My pistol hung heavy in its holster, the grip resting against my hip yet insurmountably out of my reach. The thing came closer. Vomit filled my mouth, its acrid tang surely the last thing I would ever taste. I thought of Jim Taylor, dead because of my mistake. I thought of my parents, murdered in front of me by Jedediah Cross while I sat and watched, too young and weak to do anything.

Maybe nothing had changed. Maybe I was still that scared little boy.

Hell, there wasn't even a maybe.

The thing's mouth opened, and its long tongue ran across its dry thin lips. "Time to die, kid," it whispered.

Kid.

You know something? I never realised how much I hated being called that.

I drew the pistol and brought it up, one smooth motion like Jim Taylor had tried to teach me. I'd never mastered it then. I did now. I fired my first shot as the barrel passed its navel, the noise and fury of the blast seeming to vanish inside the thing along with the bullet.

Its eyes opened wide. Its mouth, wider.

Yelling, I shoved the barrel into that gaping maw and fired again, and a third time, heard the little .31 bullets rattling inside the thick skull, felt cold, thick blood oozing onto my hand. A fourth shot, this one only clipping the top of the skull as the thing fell back. Then a fifth, straight into the left eye. The gun clicked empty. Only a five-shooter.

The second ghoul loomed over me.

And fell away as my ears rang from a sudden thundercrack of noise.

"Much obliged, Miss Blackwood," I told the woman, gently nudging her shotgun's twin barrels away from me.

She smiled, pushed me aside, and fired again. The now near-headless ghoul drummed its heels on the sand. "Shoot it again to be sure, right?"

"Yes, ma'am."

"You've come a long way," she said. "You don't hardly seem a day older than when I taught you, but…"

"You'd better get yourself back inside the school, ma'am," I told her. "It will be dawn soon enough."

I walked her back to the schoolhouse, careful to keep my body between her and the eviscerated remains of Dan Lowell. She gave me a quick kiss on the cheek, then grimaced. Apologetically, I wiped the errant vomit from my face with my sleeve and tipped my hat to her, waiting until I heard the bolt drawn closed before stepping over the dead ghouls.

Smoke drifted across the street, thick with the reek of burned meat. The sounds of gunfire had faded to the occasional single shot. Another rang out now, abruptly cutting short a wounded animal's squeal. I found one of the local farmers spreadeagled in a side street, an equally dead ghoul lying over him with a mouthful of the farmer's entrails hanging from its mouth and a fire axe driven a full four inches into its skull. A price tag fluttered from the axe's handle.

Brent Bean sat nearby, his face streaked with tears and his hands trembling. "I was too late," he murmured. "Too late."

"You did well, sir," I told him. Holmes, that was the farmer's name. I reached down and took the dead man's pistol, carefully checking it. Fully loaded. Mine had done my father proud, but I never had been very good at reloading it, especially in the dark with cold hands that were sticky with blood. "Get yourself back inside and lock your doors."

"Did we win?"

"We're still breathing, sir. I'd call that a win."

"What about you?"

"I'm going to check on the sheriff."

Once Brent shuffled haltingly back into his shop, I kept on up Main Street, the farmer's pistol cocked and ready. Somewhere in the shadows to my left I heard laughter, too loud and laced with the sheer nervous pleasure of being alive. No shots now. Just the groans of wounded men and the sobbing of new widows.

I checked on the casualties. Spoke to survivors. Helped carry the wounded to Doctor Thompson. Outside, the glow in the east seemed to drive the darkness before it. Seemed apt.

The sheriff stood where I had left him, two dead ghouls at his feet. His sword rose proudly from the chest of one. He had removed his coat again and laid it on the ground. Aaron Longfellow's neatly creased trousers and polished black shoes stuck out from under it. The sheriff's shirt was torn on his left side, four ragged slashes, damp with fresh blood.

"What took you so long?" he rasped.

"You okay, Sheriff?"

"Never better." He coughed, and spat on the ground. It

left a foam on his lips, faintly pink in the growing light of the coming dawn. "How many did we lose?"

"Three dead. Holmes, Lowell and Longfellow. Three more badly hurt. At least two of those should survive."

"Four dead, then," he murmured. "Four lives that I took from this town."

"That's horseshit," I snapped.

"Mind your language," he retorted.

"Four deaths? Imagine how many we would have lost if you hadn't come here. The Henderson Boys alone would have killed a dozen. If you hadn't come here, who knows? You might have been *leading* those things."

He stood, staring out into the desert pre-dawn like he hadn't heard me, his lips shifting rhythmically as if in silent prayer. "Thank you," he whispered.

"Thank me when you're healed," I said, smiling. "What about them? Did we get them all?"

"Almost. Not yet." He sniffed. "*He* is still out there. Close."

I peered out into the semi-darkness. Beneath the trees, maybe fifty yards away, dark pools of shadow still lingered. "It will be dawn soon. Won't the sun kill him?"

"Yes. He knows it, too. He'll make his move soon. And we'll be ready." The sheriff held his pistol by his side, seemingly ready, but I saw the way the long, thin fingers trembled.

"You should get inside."

"Not yet."

Something flashed in the shadows beneath the trees. For a single, incongruous instant I thought it was the rising sun reflecting on metal.

Then, the wet thud of impact.

The sharp retort of the rifle.

A single pained gasp.

The soft thump of the sheriff hitting the ground.

The nearest tree seemed to separate into two, a distorted figure breaking away and lurching towards me. Jim Turner's Springfield trailed from its long fingers as it broke into an ungainly run.

THE SHADOW UNDER SAD HILL

I raised my new pistol and pulled the trigger. Nothing. Just the mocking click of the hammer striking down without effect.

Never trust a gun from a man you don't know.

I pulled the hammer back, hoping the second round might fire, knowing it was already too late. The butt of the rifle flashed through the air. I tried to step back out of the way, succeeded only in tripping on a dead ghoul's outstretched arm. Pain seared through me as the wooden butt smashed into my cheek.

I heard the bone fracture before I felt it. Darkness swept across my sight, and I yelped like a damned baby goat. Air exploded from my lungs as I hit the deck. Lay there. Blinded by pain.

"Now, brother," I heard it say, "I will go back underground. Safe. I will be back, of course, tonight. And every night, until each of these mewling pack animals you call your friends has lined my belly."

Blood pooled at the back of my throat. Drowning me.

"I think I will take the little one with me now," the thing continued. "His old friend was too tough to be satisfying, and I had to share him with our brothers. Thanks to you, every scrap of this one's tender flesh will be mine alone."

But I wasn't dead yet.

"Your own flesh will be your apology for the spilt blood of our brothers," it leered. "And will taste all the sweeter for it."

It didn't see me stand, with its eyes focused only on the prostrate sheriff. It didn't hear me draw the sword, the noise of the blade slipping loose buried beneath its triumphant chuckling.

But the bastard felt it, right enough.

Staggering under the weight, I drove the heavy sword deep into the thing's naked, fish-grey back, the blade scuffing the spine before punching through its right lung. It screamed, blood spattering with every wailing note, and fell forward as I wrenched the blade free.

"I will eat your eyes first," it sputtered, rising to one knee, eyes wide with rage and hunger. "Then peel the skin from you piece by delicious piece. I will—"

I swung the blade down again, sawing it deep into the gap between thick clavicle and scabrous neck. It shrieked, high-pitched, agonised. I swung the sword again.

Again.

Again.

Blood sprayed across my face. The head lolled away from the body, severed windpipe and chalk-white bones exposed. Still the screaming continued, higher pitched and more desperate than ever, until I knew the scream was mine alone.

I drove the sword down one final time and left it there, a final tombstone pinioning the hell-spawned bastard to the ground.

"Kid," the sheriff whispered. Coming from him, the word didn't seem half so annoying.

I crawled over to him, knees still weak, trying to keep the encroaching darkness from blotting out my sight. A piece of tooth rattled in my mouth. I spat it out, along with a cupful of blood, and knelt by his side.

"You did good," he said. "The town is going to need a good sheriff. I figure you might be the man for the job. Sheriff Kid Hawkins," he murmured, weakly. "It's got a nice ring to it."

"We already got us a sheriff," I told him, my voice catching in my throat. "Best this side of the Mississippi." I glanced down at his shirt. No trace of white left, just a mass of blood. As I looked back towards the town, people were dragging ghoul corpses to throw on the fire while others tended the wounded. I opened my mouth to call to them.

"Don't," the sheriff murmured. "I don't want them to see me like this."

"But I can't get you to Doctor Thompson on my own."

"Ain't nothing that man could do. And don't bother bringing me the good Reverend, neither. Ain't no place in Heaven waiting for me. Turn me around, won't you?"

I nodded; felt a tear run down my face as I helped him

turn, inch by agonising inch, to face Mount Auburn, her neat roofs and whitewashed walls bathed in the soft pastels of the dawn. He gasped, a trickle of blood escaping his lips, but he didn't complain.

"I'm sorry," I told him.

"Don't be." He sighed. "I love this town. I loved it the moment I set eyes on it. Never dreamt it would be my home."

"There's always a place for you here."

"In the new cemetery? Buried in Mount Auburn with Holmes, Lowell and Longfellow?" He chuckled, the sound becoming a wracking cough. "I don't think so. This here accursed body has kept me prisoner too long, and I'm mighty keen to be done with it. Stick it on the fire with the others, you hear me?"

"Yes, sir."

"Not sir," he chided. "You're Sheriff now. You don't call any man sir."

Slowly he raised one trembling hand, and I took it in mine. The fingers were cold, the skin rubbery. I didn't recoil, though. Not now. I think he tried to close them around my own, but I couldn't be sure.

"It's going to be a lovely day," I told him.

"Yeah, Kid, it is. Would have been nice to see it."

I held his still hand for a little while longer. Stayed with him as the sun rose into the sky. Covered him with my coat once I felt his skin begin to bubble and blister. Wiped the blood and tears from my face.

Tipping my hat to the vultures circling over Sad Hill, I picked up Jim Taylor's rifle and Sheriff Stanton's pistol. Then, one bloody hand raised against the morning sun, I strode back to my town.

THE FALL OF DENFANAS MANOR

KC Grifant

The stagecoach raced down the side of Denfanas Manor Mountain, wheels rattling so hard in the darkness Melinda was sure they would pop off and send her and the others right over the cliff into the mist below.

"Steady!" she shouted up to the driver. Melinda knew Lance was managing the pair of horses as best he could. They had been in plenty of sticky situations before, but nothing like driving a stolen coach down a jagged mountain with a cursed family hot on their heels, intent on recapturing their prize.

Abby Agnes Prewit hadn't stopped writhing in her trance since Melinda and Lance dragged her out of Denfanas Manor and shoved her into the carriage.

"Are they close?" Lance called. His hat flew off – flapping in the cold wind like a freed bat – as the coach strained around a corner.

Melinda peeked out the back window of the coach as she reloaded her flintlock pistol without looking.

Five horse-like creatures charged down the crumbling obsidian trail behind them, their hooves thundering hard enough to feel like an earthquake. The Volcanins were rare monstrosities – they looked like chestnut mares but twice the size, and with rings of maroon for eyes. Cherry-red fur sprouted down their legs and along their necks in tufts thicker than unsheared sheep. On each of the Volcanins rode a cloaked member of the Denfanas family, brandishing their weapons of choice.

And they were barely five hundred yards from the carriage, closing fast.

"Close enough. How's it looking out there?" Melinda yelled as she pushed strands of her loose hair back. Lance's hat wasn't the only casualty; she had lost hers when they climbed out of the Manor.

"Fine as cream gravy," he shouted back in a forced tone that was decidedly not fine. "But better copper our bets, love!"

She shoved in the last bullet and winced as something banged into the side of the carriage.

"Visitor!" Lance hollered.

"Dandy," Melinda muttered, glimpsing a wing the size of a saddle. A white bat as large as a rocking chair shrieked and flew alongside of them. Instead of normal wings, the bat had four enormous crab legs extending from either side, connected by a stretched translucent membrane. Likely another exotic import the Denfanas family brought over from the monster lands. Melinda fired upwards. A warning shot, so as to not risk the damn thing toppling into their carriage. It worked; the gigantic bat soared up and away with a screech.

The Denfanas family gave whoops on their monstrous horses as they neared. Melinda took them in at a quick glance: Xander and Philip, the older twin brothers, each wielding an embellished katana; Carmine, the younger sister with a glinting machete low at her side; Markus, the father, squat and glaring with a knobbed brass mace. And in the rear, mother Lavinia in a filming white cloak. Lavinia held no weapon, but her crooked smile sent a chill along Melinda's spine. From the loose lips in Furrows Green, Melinda and Lance had learned the family collected the rarest monstrosities this side of the Hellock Mountains. Rumors were the family also enjoyed mastering the art of historic and brutal weaponry.

Melinda didn't want to think about what would happen if they caught up.

"Don't know what we got into taking this job," she said more to herself, her teeth clanking together as Lance turned the next bend. Halfway down the mountain now. *We might just make it.* Once they hit the border of Furrows Green, they'd be safe. Abby would be reunited with her family, and Melinda and Lance would enjoy a nice payout.

THE FALL OF DENFANAS MANOR

Melinda took a breath, hung out the carriage and fired at the closest Volcanin holding a brother Denfanas. The bullet buried itself into the nearest creature's neck before the flesh closed up around it. The monster horse snorted then whinnied, but only slowed a smidge. Abby shifted on the cushioned seat and gave a moan at the gunfire.

"Damn," Melinda muttered and bit her lip. She was hoping not to kill anyone if she could help it, but she had tried the easy way. With a steadying breath, she took aim again. She never missed. The bullet hit the shoulder of Xander or Philip, she wasn't sure which. It worked: the twin groaned and pulled back, injured but not killed. The rest of his family pulled ahead, flowing like water around the slowed Denfanas brother.

At least they weren't immune to bullets.

The other brother snarled and kicked his Volcanin even harder, lifting his katana.

"Oooh, how I love a good chase!" Xander-or-Philip bellowed, not even twenty some feet away. His wild black hair curled like worms, and his eyes burned under the moonlight. "Come here, buttercups!"

Melinda took another shot, this time at the hand holding the katana. The brother shrieked and veered off, his blade flashing as it pinwheeled over the side of the mountain. The rest of the family slowed, maneuvering around him.

One more bullet, three more family members.

"Faster!" Melinda yelled. They just had to get to the border of Furrows Green, where the town forbade the Denfanas family from entering on penalty of death.

The family still found ways to lure those who didn't know better up to their mountain for devil knew what. Like Abby, whose family had anxiously contracted Melinda and Lance to retrieve the girl. Melinda didn't think she'd ever forget how the ma, already dressed in black mourning, had been quietly solemn, took Melinda to the side and said she'd simply not live anymore if her Abby couldn't be rescued. A pang of heartache had hit Melinda, who had to blink back memories of her own ma, who succumbed to a monster infection when Melinda was a teen, not even ten years ago.

Abby, still muttering in her strange dream state, looked well-fed, pampered even.

After Melinda and Lance had snuck into the manor, they had found the girl bound on a lavish bed, stuffed into a lace bodice tighter than a first-time rodeo rider's grip. Her loose curls fell meticulously along two spots of red on her cheeks. She was unresponsive, her eyes rolling up as Melinda tried to wake her. A polished silver chain threaded with pearls had encircled Abby's neck and was bolted into the wall. Fruit, some rotting, piled up on a bureau on her one side, books and crafting materials carefully laid out on a desk on the other. Melinda tried not to think too much about what the girl might've gone through.

"You ain't taking our prize!" A voice rumbled behind them, deeper than an avalanche, and Melinda blinked the memory away.

She looked back, preparing to take her last shot. The father, Markus, grew closest now as he pushed his Volcanin to a gallop faster than any horse was capable. His hood flapped off, and sweat beaded onto his well-trimmed beard and along his bald head. His mace, half the length of a cane, had a head that gleamed with a dozen knobs intwined with a bronze snake. The ornate weapon looked stained at the tips.

Markus grinned at her and hoisted the mace. Melinda took aim at his shoulder when the carriage gave a violent thrust and her gun clattered to the floor, sliding beneath Abby's gown.

"Forget how to drive?" Melinda yelled.

The giant bat returned to bang against the carriage again. It screeched loud enough to make Melinda wince.

Lance cursed. "Some help!"

Melinda looked out the side door and nearly screamed. The bat clung onto the carriage, its white, crab-like legs stretched across the wood on either side of the door. Folded creases twitched where its eyes should be above a wolf-sized snout and fangs. Half a dozen smaller mouths gaped, gnash-like, across its stomach. The tiny mouths opened and closed, waiting to be fed. Melinda grimaced and pummeled her fist into the snout of the creature. Nothing—the pincers at the end of its crab legs dug deeper into the wood, harder than steel and—

A *thunk* came from behind as Markus' mace fractured the back of the carriage along the open window. Bits of the coach's wood sprayed across Abby's skirt.

"You like my winged pet?" Markus chuckled. More wood splintered forward, and his wild laugh boomed through a hole the size of a wheel.

"It looks hungry to me," Melinda said. "Maybe it wants to eat leather." She balanced herself and kicked her boot heel into one of the bat's tiny chest-mouths. The entire bat screamed and swung one of its pinchers toward her face. She dodged its snapping claw and smashed her elbow into another of its chest-mouths. A second pincer released from the doorway to strain for her throat. The bat was unsteady enough now that she readied for a full front-thrust kick to its belly the second she felt the carriage start to take the next bend.

It worked. The bat flailed off the side of the turning coach— right into Markus.

The man bellowed as the bat and Volcanin smashed together. Melinda watched the two monsters and father tumble forward, skidding into the back of the carriage and blocking the mother and sister from pursuit.

The force made the already wobbly coach tilt and Melinda sucked in a breath, preparing for the world to turn upside down.

"Hold on!" Lance hollered.

Abby woke with a shriek as they slammed against the interior before the carriage straightened.

And she kept screaming.

"Shush! You're safe now! Well, almost," Melinda said and retrieved her flintlock from the floor. The poor girl looked so dazed, she probably didn't have an inkling how long she had been gone or what had happened. "What did they do to you?"

"Please," Abby gasped and lunged forward to grab the lapels of Melinda's duster.

"We'll be in town in a few minutes. Whatever they did to you, you'll be right as rain soon enough." Melinda unwound the girl's grasp. "Your family's there, waiting. Your ma especially."

Abby blinked, confused for a second before her eyes glazed over. "Take me back!" Her hands darted forward to squeeze Melinda's neck.

Melinda wrenched off Abby's wrists, easily overpowering the smaller woman. "What is wrong with you, gal?"

"They're the only family I need!" Abby wailed. "You got to take me back."

Melinda grabbed Abby's head and pulled her close. In the streaked moonlight, the girl's face looked nearly supernatural: blown pupils, flushed cheeks, small, raised ridges of red along her jawbone.

All in all, like a woman possessed.

"You got a flask up there?" Melinda said to Lance and gave the woman a rough shake. Whiskey might help dull the edge of possession until they could get her back and examined.

"Funny time for a drink!" Lance shot back.

The roofs of Furrows Green peeked out in the distance. The mountain path, steeper now, made the horses slip. Ahead, Lance cursed as the horses stumbled over a particularly rocky path but continued their charge.

Abby twisted in Melinda's grip and howled. "Let me go! I found my real family!"

"Fight it, Abby," Melinda urged. "Whatever brainwashing they did, whatever they convinced you of, it was a lie."

Before she could reply, a screech sounded behind them.

"More bats?" Lance called.

"New problems," Melinda replied. She looked behind to see the daughter and mother had caught up and were closing the gap, near enough that Melinda could see the shine on their foreheads under the moonlight.

The daughter, Carmine, thundered forward with a shriek of delight to rip the side door open. The stench of the Volcanin hit like baked clay and swamp water.

"Where are you going?" Carmine sang in a warbly voice that made ice run along Melinda's skin. "Delectable little Abby, come back. We miss you!" Her hand stretched in, bare and muscular beneath her flapping velvet cape, her skin the color of bone.

Abby reached for the sister, but Melinda shoved her back against the opposite side of the carriage. The coach rounded a narrow, sharp turn, putting Carmine out of sight.

"I need them," Abby said. "They're my real family now." Something in her voice caught in what sounded like an old hurt.

"Listen," Melinda hissed, wracking her brain for some words that might snap Abby out of it. "You only get one ma and da in this life and from what I've seen, they care about you very much."

Abby's frown deepened. "You don't understand. We had a fight—they want me to marry—" She broke off in an angry sob. "I was more trapped at home than I am now."

"No matter what troubles you had, the Denfanases are not your friends!" Melinda couldn't help but picture Abby's mom's drawn face again. "I'm sure your ma will listen to you if you talk to her. In any case, this isn't the answer." One word kept nagging in her mind as she spoke.

Carmine had said delectable.

"Damn," Melinda muttered, then shouted. "We got vampires!"

A beat from Lance. "That can't be right!" he said back. "No bites on the girl! And townspeople saw them in the daylight."

"Must be a new type!" That was all Melinda could think.

It was said some of the new settlers made pacts with demons or used unnatural mixtures of alchemy with monster serums to become stronger, live longer. There were rumors of shapeshifters, werewolves, and the like, but Lance and Melinda had never come across honest-to-goodness vampires before.

That would explain the Denfanases' strength. And their penchant for heavy weapons.

"What did they do to you exactly?" Melinda asked the girl.

"You don't understand," Abby moaned. Her eyes still shone too brightly. "They take care of me."

"I don't know much about your life," Melinda said. "But whatever escape or comfort these monsters are promising you, open your eyes."

"They help me, and I help them," Abby insisted. "Symbiotic-like."

"Like a pampered pet," Melinda said in exasperation. "Is that really want you want? At least have the guts to face whatever plagues you and live your own life."

"Let me be!" Abby snapped.

Metal on wood screeched behind them as Carmine's machete dug into the back of the carriage next to the splintered gap.

"That's right, little sister, you tell her!" Carmine cooed as she used the embedded machete to hoist her leg through the hole her father had made.

Abby tried to reach for Carmine again, but Melinda pulled her back. "She's *not* your sister, and this is not your family," Melinda said through gritted teeth. "Remember that."

Carmine's Volcanin bolted forward, jerking the carriage.

"I don't want to kill you, but I will if I have to," Melinda spat and pointed her pistol at Carmine, who had pulled herself halfway into the coach. This close, she spotted something odd in the smirking sister's eyes: the brown irises were rimmed with white. More than that, whitish dust from Carmine's face floated forward, covering Melinda's face.

Melinda sneezed and a swirl of something intoxicating grew heavy in her chest, as if she had drunk half a bottle of brandy. An urge to sleep washed over her, like she was dozing in a hammock with Lance under a spring sun, the scent of lavender fresh in the air.

And something else. Something… *digging*… at her mind, like a quiet rat in the corner, trying to get to a plate of covered biscuits. Looking for feelings Melinda had squashed away during her life—rage, embarrassment. Grief.

"Mellie! What's happening back there!" Lance's shouts came through dimly as if she were underwater.

Psychic vampires, Melinda realized faintly. Feeding, somehow, on people's emotions, especially pent-up ones left to simmer like perfectly aged whiskey or cheese. She tried to fight it, tried to shout to Lance but her vision was dimming. She fought to steady her hand and tensed her trigger finger.

Carmine snarled and the Volcanin shoved forward again, just as Lance was about to take the last turn down the mountain.

"Too much weight!" Lance shouted as the tires screamed and something popped. "Gonna make us—!"

With a screech the carriage tipped fully this time. The white dust dissipated as Carmine grunted, trying to hold on. Before the coach flipped, Melinda managed to smash the gun into Carmine's face, sending her wailing back through the hole. Melinda tried to grip Abby and brace for impact.

Thank goodness we're at the bottom of the mountain, was all Melinda could think as the world turned upside down. She landed with an *oomph* against the side of the coach, Abby slamming into her.

Somewhere outside the coach a rock rolled and settled. A wheel creaked, its broken wood groaning. Then, quiet.

Melinda waited in the sudden silence. She fought the urge to close her eyes and rest. Instead, she sat up and pushed the hair out of her face. The carriage was on its side, and Abby next to her breathing heavily.

"Lance!" Melinda shouted while she checked that nothing was broken. Sore, but not broken. "You OK?"

Nothing.

Panic sliced through Melinda, making her actions quick as she squeezed herself out of the side of the coach. Around rose soft pine trees dusted with snow, the last stretch of the flattened rocky path a few feet behind her. She stumbled to the front of the carriage to see the two horses whinnying, unharmed.

Lance lay motionless next to them, his gray duster in a heap around his sandy curls.

She rushed over, hearing his groan as she approached. Melinda turned him over, gently slapping his stubbled cheeks. Nothing bled or looked broken, though he'd have a nice plum-sized bruise on his forehead soon enough.

"Made it?" Lance said in a daze, eyes fluttering open to reveal his baby blues a split second before he shut them again.

"You hang tight." Melinda squeezed his shoulder and turned at the sound of heavy footsteps behind her.

Now the mother was on them, her blonde curls flowing behind her atop the cloak, her wide mouth, lined and grooved, smiling cruelly. Lavinia. Melinda could tell by the careless but confident way she pulled the Volcanin to a stop that she would be the hardest Denfanas to fight.

Melinda checked herself for her gun – must still be in the carriage. She scanned for a branch or something she could use as a weapon but there was nothing on the snowy ground.

"You would make a lovely addition as well," Lavinia said. She was positively glowing in the darkness as she dismounted and strode forward.

"Abby!" Melinda called, keeping her eyes locked on Lavinia. "You snap out of it yet? Could sure use your help."

White rings lined Lavinia's ice-blue irises, and matching dust flowed forward like a swarm of pollen. Melinda tried to duck but the dust followed, turning in mid-air to cover her. She wracked her brain for anything she knew about fighting psychic vampires, but Lavinia's dust punched up the fog in her mind tenfold.

"Momma?" Abby popped out of the side of the carriage, looking about as disoriented as Melinda felt. In Abby's hand was the gun – pointed right toward Melinda.

"She's not your ma!" Melinda managed through her daze. "You got to fight the hold these psychic vampires have over you."

"Patience, dear Abigale. You may have a new sister yet. And, interesting choice of words, Melinda," Lavinia said, her eyes flashing in anger before smoothing over. "I wouldn't call it a 'hold', so much as an agreement. One you could be privy to as well. Not everyone is given the opportunity to erase their life's pain."

Agony slammed into Melinda sharper than the day her

mother died. Her mother's face, gaunt as the speckled monster infection took over, came back to Melinda vivid as a painting. And all those anguished feelings—how the days, weeks, months after her mother's passing stretched impossibly lonely, how she thought she might as well die too.

"Yes," Lavinia sighed in pleasure. "This can feed me. And look what I can do for you."

A second later the despair vanished like a wind had snatched it away. Melinda blinked, feeling better than she had, well, *ever*. As if her ma was alive and well. As if everything was in its right place. She dug her nails into her palms, forcing herself to remember how she had made it through, got on just fine, met Lance. *Lance*! She couldn't leave him there, privy to who knew what Lavinia might have in mind. She couldn't let him feel the torment she had felt.

"Why are you resisting?" Lavinia hissed. "And holding onto your misery?"

Melinda forced herself to remember Abby's parents' cracking voices, their tormented eyes. It was one thing to lose a parent—something else entirely to lose a kid.

"My ma might've passed but don't mean I want this mixed-up nonsense in my head," Melinda said. She turned to address Abby, who stood uncertainly in front of the carriage. "Your ma... misses you. Your *real* ma. That much I could tell. I saw the pain in her eyes when she thought you might not come back. Whatever suffering you got going on, it's part of life. This vampire isn't going to change that."

Abby blinked back small tears at the corners of her eyes. She tightened her grip on the pistol and shook her head as if tormented by a swarm of flies. "What did you do to my head, Momma? M..."

Melinda closed her eyes, waiting to hear the gunshot.

Abby fired.

When Melinda opened her eyes, Lavinia was clutching her chest and the Volcanin had run off.

"How—dare you—" Lavinia gaped at Abby and looked

down in shock at the blood blooming down her cloak and onto the white snow.

"You're a leech," Abby said, her voice trembling. Her eyes looked clear at last. "Damn you and your family right back to hell."

As Lavinia crumpled, the feeling of intoxication receded as quickly as it had come on. A splinter of pain shot through Melinda's temples worse than any barrel fever.

"It'll pass," Abby said, her eyes hooded. "You meant what you said?"

"I swear it. You'll see yourself how relieved your parents are when we get you back. You survived." Melinda massaged her forehead. "That's the important part. Let's get you home."

Together they hoisted Lance up.

"You both look... sad," he managed, trying to blink the daze out of his eyes.

Melinda glanced at Abby, noticing the hard jut to her jaw. She wondered if she'd ever be the same. Just then, something caught her ear. Faint howls, coming from the direction of the mountain.

Howls of grief. And rage.

Melinda glanced back at the still form of Lavinia. "Guess the Denfanas family got their own sorrow to deal with now too. But we survived," she said. "That's what matters, right?"

Lance's old grin came back. "'Til the next job," he said. "For now, let's hope Furrows Green has a saloon or two."

"Amen to that," Melinda sighed. They unhitched the horses and, under the sinking moon and echoing bellows from the remaining Denfanas family, escorted Abby back to town.

PARSONS GRANGE

David Benton and WD Gagliani

Carter studied the cards splayed out in his fist. Three fours, a Jack, and an Ace. Three of a kind was a good hand, but not a great one.

"Well, what you gonna do, Carter?" Smokey Jones said from the other side of the table, a smoldering hand-rolled smoke hanging from the corner of his mouth.

"I'm considerin', Smokey."

"You gonna consider all night?"

"I might."

"Hell, you just stallin', that's all."

Everyone else at the table had folded and turned in. Now it was just Carter and Smokey playing for the pot. Carter knew Smokey was a notorious bluffer but he also knew Smokey had been hot all night.

The door to the bunkhouse swung open and slammed into the wall, drawing the attention of everyone present away from the card game.

It was the boss's kid.

He wasn't really a kid, he was grown, but Carter didn't really consider him a man, either. Had soft hands like those of a proper lady. Livin' is easy when you're the boss's kid.

"What you want, Timmy?" Carter asked, knowing damn well the kid hated being called Timmy.

"Sumthin's spookin' the cattle, we can hear 'em cryin' all the way back at the house."

"And…?"

"And Pa wants you to go and check it out."

"Ah, shit." Carter put his cards face down on the table. "Come on, Smokey, let's go."

"What? Why do I have to go?"

"Because I don't trust you not to look at my cards while I'm away."

"Aw hell, Carter, just lay 'em down and lose right now."

"No. I'm still considerin'."

Soon Carter and Smokey were riding out into the darkness, each of them holding a hooded lantern in one hand, the reins and a rifle in the other – Carter a Model 1873 Winchester, and Smokey his trusty Henry repeater, in case the trouble was rustlers making off with cattle again. They slowed their mounts upon reaching the herd, then reined to a stop. Some of the cattle were still bellowing nervously as they milled around near the treeline, where the grassy plain abutted a thick swath of forest. The horses seemed to catch whatever was riling up the cows, making them shiver so hard Carter could feel it.

"You see anything, Smoke?"

"Just a loser at cards, that's all."

"I meant anything out of the ordinary," said Carter, grinning. Not that Smokey could see it in the dark.

"Nah, maybe a coyote pokin' around, lookin' for a loose calf?"

"Mebbe. Somethin's got their hackles up."

They rode the perimeter of the herd for a few minutes but saw nothing other than spooked cattle whose eyes were oddly wide, as if enthralled. *Or scared shitless.*

Carter was just about to turn back when his lamp illuminated a patch of flattened grass. "What the hell's this?" he muttered, mostly to himself. Not only were the blades crushed, but there were also dark patches here and there that Carter knew had to be blood. *Cow's blood?*

"I dunno, Carter, but I'm thinkin' we oughta come back here in daylight..."

"Let me jus' take a look at—" Carter started to dismount, but then pain exploded in his back.

Excruciating, tearing, wrenching pain.

He looked down at himself, and what appeared to be a fence post jutted out of his gut.

"Wha—?"

His horse reared and bolted, causing him to drop the Winchester, but Carter himself remained suspended in midair. *Ain't possible!* his brain screamed.

"Smokey!" he groaned, surprised at his own voice. But the only response was a terrible tearing sound and then the patter of raindrops all around, except it wasn't rain. Smokey was floating, too, spitted. He was sure he saw that. The horses were gone, run off in terror.

Then the pain hit in a never-ending wave.

Carter felt the warm rush of his own blood soaking his dungarees and pouring down his legs like rainwater off a barn roof. The post impaling him was a sharpened spike or tree bough, now painted black in the dim light. As he lost feeling in his extremities, the lantern slipped from his numbed hand. His vision tunneled and the sounds of cattle and screaming became distant and muffled as if he were standing near a rushing river. "I'm done," he mumbled, throat closing.

From somewhere that felt as far off as his childhood, Carter heard Smokey still screaming just before he shuffled off his mortal coil.

* *

The tall rider wore a black duster and his hat was slung low over his eyes as he traversed a narrow arroyo, part of this trail through the seemingly endless plains. He'd left Fort Leavenworth at dawn's first light heading northwest. Now, judging from the angle of the sun, it was mid-morning. He had diverged from the Santa Fe Trail and was aiming toward the Nebraska Territories with a stack of *Wanted* posters folded up and stuffed in his saddlebag. An especially dangerous outlaw was at the top of the stack.

"Someone's coming, Rex," his horse-like mount said. "From the southwest."

United States Marshal Rex Masters studied that landscape. He could indeed see a small cloud of dust approaching in the far distance.

"What do you suppose it is, Buck?"

The horse-like creature raised its long nose in the air and took a drawn-out sniff. "I smell humans. And horses. And they're all scared."

"I'll handle this." Rex swept the duster off his right hip, exposing one of his two Peacemakers holstered there. "We'll just wait here for 'em."

Buck made a decidedly non-horselike low trilling sound, a sign of his wariness.

In a short time Rex could make out the riders. Five men. Seven horses. The man in front looked much older, with long, swept-back gray hair but clean-shaven, well-dressed for these parts, and Rex surmised he was in charge. The man on the left was the youngest, his face also hairless. And he also wore fine clothing with a gold pocket watch chain visible under his suit coat. He was leading the two saddled but unmanned horses. The man on the right seemed to fall between the other two in age but was disheveled with a scraggly beard and mustache. And he cradled a rifle in the crook of his arm. Two riding behind them were nervous-looking cowhands.

Rex waited, face neutral.

"Hey there, stranger!" the eldest rider called out as they approached at a slow trot.

Now the unkempt man trained his rifle on Rex. Buck's ears fluttered, a definite sign of his preparation for defensive action.

"Easy, Buck," said Rex softly, "let's give 'em a chance."

The riders slowed their mounts to a stop across from Rex and Buck.

"Cletus, lower that damn rifle," the elder barked after glancing sideways at his companions. Presumably he'd noticed the star pinned to Rex's duster lapel. Cletus looked like a whelp who'd been cuffed by his master but reluctantly lowered the gun barrel.

"Marshal, you might be just that man we need." Muscles in the old man's face bunched as if about to burst through the leathery skin.

"What seems to be the problem?"

"Let me introduce myself. Name's Ely Parsons and this here land's my property near as far as the eye can see."

"Sorry, sir. I'm just passin' through... on official business."

"No, no, don'tchu worry none about it, Marshal," Ely said quickly. "My son, Timmy." He motioned to the youngest rider, who made a sour face. "And that there's Cletus, my ranch foreman. Back there's Smitty and Barnes. This land's Parsons Grange, the largest spread west of the Mississippi, or so they say."

Masters tipped his hat incrementally by way of saying hello. He remained wary, his hand not far from the Colt's revolver but relaxed enough to keep tempers low.

The old man glanced around. "You seen anybody else out here recently, Marshal?"

Rex squinted. "Can't say that I have. You lookin' for someone in particular?"

"Seen anything... strange?"

The muscles in Buck's back rippled under Rex's thighs. "How do you mean *strange*, Mister Parsons?"

"Why don't you come back to the ranch with us? We'll fix ya some vittles. Set up water and feed for your horse. And mayhap we can talk for a bit along the way."

"We could talk here," Rex pointed out, still wary. But Ely Parsons looked like a man afraid, not aggressive.

The old rancher looked down. "Story's kinda long and..."

"Strange?" Rex provided.

"Yessir, I'm afraid it is. I give you my word, we're in trouble here and you bein' a lawman could be a blessin' better'n anything we coulda done on our own."

"What's it about? This story, and this trouble?"

Parsons shrugged. "First glance, looks like rustlers. But there's something else happenin' besides my cattle goin' missing the last few months. Now two of my men are missing, too. All we got left of'em's their mounts."

As if on cue, the men's horses started to fuss, stamping their feet, long heads swiveling, sudden fear obvious in their eyes. Parsons' horse snorted and shook his muzzle. It was contagious, and now all the horses were stamping and shuddering in distress.

"See? Horses are afraid of whatever's goin' on around here."

Rex gently nudged Buck with his knees. The not-horse caught on and imitated the fussy horses.

Between nervous glances left and right, Parsons told his story. Starting with the most recent *event*, the disappearance of at least a dozen heads of cattle and the possible murder of two of his best ranch hands, Carter and Smokey Jones.

"They went out to check the herd, and never returned." He snorted and wiped his cheek with sleeve. "We found some… body parts and blood, though. Can't tell if it's theirs."

"Body parts?"

Parsons nodded. "You gotta see what I mean. We'll take you there."

Rex stroked the stubble on his chin. "You think rustlers?"

"Who else would want cattle?"

"Inside job?"

"No sir." Ely Parsons shook his head emphatically. "Carter and Smokey, two of my best men… somebody came and took that cattle *and* two of my best men. I was plannin' on sendin' out Cletus and my four other hands, see if they could find these rustlers, but it would surely be more helpful to have a lawman such as yourself alongside 'em. To make sure everything was handled lawful and such."

"Well, I don't know, Ely. I'm headin' west, trackin' a bunch of dangerous outlaws. Isn't there some local official you could get on the trail? A sheriff nearby, one with jurisdiction?"

"Nobody like that for two hundred miles, give or take." A sound like buzzing rose up from somewhere, and Parsons spoke fast. "Look, Marshal, let's get you a meal, all right? We can ride past where this… this *thing* happened, and show you what we seen. Ain't much. It's about what ain't there 'stead of what is."

Rex let the words filter through his extra sense, and he knew

Buck's third eye was open under his mane. So far Buck hadn't rung any bells. "Thank you, I could use a bite of dinner. But only after we take a look around. Lead the way, Mister Parsons."

After a short ride down the arroyo, past an incongruous copse of scraggly mesquite, and over a half mile of rocky terrain, they arrived at what passed for a pasture in this dry climate. Scrub-grass grew in clumps and some cows milled around, munching. But Rex – and Buck – had no trouble noticing they didn't look calm. Their heads swiveled as if searching for something. *Wary.*

"This is the outer edge of the herd," Parsons said, trying to keep his horse from bolting. The other horses were acting up, too. "Look there."

Rex followed the old man's arthritic finger and spied a large patch of flattened, crusted grass. It wasn't hard to tell the crust was drying blood. A lot of it. It stank of corruption and decay already. And here and there, the area was dotted with chunks of bloody, torn flesh. Human or bovine? Rex couldn't tell from a distance. And he didn't want to get too close.

The horses were getting more agitated, whinnying and snorting, making it hard for the men to keep them reined up. The cows lowed in fear, their eyes rolling in their sockets.

Buck whispered, "Do you smell that?" He shivered violently.

"Can't help it, it's in my nostrils," Rex muttered under his breath.

"We'd better go before they start bolting!" Parsons called out. He had a rifle in one hand now, but his other was busy holding his horse in place. The other men whirled around, grabbing their weapons. With Parsons leading the way, they galloped away from the panicking herd. As they rode, Rex heard the thunder of hooves behind them. Cows were starting to stampede, but in all directions. Terrified and confused.

"Christ, Parsons, what the hell's going on?" Rex shouted.

"Ain't sure," the rancher called out over his shoulder. "But I don't wanna lose any more men. Stick with us, Marshal!"

They rode at speed for a bit, following the arroyo until it

led to a low ridge they topped, and then they were riding parallel to a tree line, thick woods behind it. Rex had to look twice. Something was in the forest, apparently uprooting trees and tossing the trunks like twigs. But nothing could be seen. The sound of breaking trunks was suddenly deafening.

The six men, seven horses – and Buck – rode hell-bent for leather to leave behind whatever it was. The last man, Smitty it turned out, fell out of the saddle when his terrified mount stumbled, and rolled over and over when he hit the ground. Barnes turned to go back for him when *something* leaned out of the wooded barrier and grabbed the ranch hand. Whatever it was, it dragged Smitty toward the trees.

Screaming, Smitty tried to get away, but suddenly disappeared and his screams were cut off. A huge pine trunk fell out onto the trail and cut off the riders from where Smitty had disappeared. The stench was intolerable.

"Let's go!" Parsons shouted.

"I'm goin' back for'im," screamed Barnes. "Smitty!"

"Leave'im, there ain't nothin' you can do for'im now!"

Rex had to agree. Buck was hoofing it pretty quickly himself, looking like an Arabian with a rippling haze around him, his way of keeping his equine disguise in place. But for once he was having trouble doing so.

Rex had one of his Peacemakers out, but there was nothing and no one to shoot at.

They rode as fast as the traumatized horses could take them, and soon they reached their destination, bypassing a long bunkhouse next to a series of corrals and finally reining up to a massive log mansion, the heart of Parsons Grange. Rex left Buck tied up with a warning look, but not too near the horses who were skittish enough.

Bawling for his friend's fate, Barnes stormed off back to the bunkhouse while the rest entered the oversize greatroom in the two-story building and milled around with nothing much to do. Rex noticed they avoided each others' eyes as if they were afraid to see the fear that had settled on them all. But he could tell they had all seen things before.

Parsons disappeared into the rear of the house, and soon the smell of food overcame the men's anxiety. A long plank table near the kitchen was hurriedly set, and Parsons helped his cook with heavy, steaming pots. Timmy was pressed into service, handing out tin plates and utensils. Rex was served an over-flowing plate of beans and pork belly – as much meat as it was beans – plus some kind of meaty stew, nearly-fresh biscuits, and several mugs of strong, black coffee.

Two more Parsons hands, Doone and Blaylock, showed up and joined in after mentioning that Barnes was too despondent to eat.

"Well, we'll run him some vittles. He's gonna need his strength," Ely Parsons opined.

Rex said nothing.

For a while, the only sounds were of utensils rattling, and determined chewing and swallowing. When they were finished, the elder Parsons broke out a bottle of rye and passed around generous shots of the amber nectar. No one turned it down.

Afterwards, Parsons sent his men to the bunkhouse. "Get some sleep, we're goin' back tomorrow. We're gonna figure out what the hell's killin' our folks, and takin' the cattle. Timmy, you get some sleep too." When they were all gone, Parsons took Rex into his study and poured another round of rye for two. They sat across from each other at a wide desk.

Rex held his glass up to the lantern's light and watched the bronze reflections play across the room like swirling shadows. Through the prism he saw Parsons watching him, his features turned monstrous by the jagged edges.

"Come on, Marshal," the old man began, as if they'd been talking the whole time. "You know there ain't no sheriff anywhere near here. The nearest Army garrison's about three hundred miles. And now that Smitty's dead we got three men either killed or... or worse."

Rex nodded, wondering if the Parsons Grange spread had seen other strange occurrences on its wide-open spaces. But before he could express his reasons for moving on – mostly resting on needing to capture the dangerous gunslinger who also happened to be a dark mage – Parsons tried raising the stakes.

"Look, I could make it worth your while, Marshal. I haveta figure out what's happenin' to my cattle, and my crew. My ranch hands are fine men when it comes to cattle and work around the place, and no one's better at drivin' a herd to the railhead at Great Bend, but they ain't gunmen. We could use the help of a trained shooter."

"How worth my while are we talkin'?"

Ely laid a stack of ten gold coins on the desk. "And ten more for your trouble if you can retrieve my property. And ten more after that if I can see the bastards who took'em swingin' from a nearby tree."

"What about the bastards who killed Smitty and the other two, Carter and Smokey? Or is it only about the cattle?"

"Well, them too! They're the same ones, ain't they?"

Rex scratched behind his right ear. He could sense Buck's trilling from outside. The not-horse had his third eye wide open, so he could see Rex and Parsons. Probably he was shaking his long head.

Rex pushed the gold coins back across the desk.

"I'll help you because somebody's murdering your men," he said, his face set in a grim line. "But not because of the cattle. And I don't need a bounty. All I need's my oath of office and my authority as granted by the government of the United States." *And the higher authority, the same one who had matched me with Buck and given me my life's mission.* Here, now, was a part of that mission, he could see that.

Parsons stared at him wordlessly. Then he stared down at the gold coins which, probably for the first time in a long time, were worthless to him. "You… you'll help me. Us?"

"Well," Rex said, "throw in another cup of that excellent coffee and you have yourself a deal."

Rex could hear Buck's satisfied trilling. He went out to see to his not-horse's comfort for the night, a stall to himself in the long stable adjacent to the bunkhouse. He patted Buck's thick pelt. "Keep an eye out, Buck," he said by way of good-night. He meant the creature's third eye, the one with extra vision and other, even more arcane functions.

Buck nodded and cooed a quiet, "Good night, Rex," before apparently sinking into a deep sleep as he leaned against the wall of the stall.

The marshal settled down to sleep in a hay-covered corner, drawing his blanket over himself and tilting his hat over his eyes.

• •*

Early the next morning after coffee and biscuits, Rex and the ranch hands rode out to where Cletus thought the men had disappeared. Before long they arrived at the crushed and blood-crusted patch of prairie grass where the men had presumably been snatched. And likely murdered.

"They must have come out of these woods," said Rex as he eyed the stretch of wilderness spread before them.

"I reckon," said Cletus before hawking a mouthful of tobacco-dyed, brown spit.

Rex wished Parsons hadn't begged off the expedition, but the rancher had been pale and stiff and claimed ill health when he put Cletus in charge of his crew. Timmy was nowhere to be found, and Parsons frowned and shrugged. "Probably afraid, hidin' out," he said, shaking his head. "Cletus is solid, he can lead the men."

So now Rex spurred Buck gently towards the tree line. The others followed, their horses stepping gingerly.

Once near the forest's edge, Rex pulled his rifle from its scabbard and dismounted, stepping closer to investigate. It didn't take an expert tracker to see that the area just inside the tree line had been disturbed. Something had broken through the brush here. Something huge. *Or more than one something.*

The tall, scraggly grass, as well as weeds and shrubs that grew at the forest's edge were trampled flat, saplings and younger trees had had their branches snapped off, and the leaves appeared to have been violently stripped from the lower branches of the older trees. Thick trunks, recently snapped like toothpicks, were scattered haphazardly about the area.

Buck whinnied and stamped a heavy hoof. Knowing enough not to speak in front of the ranch hands, Buck still knew how to communicate. Rex regarded his faithful steed and Buck motioned to their right with his long, twitching nose.

Rex swept the black duster off his right hip and wrapped his fingers around his Peacemaker's grip. Going for one of his side irons had become a habit since his life's mission had been entrusted to him. Ready for anything, he scrutinized the nearby thicket.

"Injuns," Cletus growled from behind him.

Rex spun and saw Cletus drawing a bead with his rifle on something in the woods. The others were starting to do the same.

"Lower your guns!" Rex called out, waving them down. "I'll handle this."

The men were reluctant, grumbling. Terror was in their veins, blocking all rational thought and compelling them to violent aggression in the name of defense.

Rex calmed his rage, but not by much. "I said, put your damn guns down! Now. Aim'em at the ground or I'll shoot you clean off your saddle. I said, I'll handle this."

Grudgingly, the ranch hands complied, staring at the marshal and at the place that marked their fear.

In front of Rex, the brush parted. Silent as a whisper, a man stepped through and faced them.

He was Cherokee, of that Rex had no doubt. He wore a buckskin war shirt and leather leggings, and his long black hair was gathered in a pair of braids. He held out his empty hands in the universal symbol of peace. *At least it* looks *like peace is intended.* Others were standing stiffly, partly hidden in the brush behind the warrior.

The lawman took his hand off his pistol's grip and followed suit with the attempted peace sign.

The Cherokee warrior wore no face paint, but his eyes were intense pools of dark anger. *And well-suppressed fear.*

"Ayv, daquadoa usdi ugidali," the corporeal apparition said, introducing himself. He also used the common hand symbols known among the tribes. Which was helpful, as Rex's Cherokee was rusty.

"Osiyo," Rex replied. *Hello.* "Usganoli hiwonihi." *Please speak slowly.*

"Itsula agatisgv nasginai anisgaya agisdi agia anisgaya. Digatilvdi owenvsv. Asdudi naquu. Itsula unegutsidv tla esgaigvnehi."

"Osda, wado." *Good, thank you.*

The warrior tapped his own chest. "Usdi ugidatli."

Rex followed suit. "Rex."

Again, the warrior tapped his chest and nodded, making a small bow. Rex mirrored it.

"You speak Injun, Marshal?" Cletus asked with a sneer. It was obviously all gibberish to him. "What's he sayin'?"

"They mean us no harm," Rex said, translating to the best of his ability. "This is Small Feather addressing us. He and his braves're hunting for the men who attacked their village." Though Rex knew he hadn't said *men,* strictly speaking. He'd said, *the men who eat men,* though judging from the accompanying hand gestures they were clearly something more. And it was best to leave this detail out of the translation. Rex turned to the ranch hands, sidestepping Cletus's seething rage. "I think they're lookin' for the same men we are. They're trackin'em into these here woods. We should go with them."

"I ain't goin' nowhere with any damn Injuns," Cletus said. The others were blank-faced and seemed at least open to the idea, though they looked to Cletus, their foreman, for guidance.

"Then you go back to the ranch and tell Mister Parsons that you ran off on us." In certain situations, Rex would have made his point by just shooting Cletus through the head.

"Them Injuns probably the ones who killed Carter and Smokey and took the damn cattle to begin with!" His nostrils were pulsating. "And Smitty, they killed Smitty, too."

"No. For one thing, they wouldn't have trampled this brush. When the Cherokee travel they barely disturb a leaf. For another, we all saw what happened to Smitty and it was no war party's doing."

The foreman was turning red, scowling at the newcomers with murder clearly on his mind. He sent a brown stream to the ground between his horse and Small Feather's silent party. "You ain't in charge of us," Cletus growled.

"I'm not, but unless you kill me, I'll be telling Ely *you* started a war with the Cherokee peoples over a stupid idea born of your prejudice and hate. And you'll be hunted down like a rabid dog if you kill a United States Marshal. So what's your move?"

"Well, you tell the fuckin' savage to have the rest of them step out in the open so's we know who we're dealin' with, then," Cletus said through gritted teeth.

Rex turned back to Small Feather. "Howatsu adadvdodi digineli adohi inage adisgalodi." *Please ask your friends to step out of their hiding place.*

The brave looked deeply into Rex's eyes, then glanced at Buck, seeming to really *see* him, as no one had seen him before. Small Feather turned and spoke a few soft words. The group accompanying him appeared out of thin air, one moment almost completely concealed by the surrounding trees, and the next standing in the trampled grass and undergrowth facing down Rex and the others. They had been quite invisible to the rapid glance. They all wore knives in their belt sashes, and two carried short spears. The others carried medium bows fashioned from springy saplings and a clutch of arrows each.

There were four of them, with Small Feather himself making five. So at least it would be a fair fight if Cletus's worry about their intentions was correct. But Rex put no stock in the rabidly hateful ranch foreman or his opinions. He went on to slowly explain the situation.

"Utvdasdi…" *Listen.* He chose his words carefully: "We're looking for whoever took two men and many head of cattle from this field two darks ago. And one man last new light. We think they are *killed*. Atsilvgi. Atsilvgi! I'm wondering if maybe you and us are looking for the same people."

Small Feather turned slowly to survey their surroundings and nodded, agreeing. "Atsilvgi!" *Killed!* "Ayv atsilvgi!" *We are killed too.*

Rex waited for more before trying to translate for the trigger-happy ranch hands.

"It would be safer if we traveled together. They are close," said Small Feather slowly enough so Rex could understand.

Though Small Feather, who seemed to be the small war party's leader, was speaking to Rex, he was suddenly distracted.

Distracted by Buck.

The brave stepped forward, reaching his hand out to touch Buck's head. "Nasginigesvna sogwili!" he said directly to Buck. *You are no horse.*

The not-horse trilled and gave a tiny shake, then nodded as a horse would have.

"Nihi nasquv didahnvwisgi gigahai," Rex said. *You have shaman's blood.* He was surprised the man had been able to see through Buck's elaborate ruse. He was indeed no horse. At least no horse of *this* world.

Now Small Feather faced Rex. "My grandfather is shaman. He says I have the gift of medicine. One day I will take his place among the people." He tilted his chin at Buck. "Where did you get this Spirit Horse?"

"We are old friends. It's a long story. What about the 'men who eat men'?"

Small Feather touched Buck's snout and the not-horse tilted his head and let him. That was a first. He spoke slowly. "We must move if we want to catch them before dark. It will be much more dangerous after sundown."

Rex nodded his thanks and turned to the ranch hands, who had watched with differing levels of distress as the marshal and the Cherokee seemed to be making small talk. "Better dismount," he ordered. "We're goin' to accompany these braves in pursuit of our rustlers."

"Aw, hell!" Cletus slid out of his saddle. "You better tell'em to keep their scalping savage selves away from me."

Rex bit his tongue and turned away, lest he give Cletus a talkin'-to the bastard would never forget. He stroked Buck's neck. "You wait here and keep your eye on the horses, and us. Okay, buddy?"

Buck pawed at the ground and shook his long head. Rex knew Buck wasn't happy about it, and he also knew the not-horse was a great asset in a fight, but he'd be cumbersome in the forest, and the others might suspect something.

The war party watched expressionlessly as the white men drew rifles and joined them inside the tree line, most glaring with undisguised hatred.

Then they all pushed their way through the brush at the forest's edge, starting to track their quarry on foot, spreading out in a ragged line.

Rex stared at Cletus's broad back, carefully.

* *•*

The sun had crested and was beginning its descent when they came across the shelter. *Or whatever one could call it.*

For several hours they had traveled on foot through the forest as quickly as the wild terrain had allowed, following a swath of disturbed vegetation wide enough that even Cletus could have followed it without the Cherokee trackers' aid. Until they came across a clearing of sorts where the sun shone down unimpeded, and what initially looked like an angled clump of trees growing almost on top of each other.

But they weren't growing that way. They'd been stacked to make a primitive lean-to, one that was also strangely sophisticated. Full adult, old-growth trees had been sheared off at the bottom, sharpened at the top, and steepled together to become a makeshift building – a wooden cathedral hidden in the woods where almost no one would see it. A massive structure, it rivaled the height of the watchtowers at Fort Leavenworth.

The ranch hands were dumbstruck by the sight of it, clearly finding it difficult for their minds to accept what their eyes reported. The Cherokee braves were matter-of-fact about it, perhaps having seen it or a similar one before. For Marshal Rex Masters, it was just another stop in the long, bizarre trail on which he found himself. The voice in his mind was Buck's and indicated he was also not seeing something like this for the first time.

Oh, no, Rex, I have indeed seen this before, elsewhere, and I'd hoped I wouldn't see it here…

Damn it, Buck, you'd better tell me more.

I think it's too late.

Now you tell me…

The sound of a bellowing cow suddenly came from a corral built of felled tree trunks that took up half the clearing.

If the cows were alive – or at least some of them – the men might have survived too.

The ten men fanned out and slowly moved into position at the massive lean-to's entrance, weapons poised.

The interior of the structure was cloaked in shadow. Once their eyes had adjusted to the dim light, they were able to gauge the shelter's dimensions. The access was tall enough to stand a steam engine on end and wide enough for two wagons to enter side by side.

Rex took the lead, approaching cautiously. The others followed.

Inside, scents hung thick in the air. There was the sharp smell of the freshly cleaved trees mixed with the tang of spilled blood… as well as some putrid stench that Rex had never had the displeasure of smelling before. Its repugnant fetor made the hairs on the back of his neck stand up.

At the rear of the huge lean-to they found the missing men, but there would be no liberation this day.

They hung by their bound feet from the roof, skinned and gutted. Ripening. Carter and Smokey had been spitted by some kind of large spear… at least based on the visible damage done to their torsos prior to gutting. Smitty appeared to have been drawn and quartered, pulled apart into two halves like a chicken wing. Carved wood buckets below the swinging bodies held various quantities of coagulating blood.

Nearby sat a pile of cow bones, most of which had been split open, the raw marrow sucked out of the jagged edges. *Snapped open by brute force.* But who could have done this?

Rex had seen much in his long career running to ground bad men (and some women), but this sight rendered him speechless.

One of the ranch hands, Doone, spewed out whatever was left of his breakfast and lunch. Barnes sank to his knees next to him, retching. Everyone else could only stare, hands shaking.

Meanwhile Small Feather and his braves had turned to face a firepit, where pieces of other corpses had been roasted, their flesh and bones gnawed. Several heads with scooped-out brains rested on rough-hewn planks as if staged ornamentally. The Cherokee bowed their heads, seeing their own missing friends and relatives among the remains of a dozen or more butchered bodies.

"Tsosdadanvtli," the warrior said to Rex, his face contorted in pain. *My brother.* He pointed at one of his braves, whose stoic face was awash in tears. "Edutsi, vquina. Vquati!" *Uncle, nephew. Niece.* He pointed at another who shook, weeping. "Nigada sidanelv dinatlinohedisgi!" *All are family.*

Rex stepped back, stunned. Whatever had been here, erected this pastoral cathedral of death and cannibalism, hadn't discriminated when it came to its victims. It had no preferences. Male, female. White man, Indian. Cows.

Food.

It was *all* food to this creature. Or, seeing some depressed areas across the length of the soil floor of the place, where heavy bodies had rested or slept, *these creatures.* For there had been more than one.

Rex searched his memory for anything similar he might have faced in his past work for the US government and, more to the point, for the Elder God known on this plane as G'orrthshla... but there was nothing.

If these flesh-eaters were human, they were *large.* If they weren't human, then what kind of demon were they? He had seen plenty of those, too, here in the wide-open stretches of the Western Territories, where human habitation was sparse and creatures from other dimensions could exist – *and murder* – with impunity. G'orrthshla indeed ruled over everything, but preferred being mostly invisible. These others, they were part of the clean-up Rex and those like him had been tasked with; tracking human outlaws, but also inhuman ones, or those humans who had learned too much about the Others, or about their unholy needs, and used their knowledge for evil. Perhaps one had summoned the flesh-eaters. But why? Why would anyone wish to murder so many in such horrible ways?

Suddenly Buck's internal voice cut through his death-fueled reverie. G'orrthshla had gifted Rex with Buck many years past, and now the not-horse was trying to break through Rex's untimely distraction.

Rex! Can you hear me? They're coming back!

What the—who? Who is coming? Where are you?

I've slipped back into the woods, but… Oh, Rex, get out of there! They'll be there soon… Get out now!

Even though Buck's voice was entirely in Rex's head, he could certainly hear the creature's distress.

"We have to get out now!" Rex called out as he levered a slug into the breech of his Winchester.

"We're gonna get our dead'n bury'em," said Cletus, turning to face the marshal. "Like Christians. Stay out of our way, lawman." His face had been ashen, but his reaction to the gruesome discovery was now one of rising rage and his skin was reddening around the eyes. He swiveled his menacing gaze to Small Feather, who stood a few feet away still helping his people mourn their own dead. "And I ain't lettin' go of my notion that these savages done in our guys." He reached for his revolver.

"No!" Rex swung his rifle so the barrel covered the furious foreman.

"Why, you son of a—"

A shadow crossed the shelter's huge doorway and Rex spun on his heels.

It was a *very* large shadow.

There, in the entryway stood three near-naked men of preposterous stature. Describing them as giants straight out of a fairy tale would have been entirely reasonable because that's what they were. They each stood as tall as two grown men, perhaps twelve feet or more, yet they weren't gangly. Instead, their bodies were mostly proportionate, with arms and legs as thick around as tree trunks and chests twice as broad as normal humans. Their faces were blocky, as if sculpted from rock or marble, and grotesquely porcine eyes peered out from deep, dark caverns under their plank-like foreheads.

Their mouths, though... to Rex their mouths were straight out of a nightmare. Lips like slabs of fat, misshapen teeth badly filed to points resembling blunt fangs, and dripping tongues like gristle hung limp between their teeth.

They wore grubby, greasy dungarees that barely fit and not much else, except, Rex noted, a gold watch chain around the neck of the largest of the three.

Ranch hands and warriors stepped back almost in unison, but there was nowhere to go. The rear of the cathedral had no exit. The only way out was the main entry, and the three giants effectively blocked it. They growled at the interlopers contaminating their living quarters.

"No need trying to talk them out of anything!" Rex called out, taking aim. "Not unless you want to end up here as a side of beef." His rifle barked at the same time as some of the others' and he watched his slug drill into the center giant, the one he figured was in charge.

The creature looked down as if puzzled, then opened his hellmouth and bellowed – not in pain, but in anger. The impact of the slugs didn't knock him over, and the bullet holes didn't bleed.

"Shit!" Rex re-cocked and placed his next heavy .44-40 slug in the monster's head, to no real result.

A ragged volley from the humans in the room seemed to halt the giants' advance, but only momentarily. Small Feather's warriors added spears and arrows, but they barely registered as the giants advanced on them.

"What are they?" Cletus shouted as he emptied his piece. No one responded, and he reloaded with shaking hands, dropping a bullet before he could snap closed the loading gate on his Colt's revolver. Cocking and shooting again, he bellowed back at the monsters.

By then the giants had reached the humans, whose backs were now against the rear wall of the cathedral. Their own deaths were suddenly a more than plausible outcome.

The first giant disregarded the bullets and arrows flying around and into him, his huge fist grabbing the first human he could by the head – the ranch hand Doone. With one twist of his oversize arm, he tore Doone's head straight off and tossed it like a child's ball. With a roar he lunged and seized Blaylock, whose scream was cut off when the giant's hand plunged into his chest and extinguished his heart and his life.

Rex was on his fifth shot, knowing how many he had left in the rifle's tubular magazine, and realizing they were doomed. They were *special* bullets, helpful when fighting off *supernatural* beings, but while arguably these were not human, they weren't quite supernatural either. He put another heavy round into a giant's head, and this time it rocked him enough to make him stumble.

"Hallelujah," Rex murmured, levering another round and taking aim. "Eat this, cannibalistic bastard!"

Meanwhile the third giant had reached the Cherokee, who huddled together as if they could fight him off better this way. Unfortunately, arrows didn't slow it down, a spear shattered on his chest, and though one of the warriors screamed and attacked with his knife, the only result was a body torn in half. The others climbed on the creature's back, but he shrugged them off like insects and tore the limbs from them as if they were gossamer wings.

Inside the cathedral the screaming was deafening, and yet the giants' roaring squelched even the loudest scream. And most screams didn't last because the screamers died gruesomely and quickly under the monsters' onslaught.

Rex saw Barnes and Cletus concentrating their fire on one giant, who did falter, but then their united front only benefited Cletus because Barnes had his gun arm ripped out of his shoulder socket. As he screamed and blood gushed from the stump, the giant swatted off his head. Cletus backed up, crying as he emptied his hot revolver again.

Small Feather leaped onto the back of one giant and slit its throat, which caused a gush of green blood to curtain out and bathe the survivors. The monster railed, its mouth open in a deafening shriek. The warrior tried to hang on to the bucking monster like a bull rider, but his grip was loosening and then he would be vulnerable. Rex came to the rescue with two quick rounds to the monster's head, and again the special slugs caused more harm than the creature expected. He bellowed in pain, swayed unsteadily, then buckled under Small Feather's body. The giant was dead!

The warrior gave a quick *thank you* gesture and Rex nodded. But his rifle was almost empty, and he wasn't at all sure his revolvers, despite the same unique bullets, would have the same effect as the high-velocity shots.

The thought that he would die here today found purchase in his brain for the first time. He dropped the rifle and drew both his Peacemakers, cocking and shooting them simultaneously at the other two giants. Rex was joined by Small Feather, who had picked up a discarded rifle, and Cletus who screamed incoherently as he emptied his gun again. They were the only other humans still alive, and they poured a withering fire into the giants... but it wasn't enough.

Rex!

A midnight-black flash of muscle and teeth and hooves burst into the shelter behind the giants.

Buck had abandoned his post with the horses and torn through the woods to emerge just as the remaining defenders were about to succumb to the final two giants.

Buck's true nature – and his real shape – was mysterious even to Marshal Rex Masters, but he had seen the horse-like creature more than hold his own battling against other conjured or summoned beings. His hooves were razors that took an awful toll on the first giant he caught, slicing up its back while his own jaw unhinged like a snake's and crushed the top of the giant's head. The monster coughed up a spout of green slime and collapsed onto its ruined face.

Already on to the other surviving giant, Buck's hidden magic – aided by several bullets from Rex and Small Feather's guns – overpowered whatever lifeforce drove the cannibal's body, and soon the sharp hooves were slashing at its head and crushing its spine, flattening it into the dirt as Buck's ululating and trilling signaled its victory.

Rex was able to walk up and put a bullet through the back of the shuddering monster's head, silencing it.

I thought you could use a hand… —or a hoof or two, Rex.

Rex nodded wearily. *Thanks, old friend.*

He looked at his fellow survivors, Cletus the foreman and the warrior Small Feather, all of them splashed with human and slimy, green monster blood, and lowered his pistol.

"Your people did this!" Cletus shouted, screeching almost incoherently, turning on the stupefied warrior. "You killed them all!"

And then with a scream of rage and frustration Cletus lifted his gun and took aim at Small Feather. Rex reacted with a purely reflex motion, bringing up his Peacemaker and drilling the last round in his cylinder through the ranting foreman's head.

"I owe you two lives this day," said Small Feather, placing his hand lightly on the lawman's shoulder. Rex nodded in acknowledgment.

When they finally emerged from the wooden cathedral and the carnage inside, it was already night.

"Gvwagati dvgalenisgv." *Farewell.* With that, Small Feather turned and melted into the forest as ghost-like and silently as he had first appeared.

"It's as if time slowed down while we were in there," Rex said to Buck. They were just about to cross the tree line on their way back to Parsons Grange. "It felt like minutes, but it must have been hours out here."

Buck trilled one of his agreement sounds. "I felt it, too. Someone has been practicing the arcane arts without a license. Wherever the cannibal giants came from, their summoning disrupted the flow of Time itself."

"That's a new one on me."

Buck sighed. "I've a feeling it won't be the last time, Rex."

The dynamite charges were on long fuses, and Rex and Buck had just reached the tree line when explosions rocked the forest and flames suddenly shot up, lighting the night sky.

A fitting funeral pyre for some brave men.
And a ticket to hell for some others.

* * *

The sun had been up for a couple of hours by the time Rex and Buck reached the Parsons farmhouse.

Weary, sore, and barely able to ride, Rex wanted nothing more than to be away from this evil place. Whatever had happened here, it was beyond his mission. He had *Wanted* outlaws to chase down, starting in the Nebraska Territories.

But there was one more task to complete.

"Wait for me, Buck. Shouldn't be long."

"You always say that."

When he knocked on the farmhouse door, the commotion inside told him all he needed to know. A Peacemaker in his hand, he put a shoulder to the door.

Inside it was dim. All the curtains drawn.

He found Timmy sitting at his father's desk in the study. Ely Parsons lay on the floor, a Bowie-style hunting knife buried in his back and a widening pool of blood beneath him.

"You!"

"True enough." Rex pointed. "Looks like murder, son."

"He wouldn't sell to the railroad, and he wouldn't give me my share early," said the well-dressed rancher's son. "He had his time! It's *my* time now!"

Rex noted the boy was missing his gold watch.

"It was always you. You summoned the giants," Rex said, his gun barrel steady.

"And I can summon more!"

Timmy stood and raised his hands, his wavery voice beginning an incantation Rex recognized.

Marshal Rex Masters laughed and holstered his gun, watching as Timmy sent streams of powerful words into the air, his face reddening with the effort of untested magic. Rex waited until he'd heard enough, then he found his way through the house and outside again.

"Time to go, Buck."

"I live to serve, Marshal Rex Masters."

"Yeah, yeah…"

As they rode away, heading northwest again, Rex heard the arrival of an enraged Elder God. His boss. He knew G'orrthshla would descend like a tidal wave, black tentacles somehow seeming both substantial and insubstantial at the same time, grabbing, crushing, enveloping, consuming everything in their path. The sound of Timmy's shrieking in terror briefly filled the air as the Ancient One obliterated him like a squashed cockroach.

Sometimes Justice has a different face than most would expect.

But it's still Justice.

THE FIENDS OF TURNER'S CREEK

Alan Baxter

What the hell could have done this to a man?" Clyde Carson glanced at his son, then back at the atrocity they'd stumbled across. "Bear?"

Their horses snickered nervously.

"Daddy, ain't no bear would do that!" Jesse pointed at the ragged corpse, face down in the dirt of the trail. "His back's been peeled open like fruit. And his legs got torn off, look at those ragged stumps."

"And where's his head?" Clyde looked up from the knuckle-like bones of the dead man's spine drying in the hot sun, and stared farther up the trail. "It's less than an hour to Turner's Creek. We have plenty of daylight left. Let's bury this poor fucker."

"What's left of him anyway."

Heading off the trail into the scrubby pines to look for a suitable spot to inter the ruined man, Clyde saw something hooked up in the low branches. "Well, I'll be god damned."

"What is it?" Jesse called out.

"Found his fucking leg. One of 'em, at least."

"The other's over here. Still can't see his head though." Jesse joined his father, handed over a shovel. He held another. "Here?"

"Good as anywhere. And make it shallow. I don't want to stick around for long."

Once they'd dug a pit just deep enough and dragged the dead man into it, dropping his legs in either side, they stood looking down.

"Should we say something, Daddy?"

"Son, you're twenty-two years old. Why you still call me Daddy?"

"What should I call you?"

Clyde frowned. "Well, just Dad, I guess."

"Okay. So should we say something, *Dad*?"

"Ain't no need to be sarcastic about it."

Jesse grinned crookedly, shrugged with one shoulder.

Clyde looked down into the hole, grimacing at the sight and the quickly rising smell. Flies had begun to gather. He cleared his throat. "Well, Lord, look over this sorry bastard. No one deserves whatever the hell happened to him. But thank you, God, that it was him and not us. Amen."

Jesse chuckled low in his throat. "Shit, Dad. Amen."

They quickly shovelled the dirt back in, finally hiding the desecration from sight, if not mind.

* * *

When they rode slowly into Turner's Creek, the hairs on the back of Clyde's neck bristled. He looked over at Jesse and his son's brow was furrowed too.

"Somethin's off, Dad."

"You're not wrong." Clyde pulled his Winchester repeating rifle from its slim holster alongside his leg and sat it across his knees. Jesse drew one of the '60 Colt Army six-shooters he carried at each hip and let it hang down by his thigh.

Clyde couldn't say for sure what had him on edge, but a sense of foreboding was strong. He scanned slowly left and right.

"Too damn quiet," Jesse said.

"Where the hell is everyone?"

The town of Turner's Creek was little more than a shabby crossroads. They stilled their horses right in the centre and looked around. A saloon filled one corner, a sheriff's office and presumably a small jail diagonally opposite. General Store, undertaker's, blacksmith, all the usual things a person would expect to see in a small town, but each one was closed up and dark.

The saloon was more than dark. All the windows, first and

second storey, were boarded up and a heavy chain and lock secured the main doors.

Clyde leaned back against his saddle load—bedroll, sifting pans, shovel, hammers, everything the worthy prospector could need—and frowned up at the second-storey windows. He caught a curtain twitch in the building next door to the saloon.

"There." He nudged his palomino forward. Jesse urged his roan to follow. Dust puffed up from the horses' hooves, the dull thwack of their tread the only sound.

"Ain't even any birds singin'," Jesse whispered.

"Hey!" Clyde yelled out. He saw Jesse wince at the sudden shattering of the silence. "I see you up there. What's happening here?"

Silence sank heavy again. Jesse's roan snickered, twitched its ears.

"We need somewhere to stay. My son and I are here to stake a claim. We heard there's still pickings around these parts. Don't want to tread on any toes, but there's room for everyone, am I right?" When no answer was forthcoming, Clyde yelled, "You fixing to keep everything for yourselves, that it?"

"Will you shut the fuck up."

They twisted in their saddles to see a man in a wide hat and a seemingly wider moustache come striding out of the sheriff's office. He was maybe forty years old, similar in age to Clyde himself, and bandy-legged from years in the saddle. He had, Clyde thought, the look of the ex-soldier about him. Something in the man's bearing.

"What the—" Clyde started.

The sheriff drew a gun and levelled it at them. "I said shut the fuck up!" His tone was low, urgent, like he was trying to whisper and suppress anger at the same time. He looked up at the sky, twilight starting to turn everything to tan, and winced. "This way, and try to be god damned quiet!"

He walked past them and headed for the blacksmith's, moving almost at a jog between that building and the undertaker's next door. Clyde and Jesse shared a confused glance, then followed. As they came around the blacksmith's, they saw the sheriff at the closed double doors of a stable building.

"... can't just leave them in the street, they'll yell the place down," the sheriff was saying to someone inside.

A muffled voice came from the other side.

"Enus, god damn it, open these cocksucking doors or I'll shoot out every window in the place!"

There was cursing and rattling from inside, then the doors swung open and an old, skinny man with wild white hair and almost no teeth stood framed in darkness.

"Get your horses in and unloaded as quick as you can," the sheriff said. "There's not much time."

Clyde and Jesse rode in, returning the old man's cautious nod, and dismounted.

"Just grab yer stuff," Enus said. "I'll feed and settle 'em. Where they gonna stay, Sheriff?"

"I'll get Sally to put them up until morning."

"What's happening here?" Clyde asked. He wondered if perhaps they ought to get back on their horses and ride the hell away from this strange town.

As if reading his mind, the sheriff said, "You won't get two miles after dark. Get your stuff and when we get inside, I'll explain. Or at least, I'll try to. You chose a bad time to come to Turner's Creek, is all. A real bad time."

• ••

Sally's place was almost at the edge of the small township, and she opened the door as reluctantly as Enus had opened his stable.

"We ain't working, Sheriff Clark. Not tonight. Not any night soon."

"I know, I know. These fellas just arrived in town and need a bed, is all. You know we can't use the saloon."

Sally eyed Clyde and Jesse up and down. "They gonna be trouble?"

"Are ya?" the sheriff asked.

"No, sir. We're prospector's is all. Heard there was good claims up here. We ain't any trouble at all."

"There sure was good claims up here, but the gold rush is over, stranger. Things change." The sheriff turned back to Sally. "You can give them a room?"

"I guess. Two of my girls can bunk together and these two can bunk together as well."

"That sounds fine, thank you. Let's get in, it's getting dark." Sheriff Clark looked out into the rapidly diminishing day. "Hopefully only one more night before help arrives."

"Ain't no one coming," Sally said, voice heavy with disdain. "Nobody gives a good sweet fuck about us, and you know it." She ushered them in and closed the door, then turned a heavy lock to secure it. Several other young women sat around, eyes darting nervously between the three men.

Working girls, Clyde realised, and it all made sense. That's what Sally had meant about not working. A shame too, as some of those ladies were fine-looking.

"Jack Torrens will be there two days by now. Surely that means anyone coming can only be one day away at most. They'll get here before sundown tomorrow."

"Who's Jack Torrens?" Jesse asked.

"One of ours we sent with a fast horse to get us help."

"Help for what?" Clyde asked.

"Just a second," Jesse said. "Did Jack Torrens wear dark grey jeans and a blue shirt with a rose stitched onto the pocket?"

"He did," the sheriff said, eyes narrowed.

Jesse looked at his father and Clyde sighed. "I'm afraid your friend Jack didn't make it very far. I can't tell you what he looked like, because he had no head, and no horse for that matter, but we buried a corpse dressed just like Jesse described not fifteen miles back from here."

"Well, shit."

"I told you!" Sally said. "Ain't nobody coming."

"You still sent that letter with the last stage," one of the girls said, her voice cracking a little.

The sheriff nodded. "I did. But that was nearly two weeks ago now."

"If anyone read that letter and decided to come, they'd be here by now," Sally said.

"Just what the hell is happening?" Clyde asked.

Screams suddenly pierced the night, then rapid gunshots. *A handgun,* Clyde thought, then the deep boom of a shotgun.

"Fucking early tonight!" Sheriff Clark said. "You drew them here with your yelling!" He ran for the stairs, then paused halfway up as Sally ushered her girls into a back room. "You boys shoot?"

"Sure."

"Then get up here and pick a window. You want to know what's happening? You're about to find out."

Clyde and Jesse dropped their packs and chased Clark up the stairs. They followed him into a large room all done out with silks and lace, smelling of rose perfume. There were two windows.

Clark ran to one and pointed to the other. "One of you go there, the other next door. Shoot anything that moves."

"Anything?" Clyde asked. "What about—"

Clark spun and fixed him with a glare. "Anything that fucking moves!"

Jesse ran to the other window in the room, so Clyde ducked out and went next door. It was a smaller room but similarly decorated. He pushed the heavy drapes aside, lifted the window sash, and looked out, getting a fine view along the street. The boarded-up saloon was visible on the other side down at the crossroads. He couldn't see the sheriff's office from this angle, but the wide-open intersection was clear. And right in the middle of the road on the other side of the junction lay a body, missing a leg. Blood pulsed out, staining the dirt black in the deep twilight. The poor bastard was still alive, trying to crawl towards a building by dragging with his arms and kicking weakly with his remaining leg. A shot rang out, clearly from the room next door, and the injured man's head burst. He bucked once and lay still.

Anything that fucking moves!

What the damn hell was happening in this town?

And then Clyde saw them.

A house two doors down from the crossroads had windows broken on the ground floor. There was blood on the sill and the narrow deck and Clyde realised the poor bastard in the street must have escaped that way. Must have been where the gunfire had come from too. But now, out of the window, came two, then a third, then fourth creature. Tall, thin, gangly almost, with heads too long and hands too long, and hard muscles for all their wiry stature. Their skin was pale grey like an overcast day, their eyes a bright, almost burning green. They opened long, black maws emitting howls that made Clyde's bladder weak.

The first two looked left and right, then gunfire burst from all around. Some from the room right next door to Clyde, some from various other places around the town, people hiding in upstairs windows taking their shots. The first two creatures danced and bucked as bullets struck them, then the second two turned to the window and dragged out the body of a woman. They held her up high and wrenched on her limbs, pulling one leg and one arm free to gout crimson across the pale wooden wall of the house. The woman didn't make a sound.

"Fuck me," Clyde spat, and sighted along his Winchester and fired. The top of one of the creature's head burst in a mist of red, and Clyde worked the lever-action and aimed again. The first two had fallen and lay still, but the one Clyde had already shot still staggered left and right despite half its head missing. Feeling his gorge rise, he aimed but the creature jigged and jagged as another volley hit it from various sides. He quickly resighted on the last of the things that was loping for the shadows. Several other shots rang out, but all missed. Clyde drew a deep breath, then let it out and fired. His round took the creature dead centre between the shoulder blades and it pitched forward. It cracked into the upright at the corner of the house veranda and spun, staggered to the street, then kept going. Bent over, limping, but the damn thing kept moving. Clyde racked and fired again, even as more shots accompanied his. But he knew it was his bullet that took the creature's head almost clean off at the base of the neck.

This time it went down, the long, sinewy body twitching, then slowly falling still. A tense silence descended over the town.

"Nobody move." Sheriff Clark's voice was strong but subdued. Loud enough to carry without being a shout. "There'll be more."

The tension built, but not for long. Movement at the door of the house with the broken windows caught Clyde's attention, then the long, grey things were pouring out. More tumbled from both windows. Clyde racked shot after shot, then dropped the Winchester to the floor when it ran dry and pulled his Colt from its holster under his left arm. He emptied that three times, rarely missing a shot, but these ungodly fiends often took two or three or even more to go down. Even head shots didn't always stop them.

Despite the heavy crossfire, he saw two of the things duck and run right across the street, then the sound of breaking glass. Screams punched through the gunfire. More of the creatures, despite multiple gunshot wounds, ran to join their friends. Clyde hung dangerously far out of the window to get a look just in time to see three of the things come back out of a house on that side. They carried a young couple, thrashing and scream-ing in their long-fingered grip, then others joined them and the atrocious creatures simply ripped the man and woman to pieces. They pulled limbs free, dug pointed fingers into flesh and tore strips of meat away, punched in and pulled free with handfuls of looping intestines. Then they were finally felled by the gunfire from all sides.

Clyde realised, with a flash of shame, that he hadn't fired a single shot while he watched those two torn to pieces. Finally, stillness fell again. Clyde's breathing and heartrate began to settle back to something like normal and he returned to the room with the sheriff and his son.

"Come on," Clark said. "Work to do."

Clyde and Jesse exchanged a glance. Jesse's eyes were wide, his skin chalk pale. They had no words.

* * *

People moved fast, with practiced ease. They swiftly boarded up every window in both houses that had been attacked. Others loaded up the bodies of the dead, human and fiend alike, onto flat wagons, and hurried them to the outskirts of town where a blackened pit stared into the darkness like a dead eye. The bodies were thrown in and burned, an oily column of black smoke drifting up to the stars.

Clyde followed the sheriff back into the first house, the front door the only part not boarded up, and saw the floorboards in the main room all broken upwards, a dark hole underneath.

"You want us to nail some planks down over this and then the door?" asked a young, skinny, jittery fellow with raggedy blond hair. Another man, his opposite in every way—bald, fat, seemingly unperturbed—stood to one side, eyes hooded.

"Yep," the sheriff replied. "Seal it all up."

"Ain't gonna do much to hold 'em," the bald man said. "Or they'll just come up elsewhere anyhow."

"We're keeping a lid on things until help comes, that's all."

"They come from underground?" Clyde asked.

The sheriff nodded. "Ayup. Never know where they're going to come up next. Usually outside of town and they sneak in, but this isn't the first time they've dug in through a building."

"The saloon?"

"Yep."

"They live underground or tunnel in from somewhere?"

"No idea."

"What the hell are they?"

Sheriff Clark turned a hard eye to Clyde. "You think I have any kind of answer for that either? You saw them. What do you say they are?"

"Some kind of demon from Hell. Goddamn fiends."

"That's as good an explanation as any other. Pure fucking hate, that's what they are. They just kill. Violently. They don't even feed."

"How long they been coming?"

"A couple weeks now. If we're quiet at night they sometimes don't come. Any loud noises always seem to attract them. It's like they forget we're here, then discover us anew every time, especially if we make noise."

Clyde looked down into the yawning hole. "You've tried to find the source of them?"

"We keep sending out parties during the day, because we only ever see them at night. Maybe they don't like the sun. But we can't find anything."

Clyde pointed to the hole in the ground. "What about that way?"

Clark looked from the hole to Clyde and back again. "Go down there?"

"Sure. It must lead to something, right? That's a way to find out where they came from."

Sheriff Clark barked a humourless laugh. "Be my fucking guest, stranger." He turned and walked to the door, then addressed the skinny guy again. "If he wants to go down there, you board it up behind him, then this door."

As the sheriff went to step out the door, the bald man spoke again. "Ain't no one coming, Clark."

The sheriff turned back. "What's that you say?"

"You were a big hero in the war and you think you're some kind of big man now, but you ain't."

"Cecil," the sheriff said, "you'd better clip that tongue of yours quick smart."

"No. I won't. I see it your eyes. I was in the war too, I saw what happened. And I see it in you. You're fucking scared. The war broke you."

Clark took three long strides across the room, face like storm clouds, but Cecil puffed his chest, stood his ground. "Say what?" the sheriff demanded.

"You heard what I fucking said. The war broke you. You pretend, but you're scared. Too scared to face up. You keep saying we wait for someone to come while almost every night now we lose more people. Or in the daytime, people leave. And who can blame them? Ain't no-one coming. We're on our own. This stranger here got better ideas and more balls than you ever did."

Clyde watched the sheriff's hands trembling as he clenched them into fists, watched his eyes. Cecil had the measure of the man, he was indeed terrified.

"We could get a posse together," Jesse said.

Clyde looked over at his son, now in the doorway. "A posse?" he gave a lopsided grin.

"Well, the same thing, right? I heard what you said, about going down there and tracking them to their source. Enough of us, with enough guns, we could end this, couldn't we? Go in the daytime, catch 'em sleeping."

Clyde nodded. Sometimes people needed the precociousness of youth. "You have a point." He turned to Clark. "You may or may not want to join us, Sheriff, but I think it's a good idea. What about we guard this tunnel until sun-up, and in the meantime gather as many able-bodied and willing souls as we can. Cecil is right, no one's coming. We told you what happened to your Jack Torrens."

Sheriff Clark looked from Clyde to Cecil to Jesse framed in the doorway and back to Clyde. He had the manner of a rabbit caught between predators, nowhere to run. Clyde thought perhaps the only courage the man had left was shown in the fact that he hadn't yet slipped away from the town. Staying put took bravery, but he sat doing nothing hoping for help that would never arrive.

"You don't have to come, Sheriff. Someone needs to watch the town and protect those left behind. But we should—"

"Don't patronise me, son!" Sheriff Clark sniffed, drew himself up tall. "Perhaps you're right. Maybe it is time to take the fight to them. Let's gather us as many people and weapons as we can and get to it." He pointed at the hole in the floorboards. "We'll go that way at first light."

* *•*

The ragged band gathered in the old house at dawn didn't fill Clyde with glee. He'd hoped for a better force than the one fidgeting and shifting from foot to foot. To his credit, Sheriff Clark was there with a Winchester rifle and a Navy Colt six-shooter on each hip. A Chinese guy by the name of Lau Wing, a heavy, metal meat cleaver in each hand but no guns visible, looked about ready to kill the first thing that moved. The man was clearly determined.

Cecil was armed just like the sheriff, except his rifle was an old Whitworth, and his skinny friend, whose name apparently was Spook, though Clyde had no idea why and no inclination to ask, had a breech-loading side-by-side double-barrel shotgun and a bandolier of cartridges across his chest. Spook also had a large, wicked-looking knife jammed in the back of his belt. Jesse had his two Colt Army Revolvers, one on each hip, and Clyde had his Winchester repeater and Colt Army six-shooter. They carried all the ammo they had with them. Lastly, there was Sally, the madam from the brothel, wearing leather pants and jacket, also armed with a Winchester.

"Are you sure—" Clyde started and Sally pinned him with one pointing finger.

"Don't you dare suggest I ain't coming because I'm a woman. I'm a better shot than all o'y'all and I have my girls to protect."

"She is a damn fine shot," Spook said, nodding.

"Well, fair enough." Clyde turned to the sheriff. "You want to lead this party?"

"I guess that would be my job. Okay, let's go."

The sheriff stepped around the broken floorboards and slid his way down rough and broken earth into darkness. Lau Wing followed him, then Sally, then Cecil and Spook. Clyde gestured for his son to go next and Clyde himself brought up the rear. In single file, a couple of kerosene storm lanterns lighting the way, they moved slowly forward.

It was dry in the subterranean tunnel, and cool. The rock and earth had been hauled away haphazardly, grit and stones frequently raining down on them as they passed. A tense silence hung between them as they walked, often having to crouch almost double. Sometimes large rocks blocked the way and the fiends had dug around those, the tunnel meandering with the geology of the landscape.

"What are you two even doing here?" Cecil whispered over his shoulder to Clyde after the silence became too heavy to bear.

"Same as most," Clyde answered in a whisper. "Looking for our fortune."

"Gold?"

"Yeah, of course."

"The gold rush is over, friend. Even Wing up there gave up on his claim and came to stay in town. He did okay though, probably one of the wealthiest among us."

"That right?" Clyde's estimation of the man rose. Armed only with heavy cleavers and enough money to leave, still he was here to fight.

"Yep. But you're shit outta luck, stranger. No gold left in these hills."

Clyde shrugged. "Guess we'll take our chances once this whole mess is dealt with."

Cecil nodded but said no more.

A few minutes later the column shuddered to halt. Sheriff Clark raised his lantern, shining the light all around. "Big fucking cave," Spook said.

Water trickled over rock somewhere and the cool air had a new chill to it. As they emerged into the cave, they spread out to look around. Stalactites speared down and several other holes led away from the wide, irregular space.

"These their other tunnels?" Sally asked.

"Looks like," Cecil said.

"Zài qiǎn dòng lǐ, yǎn shǔ huì yúnòng long," Lau Wing said.

"What's that now?" Sheriff Clark said, frowning at the smaller man.

"Chinese proverb," Wing said. "In shallow holes, moles make fools of dragons."

"What the fuck is that supposed to mean?" Spook asked, a nervous tremor to his voice.

Clyde thought he understood Wing's point, but they didn't get to discuss it further because all hell broke loose.

It started with Cecil's scream. The big man had been standing off to one side of the group and he flew sideways like a sudden wind had blown him away. His Winchester flashed and barked in the darkness, then a sound like water splattering over rock, and Cecil's scream cut off. Sheriff Clark ran sideways, raising his lantern to illuminate a hollow to one side of the cave. It was infested with fiends, their rough grey skin reflecting the lamplight as they squirmed and swarmed over each other like mealworms in a barrel of oats. Some had emerged from the mass and pulled Cecil into several pieces. His eyes were white, staring from a head torn raggedly from the neck. His entrails spilled over a rock and all four limbs were simply gone.

The remaining party began firing, the reports deafening in the echoing cavern. Muzzle flashes went off like lightning, Spook's shotgun boomed like thunder. Grey meat and limbs flew. Wing stayed to one side of the barrage of gunfire but kept the fiends from flanking the party on the open side by hacking them down, his arms swirling in mesmerising patterns, loops and figure-eights, chopping the fiends down left and right. He hopped from rock to rock, always outmanoeuvring the creatures.

Clyde moved as if in a dream, racking and firing the Winchester, always aiming for head shots, reloading, firing again. Jesse was beside him, grim-faced but determined. He was becoming a man Clyde could truly be proud of.

The fiends themselves were silent, but relentless. Long limbs ending in long, pointed fingers reached for the posse. Their elongated heads swung side to side, large green eyes searching, but wincing away from the light of the storm lanterns. Their wide mouths were filled not with teeth, but a thick ridge of bone top and bottom. The only sound they made was the clack of those bony ridges as they snapped their jaws in fury.

Clyde thought the theory about them not liking the daylight was correct. They should have brought more light.

Clyde backpedalled, scrabbling for more ammo, then realised a kind of calm had settled.

"Did we get 'em all?" Spook asked.

Sheriff Clark and Sally each lifted a lantern and turned the wick up as bright as it would go. The cavern swelled with brightness. Body parts littered the ground, blood gleamed black against the stone.

"Shit, Wing!"

Clyde turned to see Spook run over to Wing, who grinned crookedly. Blood soaked his shirt.

"I'm okay. Superficial." He lifted the shirt aside to show two gouges across his chest. "Their fingers like stone," he said. "Not natural."

"Here, hold this." Sally shoved her lantern at Jesse and began patching up Wing's wounds.

"Is that it?" Spook asked. "We got 'em all?"

"Shoulda done this weeks ago, Sheriff," Clyde said.

"It ain't over," Jesse said quietly. He lifted the lantern higher and it lit up the far wall of the cave. Except it wasn't a wall, but a large opening leading somewhere. Heavy breathing noises and scuffling echoed from it.

"They don't like the light," Clyde said. "Keep the lanterns turned up and keep them at the front." He crouched and picked up the arm of one of the fiends—long, hard, and rough to the touch. He tore up some of Cecil's bloodstained shirt and wrapped it around the bloody stump, then gestured for the lamp oil from Sally.

"I get it," she said and pulled the bottle from her bag, drizzled it over the material.

Clyde lit it from the lantern wick and had himself a sputtering torch coughing black smoke. But the flame was bright.

"That's fine thinking, Dad." Jesse did the same and armed with two storm lanterns and two fiend torches, they set off into the bigger tunnel.

It wasn't long before they found themselves at a kind of T-junction. To their left, the sounds they'd heard before. To their right, a tumble of rocks that looked strangely unnatural. Clyde paused, moved nearer for a better look.

"This isn't a natural cave tunnel," he said.

Sheriff Clark came to see. "What do you mean?"

"This didn't form naturally. Looks like someone blew through here somehow."

"Blew through?"

Spook looked beyond the fallen rock wall. "So that's where Darcy Bellow had his claim."

"What?" the sheriff asked.

Spook pointed. "Look out there. I see his bags and stuff in the cave beyond. And that wooden crate in the corner? Remember how he got hisself some TNT? There it is."

"Darcy Bellow?" Clyde asked.

"Prospector," Sheriff Clark said. "Left town a few weeks ago, we thought."

"I can see a hint of daylight that way," Spook said.

"I'll check." Before anyone could stop him, Jesse clambered over the fallen rocks and disappeared. A few moments later he came back. "Yep, that cave leads to a tunnel that has clearly been blown open with explosives same as this one. And that leads to the surface about a hundred yards yonder."

"I don't think your friend Darcy left town," Clyde said. "I think he woke something up."

As if in answer, the noises from behind them increased. The group turned to face whatever lay that way. It was wide enough that the six of them could advance in a single line abreast. Whatever it was seemed to be breathing heavily, like it was exerting itself. The chill of the caves, Clyde noticed, had given way to a kind of humid warmth.

"You have got to be fucking kidding me," Sheriff Clark said as they emerged into another wide chamber.

Before them was a deep, bowl-like hollow in the floor. At its centre sat a huge, fat, glistening version of the fiends they'd seen before. This one had to be twenty feet tall, rolls of bulging grey meat hanging off its bones, heavy teats all down its front leaking ichor. And it was busy. It leaned back against the curved edge of the rocky bowl, its legs bent at the knee and fanned out to either side. Between its legs, wet folds of grey flesh flexed and pulsed and a squirming fiend slowly extruded to slap onto the slick ground. The huge, gasping motherfiend let out a rasping howl, lifting one arm to shield its huge green eyes from the light. Several slimy-looking fiends, fresh-born, were curled around the motherfiend's hips.

"End that ungodly fucking thing!" Sheriff Clark yelled, and the group did not hesitate for a moment.

Freshly reloaded, they began firing everything they had, pumping round after round into the heavy, gravid creature. The newly-born fiends raced forward, bony tooth ridges clacking, and were gunned down too. The motherfiend howled as black blood burst and spattered from every gunshot wound, its own thick ridge of bone clacking as it leaned forward to snap at them.

Bigger than they realised even, it swept one long heavy arm around and its hand, the size of a wagon wheel, hit Sheriff Clark and snatched the man up. He screamed, high and shrill, firing repeatedly at the thing as he was carried to its maw. One of his shots managed to burst one of the motherfiend's bulbous eyes, then the sheriff was chomped in half at the waist. The top half of him vanished down the motherfiend's gullet, while his legs fell to the floor as the fiend slapped her hand over her ruined eye and screamed. Clyde's ears strained fit to burst with the noise.

Her other hand swept blindly back and forth and Lau Wing danced in, both cleavers whistling through the air. One found its target and a long, hard, grey finger spun away from the hand and the motherfiend howled again. But for all the wounds, she didn't seem to be slowing.

Clyde blew away the fiend she had just birthed and then yelled, "Back up! Get to Darcy's claim and the light!"

The motherfiend tipped herself forward onto her knees and began to rise, but restricted by the size of the birthing chamber her movements were slow.

The group turned and ran, tripping and stumbling back the way they'd come. The motherfiend scrambled after, grunting and coughing pained, furious shouts after them. In a shower of stones and dirt, Clyde ducked sideways as something swept past him and realised she'd caught up faster than he thought possible. Her arm, having missed him, hooked back and collected Spook on the way. He pumped two shotgun shells into her, the grey flesh of her shoulder bursting with black sprays of blood, then he went the way of the sheriff.

They ran in a blind panic, heading only for the soft glow of daylight somewhere ahead. The makeshift torch Clyde carried sputtered and went out, so he dropped the fiend's limb, glad to be rid of the feel of it. He turned as he ran, fired two more shots aiming for the motherfiend's good eye as she scrambled on hands and feet after them. His first missed entirely, his second gouged a black furrow across her ridged brow and she bellowed. It was, he realised, his last bullet. The party burst through into another cave and glorious daylight came from above.

Clyde's elation swiftly drained away. "This is a dead end."

The cavern was quite large and a crack high above them admitted bright daylight in a wide shaft that pooled close to the rear wall, but the rest of the cave was dark and there were no exits bar the one they'd entered by. The one now filled with the bulk of the motherfiend as she snatched at them and grunted her fury.

"This isn't what I saw!" Jesse said. "We must have got turned around, come a different way."

"Now what?" Wing asked.

The motherfiend drove herself hard against the entrance to the cavern they were trapped in and rocks tumbled down around her, then she was inside.

The four of them pressed themselves back hard against the far wall as the motherfiend advanced, but she came up short, hissing and snarling at them from the other side of the shaft of sunlight. She tentatively reached forward, but the moment her hand came into the light she hissed and snatched it back. Slowly, she moved sideways, trying to circle the light to get to them.

The party of four circled with her. She moved the other way, and so did they.

"I'm out of ammo," Clyde said. "You all got anything left?"

"I'm out too," Jesse said.

"I've been out since we first found her," Sally said.

Wing looked at the cleavers in his hands. "Well, fuck," he said softly. He drew a deep breath and went to step forward, but Jesse put a hand out to stop him.

"No, you can't beat her with knives."

Wing arched an eyebrow. "Really, you think so? You'd be surprised who and what I've beaten with knives. How long you think we can keep this up?" He indicated the shaft of sunlight and their slow movements left and right. "Besides, the sun will move in the sky and this column of light won't protect us for long."

"Just keep her occupied," Jesse said. "I only need a minute." He looked up to the small hole in the roof and then down at Clyde. "I reckon I can fit through there, don't you?"

"And do what?" Clyde asked. "I mean, even if you can climb up there and get out, then what?"

Jesse grinned and held up a stick of TNT, a short fuse sticking up like the wick of a candle.

Clyde smiled. "Damn, son. Good thinking. Reckon you can make it?"

"I'll give it a wild try."

"Be careful!" Sally said.

"I will. And I'll get us out. I saw a lady in your place who rather took my fancy."

"Get us out of this and the discount will be generous," Sally said.

The motherfiend hissed and shifted quickly to one side. The four of them danced swiftly around the wide column of light and Jesse took his chance. He bolted for the back wall and leaped up, grabbed a handhold and began to climb.

The motherfiend spotted the movement and made a grab for him, but Wing sprinted to intercept, his double cleavers flashing in the sunlight as he chopped left and right, carving great gouges in her arm and wrist. She bellowed and staggered back, thick oily blood pulsing from her wounds, striking out with her other hand in defence. That hand passed through the sun and her skin blackened and crackled, smoke pouring off it and she staggered further back, but not before her wild blow had struck Wing across the hip. The small man sailed sideways, crashed into the rock wall and fell limp to the ground. Blood ran from a nasty wound above his eye and he didn't move.

Sally ran to him, dragged him back to them and tried to stem the blood from his head wound with a strip of cloth torn from her shirt.

"He's out," Clyde said, pointing up to where his son, like some gangly rock spider, had reached the top of the cave wall and managed to squeeze himself out of the gap.

"Brace yourselves for rocks falling!" Jesse said, then there was a moment of silence before the TNT blew.

Clyde and Sally threw themselves over Wing's unconscious form, all three of them jammed in under the edge of the wall, as rocks and dirt and gravel hammered down from above, striking like punches into their backs and shoulders. And then sunlight filled the cavern like a flood.

The motherfiend screamed as the sunlight drenched her. Her grey skin blackened and blistered and cracked apart like dry earth in a drought. Her flesh ignited, the flames green and black, and she thrashed and wailed and cooked and finally fell still.

Wing blinked slowly awake as Sally and Clyde stood and brushed rock and dirt off themselves. Where the motherfiend had been, only blackened bones remained.

"Okay down there?" Jesse called from the now wide-open space above.

"I think so," Clyde said.

"You think we got them all?" Sally asked. "The ones she birthed, I mean?"

"We certainly killed all the ones we've seen," Clyde said. "If there are any others lurking around, I guess they can be picked off now. At least she won't be making any more."

Wing, a hand pressed to his head, said, "Let's get back and patched up, then maybe we can scour these tunnels, make sure they're all gone."

Clyde nodded. "As good a plan as any. Let's get the hell out of here."

• ••

"You going to stay?" Sally asked the next morning over a generous breakfast. Almost as generous as the discounts she had promised and come good on after they'd returned and swept back through all the tunnels, fully-armed, and found them empty. Although Clyde couldn't help wondering if maybe there weren't more mothers out there somewhere, underground, waiting.

Clyde, Jesse and Wing sat around the table with her, cleaned and patched up and altogether satisfied.

"I don't know," Clyde said. "What do you think, Jesse?"

"I could get used to this place."

"We do need a new sheriff," Wing said. "You know, if you thought you might need a job. I don't think they'd accept me for it."

Clyde smiled. "I'll think about it."

WHERE THUNDER DWELLS

Edward M Erdelac

Believe I'm ready to settle up," said Lieutenant Coleson, reaching for his wallet. "Storm's comin' in over the Huachucas and I wanna get back to the post."

Haayashi nodded, her thoughts drifting to her husband, Ves. She hoped he'd seen the thunderheads too and was planning to get back accordingly.

"Think she'll like it?"

She smiled at the young officer. "Oh I expect she will, Lieutenant. Be a nice surprise."

Haayashi finished tying up the parcel of gingham just as the lieutenant's forehead blew open and splattered her shop apron and the counter with dark red brains that quivered like a litter of newborn things shuddering at the cold.

She backed against the shelf, rattling the hard rock-candy jars as the cavalryman, still smiling, slumped to his knees, bashed his chin on the countertop, and tumbled out of sight.

The gingham had been for a new dress for the lieutenant's wife. He would never see her in it now.

A scruffy N'daa man with a head of curly orange hair stood in the doorway, lowering a big pistol and grinning like a delinquent with a slingshot who'd just busted an upstairs window.

Haayashi rushed around the counter and made a grab at Coleson's sidearm, but the N'daa headed her off and kicked her in the side so hard she tipped over the medicinal bottles stored there, smashing them to pieces.

She curled on the floor, gasping.

The orange-haired man took Coleson's pistol, tucking it into the front of his pants.

Nach'aa, her old father, incongruous in his white man's suit and spectacles with his long, slate grey hair spilling wild from beneath his broad red Apache headband, crept out of the backroom with his Whitney rifle. He would have killed the orange-haired N'daa if a Mexican hadn't stepped inside and shot her father's leg out from under him, spoiling his aim. As it was, the N'daa cried out and fell over Coleson's body, clapping a hand to his side.

"Jesus Christ, Swifty," a third man said in disgust, pushing past the Mexican. This one had long, greasy yellow hair and a rattlesnake skin hat band. *Snaker Pista.* He had been in her father's store a few times, buying bullets and tobacco and trying to bully him into purchasing his rotgut moonshine whiskey. Every time Snaker had come in it had been like letting a wild coyote wander around the store. Nach'aa would lean his Whitney against the backroom door frame at his approach. Only when Snaker left did her father put it back on the wall.

"We need the old man alive," Snaker said, glaring at Swifty rolling on the floor.

"Pelado shot him," Swifty groaned. "The old bastard nearly put me under. God, I got a hole in me!"

"That is the aim of a bullet," Snaker said matter-of-factly. "You sling 'em around so damn regular don't be surprised when somebody pitches one your way." He looked to the Mexican called Pelado as if for an explanation.

"It was just the leg, Snaker." Pelado shrugged. "He'll live."

Snaker tipped his hat to Haayashi and stepped over Coleman's corpse. "Hello, Haayashi. Good to see you again. Where's your husband?"

"Out hunting you," Haayashi growled.

"You underestimate your man. If Ves Payne was after me, why, he'd be right there," Snaker said, throwing his thumb over his shoulder. He grabbed a fistful of her long black hair and yanked her head up to look him in the eye. "Where is he?"

"Out at the Lazy S, looking for rustlers," Haayashi hissed. "I just figured it was you."

"Ain't no two-bit cow thief, girl. Bigger and better things." He spat on the floor and dragged her behind him to stand over her father. "Dagotee, y'old bandit. How's tricks?" He let her go, reached down, and smacked the old man's face.

Nach'aa made no sound. The back of a hand was like a mother's kiss to a Mimbreño Apache who had ridden with Victorio.

Haayashi got up on one elbow and strained to watch as Snaker pulled her father up by the shirt front.

"Is it bad?" Swifty whined to Pelado. "Am I dyin'?"

"We're all dyin,' chavo," said Pelado, disinterested. He had picked a can of peaches off the shelf and chopped the top off with the machete he kept tucked in his sash. "Hey," he laughed, as he put the can to his lips, "maybe you ain't so swift, ah?"

"You bastard!" Swifty half hissed, half sobbed through his teeth as he got to his knees and clenched his eyes at the pain. There was a dribbling hole in his side, just above his belt. "Oh Lord, Lord… am I done for?"

"Haayashi'll plug your hole, Swifty, just don't get tiresome," Snaker said, not even sparing him a look. "First, girl, you get on over here and fix up your daddy's leg. He's got a long ride ahead of him."

Haayashi rose and limped over to the boxes of linen bandages, testing the stitch in her side with her breath. Pelado's eyes followed her over the tipped can of peaches.

Snaker stood back as she knelt and bound up her father's leg. It was bad. The bone was shattered just below the knee, the dirty bullet still lodged in there somewhere. The lead might get black in his veins and find his heart if they waited too long to treat it or saw it off. She looked into her father's dark eyes.

He read her prognosis, unblinking,

"I know you won't talk at me or Pelado, old man," Snaker said, "even though I know you understand. That's part of the reason Haayashi's gonna be goin' with us." He idly took out his own pistol, spun it on his finger so it came up cocked, and pressed the muzzle to the top of her head.

She stiffened at its touch, locked eyes with her father. His black irises flared like a pair of gun bores. Haayashi shook her head. If her father made a move, they'd both die.

"This is the other reason," Snaker said. "You sabe?"

Nach'aa looked up at Snaker and bobbed his chin once.

Haayashi turned her gaze to the outlaw. "Where are we going?"

"I know you ain't as tame as you let on," Snaker said to her father. "Just 'cause you scouted for the yellowlegs and married you a Dutch widow and took to runnin' this store. I know you funneled them Bronco Apaches up through the Huachucas and down into Old Mexico on the sly. You're gonna show us the way, old man. You're gonna do it, or you're gonna bear witness to the slow death of your daughter. Comprende?"

Nach'aa answered in Apache, even, and without a hint of distress or pain, as if explaining the passage of the seasons to a child. "I will take you, white-eye. I will take you where I took the Broncos – to The Place Where The Thunder Dwells. If you harm my daughter, I will take you there all the sooner."

Haayashi frowned. Of course she knew her father had helped the renegade Apache, the Broncos who would not surrender to Crook and board the train to Florida. He'd done it for years. Sometimes it was with bullets and feed and bandages from her mother's store. Other times they had come under the cover of night, half-starved with their bandoliers empty and the hooves of their tired horses wrapped in buckskin, and the white law thirsty for their blood. Some would come asking for the secret way to sanctuary, the hidden stronghold, The Place Where The Thunder Dwells.

After a few low words, Nach'aa would set out with them in the dark to show them the way. Always by morning he would return alone. Massai and The Apache Kid, who were still being blamed for every act of murder and thievery from here to Flagstaff, had been taken to The Place by Nach'aa. He had never spoken to her about it, nor to her late mother, nor to any other man so far as she knew.

"He said he will take you," Haayashi said.

Snaker laughed. "He said a lot more than that, but OK. Pelado, go outside and tell Emory to switch out the horses. Grab all the cartridges and victuals you can carry." He went over to a stack of turpentine cans and twisted the top off one, wrinkling his nose. He finally looked at Swifty with disgust. "Get your ass moving, Swifty, or you'll burn with this place." He upended the can, sprinkling the counter as if he were generously watering a bed of flowers.

"Who gets the lieutenant's pony, Snaker?" Pelado asked.

Snaker paused and regarded the corpse. Then he smiled. "Why, the lieutenant."

• •°

The adobe store burned, spilling an ink black cloud across the sky that could be seen for miles. Flame bloomed in its broken casements like a cooking fire poking out of the pot belly of a squat Pueblo horno.

Vester Payne wheeled his pinto about, staring fixedly at the ground, ignoring the sight. Every inch of his heart hammered and sent the blood thumping in his ears like war drums. Every sign and spoor was a goad urging him to kick his horse in the ribs and shed blood before Snaker Pista and his gang laid hands on his wife, his Haayashi; his sweet, black haired danohshoni.

He was conscious of the eyes of the other men alternating between the fire and the back of his neck. He wasn't sure which was burning hotter. Vester had spied the smoke of his father-in-law's burning store and abandoned his frustrating investigation of the Lazy S's disappearing cattle. He'd ridden like hell, running smack into Marshal Ray Barraclough and his posse, chasing down the Snaker Pista gang. Snaker's bunch had just robbed the Drucker and Dobbs company office in Delirium Tremens and gunned down the marshal's younger brother, Andy, in the doing.

The posse had welcomed him in the way white men ever

welcomed the assistance of a Negro; ranging from begrudging acceptance to naked distaste.

Barraclough was a shady fellow, happily wringing the failing mine and the town's slowly departing industries dry with the help of his bean-counting brother, but shooting said brother had put the wrath of God in the marshal. Ray Barraclough wanted his money, and he wanted blood for his kin.

He had his deputies with him. Luke Holt and Charlie Lowell were a vicious pair, quick to kill and slow to question. Barraclough had been Lowell's captain in the war, and although Holt was too young to have fought, he had been orphaned by it, and idolized the two old Rebels as surrogate fathers, eating up their war stories. The threadbare, butternut sack coat Lowell wore, replete with his faded sergeant's chevrons, and their undying nostalgia for The Cause slipped across the border of mawkishness into homicidal irrationality.

For Lowell, the war had not ended, it had simply entered a passive phase. They spat at the Negro soldiers who passed the marshal's office, and made the piano player at the Gone Green Saloon play Dixie while they put their backs to the wall and silently dared anybody to object. They were despicable snakes, and although Vester had been born free the year after Emancipation, his Federal-issue belt buckle from his days as an Army scout incited them about as much as his black skin.

Barraclough's pet bounty killer, the Englishman, Alwyn Frees, was along for the ride on his postage stamp saddle. The man sold prisoners from Barraclough's dungeon for the price on their heads in neighboring counties, splitting the take with the marshal. Jose Chapol was there too. He had once spilled a man's guts in the sawdust of the Todos Mis Amigos cantina and never even had his knife taken away because he rode for the Barracloughs.

"Well, boy?" Barraclough called. "Where'd they go?"

Vester ignored the jibe. He had more pressing worries.

"East," said Frees. "It's as plain as the day."

"I don't believe so," said Vester. "They switched out the

horses with the remounts the old man keeps in the corral out back for the stage line. They ran their spent ponies off east, hoping we'd split up and chase after 'em. You can tell by the depth of the depressions they ain't but one rider. They's two blood trails. The one headed east, probably just a body tied to the saddle."

Frees raised his eyebrows and tipped his bowler to Vester.

"You figure that'd be the old Injun or your squaw?" Barraclough prompted.

"They took my wife and old Nach'aa both," Vester said. "Dead man might mean one less of the gang, but I reckon it's some customer got caught unawares. Maybe a soldier from Huachuca. Horse's shoes are Army issue. The other trail... somebody wounded, sure, but alive."

"The woman I understand," said Holt, "but why take the old man?"

"He's 'Pache. No torture could make him take them where they going, and he took an oath not to talk to whites or Mexicans in they own tongue. It's part of his Power oath. They figure threatenin' his daughter'll make him comply."

"Excuse me, power oath?" Frees asked.

"'Paches sometimes take an oath or follow a vision, grants 'em a special power," said Vester. "Like Samson, you know?"

"Who?" Holt said.

"From the Scripture, ya goddamned heathen," said Lowell, swatting his leg.

"What's the old man's power?" the Englishman asked.

"Ain't a thing no 'Pache will tell you readily," Vester said. "Knew a woman who could see the future if she didn't harm no snakes." He looked anxiously off towards the Huachuca Mountains, where thunderclouds were brewing way up over the ridges. "I reckon he's leading 'em to them mountains."

"I've never heard of a way through the Huachucas," Frees said.

"Old Mexico's on the other side," Barraclough said. "Do you know a way, boy?"

"No," Vester admitted, "but I believe Nach'aa might, and I can follow him. We best hurry. If them clouds spill, gonna be hell trackin' 'em, never mind gettin' up them mountains in the rain. They only a hour or so ahead."

"Well, then, let's ride," Barraclough said, and whupped the rump of his chestnut.

Vester spurred up alongside him. "I'm along for my kin, Marshal. Can't be no shooting till I get 'em clear. And I can do it, but you got to give me the chance. I got your word?"

"Sure, sure," said Barraclough, not even looking at him. "We'll spare your kin. My word."

Vester bit his lip as they rode on towards the foothills. He didn't put much value on Barraclough's word.

    *   *   *

Swift Tom whimpered and leaned way over the neck of his horse. "I can't go no further," he announced from the back of the train. "I won't. God, it hurts so damn much!"

They were high up past the foothills, and there was a spot on the horizon from the direction of the burning store growing steadily larger, kicking up dust on the desert plain below.

Haayashi held her breath and risked a look at her father, tied to another horse. She had bound up the orange-haired N'daa's wound in such a way that he continued to drip blood on the stones. There was no doubt in her mind Ves had come at first sight of the fire, and that he was tracking them now.

Snaker sighed and nodded to Pelado, who dismounted and half-slid down the steep trail, sending shale cascading till he got to Swift Tom. Pelado pulled his machete and neatly flicked it under the horse's chin, gripping its bridle so it wouldn't rear.

It fell to its forelegs, spurting torrents of blood from its cut jugular, and gradually crashed on its side.

"What the shit!" Swift Tom croaked, barely avoiding getting crushed under the dying animal.

"You got the Injun's repeater and now you got yourself a breastworks," said Snaker, rolling a cigarette. "Sell it high, Swifty. Get as many as you can when they get in sight. Make a point of getting that sumbitch Barraclough if you can."

"Y'all are just gonna leave me?" Swift Tom whined.

"You said you can't ride," said Snaker. "So stay and shoot. You can join us up the mountain if you live. Don't waste no bullets on us or we'll kill you right here." He kicked his horse up the draw while behind him, Emory, the big-bellied Scot, laughed through his prodigious whiskers and followed.

Pelado got back on his horse and motioned for Nach'aa and Haayashi to get a move on.

"Pelado," Swift Tom groaned, reaching out, beseeching. "I can ride."

"Lo siento, chavo," Pelado said, opening his hands and pouting in mock sympathy. "We're shy of horses now. Vaya con Dios."

As Swift Tom's curses dwindled, Haayashi watched her father jam his thumbnail between the bandages on his leg. The blood flecked the stones, unnoticed, as they rode.

• ••

Swift Tom listened to the grunts of the horses and the slide of stone on stone till he could hear it no more and cursed to himself. Lying against the cooling carcass of the horse, the blood from its cut throat ran down the hillside in a twisting red creek.

Small, scared sounds tumbled from Tom's trembling lips as he clumsily stuffed cartridges into the Whitney rifle and filled his belt loops from the box in his saddlebags. His hands were pale and shook from blood loss. Would he die before they got here?

He pulled a pair of his whitest-looking drawers from his bags and tied it about the muzzle of the rifle, ready to wave it when they got in sight. Swift Tom knew he couldn't get more than one of the pursuing posse – at best – before they overwhelmed him, breastworks or no. He was no great shot at a distance.

Damn Snaker. Swift Tom would lead the posse to the gang. Barraclough didn't know it was Tom who'd killed the marshal's brother. Andy Barraclough had reached for something in a desk drawer… A key, it turned out, but how could Tom have known?

A shadow passed overhead and he flinched instinctively, glimpsed some sort of big bird. Probably a turkey vulture or something attracted by the dead horse. It wheeled down and landed with a fuss and scrabble somewhere below and behind a bend in the rocks.

Yeah, Tom would tell Barraclough it had been Snaker who had killed Andy, and would take no small pleasure in that son of a bitch getting drilled to death by the lawman. Barraclough was a hard man. Hell, maybe the marshal wouldn't even stop shooting for a white flag. Still, Tom had an ace up his sleeve; that box he'd taken from the mining office. The two jars inside could make things interesting real quick.

Another shadow swept across him and remained. Something perched on a ledge a few feet above his head. It shifted with jerky movements. He squinted up at it. The thing was about the size of a dog, all sharp angles with an unsettling lack of feathers.

He shooed it.

It hopped back a bit, but stayed between him and the sun.

There was an insistent squawking below him, and he turned to see something strange poking its head out from behind the rocks. Some kind of featherless bird, long nosed with a strange, tapering head. It poked and dipped the end of its beak in the horse's blood, then hopped out like an oversized sparrow. Sparse brown feathers littered its body, but its wings appeared to be bare and leathery like a bat's.

Lapping hungrily at the running blood, it bounced lightly up the stones, stopping to taste. It spread its wings to regain its balance, cocking its head to observe him like a skittish pigeon. Goddamn ugly little thing, quite unlike anything Swift Tom had ever seen. It had beady black eyes set back on either side of its long head, and feet bigger than a turkey's; its talons looked sharp as a hawk's.

As it neared, he decided he didn't want the thing close to him. He pointed the rifle and fired when it got within six feet, blowing its body open and sending it whipping off down the mountainside in a cloud of blood and dust.

He breathed in relief.

Then the shadow above his head shifted. Swift Tom whirled in time to see the second one's sharp beak diving towards him out of the sun an instant before it plunged deep in his left eye; so deep it felt as though the sun itself were burning a hole in him. He uttered a dwindling shriek as wheeling shadows converged on him, then the end of the beak punched entirely out the back of his skull.

* * *

"Gunshot," said Frees.

"Somebody had a disagreement," Vester agreed.

"Might could've been thunder," said Holt. "Look at them clouds."

Big black thunderheads were tumbling over the mountains now, smudging and flashing inside as if they had torn themselves open on the peaks and were bleeding rain.

"Thunder sounds like thunder," said Barraclough. "Nothing else sounds like a gun."

They made the base of the foothills and urged the protesting horses up the sloping draw. They did hear thunder now, rolling far above them.

"How we know they ain't gonna shoot us comin' up?" Holt said nervously.

"They ain't waiting if they can help it," said Vester. "Leastways, nobody gon' volunteer to hang back. All that money they got gon' keep 'em on the move."

The blood trail was thicker the higher they climbed above the plain. But then a deep, cooling shadow fell across them and with it came a furious downpour the likes of which was rarely seen in Arizona.

* * *

Snaker and the others cursed the shuddering rain that bent their horses' necks, and made them slip and stumble on the uneven path. It finally narrowed to nothing more than a gap in the high, sheer stone – a dark entrance to a slot canyon in the face of the escarpment that could only be traversed single file. On foot.

Haayashi and Nach'aa shared a look. The water was steadily washing the blood trail away. "Fix your bandage," she urged in Apache.

Her father looked pale and weak as he fumbled with it half-heartedly. "Tell them this is the way. Tell them to leave the horses."

"What'd he say?" Snaker demanded.

"He said we have to go on foot from here," she answered.

Emory snorted and wheeled on Snaker. "You didn't say anything about having to walk into Mexico."

"This the only way?" Snaker eyed the narrow passage uncertainly as he dismounted. "Don't these things tend to flood in a storm?"

Nach'aa nodded, eyeing the high stone surrounding them on three sides.

"This is the way the Broncos went," Haayashi confirmed.

Snaker cursed.

"We ain't going to be able to carry it all," Pelado said, unhooking money sacks from his saddle.

"They'll carry what we can't," Snaker said, gesturing to Haayashi and her father. "You understand?"

"Look at him," said Emory. "That old man can barely carry himself."

"Leave the extra cartridges on the ponies," said Snaker. "Just load up your guns and your belts and your pockets. Water and money. Nothing else."

They scrambled to acquiesce, rain drenching them to the bone. Then one by one they slipped between the press of the stone, Nach'aa leading the way.

• •⁕

The rain came down hard and rattling, warm as bathwater. The pinions and the scrubs took to dancing in place. Vester cursed as the big drops splashed steaming on the sunbaked stones and washed the blood away.

Frees gave a shout that stopped their ascent. They gathered near, bending under the rain to observe a strange carcass lying in the rocks.

"What in the fuck is that?" Holt exclaimed.

Vester toed it with his boot. It was some kind of bird. Big as a hound dog with featherless, bat wings the color of the desert and a thin, tapered head like a pair of scissors. "Dunno," he said, his short hairs standing up. "Never seen nothing like it."

"Is it a condor, maybe? It's got a bullet in it," Frees observed. "Somebody shot it but didn't collect it."

"Will they stop for the rain?" Barraclough asked.

"I don't know about Snaker Pista," said Vester, "but Naa'cha won't, no."

"Then why are we stoppin' for a goddamn bird?" Barraclough said, and kicked his complaining horse up the draw.

Rain pelted the ground now, coloring the stones. The posse hadn't got more than thirty feet before Barraclough drew his rifle, cocked it, and aimed at the ground behind a boulder.

"Dead man here," he announced after a bit.

Vester swung down from his saddle and turned the body over. It was a mess. Torn to bits, eviscerated, the eyes and tongue gone, the body perforated in dozens of places as if by spears, as was his horse, whose guts were strung out among the dark wet rocks.

"Anybody recognize him?" Barraclough asked.

"By that hair," said Frees, "I surmise it to be one Swift Tom Posner. Two hundred dollars for armed robbery."

"What the hell did that to him?" Holt said.

"Shit, gotta be Broncos," said Lowell, drawing his gun a little nervously, glancing about the rain-washed rocks, expecting Indians to come charging at him.

"I bet that old 'Pache's got friends hidin' up here," said Holt. "I bet he led Snaker into a trap."

Frees frowned. "I've known Indians to worry a body, put a man's eyes out to blind him in the sweet hereafter," he said cautiously. "But I've never known them to leave behind guns and cartridges, or to do that to a perfectly good horse."

"We in agreement," said Vester. "Its throat's been cut. And that there is Nach'aa's Whitney rifle."

"Why the drawers tied to the barrel?" Barraclough said. "Was he surrendering?"

"Might could've been his intent," Vester allowed. "And this," he said, pulling out the double-action revolver tucked into the dead man's pants. "New Army .38. Cavalry issue. No holster. 'Reckon it *was* a soldier they kilt at the store."

"So what happened?"

Vester looked around. The rain had rendered any talkative signs on the ground dumb. The perforated carcass of the horse, the dead man... they looked like they'd been set upon by scavengers. There were slash marks. Claws. Maybe the posse's approach had scared off some kind of varmints. Holt's guess about Broncos holing up in these mountains wasn't without merit. Maybe old Nach'aa ferried them up here to some hidden stronghold, brought them provisions from the store. But something didn't make sense. Apache didn't kill like this.

"What about the bird?" Chapon said, startling all of them, for the Mexican hadn't said a word the whole ride.

They stared at him.

"The bird he shot."

"They'd have to be a whole passel of 'em to do this," Vester said.

"Quit jawin'," Barraclough said, "and let's get these bastards."

"We should check his saddlebags for loot," Frees said. "Shouldn't we?"

Barraclough said nothing, but it was plain to Vester that recovering the stolen money was far from the marshal's mind. That made Vester all the more nervous about catching up with Snaker.

Vester had to get in front of Barraclough. He didn't want any harm coming to Haayashi.

"Hey, yeah," Holt said, unbuckling the bags still tied to the dead horse's saddle. After a bit of rummaging, he looked disappointed. "Nothing but possibles, clothes, and this here box of moonshine." Holt held up a small wooden crate full of packing straw and two clear jars of liquid.

"Jesus Christ!" Lowell hissed. "Put that down easy, you goddamn fool! That ain't moonshine, it's nitroglycerin! We're lucky the whole damn side of the mountain didn't come down on us when that horse fell."

Holt went whiter than white, closed the lid, and slid the box back into the saddlebags like it was a sleeping baby.

"He must've took it from the mining office, Captain," Lowell said. "Dumb asshole. If he hadn't been kilt, he'd have blown himself to Abraham in another minute ridin' up this mountain."

"Leave it be and let's ride," said Barraclough.

Vester put the double-action through his belt, took up his father-in-law's rifle, and got back on his horse.

* * *

Haayashi and her father emerged blinking from the dim stone passage to find themselves at one end of a long, white canyon that twisted off around the rocks ahead. After slipping through the narrow way between the stone with the darkening sky a faint twisting line high above, and rainwater at times up to their chests, it was like being born. Several times they'd had to pause while fat Emory sucked in air and squeezed himself through, all in a panic that he would be trapped and unable even to go back. Pelado cursed and kicked Emory from behind, but they had lost much time with the Scot's nervous scrabbling.

"To hell with that!" Emory gasped, red in the face when he came through at last. He dropped his sacks of gold dust, panting. "And never again!"

"What is this?" said Snaker, curling his lip and looking about the slush floor of the canyon. "It ain't snow."

It couldn't be. They weren't high enough for snow and it

wasn't cold enough. Yet the rocks and ground were covered in a thick, greyish-white substance that gave like soft mud beneath Haayashi's boots and crept up over her ankles. It was slippery, and had a bad smell, even in the rain. It coated everything here. There were bones scattered throughout the strange mire – broken skeletons of buffalo, cattle, and horses.

She looked up the white-stained walls. There was a lip beneath which the rain did not fall. High over the canyon lips rose a series of conical stone formations like teeth. There were three in all. Set atop one was a massive, circular tangle of brush and tree branches, like a thorny crown.

"What in the hell is that?" Snaker said.

Haayashi looked at her father.

"The abode of the Thunder-Makers," the old man murmured to her in answer. "When there is no place left for an Apache to go, when he will not surrender and go into the belly of the iron horse, when he will not grow corn and there is no wickiup beneath which he can lay his head, they come to me, and I bring them here, to The Place Where The Thunder Dwells. To die."

"What'd he say?" Snaker whispered to her, unnerved by the strange shapes atop the pinnacle stones.

"He said the way down to Old Mexico is at the other end of this canyon," she said, breathless.

"That ain't what he said," said Pelado, cocking his pistol.

They all turned to where the Mexican stood with his money sack over one shoulder and his back to the slot in the stone.

"You think I don't learn a word of Apache, growin' up along the border?" Pelado grinned, the gold caps in the corners of his mouth glinting.

"What did he say?" Emory asked.

"He said he brings men up here to die. What'd you do to the Broncos you brought up here, Viejo?" Pelado snarled. "You kill 'em and take their goods? Sell off their horses? Maybe you got a deadfall set up in this canyon, eh?"

Emory, meanwhile, had been toeing at the viscous slurry at their feet, and suddenly gave a curse, and stooped to pull something free and dripping from the muck.

A long, white leg bone, swinging easy on a loose thread of old sinew, a leather boot dangling on one end.

"Ooooh, yeh bugger!" the Scot said. "Will you look at this?"

Snaker drew his gun.

• •⁎

The ascent had grown too treacherous to ride the horses, so the posse led their ponies up the mountainside on foot. Vester was out front and steadily approaching a sheer escarpment when he held up his hand for the others to halt. He peered warily at a huddled mass of moving shapes on the ground before a tall, narrow crack in the stone.

Barraclough and Frees handed their reins to Holt and crept forward with their rifles, while Lowell and Chapon kept watch.

The sun had slipped into the desert, but lightning splashed an unsteady light across the moving shadows near the stone wall. Vester glimpsed slick, dark shapes shuffling over a number of jumbled mound-like boulders.

"What are they?" Frees whispered.

Vester shook his head. "Dunno. Look like… a whole lotta… birds. Vultures maybe?"

Thunder rolled over the mountain, and the things hopped and shifted erratically, but went on about their business beneath the downpour.

"That the way over there? Through that crack?" Barraclough said.

"Only way they could've gone. But their horses…"

"Well, they're in the way, then," Barraclough said. He levered his Henry and fired twice in the air.

The effect was immediate but not at all what the marshal intended. The things on the ground fluttered en masse, unfolding bat-like wings, lifting off from the carcasses of half a dozen dead horses to take briefly to the rainy sky like a flock of startled pigeons. They hopped nervously about a bit, then swiveled their sharp heads side to side, spotting and sizing up the three men.

There had to be two dozen or more of the things. Just like that strange creature they'd found shot to pieces where Swift Tom had been killed. That carcass had been an oddity. This group, with their sharp beaks and beady eyes glistening in the rain, curved talons scrabbling on the stone, were a threat.

The things uttered a few interrogative squawks amongst each other, then charged the three men, hopping awkwardly like bats along the ground.

"Oh shit," said Barraclough, stumbling back.

Vester fired the Whitney and blasted one out of the air as it sprang, but a second came directly for him in its wake and he threw the rifle up crossways, barring the clawing, pecking thing from his face. The weight of it bowled him over, and he fell backwards, others flapping and hopping over him.

Frees yelled and fired. Barraclough grunted. Somewhere behind them, more shots and unintelligible shouts. The horses shrieked in terror.

The thing in Vester's arms was all sharp, stabbing, ripping angles. It tore his sleeves and arms and slashed at his face; he took a glancing jab from its beak beneath his collarbone. He rolled on top of the thing, pinned it by the throat with the rifle, and wrenched its head sideways, breaking its neck.

He looked up just as another whiplash of lightning painted a horrific scene. Holt's horse reared. It was covered with the clinging, slashing things, flapping demon wings obscuring the deputy as he screamed and fell backwards, still clenching the reins of the other horses. He and his mount tumbled down the mountainside dragging the others with them in a violent tangle. Holt gave a pretty good approximation of the old Rebel Yell as he went.

Lowell made a desperate grab for his partner and was brought down under a flapping swarm.

Chapon, unmounted, clung desperately to his horse's head as it wheeled about madly, its eye sockets empty and streaming blood. He was flung against a boulder and lay senseless as the animal collapsed under a heap of beating wings and stabbing heads.

Beside Vester, Frees swung his rifle by the barrel and missed, smashing the wooden stock to splinters against a stone. His target spread its wings magnificently and leapt at the Englishman's face, but Vester shot it away. Frees pulled his revolver and blazed madly.

Muzzle flashes and lightning lit the scene.

Barraclough got to his feet, the side of his face torn open to the teeth, his lower lip hanging from his chin in two ragged halves, a pistol in each hand. He killed another of the savage birds, then high-tailed it for the crack in the stone, which was spilling white water like a river source.

Vester spun to see if he could help Lowell or Chapon as Frees followed the marshal. Old Lowell was twitching faintly beneath a squirming pile. Chapon had his pistol in one hand, his knife in the other, and was bleeding from half a dozen wounds. One bird clung to his back, stabbing its beak again and again into his shoulders.

Vester ran over, drew the double-action from his waist, and shot the thing in the head point blank. He pulled the dazed Chapon up the incline, stumbling over dead horses and fighting the current of water tumbling from the slot canyon.

Chapon hung from Vester, batting the birds away with his knife as they leapt at them. They reached the crack just as Frees pulled himself inside.

The way was desperately narrow and choked with water up to their armpits. They had to wedge themselves between the slick stone to keep from being washed back. Barraclough and Frees pushed on ahead, their guns held awkwardly above their heads, fleeing the horror behind them.

Vester came next. He had to turn sideways and shuffle, the stone brushing his chest and back, barely room to turn his head and look back as Chapon screamed and fired his revolver at the entrance when it filled with two of the hungry things scrabbling high along the walls to get at him. It was deafening in the closeness, and all of them screamed for him to stop, but he didn't until his pistol ran dry.

They made their way in the wet, narrow darkness, ears ringing. Vester didn't even hear Chapon die. He just happened to look back and note the man's absence.

All Vester knew next was the scrape of the stone, and the water, cold in the dark.

Gradually, the heave of their breath and the steady trickle of the dying rainstorm returned with his hearing. There was a rumble of departing thunder.

A dim shift in the light appeared up ahead, a distinct paleness. Then he heard shooting again, and pushed on. *Haayashi.*

• ••

The storm passed over the mountain, the clouds breaking and letting the early-night stars and the bright moon shine down into the pale canyon.

Haayashi and Nach'aa knelt before Snaker and Pelado, staring down the black barrels of their guns, her old father leaning heavily against her.

They waited in silence as fat Emory returned. "There ain't nothing up ahead but the other end of this canyon and more bowfin mud. It don't go anywhere!" Emory panted. "Now what're we gonna do?"

"Shut up, Emory, and let me ponder a while!" Snaker snapped.

"Maybe we can hold up here a little," Pelado suggested. "Maybe Barraclough had to stop for the storm. Maybe they didn't find the slot."

Before Snaker could answer, Ray Barraclough himself came storming out of the crease in the back of the canyon. True to form, his bullets preceded his appearance, ricocheting off the stones and sending them scattering for cover in the white, bone-strewn mud.

All but Haayashi and her father. They knelt in the center, still bound, and she shuddered and looked down to see blood spreading across her stomach.

The dim silver canyon, the star speckled sky, they wheeled, and she fell on her side in the cool muck, unable to regain her balance. It seemed to swallow her, drawing her down deep.

She was aware of her father calling her name in ever increasing volume, then she knew only a black blacker than the oldest shadows of night.

* * *

"Behind them rocks!" Barraclough shouted, banging away with both pistols. "This is for my brother Andy, you son of a bitch!"

He took cover behind a white boulder. Alwyn stumbled out, slinging wild shots as he dove in the mud on the opposite side behind a pile of bones.

Vester emerged last, the dreaded voice of his father-in-law the only yelling he heard.

"Haayashi! Haayashi!"

He joined in the shouting of her name, firing the Whitney rifle to keep heads down as he made for his wife. Vester fell to his knees in the mud, joining the old man cradling her body. Haayashi lay limp in his arms, dripping muck, her beautiful black hair frosted white with it, her face slack, the front of her blouse dark with blood.

Vester shook his head violently, heedless as Snaker Pista and Ray Barraclough traded lead that bounced off the stones and plopped into the mud all around them. He blinked at his father-in-law through eyes heavy and bulging with tears, his heart dropping in his chest and plunging into his stomach.

The old man looked up from the body of his daughter, his face as empty and inanimate as if it were her own. His expression was hewn in red rock, his sunken cheeks, his thin mouth, his narrow shoulders, even his long silver hair seemingly weighed down with the heaviness of the loss. The agate eyes behind the cracked spectacles were as dead as abandoned rooms behind the broken casements of a derelict house.

Nach'aa didn't seem to see Vester as he flung down his spectacles, got to one unsteady leg, rose to his full height, and turned, the bullets whizzing about him.

A bullet passed close enough to slash his cheek. The old man barely registered it. He raised his arms like a Pentecostal knee-deep in baptismal water, and cried out in fluent English, his voice resounding off the canyon walls, dulling even the snap and crack of the gunfire until they ceased as if embarrassed to carry on in the face of his proclamation.

"White eyes! Listen to me, White eyes! Hear my words! I am speaking to you! You are in The Place Where The Thunder Dwells! I, Nach'aa have brought you here! And now I have come myself as I came before, as I brought men and women who wanted to come at last to Usen! But this time I am staying! Nach'aa is staying! And you are staying with me!"

Barraclough, Frees, Snaker, Emory, and Pelado all poked their heads out from behind their cover at opposite ends of the white canyon. They looked from the old man standing with his hands in the air staring up into the night sky, then to each other.

Snaker pointed his pistol at Nach'aa and shot him dead.

The report echoed up and down the length of the canyon, and Nach'aa flopped flat on his back, arms still outstretched.

The outlaws and the posse were quiet a moment.

Then they began to laugh, and their laughter overtook the echo of the gunshot and bounced playfully back and forth off the pale stone walls, till they were doubled over where they crouched, their vengeance and avarice momentarily forgotten in the face of the killing of the crazy old Apache. Maybe a parley would replace lead. Maybe they'd pat each other on the back, split the money, and go their separate ways.

Only Vester Payne didn't laugh.

He stared hard at Marshal Ray Barraclough, who had given his word. Vester took out the double action New Model Army and shot Ray in the neck.

The marshal clapped one gloved hand over his spurting throat, and stared wide-eyed at Vester, enraged. He stood and swung his other pistol to bear.

WHERE THUNDER DWELLS

A broad shadow enveloped the canyon and blotted out the stars and the moon, right before the unearthly bellow of a longhorn steer broke the silence and the two-thousand-pound animal plummeted to earth right out of the black sky. It crushed Marshal Ray Barraclough flat where he stood.

The broke-backed, broke-legged steer flopped and rolled, lowing pitifully, dragging its burst organs across the crushed corpse of the marshal, wallowing in his pasted remains. Vester numbly recognized its Lazy S brand.

Then every head craned, and every skeleton shivered in its scabbard of muscle and blood.

Perched in the midst of the strange bramble corona atop the narrow stone pinnacle, an immense dark shape spread its membranous wings. A great, sharp head rose on a tremendous neck and hooked claws the size of ancient desert daggers clenched the tangled edges of its nest.

The things that had driven the posse into the slot canyon had come from this great sire. It tipped back its head, parted its long beak and let out a long, piercing shriek that filled their ears.

It was a call to feed.

Vester heard a fluttering of many wings, and black shapes broke the light of the stars. Flocks of the gargantuan thing's brood, poured down into the canyon, streaking like bullets.

Some lit on the proffered steer, picking it to death. But others spied the men and wheeled for this unexpected repast.

Emory Cashe had no time to shoot as two of the creatures pinned him to the ground by his shoulders. He screamed as others ripped wide his prodigious belly, spilling its contents across the canyon floor. One yanked his intestines free and tried to take flight, but was jerked comically back to earth like a dog on a short leash.

Pelado screamed and hacked at the wild sky with his machete, cutting down a half score of the things before he was pecked full of holes and collapsed behind a stone.

Snaker Pista emptied his gun then was borne into the air by a dozen of them. He screamed and cursed as they tugged his limbs in all directions until he split and burst and fell in a crimson rain of scraps and blood.

Alwyn Frees scorched his lips on the muzzle of his revolver and swallowed his last bullet.

Vester stirred as they came for him, and blew three out of the air, but then placed his gun to his own temple, prepared to follow the Englishman to Hell, when the faintest tug at his wrist brought him from the brink of self-destruction.

He looked down at his Haayashi, his danohshoni. She didn't move, but that one finger curled around his, and her eyelid twitched.

That was enough.

He spent his last bullet on one of the cawing little terrors, dropped the stolen pistol, and gathered his wife up, extricating her from the sucking filth.

Vester made for the slot canyon as fast as he could, stooped over, cradling Haayashi close. The birds stabbed at his back, their claws tore at his coat and his arms. But they didn't touch her. He staggered when one lit upon his shoulders and drove its beak halfway through his shoulder. He fell against stone, nearly passing out, but saw the gap and pushed Haayashi into it.

Then he turned and bashed the thing on his back against the rock until it slid from his bleeding shoulders.

He blocked the opening with his body, blood running into his eyes. Vester drew his own pistol and fired till his fingers were torn from his gun hand and he had to border shift to his left. He barred his eyes with his arm and pulled the trigger till it was empty, then swung it back and forth like a sap, knocking the things back, trading punishment for punishment, repaying stabs to his chest and stomach with broken beaks and crushed skulls.

Then he was drawn back, pulled into the slot by familiar arms.

He staggered, only the smooth stone keeping him on his feet.

"Come on, Shijii," Haayashi whispered in his ear. "Come on!" She grasped his hand and tugged him along the narrow passage.

Some of the things tried to force their way in, mad to get at him. He punched them, driving them away as best he could. One darted in under his arm and he cried out, pricked, but he slammed his elbow down, felt its neck snap. Fury had him dig his fingers in, twisting. He ripped the head away and cast the thing behind him. The others tarried to dig and tear into it, heedless of its origin, sated with hot blood and flesh.

The return through the slot canyon was perceived by Vester only in increments of wavering consciousness. Haayashi bore him to the entrance till they stood before the sheer escapement amid the skeletons of the horses, gazing down on the moonlit desert. She set him down and tore her clothes, tying the scraps tightly around his wounds. He only bled, saying nothing, awkwardly pushing cartridges from his belt into his gun with his off hand, mostly to keep his brain and body functioning.

They trudged heavily down the mountainside, husband leaning on wife, in silence, exhausted.

They'd made twenty feet or so when the shadow fell across them, and the withering cry sounded high above.

Haayashi shook her head and pulled her dazed husband aside as the wind began to rush and scream like a falling artillery shell at their backs, the shadow widening around them.

Then he pushed her to the ground and spun, firing the pistol upwards.

Three shots.

Four.

Still it came, unwavering.

He dove flat.

The thing tore his slouch hat away.

They lay on their bellies, staring across the space at each other. He had dropped the gun, his fingers too weak to hold it as he fell.

It lay between them.

They watched the monster wheel in a wide, dreadfully slow arc against the sky, tilting its broad wings as it made to return.

Vester laid his head against the rocks, too weak to move. Too weak to stand. The bullets were mosquito bites to that thing.

His eyes went from the gun to the slope of the mountainside, looking for an overhang they could roll under.

Instead, he found Swift Tom's dead horse.

The open saddle bags.

He tried to push himself up, fell.

Haayashi crawled over and laid her cheek against his, hushed him.

"No," he said. "No. In them saddlebags. See the box? The box!"

"Yes."

"It's nitroglycerine. You know?"

"I know!" Her lips brushed his cheek, swept through the cuts and the blood and pressed against his ear. Then she was on her feet, limping towards the horse, waving her arms, shouting a wild Apache trill.

The huge thing angled ever so slightly and bore down.

Vester Payne prayed.

Haayashi climbed unsteadily onto the carcass of the horse, still trilling, still waving her arms. The place where the bullet had gone into the left of her belly and come out her side sang in its own harsh tongue.

Oh God. Oh dear God.

She seemed to jump directly at its gaping beak, but turned sharply downward, headlong.

It passed inches from her heels, so close it might have snagged her with its hallux as an afterthought. But its beak struck the horse. Tore into the saddle, into the bags.

The smooth lines of its avian face, fashioned in ancient times to make it cut through the wind and the clouds, was obscured in a sudden burst of fire and sound and smoke that splayed open its beak, filling the sky and painting the rock with blood. It ploughed headlong into the side of the mountain like a meteor, its wings folding haphazardly about it. Its rear end doubled over; skeleton cracked open. Flesh tore, gargantuan organs tumbled and burst, contents cascading down the gullies and slopes.

And in the midst of the cataclysm, Vester Payne, rolling and scrambling to get out of the way, was engulfed in blood and bone and sound and stone.

When next he knew anything, the sun was high and bright behind the battered face of Haayashi looking over him.

"Are you alive, Shijii?"

"Yep," he mumbled. "Danohshoni."

Her smile was brighter than the sun somehow. "Well good. Can you walk?"

"I think so. Can you?"

"I got a hole in me," she said, pulling him to his feet.

"Just one?" He groaned, looked around, confused. "I think I got somethin' in my eye."

"You got nothing in that eye," Haayashi said. "It's gone. It's OK, Shijii. Now it'll be just like you're winkin' at me all the time, like that first time you come into the store."

He chuckled and leaned on her, but was frowning by the time they'd gone five steps, and stopped. "Snaker burned out the store."

"Yeah, he did."

"And Papa Nach'aa's gone."

Haayashi lowered her head. "He's with Usen. And Momma too. And all them Broncos that asked him to lead him up here."

"Well, but they's a fair amount of money and gold dust layin' back on the other side of that slot canyon."

She looked at him, and turned him slowly around so he could look back.

Between the explosion and the creature driving itself into the face of the escarpment, the fissure in the rock had collapsed.

"The Thunder-Makers have it now," she said, shrugging.

"Well," Vester demured. "You think Old Saunders'll still pay out that reward money when I tell him what's been nabbin' his cattle?"

Behind them, the immense, ruined carcass shifted almost imperceptibly. The hide of its back began to gradually rise and fall in a dozen or more places, as though long, sharp fingers probed the elasticity of its skin, the first, questing explorations of the unborn testing the boundaries of their incubator.

SNAFU: DEAD OR ALIVE

Hayaashi and Vester were too far down the mountain to hear the tear of leathery skin, nor did they see the bloody beaks burst through the body, followed by the stumbling, angular creatures, unfolding and beating their vampiric wings free of the viscera of their dead sire as they clambered in squawking droves into the lightening sky.

MERCY

John W Salvage

The gallows told me everything I needed to know about the people of Mercy. I turned an outcropping of rock and there they was. The tall wooden pillar, the body dangling from its crossbeam, and the town framed between.

It couldn't have happened more than a half hour before. The vultures hadn't yet eaten his eyes. They stared at me with a blind agony amidst the bloated face.

A girl, must've been about seven, gazed up at the dead man with a distant smile on her lips. She poked at the corpse with a stick and giggled.

"Leave that!" I hollered. She turned to me, surprised. Not looking like she was caught at something she weren't supposed to be doing, but shocked someone was minding her at all.

"We're gonna catch a buzzard," a voice said from a nearby rock. I turned to find a boy of maybe twelve working some twine into a snare. On his head rested a war bonnet made of vulture feathers.

I spurred my horse, Hopper, and rode on.

Beyond the gallows lay some shallow graves with stones piled over them. Not all them that hung made it to the grave. The bones lying amongst the scrub proved these people sometimes let a body rot until it fell.

It never did sit with me well the way some folks like to make their point linger. I ain't never been one to let a man live that needed killing, but once it's over, it's best to be done with it. Lingering on his death raises a man's legend. Sometimes it'll raise 'em right out of the grave.

I seen things like that. Things that don't have no earthly right to happen. After Shiloh I thought I'd turned lunatic. Got help from a feller I'd heard about. What you might call a spiritualist, by the name of Pete Anderson. He told me the truth about what I'd been seeing. Eventually, he inducted me into the Brotherhood.

Me and my brothers investigated the dark shadows eating at the corners of the world. Most of it was humbuggery, but we dealt with evil darker than I ever imagined. I buried a man twice then burn him lest he rose again. Done killed a man so evil milk curdled in his wake. Met a woman who could heal with a touch and another who caused limbs to wither and rot.

Pete ordered me to this Godforsaken place to back up another member of the Brotherhood, Henry Pozan. Along the trail I heard tell Henry'd been hung. Now I can't say me and Henry was friends. Associates is about as close as I'd come, but that didn't mean I could ignore his murder.

Made my way to the saloon first. The whitewashed walls had been stripped to bare wood by the hot winds while dry rot ate at the windows and door frame. The whole town suffered like a twig drying in the hot sun. The wood bleached to the yellow-white color of bone.

I led Hopper to the hitching rail but didn't bother fastening her to it. She wouldn't wander.

Inside, a fat man stood atop a chair, talking at the room. He was bald and sweat a lot, but at that moment he looked happier than a hound gnawing a soup bone. He was jawin' on about how Mercy was a safe town once again, about how the prosperous days would return, and on and on. I don't know how long he'd been at it, but he still had a lungful coming.

When I ordered a drink, the barkeep seemed happy enough to turn away from the speech, but the rest of the crowd hung on every word. Figured they was eager for a free drink after he stopped jawin'.

"I'm looking for the marshal," I told the barkeep, and his eyes lit up with surprise.

"Marshal Larouche is dead."

"Come again?"

"He died two days ago," he said before a grin crossed his lips. "But we caught the bastard that did it! Strung him up on

Old Justice not yet an hour ago." His eyes glowed with wild delight.

"Who's in charge then?"

"Mayor DuPont," he said, nodding to the man speaking atop his chair.

I turned, half listening as I scanned the room. I weren't looking for anything in particular, but like Pete once told me, "you'll always see nothing if you ain't looking for something."

There weren't nothing particular I saw that I could point my finger to, but something was off. I felt it in the way my back teeth hummed. Saw it in the adoring looks the townsfolk gave the mayor. I seen people testifying at church wearing looks like that, but I ain't never seen it on a man listening to a politician.

After the mayor finished his yammering, he come up and clapped me on the back. "Good afternoon, friend," he said, talking to the room as much to me. "What brings you to Mercy?" Then, raising his voice, he half-turned to the crowd around him and announced, "I sure hope you aren't planning any deviltry like that feller out yon." Those around him laughed and saluted him with raised glasses of whiskey.

I didn't give him a reaction a'tall.

"Oh now, don't take offence," the mayor said. "We're celebrating swift justice today."

I just looked at him, taking his measure. The sweat on his forehead beaded like dew and his eyes darted in his sockets as he searched my face. His smile faded, locking in the sour breath that oozed from his lungs.

"So, what brings you to town?" he asked at last.

"I'm here to find a killer."

"Ah, well," he replied, his face lighting up again. "Maybe that's why you're so glum! We beat you to it! There ain't no bounty for second place." Again, his laughter was infectious.

I stopped myself from saying what I wanted, and instead said, "Got a question for you, Mayor."

"Oh?"

"What happened the night you killed Henry Pozan?"

After I said it, the mayor didn't need to raise his voice for the whole room to hear. The silence was so great he'd have a hard time passing a whisper.

"What? What do you mean?" He stuttered over the words while backing away.

"I mean," I said, stepping closer. "Something happened the night you and your posse killed Pozan. What was it?"

Well, I must have struck the right chord because his eyes got distant and glazed. Then he started talking in a low voice while them around us moved away.

He talked for a good half hour. Some of what he told me I already knew. I'd read the letters Henry'd sent before he'd been hung. More important, I knew why Henry'd come in the first place.

Henry was a founding member of the Brotherhood. He'd been studying what he called 'spatial anomalies', which was places around the world that didn't hold tight to Natural Law. Henry told me these places were where our world butted up against another 'realm of existence'. His words. Said it was kind of like when two tree limbs rub together until they conjoin.

He studied a number of these places around the world, particularly in England, Egypt, and southern China. When his research showed he might find one around here, he jumped at the chance.

Henry sent several letters before he died. He wrote about his travels and his troubles finding the anomalies. Also talked about the people of Mercy. About how vicious their fights got, how loose the livery owner was with the whip, and the sadistic nature of the children's games. It didn't mean much at the time, but I was beginning to understand what he meant by their casual cruelty.

"I pegged him as a queer duck right off," Mayor DuPont told me. "He was asking a lot of strange questions about the land around Mercy. Wanted to know if we'd ever seen anything unusual. After a while he started asking about the mines. Not the copper mind you, but the mines themselves. He even hired Ned McBride to take him down into a couple for a look-see."

"Did he find what he was looking for?"

"I don't rightly know. Ned said that he wandered around looking at his compass and scribbling notes."

"What else did he do?"

"Not much. He made camp outside a different mine every night and scouted it out during the day."

"What changed?"

DuPont hesitated before continuing. "One night Johnny Cobb heard some strange singing coming from the hills. Fearing an Indian war party, he snuck up to get a gander. Over the rise he spied Henry dancing around a fire. Then Henry turned and walked into the flames. He should've burned up. Instead, he stood there chanting in a voice that weren't his own. The fire changed colors, burning cherry red and yellow and ghostly orange until the flames turned black.

"Now Johnny wasn't more than a kid. What he saw scared him so bad he turned tail and ran all the way back to town. He came to see me—"

"Why you?" I said. "Why did he come see you and not the marshal?"

"Well," Mayor DuPont said, his knowing smile relishing his own words. "Marshal Larouche had only been with us a couple of months. I've been mayor for years. It's not unusual for people to come straight to me."

I nodded and motioned for him to continue.

"So, we got a posse together and Johnny led us to him," DuPont said. "Sure enough, it was like he said. We caught Henry, roped him, and dragged him to the gallows."

The mayor swallowed hard, his lips pursed while he considered how to continue. Rather than talk about the hanging though, he moved on to what happened after.

"Johnny Cobb died first. Frank Morris found him hog tied and dropped down an abandoned mine. They found Stewart Blair tied to a tree and scalped. Whoever done it didn't stop at the scalp. They peeled off his entire face. They started dropping like flies after that." His voice fell to near a whisper, and I had to lean in close to catch the rest. "Frank Morris got stoned to death. We found Ned McBride impaled on the stump of a Jack pine. Then, two days ago Marshal Larouche was found up past Stony Gap. He was dangling above from a rope fixed to a branch some fifty feet off the ground. Nothing was missing except the marshal's hat."

It was the hat that damned Jake Wellings, the man they hung the day I arrived. He was wearing the marshal's hat when he come to town. Said he found it amongst the pines. Nobody believed him.

"How many of the people in the lynching party are left?" I asked after he'd finished his tale.

He thought for a minute. "Oh, I guess there's just me and Preacher Kinney."

I put away my notebook, thanked him for his time.

"Any time, friend," he said, talking loud again. "Too bad you weren't a little faster in getting here. You could have seen that murdering bastard hang."

"You killed the wrong man," I said as calmly as I could manage. "I reckon that makes you a murderer, too."

His fat head shot around. His soft jowls flapped, and his face grew red as he shook with anger. "That man got what he deserved! All the proof we needed sitting on the top of his head."

"I guess a hat never blowed off your head before. Easy enough to happen in town, and a whole lot easier up on a windy ridge, especially if there ain't a live hand to hold it." He looked at a loss for words, so I pressed. "And what kind of killer comes prancing into town wearing the dead man's hat? Criminals are stupid, but not as stupid as scared politicians."

"You can't speak to me like that!"

"Just did."

I wouldn't have been surprised if he went for his gun. Had he been drunker or braver he might have. Instead, he tried to draw strength from those around him. "You best be moving on, mister. This town don't take to strangers raising a fuss."

"I'll be moving on when my job's done."

MERCY

Outside, the sun beat down on the dusty street like midsummer instead of the end of May. I turned right out of the saloon and headed toward the sound of the bell ringing the noon hour. The church's belfry towered a good twenty feet over the other buildings. Built when the town was flush with money, the people of Mercy spared no expense in its construction. The same couldn't be said for its upkeep.

I opened the door as the last of the bell's steely clangs faded and heard someone gasp in the inky darkness. As my eyes adjusted, I found Preacher Kinney leaning up against the wall of the vestibule, his eyes wide and his mouth agape.

"Guilty conscience, padre?"

"Pardon?" he replied in a shaky voice.

"You're a mite jumpy."

He stood straighter immediately, his hands brushing his pants' legs smooth. "Oh no, you surprised me is all. I don't normally get many visitors this time of the afternoon. Too hot for most folks, I imagine."

"It's hotter in hell."

He looked at me for a moment then gave me a thin, tired smile. "Very witty. I shall tell my parishioners as much this Sunday." We stood studying each other for a few moments before he finally asked, "And how may I help you Mr...?"

"Tanner," I supplied. "Barret Tanner." I reached out my hand and received an honest handshake.

"How may I help you, Mr Tanner?"

"I want to hear about the hanging of Henry Pozan."

His face turned ashen. Had the wall not been there to catch him I believe he would've fallen. "H-Hen... Henry..."

"Pozan. You was there when they lynched him."

"Sweet Jesus," the preacher moaned. He didn't say nothing for a minute or so, but when I was about to prompt him, he spoke up again. "Come. Let's go back to my office."

Before I hardly sat, he was already fishing around for a bottle of whisky he'd stashed in a drawer. He poured two cups about three fingers high and downed most of his before handing me mine.

According to Preacher Kinney, he was settling down for the night when he heard the hullabalo outside his window. He seen the posse dragging a man behind them and knew what they was up to. So he gathered his bible before running outside to try and stop them. By the time he got there, Marshal Larouche was already trying to break it up. It wouldn't be easy. The mayor was keen on murder and was used to having his way.

"The mayor's a bit of a bully," Preacher Kinney confessed. "He would have been marshal and mayor if marshaling wasn't real work. Instead, he hires people to do his bidding. He miscalculated with Larouche, though."

"You ain't lynching anybody today!" The marshal reached to pull Henry loose from Stewart Blair's grip, but Blair held tight.

Mayor DuPont stepped between the two men. "Marshal Larouche," he thundered in his big campaign voice. "I order you to return to your office and let us resume our business."

"Order?" The marshal nearly spit those words. "You may have hired me, but I work for the town, and you're disturbing the peace."

"You don't know what he's done," Johnny chimed in. "He danced on fire, Marshal! He danced on black fire!"

"Hang him!" Someone yelled from the back of the mob. Others took up the call and suddenly they was in motion. They didn't get ten feet before a gunshot took the fight out of 'em.

Acrid smoke wafted away from the marshal's big peacemaker. Once he claimed their attention, he aimed his gun squarely at Mayor DuPont's chest. "Listen here, Gerald. This is your crowd you whooped up into a frenzy. You talk 'em down or we're going to need a new mayor." DuPont's mouth hung open, so the marshal continued. "Ned, you take that gag out of his mouth. I want to ask some questions."

"You're making a mistake," Mayor DuPont said, his smile widening to a sneer. "Your days are numbered, my friend."

Marshal Larouche ignored him, turning his attention to Henry, who was kneeling down in the dirt and breathing hard but weren't saying nothing. The marshal called to him.

That's when Henry lifted his head.

"What I saw," the preacher told me between sips of whiskey, "I can't ever forget. I wake up and feel it weighing down my soul."

When Henry looked up, blood was coming down his face in a stream. He snarled like an animal, but it was his words that undid them.

Henry spoke in a strange mixture of languages. The preacher recognized English, French and Latin, but he also heard others he couldn't identify. He flopped back and forth between them, sometimes mid-sentence. It weren't what he said that spooked everyone though, but how he said it.

"It was like no Earthly voice I ever heard," the preacher told me. "A long, base rumble that made my stomach turn in on itself." The preacher couldn't drink for the shaking of his hand. "The anger in his voice… malice darker than the loneliest cell in hell."

Frank Morris was the first to get his wits back. He stepped forward and punched Henry, shattering his nose. Blood shot out of it like a slaughtered lamb's throat. That's when the rest of the men regained their courage. They came kicking and punching, trying to make that damned voice stop. Eventually it did. For a time anyway.

"Let's hang him," Marshal Larouche said.

Now a hanging, if it's done right, will snap a man's neck as quick as lightning. A little gallows two-step and it's all over 'cept for selling post cards. When a man's neck don't break though, it's a different thing. He dies slow and silent except for the choking.

That's how it was with Henry Pozan. All except for the silence, that is. Once he was dangling by the neck, his voice called out clear and long, though it shouldn't have with the rope crushing his throat. He swung there for the better part of ten minutes while he turned blue and poured out a waterfall of curses.

"What was he saying?"

"Threats mostly. Telling us he would feed us glass… bathe in our blood."

Ned put two bullets in his chest to shut him up, then they left him there to rot. He hung there for over a week before they cut him down. The buzzards never did go after him. Even the flies and the worms steered clear.

Preacher Kinney was slurring his words and could barely sit upright by the time he finished his tale. It weren't just the drink, neither. His eyes were empty and glazed like them who survived the rebel shot and shell whilst friends died all about 'em.

The man Preacher Kinney described didn't sound like the Henry Pozan I knew. I saw a man act similar once though, and I feared what it meant. "Where'd they find Henry?"

"About a half mile north of here. There's a trail that will take you past a big tree stump. The mine shaft's about two hundred yards north-east of the tree."

I turned to leave but stopped when he spoke one last time, his voice broken from misery. "What should I do?"

"Pray," I told him. "And don't leave the church."

I whistled for Hopper, and she came running. Had just started out of town when I heard someone yelling for me. I turned and spied the mayor strolling out from the saloon with a couple of cronies at his side. Ignoring him, I headed out of town.

When I found Henry's camp, I approached it slow. The canvas he'd been sleeping under was sagging and torn. All his belongings had been rummaged through and broken.

Bypassing the mess, I headed toward the mine shaft. A tingle grew around my throat and spread down my spine as I neared. I stopped and drew a breath, my hand automatically going to my sidearm even though it would do no good.

I recited the Lord's Prayer. When I was done, the tingling abated and I sighed in relief. The evil I felt was only residue, like the lingering glow after a lightning strike.

My eyes adjusted to the darkness after I crossed the mine's threshold. The air was stale, but no worse than other mines I'd been in. The hungry presence I felt had slackened some, but it still lurked deeper down the shaft.

I found the large rock I'd expected about ten feet in on the right. If the mine'd been active the rock would have been taken out long ago. This one was brought in. Beneath it I found a sturdy but well-worn leather-bound book. The cover displayed the emblem of our Brotherhood — the Seal of Solomon — just like the one I'm writing in now.

There weren't much written in that notebook, but what was there filled me with dread. Henry managed to locate his spatial anomaly. I cursed myself for a fool when he described it.

The very spot where they built the gallows.

What he was really looking for was underground though. Since he couldn't start digging up the gallows, his search took much longer. That delay gave him time to see how the anomaly was warping the people of Mercy.

Maybe the anomaly drew violence to it. Maybe putting the gallows on top of it somehow warped it, turning it foul. Maybe the evil was waiting all along for a chance to reach out into the world. Henry didn't know, and he was smarter about these things than me. He figured the violence and the anomaly fed on each other, gaining strength and spreading like a pox.

What madness drove him to seek it out alone? He wrote of protections and wards, but they wouldn't mean shit to the thing lurking down there. He should've known better.

Though it weren't written down, I reckon I know what happened. He must've found the source and overstepped himself. Maybe it tempted him. Maybe it tricked him. Maybe there was some sort of accident. Whatever happened, something escaped and possessed Henry.

"You can't fight spirits with bullets," I said, remembering Pete's words. That was true of the bullets I had. If the preacher were to bless them though...

There was only a few people on the street when I rode into town. The boy I saw setting snares earlier spotted me and went running off down the street. I figured him for telling the mayor I'd come back.

I climbed off Hopper and retrieved my rifle from its scabbard so the preacher could bless every bullet I had. Hopper remained untethered as I went on to the church.

Soon as I opened the doors the stench of copper and shit filled my nose. I raised my rifle and squinted until my eyes adjusted to the darkness. Took slow steps across the vestibule until I touched the door handle to the nave. Drawing a breath, I pushed the door wide.

The preacher's ankles was tied and strung over the top of the cross. His body hung upside down with his hands nailed to the wall. If he'd had a head, it would have dipped below the cross, but it had been cut off and placed in the middle of the altar. Preacher Kinney's face looked out, his eyes wide with terror while his blood soaked the bible it rested upon.

I stood there for a spell, not moving. Don't know why. It ain't like I never seen a dead body before. It ain't even like I never seen one as broke up as the preacher's. When I left him, I told him to stay in the church. Figured it would keep him safe, but that thing was strong enough to walk right through those doors, kill the preacher, and defile sacred ground.

"Come on out with your hands up," a voice commanded from outside.

I rushed to the window and peeked out. Armed men ran hither and yon. A man with a rifle climbed to the top of the saloon across the way whilst others stood at a distance with cudgels and axe handles.

"Come out easy and we'll make sure you get a fair trial."

I moved up to the front door wishing there was windows. Near the bell rope, a thin stream of light shone through a chink in the wall. It allowed me to peer into the thoroughfare. Mayor DuPont was standing to the side of an upturned cart.

"What you arresting me for?" I called out, laying my rifle near the door. I ran back into the nave and pulled one of the heavy pews into the vestibule.

"For murder, you villainous cur!"

I turned the pew on its side and pushed it up against the wall to the right of the door. "Who'd I murder?" I asked before returning to gather a second pew.

"Preacher Kinney!" The mayor's declaration sounded more like a whoop for joy than an accusation.

"The hell you say!" I shouted back while trying to stack the second pew on top of the first. "I just got here."

"You were the last one to see him. We all saw you leave town like the devil was biting your ass."

"You promise I'll get a fair trial?"

"Judged by a jury of your peers."

"All right!" I called, hunkering down behind the stacked pews. "I'm coming out." I turned the doorknob slowly then pushed the door open hard.

"Fire!" Someone screamed and the air filled with thunder. Bullets thudded into the door and walls. The pews quivered under the impact. In the nave, windows shattered as they poured round after round into their place of worship.

At last someone yelled "hold your fire", and the shots began to die off. All around me the sun shone through bullet holes, filling the room with strangely beautiful rays of light.

Peering through one of those holes, men hurriedly reloaded their weapons. Mayor DuPont gave orders to some. Kept pointing to the church. With each wave of his hand, the mayor drew himself out from behind the wagon. I edged slowly to the opening.

Started counting. When I got to thirty, I took a deep breath knowing it could be my last. In one smooth motion I turned, bringing the rifle to my shoulder. I let instinct take my aim and squeezed a single shot.

A fine spray of red confirmed my hit. Everything was silent for a spell, then the screaming began.

I hoped shooting DuPont would end it. Figured the demon jumped to him when Henry died. Maybe killing him would kill the demon. Maybe if the preacher'd been able to bless them bullets it would have. That weren't the way it happened though.

"He killed the mayor," someone yelled. "Fire!"

I dove to the floor as the bullets slammed into the church. This time I didn't have the luxury of hiding behind the pews. I took a bullet in my leg. It struck me solid and would have broke my bone had the wall not slowed it. Sharp stings lashed across my body as flecks of wood shrapnel struck me in a dozen places.

When the firing stopped, I peeked through one of them holes. They wasn't approaching, but some of them scurried around the upturned wagons.

Their eyes caught a strange glint of twilight from the setting sun. At first, I thought I imagined it, but the more I watched the more distinct that light became. When the sun set, that glint became a glow and I knew the truth.

That thing in the mine didn't possess just one man. For more than a hundred years it drew life from the town and breathed out anger. It must have captured the souls of everyone who died on that gallows, and likely a fair share of others.

When Henry come along and freed it, it didn't need to go far. It might have taken over Henry's body, but the town was already his. The mayor might have been right in his instinct to kill the demon, but when it escaped Henry's body, it found a ready host in DuPont.

But why kill the posse?

Maybe it was mad they killed his vessel. Maybe it wanted to drive the town to madness. Maybe it was just eager to murder. That seemed right. The opportunity to kill must have been overwhelming after what was likely eons trapped underground.

Now that DuPont was dead, the demon spread itself across the town. I could see it plain in their glowing eyes and hive-like efficiency.

"You best stay back!" I hollered. If they knew I was alive it might buy me some time. I yanked my belt free and cinched it around my leg to staunch the blood.

A group of men stepped out from the general store toting a passel of unlit torches. Another two carried tins of whale oil. If they couldn't shoot me out, they'd burn me out.

That was when I saw Hopper galloping around the thoroughfare. She was panicking, running rampant while two men tried to corner her.

I whistled loudly and she jerked her head about searching for me. When I whistled again, she barreled through the men, knocking them to the ground in her desperation.

MERCY

The men on the porch was lighting their torches. The whale oil tins was already open. I leveled my rifle and took careful aim.

My bullet caught the tin of oil. The can burst in a fine mist that hit one of the torches making it blossom into a fiery rose. Two of the men was caught in the blaze while the others tripped over themselves getting clear.

I squeezed off my second shot and nicked the second tin. The oil sprayed against the wall of the general store. One of the burning men stepped on the oil trail and ignited it. When it caught, I heard the whoosh all the way from the church.

The town shot back, and I couldn't hide from the volley. I hobbled out of the vestibule and dove into the nave. Crawled to the wall then peeked through the shattered window for my horse. One man pulled on her reins while another tried to calm her. I shot the man holding her then whistled.

Her head turned wildly as she searched for me, and I clambered up on one of the pews and waved my arms about. Hopper spotted me, but she weren't the only one. A bullet missed my head by an inch. Others followed, turning the nave into a hornet's nest of lead.

The shots stopped and I barely had time to lift my head before the first two torches was flung through the window. A can of oil and another torch followed. The oil ignited in a wave of heat. The sun-rotted pines snapped angrily as the flames ate fuel and air.

Looking out the window, Hopper darted toward me. Most of the wall was engulfed in flames. I scrabbled atop one of the pews then dove right through the shattered window, my hair singeing from the wall of fire.

Reckon nobody expected me to emerge through the flames, which is likely why I'm alive to write this tale. I hit the ground hard, and rolled, coming up to one knee. Bolts of pain shot through my wounded leg. Hopper raced up to me, barely slowing to a trot as I rose. My foot caught in the stirrup, and I was up and in the saddle before the townsfolk knew what happened.

They didn't dally long. Shots fired all around me. The

bullet from the man up top of the saloon shattered my shoulder, making me drop my rifle. Hopper leapt and stumbled as buck shot struck her in the rear. She kept her footing though and got me out alive.

When we got to the gallows, I spared a look behind me. The sky was thick with black smoke and the screams of people shouting for water. There weren't nobody coming after me, though I didn't figure that to last.

I urged Hopper on, though to my regret I pushed her too hard. When the spur and the quirt couldn't urge her on, I stepped down from her. Her back and legs were wet with blood. Besides the buckshot, three bullets caught that magnificent beast as she bore me to safety. Even as I lay a calming hand on her head her legs slipped out from under her.

I spared a bullet to put her out of her misery. Maybe it ain't right to say a prayer for a horse, but I done it.

Gathering my saddle bag, I moved into the rocks, climbing until the loss of blood made me too weak to go on. The town of Mercy burned in the distance, the alkaline air glowing orange. The men was busy putting out the fire now, but they would hunt me soon.

I heard them creeping up the barren hill before noon the next day. I only had my pistol, so I let them come close. Killed two before the rest scampered away to regroup. Over the day I turned away no less than five charges and killed near a dozen men.

Still, that didn't stop them. They're down there now behind the ridge.

They'll be after me tomorrow morning, and this time they'll get me. I'm down to less than a dozen rounds, and a fever has taken hold from the infection in my leg.

Dying don't bother me much. I seen enough to know the glory that lay ahead and the suffering I'm leaving behind. I tried to live right by the Lord, and believe He will forgive my sins, numerous though they may be. My only regret is that I didn't burn Mercy to the ground. Maybe its ruination would've ended the curse.

MERCY

I'm going to stow this ledger under a rock. Figure in a week or so Pete will send someone to find me. I hope whoever comes is smart enough to bring back-up. Once they learn where I made my stand, they'll find this ledger.

To whoever finds it, you've got to burn the gallows. Uproot the timbers. Scatter the ashes. Dynamite the mines. Burn what's left of Mercy. Kill every last man, woman and child who called this place home. They don't know the evil eating away at their souls any more than they can be saved from it.

May God have mercy on our souls.

SNAKE MEN ON A TRAIN

James A Moore and Charles R Rutledge

B en Logan brought his hands up just in time to keep from slamming his face into the seat in front of his when the train gave a sudden lurch and began braking. The wheels screeched, drowning out the frightened yelps of some of the passengers. He glanced across the aisle at his fellow Pinkerton agent, Dave Cobb, and said, "If it's Ketchum's gang, they picked a good spot. We're miles from anywhere."

The train was on the loneliest stretch of the run between Santa Fe and Colorado. Nothing out there but Juniper trees and coyotes. Not that Logan could see any of that outside the windows. Between the night and the dense fog that had rolled in at sundown, there hadn't been much to look at since leaving Lamy.

Logan had read somewhere that fog in New Mexico was really low hanging clouds. A man with a more poetic turn of mind might have found the idea of taking a train through the clouds romantic, but to Logan it was just a damn nuisance.

When the train stopped moving, Logan rose from his seat. He pointed to Jake Morris who was sitting at the back of the car. "Keep an eye out. Dave and me will go see what's going on."

The passengers were in a panic, and one of the train's two conductors was trying to calm them down. The other conductor was at the door, getting a lantern ready. There were less than a dozen passengers in the car, and about the same amount in the second passenger car. Logan had walked the length of the train before they had left Santa Fe. Not a big train. Three passenger cars, two cargo cars, a coal car, and the engine.

"What's the problem?" Logan said to the conductor at the door.

"Just going out to see. Engineer says it looks like a landslide blocked the tracks."

"Let's have a look, then. Name's Logan, I'm with the Pinkerton guards."

"Abe," the conductor said. He opened the door and stepped out into the dark and the mist.

Logan and Dave followed Abe as the man walked to the front of the engine. The yellow light from the lantern made a feeble circle and threw dark, wavering shadows along the sides of the train cars. The fog swirled along the edges, offering half seen shapes that danced in the lamp glow.

Abe said, "Yep, rocks on the track. Must have come from that slope there to the right."

Abe held the lamp high, and Logan spotted some good size boulders across the rails. Then he looked at the ground and his hand went to the butt of his Colt.

Logan said, "Wasn't a landslide. No rocks between here and the slope. Somebody carried those boulders here."

He suddenly felt very exposed in the lantern light. Logan and Abe would make admirable targets to someone hidden by the fog. If it was Ketchum's boys, they could pick off anyone trying to clear the track.

"Dead man over here," a deep voice said from Logan's left.

Logan started at the unexpected sound and his Colt cleared its holster. He spun toward the voice and saw the biggest man he'd ever seen crouched by a dark shape on the ground. There were two other men with him, but Logan couldn't make them out in the fog.

"Who the hell are you?" Logan said.

"I'm Kharrn. I was in the second car. Tell your friend to bring the light over here."

Logan didn't much like being given orders by a civilian, even one as big as a horse, but he nodded to Abe and the conductor walked over to the big man. Logan held his gun down by his leg. The lantern light did indeed show a dead man. Or what was left of him.

"Jesus Christ," Abe said.

Logan was thinking much the same. The body on the ground had been stripped of clothing and most of its flesh. It looked like a butchered steer, and blood had soaked into the sand under it, leaving a dark stain.

Logan took the lantern from Abe and crouched beside the giant, the light held close to the dead man's face. There was enough flesh left to recognize the features.

Logan said, "This is Bob Cole, one of Black Jack Ketchum's boys. They must have planned to storm the train here."

Dave said, "But what in God's name happened to him, and where's the rest of the gang?"

"Well now," one of the other strangers said, "That is the question, isn't it?"

In the lantern's light, Logan could now see the other two men more clearly. He sort of wished he couldn't. The one who'd been talking was plain as the day was long, brown hair, brown eyes, tanned skin, and spectacles but the one next to him was almost as tall as Kharrn, if only half the width. He looked like a corpse, with shoulder length dead white hair and skin, cold blue eyes half-lidden in the lamp's glare, and a cadaverously thin body.

The albino corpse half-whispered, "I expect they might have run away, or found themselves in similar trouble. There are a lot of tracks here that don't look right, Mister Crowley."

"How do they look wrong, Mister Slate?" The plain man, Crowley, responded.

"They aren't human, and they aren't wearing shoes."

Crowley looked at Logan, "Sounds like you were expecting trouble. Is that why there are so many Pinkerton men on the train?"

Logan stood from his crouch. "How would you know that?"

Crowley smiled, and all thoughts that he was plain, vanished. That was, hands down, the most sinister smile Logan could remember seeing in his life. "You all wear badges under your coats. There are at least three 'Pinks' on the second car where my associates and I were seated. I assume there are more in the other two cars."

"You're a smart fella. How do I know you're not working with Ketchum?"

"He thinks we're train robbers, Mister Crowley," Slate said.

"Where did you three get on board?" Logan said. "I walked the train in Lamy and I'd sure as hell remember you."

Crowley said, "We boarded at Romero. Would you like to see our tickets?"

Kharrn rose to his full height, which Logan judged to be near seven feet. "We should get back to the train. We're too exposed here."

"Kharrn has a point," Crowley said.

"All right, but I ain't done with you three," Logan said. He held the lantern out to Abe.

Abe never got the lantern.

Something came out of the dark and grabbed Abe, sank sharp fangs into his neck. Logan stepped back, and the lantern flame guttered, so that the creature latched onto Abe's back was revealed in flickering light.

It bore only a slight resemblance to anything human, having two arms and two legs. But its body was long and gaunt, with feet more like hands. Its skin was mottled and squamous, and its eyes, Good Lord in Heaven, its eyes. They were large and amber colored with red irises. The eyes of a snake. The creature's wide mouth was like that of a snake too, yellow lipped, with prominent fangs.

Logan only had a moment to be shocked because a throng of similar monsters came running from the darkness. He was still holding his Colt and he swung the gun up and fired at the closest creature. Dark blood spurted, but the thing kept coming. He fired again and this time the snake man fell. Another took its place, and he shot that one in the head.

Dave Cobb's pistol hadn't even cleared its holster before he was overrun by three of the things. He went down screaming as their fangs bit into him. Logan fired twice more and then he was out of rounds. Two more of the creatures ran at him, hissing as they came.

Logan threw his arm up, knowing he couldn't ward them off. Then something big moved between Logan and the two monsters. Kharrn swung a massive fist and one of the things went flying. The second snake-man leaped onto the giant, but he caught it by the throat and Logan heard bones snapping. The giant tossed the lifeless creature aside.

"Run for the train," Kharrn said.

Logan did as he was told, but in the light streaming from the passenger cars he could see some of the things had gotten between him and the train. Then he saw Crowley and Slate. Crowley's smile was broader than before, and the man's face looked demonic as he grabbed one of the snake-men and caught it by the throat before it could bite him. That mouth opened impossibly wide, and venom dripped from fangs the size of daggers.

Slate let out a startled noise as one of the snake men pounced on him. He grabbed at the writhing torso of the creature. Its body whipped back and forth, moving in ways no human being ever had. Slate's face shifted into a mask of cold fury, and the albino dug long, thin fingers into the chest of the creature, tearing at scaled skin and splitting the thing's breastbone in half. Even as the nightmare writhed and died, two more came out of the darkness.

Crowley grunted and the snake-man's spine snapped. His strength was not human. He was no larger than Logan, but Crowley broke the monster's back with unsettling ease.

"Come on," Crowley said. "There are too many of them."

Logan couldn't hear what the pale man said, but he saw one of the creatures stagger back, shrieking as its scaly hide burned.

Crowley led the way, and Logan and Slate ran close behind. Kharrn brought up the rear. They reached the front passenger car and just managed to get through the door and close it before the creatures slammed into the panel.

"It won't take them long to get in here," Kharrn said.

"Got something that might help. Jake, get the rifles."

"What's going on?" Jake said. "Is it Ketchum?"

"Just do like I tell you."

Jake went to a long, wooden crate near the back of the car. He unlocked a padlock and threw the lid back. From within the box he withdrew a Winchester repeating rifle and tossed it to Logan. Even as he did so, Logan heard windows shattering. He worked the lever as he turned and fired as one of the snake-men pushed its head through a window. A big chuck of its face was blown away.

"Jesus Christ," Jake said. "What the hell was that?"

Logan could barely hear him for the screaming of the terrified passengers. He opened his coat to show his badge. "We're with the Pinkertons, folks. Everyone get down on the floor and stay out of the way."

He went to the window and shot any of the things he could see in the dim light. They backed off some, but didn't go far. Logan turned to Crowley and the other two. "Can you use one of these?"

"Very well," Kharrn said.

"Passable," said Slate.

Crowley just smiled and nodded.

Logan said, "Give these men rifles, Jake." He looked out the window again. There were dozens of the creatures out there. More than they had ammunition for. The gunfire had cowed them for a moment, but they were creeping forward. He selected one close to the front of the group and took aim.

From beside him, Crowley said, "It's best if you don't excite them."

Logan jumped. "Don't sneak up on me like that. You know what those devils are?"

"Not devils," said Crowley. "They're called Sithana or the children of Sithanas."

"Children of what?"

"Sithanas. One of the outer ones. An old, dark god. They shouldn't be here. They've come up somehow from the depths of the earth, and make no mistake, they'll get over their fear of the guns and then we'll be overrun."

"I'd call you loco, but those things are real. How do you know all this? Who the hell are you?"

"Someone who's been around a long time. I've run into these things before. Whatever drove them to the surface, they're angry and they're hungry. That's a bad combination."

Logan said, "You mean they eat people?"

"If that's all they can get. We have to get out of here."

"Mister, in case you missed it, the track is blocked. You were right. I had eight men on this train in case of a robbery attempt. It's carrying payroll for a cattle outfit in Dodge City. From the look of things, Black Jack Ketchum's gang blocked the tracks just before those monsters found them."

"Then we have to clear the tracks," Crowley said. "And we have to hope the Sithana haven't found the engine's open or we won't have anyone to drive the train."

Kharrn said, "Jonathan, they look like they're massing to attack again."

"Kharrn, if Mister Slate and I can get the track cleared, can you get to the engine and keep the engineer alive?"

"Yes," said Kharrn. "But I'll need my ax. It's in the next car."

Logan heard a hail of gunfire from outside, and glanced out the nearest window. "Goddamn it. They're attacking the second car. My men don't know what's going on."

Kharrn said, "They'll find out soon enough. I'm going out the back door and into the second car."

Crowley said, "Go. I'll lay down covering fire."

Logan got the idea these two men had worked together before. Maybe even served in the military together. The big man hurried down the aisle and unlatched the back door. Crowley followed. When Kharrn ducked through the door, Crowley stepped out onto the small platform at the end of the car. He raised the rifle and fired twice at targets Logan couldn't see.

He *could* see several snake men on the platform of the second car. Kharrn plowed through them, knocking them from the platform, and disappeared into the other car. The man's strength was frightening.

Logan turned to Slate. "Did Kharrn say he was going to get an ax? What the hell does he think he can do with an ax against these things?"

"Wait and see," said Slate. He leaned out the back door of the car and fired once.

* *•*

Kharrn leaped across the narrow space between the two cars and landed on the platform. There were three Sithana outside the door. They were too close for him to bring the Winchester into play, so he slammed into the closest one with one massive shoulder, knocking the hissing creature from the platform. Even as it fell a bullet from the first car took its face away in a blur of red.

He struck another of the things in the face with the butt of the rifle and kicked the other one as it tried to latch onto him. Then he went through the door into the second car. The three Pinkertons and the other passengers hadn't had any way of knowing what was coming and the snake-men had poured in through the doors and windows.

Most of the passengers were already dead and a group of four men were pinned in the back corner by a mob of Sithana. Three of the men had Winchesters identical to the one Kharrn carried and were firing into the writhing mass of snake men. One of the shooters sighted on Kharrn as he came through the door but recognized him as human and shot another Sithana instead.

Kharrn levered a round into the rifle and shot a snake man who was climbing through the window. He moved through the car, levering and firing as he went. The Sithana's numbers seemed endless. The Winchester's fifteen rounds were soon exhausted.

But Kharrn had made it to his seat, reached between it and the wall and extracted a long, flat leather case. Even as he was unlatching the case, a heavy weight landed on his back and then twin points of agony lanced his shoulder. He reached behind him, grabbing the snake-man on his back and threw it over his shoulder. He stomped its head before it could get up again, crushing its skull.

The venom of the Sithana was incredibly powerful and another man would have already been dead, but Kharrn was the paladin of the goddess Samra. Thousands of years in the past he had struck a bargain with the Goddess of Vengeance. She had granted him the ability to heal almost any wound. He wasn't invulnerable, but it took a lot to kill him.

Still, he felt his injuries as any man would and he gritted his teeth as fire ran through his veins, radiating from the bite. He threw back the last latch and opened the case. He sensed, more than saw more of the Sithana closing on him as he pulled his twin-bladed ax from the case.

Kharrn whirled, taking the head from the closest creature, and then disemboweled a second one with his back swing. His vison blurred from the venom, but he waded into the crowd of Sithana, hacking and cutting as he went, painting the walls with brackish blood.

When he reached the men in the corner only two remained standing. Kharrn said, "You're the Pinkertons?"

"Yeah," one of them said. "What in the name of Jesus are these things?"

"I'll explain later. Right now we have to get back to the front car. Your boss is there."

"Logan's still alive," the agent said. "Good to know. Can you buy us a minute to reload?"

Kharrn turned to find more snake men coming through the door. "I can."

* * *

The snake creatures had stopped their assault, but Crowley assured Logan they were merely regrouping. The Sithana never gave up. Logan jumped as the back door swung open, but then he saw it was not more enemies but Kharrn and two of Logan's men, Travis Bedford and Otis Slocum.

Kharrn lumbered down the aisle and Logan saw he now carried a big ax with two blades. Those blades were covered with dark blood and gore. The big man was smeared in blood too, and his blue eyes glittered with something akin to madness.

"Everyone else in the second car is dead," Kharrn said. "I'm going to make a run for the engine."

Crowley said, "The rest of us will try and clear the tracks."

"What about the third car?" Slocum said. "There might be somebody alive back there."

Crowley said, 'There won't be anyone alive in here if we waste any more time. One of you can stay with these passengers, but the rest of us need to move."

"Shouldn't one of us go with Kharrn?" Logan said.

Kharrn said, "You'd just be in my way."

The big man turned and went out the front door into the dark.

Slate, the other freakishly tall man, lowered his head slightly as he slipped from the car, moving into the darkness. Crowley followed on his heels, neither of them stopping as they left the relative safety of the train.

The night was alive with nightmares, and Logan watched on as Slate unloaded shell after shell into the snake-men, barely seeming to waste his time with aiming, merely levering and firing and dropping another of the beasts until his rifle clicked on empty.

Slate reversed his grip on the Winchester, grasping it firmly by the hot barrel, ignoring the heat that must have been enough to scald his palms, and lashed out with the hard wooden butt of the repeating rifle, shattering the skull of one of the creatures as he moved forward. The thing fell to the ground, thrashing as it died.

Crowley moved next to him, working the lever, aiming and firing. He drove the tide one shot at a time and Logan did the same until the rifles were suddenly useless. By that point they had reached the blockade, and Slate hauled a rock that had to weigh as much as he did aside with one arm, using it to smash a Sithana even as the thing came for him.

"They're everywhere!" Slocum's voice broke.

"Stating the obvious is hardly necessary." Crowley reached into his pocket and pulled out a small package of dust. Whatever the fine powder was, he held it in his hands and spoke softly before casting it towards the closest Sithana.

The thing shrieked and retreated as its skin caught fire, fine scales hissing as they burned. It ran towards more of its kind, scattering them as they tried to get away from the overwhelming pain of burning alive. Logan squinted, unable to look away. Each step drove the burning thing deeper into the snake-men coming for them, forcing the others to retreat, if only for a moment.

Slate let out a grunt as four of the snake men tackled him from different directions, driving him to his knees in the darkness. At least two of the things bit into him and he screamed his eyes flying wide and his gaunt face drawing into a mask of pain.

One hand captured a snake-man's face and hauled the creature away from him, slamming the entire length of the thing into the dirt and the railroad tie underneath him.

"Mister Slate!" Crowley moved closer, his smile fading away.

The gaunt man spoke in a language that was little more than gibberish to Logan, and caught the next of the Sithana in both of his hands, screaming at the writhing monster as it snapped at his face.

The snake-man lunged again, its long neck extending, and it would surely have bitten the man in his face had Crowley not lashed out with his rifle, driving the barrel into its eye.

The damned things were everywhere, a wave of serpentine flesh.

Crowley spun and used the barrel of the rifle like the tip of a sword, impaling another snake-man as it came for Logan. The thing shrieked and thrashed and bled even as Crowley threw both it and the rifle backward.

"Watch yourselves! I'd like to live through this affair."

"With apologies, Mister Crowley." Slate's voice was barely audible over the hisses and odd noises from the Sithana. "I find I am distracted." Slate stood back to his full height, one of the snake men on each arm, held back by those pallid hands gripping at flesh. A third of the things had half wrapped itself around him, more like a snake than a man in the way its body moved. It lunged forward and bit into the poor bastard. That was three bites, and he was surely a dead man.

Slate hissed and drove his forehead into the face of the snake-man, his teeth bared, his face once again made into a mask of fury.

Logan spun away and pulled his Colt again. Only six rounds. Still, no choice but to shoot the damned things. They were overwhelmed and there was no two ways about it.

* *

Crowley shook his head and concentrated. The problem with fighting an army was not having an army to fight back with. There were five of them. No. Four. Bedford let out a yelp as he was bitten by a Sithana and already it was too late for him. He'd be dead in a few seconds.

Slate was likely a dead man. He'd taken several bites. There was still too much they did not know about the pale man's abilities, but venom was venom and most of them would be killed by that sort of poison in their systems.

Then Slate said something in a different voice, the voice of the Skinwalker that possessed him, and all three of the Sithana touching him went into seizures. The remaining Pinkertons were too busy to see what happened, but Crowley was not. The snake-men twitched, their mouths snapping open and closed in aberrant fits, and their impossible spines bending in ways that were beyond even their range, and Slate stood to his full towering height, glaring his hatred at the surrounding creatures.

He spread his arms and spoke again, and all around him the Sithana fell to the ground, bodies jerking in fits and spasms.

Crowley took in a deep breath and collected himself. There were more of the damnable things coming, spilling from somewhere below ground. Only death would stop the creatures, and while he could likely make that happen, he could not do it if *he* were dead. Maybe Slate could stop them, but there was no way of knowing if he would. The Skinwalker was an unknown variable. Lucas Slate was a genuinely good man but he was not in control of all his actions.

A gesture, and Crowley's Peacemaker revolvers were in his hands. He aimed and fired, killing a Sithana even as Slate's body spoke in the Skinwalker's voice again and more of the horde staggered back, choking as if they could not breathe. He knew nothing of how the Skinwalker's magic worked, only that it was powerful stuff.

Another bullet and a snake-man fell back, half of its insides painting the air around it.

The Pinkertons fired again and again and then paused to reload.

Slate staggered and said something else, and a pale light surrounded him. From under his dead-white skin lights flashed and burned and Crowley guessed whatever he was doing was meant to fight the venom coursing through his veins because he could see the blood in the man's body glow for a moment.

Enough. "Mister Slate, the rocks, please."

Slate merely nodded, reached for the closest of the boulders, and hurled it from the tracks, knocking down three of the Sithana in the process.

Crowley grinned and looked around briefly.

Slate's voice was impatient. "I could use a hand, Mister Crowley."

"Just as soon as I can, Mister Slate."

Whatever respite he'd hoped for was done as soon as bullets stopped hitting the snake-men. The creatures came forward again, moving with the same simple goal that always seemed to fill them – to eat whatever they could find, to fill their insatiable stomachs with fresh meat.

The Pinkertons did their best to brace for the coming wave, but they wouldn't survive much longer. They did not have the advantages both he and Slate had, or Kharrn for that matter.

"Mister Logan. I need you to ask for my help."

"What?" The man looked at him for scarcely half a second.

"Ask for my help, please. My assistance."

"I'm a mite busy here, Crowley."

Slate grabbed another of the large rocks and pushed it away from the tracks. The stone, roughly the size of a water barrel, rolled and bounced into the crowd of snake-men, knocking several of them over and crushing two. "Just do it, man!"

"Mister Crowley, please help me." He spoke automatically, as he watched that stone come to a halt.

Crowley smiled. He had done it to himself a great deal of time back, and to this date was not sure if he could reverse it. Had made certain he would never abuse his abilities by putting certain limitations in place. Many of his greater powers could not be used unless he was defending himself or coming to the aid of those who asked for his assistance.

He had been asked.

Crowley moved forward and drew forth the power that had been restrained until now. The desert ground contained little of what was needed for raising a crop. But he hardly intended to plant one. He just needed the plants for a few moments.

The seeds had been picked in a vineyard several years earlier, and had been stored away for if he ever wanted to plant grapes. Now was a good enough time. In reality, without his abilities the seeds would likely have been useless.

He spoke the words and cast his seeds then summoned his power and released it.

The vines dug into the ground and rooted themselves even as they exploded into life – a writhing, dance of growth that pushed into the mass of snake-men and caught them, wrapping around thrashing limbs as if they were catching onto trees.

The largest of the stones had been cast aside by Lucas Slate, and Crowley moved quickly to his side, even as the plants tangled the confused Sithana, trapping them in thickening growth and shoving them back as the vines continued to grow at impossible speeds.

They would not last long but hopefully long enough.

"Now, gentlemen! We need to move the rocks now, before they come back."

"What did you—?"

"Now! Move!"

The Pinkertons listened half in shock, but used to following orders, they did as they were told.

Now, if Kharrn could do his part, they might yet get through this.

It was a minute before the tracks were clear enough and Crowley headed for the engine and Kharrn. There was no time to lose, and the horde would be coming back.

* *

A wave of the Sithana came rolling toward Kharrn even as his boots hit the sandy ground. What had made them so ravenous? It didn't matter. He had to get past them.

Most of the effects of the bite had worn off but he didn't relish the idea of being bitten again. Enough bites could kill even him. He hefted the ax and waded into the press of snake-men.

He advanced with great sweeps of the double-bladed ax, smashing and cutting through the horde of creatures like a farmer harvesting his crop. When he had fought in the Third Crusade, both the Crusaders and the Saracens had called him 'the reaper'.

Of course the Sithana had one advantage. Any human foe hoping to attack a man with an ax knew he had to get within the sweep of that weapon, risking injury or death. The snake-like things didn't care.

Kharrn stayed close to the train as he ran past the coal car. That kept the snake men from attacking him on one side. They had to come at him from his left. He was close enough to see the engine now. Could make out some light from the fire in the boiler, but he didn't see a lamp. No engineer or coal man in sight. If they were dead, there was a good chance Kharrn and his companions would be too. Very soon.

A group of five snake-men rushed in. Kharrn killed two but the other three managed to get hold of him and, for a moment, his arms were pinned. He drove an elbow backward into the face of one, dislodging it and freeing a hand. Kharrn wielded the ax one-handed and used the point on the top of the weapon to skewer a second creature. The third drew its head back to bite.

Kharrn dropped the ax, grabbed the snake man by the throat and lifted it off the ground. He turned and threw the creature at two more Sithana who were closing, bowling them over. He snatched up the ax and vaulted into the engine. A bullet whined past his ear.

"Sorry, mister," a voice said from a corner of the engine. "Thought them things had finally come for me."

"You're the engineer?"

"Yeah. Silas Kemp."

"Get ready to get this train moving, Silas," Kharrn said.

"What about—"

"Don't worry about the snake-men. Just do what you need to do."

Kharrn went to the open back of the engine and leaned out. The Sithana had seen him enter, but they had other problems. Crowley and Slate had come upon them from behind and were wading in. Kharrn jumped to the ground but stayed by the engine. They needed Silas Kemp alive.

* * *

Logan's Winchester would never shoot again. The barrel was warped, and the stock was busted and slick with dark blood. He'd have to remember to write Mister Winchester a nice letter and tell him what a fine club his repeating rifle made. He kept making use of it as he followed Slate and Crowley toward the engine.

SNAKE MEN ON A TRAIN

He was trying not to think too much about those two strange men, because to do so would be to risk running mad in the middle of this fight. Later, he could try and reconcile what he had seen with his former idea of how the world worked. Or better yet, he could just get very drunk. Right now he had to stay alive.

Travis Bedford was dead, so now only he and Slocum were left of the Pinkertons from the first two cars. He didn't hold out much hope for his men who had been in the back passenger car.

"Hurry up, Mister Logan," Crowley called. "I see that Kharrn has secured the engine and presumably the engineer. Be a shame to die within sight of your salvation."

Logan didn't answer. Crowley seemed to enjoy being sardonic. There was no point in rising to his baiting. He broke the rest of the stock on a snake-man's head and ran up to join Crowley and Slate at the engine. The ground was littered with dozens of dead monsters. There seemed to be no end to their numbers and no end to the amount the three strangers could kill.

"The track's clear?" Kharrn said.

"Did you have any doubt?" said Crowley.

Kharrn grinned a wolfish grin. "Maybe. Now let's get moving."

As Logan climbed into the engine, the engineer said, "One of you is going to have to shovel coal."

"I'll do it," Logan said, shrugging out of his coat.

"They're coming, Mister Crowley," Slate said, raising one long, thin hand.

Logan looked to where Slate was pointing. A mob of snake-men was rushing toward the engine. Logan would have given his left hand for a gun, but that wasn't an option just then. He heard a long hiss of steam releasing and then the train gave a shudder and began to move.

"Come on," Logan said under his breath, willing the big engine to go faster. "Come on."

The wave of Sithana reached the train. Some of them tried to get into the engine but Kharrn was there to stop them. A greater number leaped onto the coal car and the first passenger car and began to scramble forward. The train was rolling now and beginning to pick up speed.

Kharrn and Slate climbed on top of the coal car and knocked snake-men from the train. Crowley stayed with the engine to keep the engineer safe. The train was moving fast enough now that only a few more of the creatures were able to latch on to the coal car and scramble up. It was starting to look like they might actually make it.

The engineer screamed.

Logan whirled and looked where the terrified man was staring. Something was breaking up through the ground several hundred yards ahead.

Something big.

Logan wanted to scream too, but his voice wouldn't come. The thing from underground was like some huge serpent but covered with writhing tentacles. Logan had seen people eating squid in Chinatown in San Francisco. The thing looked like a cross between a squid and a giant snake. The worst part was it glowed with a bluish-white luminescence. And it stank. Good Lord in Heaven it stank like a thing from the pits.

"Now we know what the Sithana were running from," Crowley said from beside him.

Then there wasn't time to say anything as for the second time that night, the engineer threw on the brakes and the train wheels screeched like tortured souls. There wasn't enough room to fully stop. Logan threw himself from the train just as the front of the engine rammed into the giant monster.

The engine left the rails pulling the coal car with it. The passenger cars jumped the tracks and fell sideways onto the sand, breaking up as they went. Snake-men were flung in every direction. Logan saw Kharrn hit the ground hard, but he staggered to his feet.

Logan yelled, "Kharrn, what is that thing?!"

The big man ignored him. Just hefted the ax and ran towards the monster. The thing was still emerging, pushing up from below until it looked fully as long as the train itself. The monster twisted around, its tentacle-like feelers spreading out. As Logan watched, the wriggling arms began snatching up snake-men and feeding them into its wide maw.

Now that the creature was closer, Logan could see the end of each tentacle held a lamprey-like mouth and the undersides of the feelers were covered with hooked claws. He also realized the thing didn't have eyes. It wasn't meant to be on the Earth's surface.

One of the tendrils came questing toward Kharrn. The big man lopped the end off with the ax. The creature shuddered and three more tentacles struck out like whips, knocking Kharrn from his feet and sending him rolling across the ground. The great beast turned back toward the fleeing snake-men and began scooping them up.

Kharrn was on his feet again. The giant's vitality was truly amazing. Out of the corner of his eye Logan spotted a familiar looking box that had been thrown clear of the train in the crash. He ran over to it and righted it. There were two Winchesters inside. The barrel of one looked to have been bent by the impact, but the other seemed intact. Logan grabbed the gun and checked the action. Everything looked fine. The weapon was loaded but he grabbed up a handful of cartridges from a tin box and stuffed them into the pockets of his coat.

"I know I said I'd give my left hand for a gun, Lord, but we can talk about it later?"

Logan trotted after Kharrn, who was already running back toward the giant monster.

* * *

Lucas Slate crawled from his hands and knees to a standing position. The train's conductor looked to be unconscious or dead, it was hard to say which as the dust settled in the moonstruck darkness.

Not ten feet away, Crowley was already standing, looking at the massive serpentine nightmare that was eating every snake-man around them. Apparently, they were the preferred food of the creature. Slate paused as well for a moment, to look at the thing slithering from the earth, a monumental serpent with tentacles and mouths that defied every belief he had about what was good and right in the world. It was a blasphemy made flesh, and his mind was repulsed by the very notion of its existence.

"What exactly are we seeing, Mister Crowley?"

"I assure you I have no idea, Mister Slate, but I expect we should be killing it, regardless." Crowley stared at the thing, but if he felt the same revulsion as Slate himself, he hid it well. "I'm just not sure how, and frankly, it's making short work of the snake-men."

"I would consider the latter a boon."

"Yes, but if it runs out of snake-men it might decide we'll make a fine repast, and I choose not to be anything's dinner if I can avoid it."

Crowley shook his head, picked his gambler's hat from the dust, set it back on his head absentmindedly, and then started toward the gigantic worm-thing. "Whatever it is, I suggest we cause it some harm, Mister Slate."

Slate nodded and started forward, the song that kept him company at all times growing louder as the Skinwalker tried to decide how to fight a blasphemy that simply should not have existed in the world around them.

One of the heavy tendrils moved in his direction with a lazy sort of grace that belied its speed, and Slate danced back before the mouth at the thing's tip could bite into his flesh. Those jaws snapped shut and opened again a half dozen times with a sound like wet castanets.

When the tendril came for him the second time, Slate felt the Skinwalker he shared space with react. Both of his hands reached out and caught at the slimy-slick hide of the abomination, holding tight even as the damned thing rose into the air and took him with it. Three feet off the ground and his mouth opened to utter words that came from the Skinwalker's endless song. Those words rang through his body like a church bell calling for mass, and the tendril tried to pull back, lifting higher still. Seven feet off the ground and Slate let go of his prize, falling back to the ground before he could be taken higher still.

The tendril blackened where his hands had been, and the eerie luminescence of the thing flickered and faded where he had touched it. Unnatural flesh rotted and decayed in seconds, offering up a stench even worse than the creature emitted on its own. It was the stench of decay, of rot, and Slate watched the decomposing flesh of that limb continued to blacken and weep putrescence.

The whole creature shuddered, but that one limb thrashed as if trying to shake away a fire that had caught it.

Slate felt a grin start on his face and shook his head. The Skinwalker wanted control of him, and he could not allow that, dared not give in to the temptation for fear he would never find himself in control of his fate again.

Jonathan Crowley could have used sorcery but chose not to. He moved his hands and the Peacemakers he hid away were suddenly there, as if drawn from a hat by a magician. The weapons fired and blew holes into the hide of the creature, but it barely seemed to notice, far more offended, apparently, by what Slate had done and by the damage caused by Kharrn's massive ax.

Crowley frowned and sighed, and the weapons vanished as the man considered his options.

Rot raced along the tendril Slate had touched, sliding along the length at a furious pace, but the creature was not so easily vanquished. Two of the other tendrils reached over and tore the limb away before the corruption could spread to the rest of the creature. It was either instinct, or the monster was smarter than Slate had hoped.

Before Crowley could attack, one of the writhing limbs turned toward him and he was forced to retreat, whatever plans he was making immediately set aside as he avoided the attempt to bite deep into his flesh.

Crowley stepped back farther, moving over the debris and

wreckage of the capsized train engine. His eyes stared at the coal spilled from the bin and he looked back at the creature, then back to the coal.

A moment later he gestured and spoke softly; a stream of coal nuggets rose into the air and hurled themselves toward the towering snake-worm-nightmare. As they launched toward the beast, the coal burst into streaks of burning fuel that hit the creature and bounced in some cases, and stuck in others, searing flesh and igniting it.

The fires would have been more impressive if they did not seem like mere pinpricks against the sheer size of the monster.

"It's not enough, Mister Crowley!"

"I am aware of that, Mister Slate, but I'm hoping to distract this thing from Kharrn and from you. I should rather not lose good companions today."

"How do we get rid of this thing, sir? We need to cast it from our world."

"I'm not sure if we can. First, we have to reach the point where it comes into our world and that seems to be far below ground."

Kharrn wreaked havoc with his ax and Slate considered where best to strike the thing again assuming he could get close enough. The creature was bloodied and burnt and hardly seemed to care in the least. It was massive, and there seemed no end to it. A great loop of the writhing body slammed into the ground and the massive tip of the body turned and drove down toward the ground as if to swat them all aside.

The beast turned toward Slate and lunged, shoving earth aside as it came for him. He could no sooner dodge the gigantic thing than he could a runaway train.

• • •

Logan thought he had exhausted his capacity for disbelief. But now, seeing what Crowley, and particularly what the man called Slate had done, he knew he had to be going loco. But even they couldn't stop that big bloody bastard of a snake. The thing was just too huge. Even setting it on fire hadn't...

An image flashed in Logan's mind. When he had walked the length of the train back in Lamy he'd looked in both cargo cars. One of the cars held several crates addressed to the Cripple Creek Mining Company. Logan turned from following Kharrn to certain death and started back toward the train.

Most of the snake-men had fled as the giant serpent had appeared, but the ones that were left were just as bad tempered as ever and they charged at Logan as he ran. He levered the Winchester and fired again and again until he bought himself a little time and room.

Logan found the right car and thanked God it wasn't on its side like the others. He shot the padlock off the sliding side door and rolled the door aside. He made a quick look behind him but none of the Sithana were close, so he climbed into the car. Considering what he was looking for, he didn't want to light a match, but he had no choice. Time was running out.

The flickering light fell on the box he was looking for. Logan blew out the match and grabbed the box of dynamite by feel.

*　*　*

Kharrn's ax was lodged in the side of the great serpent when it wheeled back toward Slate and for a moment he was dragged along. Then the blade tore free, and he dropped to the ground. Slate was off balance and wasn't going to get clear of the monster's descending maw.

Kharrn threw the ax to the ground and sprinted into the snake's path. He caught Slate by the collar and dragged the pale man clear just as the massive beast's mouth snapped shut. The two men went rolling.

"My thanks, Mister Kharrn," Slate said in his ragged voice.

"I keep telling you, it's just Kharrn."

He rolled to his feet before Slate could answer and took off to retrieve his ax. Kharrn had been carrying it for the better part of twelve thousand years and was loathe to part with it. But the great serpent wasn't done. For something so huge it could turn quickly, and it seemed determined to reach Slate. Perhaps something in the pale man's eldritch makeup drew the thing to him. Perhaps it was just a vindictive son of a bitch.

Several of the thing's tentacles reached out. Without his ax, Kharrn had no real way to ward them off. He prepared to try anyway.

At that moment Kharrn heard a loud roaring sound and felt a shudder run along the length of the serpent. The thing twisted and went in another direction. Kharrn saw the Pinkerton, Logan, lighting a stick of dynamite from the end of a cigar. He had apparently already hurled one such missile.

He threw the dynamite as the serpent's head swung his way. The monster flinched, but its mass and momentum carried it forward, and truly, the dynamite didn't seem to have done it much harm. Logan managed to leap aside at the last possible moment. He rolled down a rocky slope and lay still. Kharrn ran toward the fallen man. As he reached Logan, Crowley ran up as well.

Kharrn checked Logan's pulse. "He's still alive."

Crowley said, "He had the right idea. Just not the fire power."

"Let's see what we can do about that."

Kharrn ran up the slope and found an entire box of dynamite. There were probably twenty sticks of the explosive, give or take a few. He lifted the box. "See if you can get that thing's attention."

"I can," whispered Slate. He had arrived without a sound. "It seems fond of me."

The pale man raised his hands and a baleful glow played about his fingers, spiraling upward like the light from a thousand corpse candles. Kharrn grimaced. He had traveled with Slate and fought beside him, but sometimes he still felt uneasy around the man.

They heard a hissing roar and then the great serpent came hurtling out of the darkness, drawn by Slate's light or just his presence. Kharrn saw the maw they had only recently evaded, open wide.

"Going to need some fire, Jonathan," Kharrn said.

He hefted the box and hurled it down the serpent's oncoming throat. Out of the corner of his eye, Kharrn saw Crowley gesture with one hand and mumble some words in an ancient tongue. Then the serpent's jaws closed over the trio and a half second later the world turned into a wave of roaring fire.

 ● ●●

When Ben Logan awoke it was daylight. His head felt like he'd been on a three-day drunk. He sat up, looked around, and saw the wreckage of the train all around him. He doubted there were any survivors on the cars, but he would look to be sure just as soon as the world stopped spinning.

"Still with us I see, Mister Logan," he heard Jonathan Crowley say. He turned his head to find Crowley, Kharrn and Slate standing a few feet away. They looked considerably worse for the wear. Their clothes were tattered and even looked scorched in places.

The giant man tossed Logan a canteen. "We found water. That should hold you until someone from the railroad gets here. There's some food piled over there in the shade."

"You're leaving," Logan said.

Crowley said, "We were on our way to Dodge City. I suppose we'll continue on. From there Kharrn is heading east. Mister Slate and I are undecided."

Logan got painfully to his feet. "You have to tell me, what were those things?"

Crowley said, "The Sithana are denizens of a subterranean world. The great serpent is their most dangerous enemy. This is the first time either has been to the surface in centuries. Just an unpleasant quirk of fate we were there when it happened. The snake-men have gone back below. The serpent is dead."

"You killed it?"

"We followed your plan," Crowley said. "We just enlarged upon it a bit."

"No one else survived," Kharrn said. "Don't waste your time looking. We already did." The big man slung a canteen and a bag of supplies over his shoulder. "Take care, Logan."

Slate nodded and Crowley just smiled his unsettling smile. The three men turned and began to walk away.

"Wait," Logan said. "Who are you? What are you?"

Crowley looked back over his shoulder. "Someone you'd best forget. Farewell, Mister Logan."

UNFINISHED BUSINESS

Benjamin Spada

It really got under Woods' skin when tasked with assassinating the same target twice. Especially since the first attempt had, by all accounts, been a success.

He wasn't so naïve as to say he was proud of his line of work, but he continued to answer the call twenty years on because it was a job that needed doing. Woods was one of the longest serving operators of the Black Spear Initiative – America's deadliest black-ops unit. He had acquired some professional pride in his skillset, which was why his current assignment was a bit of a blow to his ego.

Two decades with the Initiative had brought Woods face to face with everything from soldiers enhanced with bleeding-edge cybernetics, to rogue scientists funded by doomsday cults to engineer their own plagues. Bottom line: Woods' threshold for believable was a few tiers above most.

Then the boss told him black-market geneticist Jasper Ulrich was still alive. Ulrich was a modern-day Dr Moreau who spliced together animals to make monstrous guard dogs for criminal underworld VIPs. Living designer weapons customized to serve whatever perverse desire the buyer had. Billionaire heiress's had purse dogs; cartel lords had Ulrich's beasts.

A double-tap through Ulrich's heart and a kill-shot through the man's throat had seen it done. But if the boss said Ulrich was still alive, then Woods was less concerned with figuring out how and more concerned with correcting that oversight.

He'd packed a bag, loaded up, and punched out.

Six hours on the road and Woods pulled over to grab a coffee from a roadside diner. It was the perfect spot: hole in the wall, nondescript, and best of all no CCTV cameras. Black Spear's skill at erasing its operators from security footage was unparalleled, but Woods preferred to avoid the issue entirely.

Latest intel had Ulrich holed up in an old ghost town called Jericho Springs. There was nothing special about it. In this area of the southwest there were dozens of similar prospects which'd been abandoned over a century ago. Satellite footage of the town showed a semi-trailer with four large cargo containers, which meant Ulrich hadn't yet had time to offload his latest product.

The *ching* of boot spurs snapped Woods from his thoughts and to the man walking through the front door of the diner. It wasn't uncommon to spot a cowboy enthusiast in these parts of the country, but this particular person was pulled right from a spaghetti western. From the wide-brimmed hat dipped low, duster coat, to the matching deep-red jacquard vest and silk ascot tie. His black boots *chinged* with every steady step.

The stranger sauntered towards Woods, raised his chin slowly to give him a steely-eyed stare, then eased uninvited into the seat opposite.

"Major," the cowboy said. "I reckon you and I may be after the same man."

Nobody should have known he was here, or why, and his military rank hadn't been public record in decades. Refusing to let his face betray his surprise, Woods took a long sip from his coffee while his other hand went to the .45 semi-automatic holstered on his hip. "I think you may have me mistaken with someone else, friend." He was firm, but polite. No reason to instigate a confrontation. Should one occur, his .45 would be ready regardless.

The stranger steepled his hands on the table and gave Woods a wide smile that showed both rows of polished whites. "We can be friends. If you play it right, that is."

Woods knew how to gradually ease the pressure onto the pistol's hammer to avoid that telltale click, but instead let it be loud enough for the two of them to hear.

"Easy now," said the stranger, holding up both hands. "I come in peace."

"And you can go in peace, too. I'm just trying to enjoy my coffee and we can both be on our separate ways."

"Yep, except those separate ways have a common destination." The stranger twirled his fingers, then out of thin air produced a nickel and casually began to polish it on his shirt. It was a cute trick. He gave Woods a wink. "Tell you what: call Rourke, tell him you've got Ethan Cross sitting at your table. He'll vouch for me."

More and more unsettling. Name-dropping Black Spear's head honcho was indicative that Cross was read in on some pretty exclusive circles. Without taking his eyes or pistol off Cross, Woods pulled his phone out and called the boss.

Rourke answered on the first ring. "Status update?"

"I'm about twenty miles from Jericho Springs, but I've run into a bit of a complication."

There was a pause. Complications in their line of work rarely meant anything good. "Explain."

"Got a gentleman across from me who might be hunting the same game. Seems to fancy himself something of a Doc Holliday, says you know him. One Ethan Cross, sir."

Another pause, longer this time. Which was telling considering how rarely Rourke was ever surprised by anything. "He have an old six-shooter with ivory grips?"

Cross parted his duster like he'd heard the question and revealed the pistol in question in a sun-tanned holster on his hip. Sure enough it had a pearl-white ivory grip with a gold scorpion filigree laid into the handle.

"Indeed, sir."

"That's him. Let him tag along, no point trying to shake that one."

Once more Cross seemingly heard Rourke and his smile spread even wider. "Told you we'd be friends, amigo."

* * *

"We'll take your car," Cross said, snapping and pointing to the sedan.

Woods half expected to see a black horse tied up out front of the diner when they walked out, and was partially disappointed that there wasn't one. "What's your business with Ulrich?" he asked as they reached the car. Cross dodged the question, so Woods hit the lock button on the key fob just as the man reached for the door.

Cross grunted at the inconvenience then tilted his head. "That's real mature, Major."

"Ulrich."

"Right. Mister dog-trainer-creature-maker extraordinaire. He's fixin' to sell some rather volatile products what don't belong to him. Said products' rightful owner is having me bring him in so he can answer for what he's done."

Woods unlocked the car and slid into the driver's seat. "We appear to be at odds then, Mr Cross. I'm aiming to put him down, not bring him in."

The cowboy chuckled to himself and plopped into the passenger seat. "You know, I think by the end of this there will be a way we can both walk away satisfied. Call it a gut feeling."

Woods found the comment curious, but he'd kill Ulrich either way and then Cross would have to answer to whoever his employer was. Which also sparked another question. "So you're what, an independent contractor?"

"Of a sort," Cross answered. "I've helped Rourke a few times hunting down some folks that not even you people had any luck spotting."

"Yeah? Maybe you can tell me how you found me."

"Anyone's easy to find if you know how to look."

"I'm really good at not leaving a trail."

"Well, I'm better'n most at finding one."

The engine turned over and Woods steered the car to the highway, kicking up a cloud of dust as they headed for Jericho Springs. This hit was supposed to be a solo run, and Ethan Cross' inclusion was a ten-gallon hat-sized pain in that plan. Woods was in no mood to babysit anyone, nor was he willing to compromise the mission if the cowboy got himself hurt. Or worse. He knew too well what Ulrich's beasts could do.

UNFINISHED BUSINESS

As the stretch of miles to their destination closed, Woods once more found himself thinking back to the events that led to him killing Ulrich. Or, attempted to kill rather.

Two months prior, and clear on the other side of the world, Woods' team was tasked with eliminating a Russian oligarch. The mission itself was straightforward: stealth infil, take down the target, and exfil.

The only problem were the guard dogs.

No one could've expected a dog the size of a Doberman to have the bite force of a gorilla, or that they'd be resistant to tranq darts. Woods' lieutenant, Hudson, learned that the hard way. A single bite to the leg had crushed his tibia and nicked the Popliteal artery. He bled out in under a minute. Woods had been gunning with Black Spear for twenty years; Hudson had been at his side for fifteen of them.

It took two loads of buckshot to put the dog down.

The after-action report determined that finding the dog's source was a new priority. He took his men's lives personally. When backtracking, the dog's bill of sale led to Dr Jasper Ulrich, and Woods accepted the assignment eagerly with one condition: he'd do the deed alone.

As the geneticist got into his car Woods had come out of nowhere, masked by the shadows, steps hidden by a heavy downpour, and fired three rounds through the windshield. The first two were a hammer-pair that landed mere millimeters apart over the man's heart, the third to the carotid. The resulting blood spatter painted what was left of the windshield red; Ulrich's limp feet on the gas sent his car rolling into the water nearby.

Woods had replayed that moment a thousand times in his head since told of the botched job. His .45 had a twelve-round capacity. He could've burned the remaining nine into Ulrich's body to make sure the job was done. Hell, that close a distance he probably could have put them all in Ulrich's skull just to be certain.

This time he wouldn't make any mistakes. For Hudson, there would be no half-measures.

The car lurched to a halt and Woods put it in park. They'd stopped about half a klick from Jericho Springs so they could infiltrate the ghost town unseen. The sun was growing low but hadn't quite set. The waning light would make their approach that much easier.

He hopped out and popped the trunk. Cross took a peep inside and whistled a note of appreciation. From the trunk Woods retrieved a ballistic vest and threw it over his t-shirt, then stashed three grenades in pouches along his belt. Two were flashbangs, the last a frag. There was time for covert, and there was time for overt. Out here in the middle of nowhere with no civilians nearby, Woods wasn't too concerned with kicking things up a notch.

With that in mind he grabbed a compact AUG bull-pup assault rifle and stuffed two extra magazines into pockets on his vest. Ulrich's previous creations were tough bastards to put down, and Woods wasn't about to take any chances. While he was gearing up, Cross seemed content to meticulously load six rounds into his revolver and give the cylinder a spin.

"That all you're bringing?" asked Woods. "Little out of style."

"At least I know mine will work," said Cross, pushing the brim of his hat up with the tip of his barrel. It was an odd thing to say, but Woods knew revolvers had the advantage of never jamming.

Not a word was spoken as the two crested the hill overlooking the long-deserted town. The sun was strategically at their backs; if anyone were to look up, they'd be blinded by the light before they could spot either Woods or Cross. A dead tree was nearby, and Woods leaned into it for cover, then brought the scope of his rifle to his eye.

The semi-truck and its cargo were still in the center of the town remnants, but it was now joined by a few high-end SUVs. *Potential buyers?* He made a mental estimate of how many shooters might be below based upon the vehicles, and was all the more grateful he'd came loaded to bear.

"Any sight of him?" Cross asked. He polished that same nickel from the diner on his shirt. It was a queer sort of nervous tic.

Woods scanned through broken windows and along dust-covered balconies. Nothing. "Not yet, but if I were hiding that would be my spot." He pointed to the old frontier church that lay at the end of the town strip. "Clear view of main avenues of approach, solid sniper's perch in the tower. Yeah, that's where I'd be."

Cross spat on the ground. "Well, shit-fire, let's get this party cooking."

Woods covered Cross with his rifle as the cowboy descended upon the town. Cross hugged tight to what was once a general store, then waved Woods down. With each step closer to the town, the more uneasy he got. A wretched knot twisted itself up in his gut and refused to let go. It was an unfamiliar feeling, but undeniable.

Then there was the smell. Like ground meat, gone bad. And something else. *Rotten eggs?* Whatever the foulness, it drifted across the wind and made Woods gag. He choked the reflex back and gave Cross a querying look. The gunslinger was unfazed and pointed them both on towards the truck.

The stench grew worse as they neared. Woods rounded the other side of the truck, expecting to find Ulrich's buyers unloading the cargo, but instead simply found pieces. That was the only way to describe what was left. To call them dead bodies would've been an exaggeration of how meager the remains were. There was a lower leg wearing a fine Italian leather shoe near one of the SUVs. Two fingers and a thumb were all that remained of a hand near the truck's tire. Scraps of shredded clothing here and there. Everywhere, blood.

Blood, blood, blood.

If there was a message the gore was painting, then Woods was dumb to it. He plucked the piece of hand up. Bite marks.

"Shit," said Cross from behind him. "Now this here is what we call a complication."

Woods followed the man's gaze: all four of the cargo containers were open and empty.

"Ulrich's latest are an improvement," Woods said, examining the leg. "This went straight through the muscle and tibia in a single bite. That's... that's one hell of a bite."

Woods tried to keep his head in the game but couldn't help thinking of Hudson's own leg.

"Major, I don't know how keen you are on shooting dogs but I reckon this might be an exceptional circumstance."

Woods gave him an agreeing nod. Forcing the seasoned soldier to put down dogs, however mutated and unnatural, was but another reason he was looking forward to sending Ulrich to the undertaker. Though more and more it was looking like it'd be a closed casket funeral once he was done with the geneticist.

That rotten smell grew stronger, and Woods knew it meant one of the beasts was close. The stink was a combination of wet dog, freshly spilled blood, and some earthy scent he couldn't place. But it was getting nearer.

Then came the bark. Except to call it a bark wasn't quite doing it justice. Its savagery was more like if a lion and a pitbull had been crossbred. Short, angry roar-barks that resonated through the town as if Jericho Springs was one chaotic tuning fork. Woods became painfully aware of how tactically undesirable their present location was: smack dab in the center of the town.

All thought for strategy disappeared when the thing lumbered into view from behind the saloon. It stood five feet at the shoulder, nearly twice that in length. Its body was packed with muscle, and its grayish-black skin was littered with patches of long fur. Woods couldn't even determine what breed it had once been. The head and jaws were huge and wide as a bulldog's, but the snout was too long and its ears were almost wolf-like with how pointed they were.

Thick ropes of saliva dripped from its maw, and in its jaw was an entire human head. The monstrous hound tossed its head back and swallowed the thing whole. Like a treat. Then Woods saw its eyes for the first time. They were dark but rimmed in red like smoldering coals. When it saw him, those eyes went wide with hunger.

The brief moment of shock passed, and Woods' training took over. He brought his rifle up and fired a three-round burst into the beast's face. The bullets punched into the dog's head, and seemed to cause about as much pain as bee stings.

It charged.

Woods fired again and again. Small holes pockmarked the dog's face, and sickly yellowish fluid spilled from the wounds. Its jaws opened wide. Those fangs would've been more at place in a dinosaur's skull than any modern animal. Refusing to panic, he adjusted his aim and the beast's eye exploded. This time it staggered, but only briefly.

It pounced for him, and the only thing going through Woods' mind was doing whatever he could to protect himself from those saber-like teeth. He threw his rifle up to save his face, and the jaw snapped shut with the force of a sprung beartrap. The beast slammed him to the ground, its full weight pushing every breath from his lungs.

Woods kept the rifle wedged between the beast's teeth as it worried its head back and forth. The metal strained against those powerful jaws, strained and impossibly began to bend. He knew it wouldn't hold, so when the beast shook its head once more to the left, he slipped and rolled to the right.

He came to a rest on one knee, drawing his pistol. The beast's remaining eye glared at him, then its jaws crunched down on Woods' rifle and rent it in half. He tried to run the numbers on what kind of bite-force it would take to accomplish such a feat, then tried to deduce what type of splicing Ulrich could've used to create it, but then let go of any desire to figure it out and instead just wanted to end it.

Woods fired five shots into the dog's face.

If he'd thrown marshmallows at it instead, it would've had the same effect. That roar-bark came again. So loud, and so deep, Woods could feel it boom against his chest. Again, it leapt at him with hungry jaws, but Cross' .44 revolver roared louder as the cowboy fired a single shot.

The round struck dead center between its eyes, and the beast skidded to a halt at Woods' feet. It trembled, one monstrous claw pawing at its head, then shuddered to a dead rest. Amber blood dribbled to sizzle against the desert floor like hot grease in a pan. That sulfur smell burned the inside of his nose.

"Told you mine'd work," said Cross, offering Woods a hand to his feet.

"I've put Ulrich's work down before," he said. "This is different."

"New dog, new tricks," said Cross with a laugh. "Wait... that's not the saying?"

Woods leaned towards the corpse that was quickly turning an ashen gray. Not for the first time he felt Cross knew more than he'd been letting on this whole time. "Is that the trick, bullet has to be right between the eyes?"

"Something like that," he said. "Tell you what, hand me that smoke wagon."

Woods thought about it for a second, then cautiously handed Cross the pistol. The man hummed to himself as he ejected the magazine, then whipped a small leather-wrapped bottle from his pocket and proceeded to drip it onto the tips of the bullets.

"That'll put a little extra pep in your step," said Cross. "We'll need it. Four crates, only one dog. Easy math, amigo."

Woods slapped the fluid-tipped rounds back into his gun and fed one into the chamber. "You coat your rounds with some kind of venom? Is that it?" Whatever Cross had laced his bullets with was impossible to identify. It had no scent, no color, and was as viscous as water.

"Ah hell, Major," said Cross, "quit worrying about what and how and just appreciate the end result."

The strangeness of his companion was beginning to bother him. The series of bestial roars that boomed into the air were far more bothersome, though. Those sounds had no rightful place in this world. Whatever Ulrich had birthed had gone beyond science. The three remaining hounds were an affront to every law of nature.

"We can make our way to the church," suggested Woods. "Ulrich always had a safeguard built in using pheromones or something. The hounds won't harm him, which makes his little holy shelter over there just as friendly to us."

"Pheromones? Shit, Major, you sure he doesn't just have a dog whistle?"

The sound of heavy footfalls sent both men back-to-back. Something was just on the other side of the buildings, circling around them.

"Watch your foot," Cross said.

Woods saw his boot-tip nearing the pooling yellow blood of the dead dog. A moment ago he'd thought it sounded like hot grease, but now he saw it hissed more like battery acid. He pulled his shoe away from the blood, not willing to find out just how similar it was.

"It seems Dr Ulrich has watched one too many Ridley Scott movies," Woods said. "Or was that your boss' idea?"

Unsurprisingly, Cross didn't answer.

God that stench, though. Somehow that foul blood smelled worse with the dog being dead. It was as if every whiff clotted in his nostrils and coated his throat.

A guttural growl from above showed Woods' mistake. Gobs of spit trailed from a second hound perched atop the truck beside them and splattered onto Cross' shoulder.

Cross shouted some indiscernible curse as he turned, firing from the hip. The round ricocheted off the truck as the hound leapt. The beast bulled at Cross before the man could adjust his aim, and the gunslinger was flung onto his backside. The scorpion-handled six shooter flew from his hand.

The second hound whirled on Woods. Everything had happened in the span of half a heartbeat, and all within arm's reach of each other. He backpedaled to create some distance. Needed a clean shot for Cross' venom to do its trick.

But that monster was too fast. It snapped its head to the side, and its impossibly large jaws bit down on Woods' entire torso.

Its mouth entirely engulfed his chest. He was held between it like a pooch would carry some small toy. The only thing that saved him was his body armor, but the plates themselves crushed his ribcage like a vice.

It thrashed him about like a ragdoll. Woods fired two wild rounds, and managed to clip it in the foot. Two toes were blown off and the startled hound threw him through the air. He soared right for a window to the saloon, and tucked himself into a ball as he crashed right through. Shards of glass raked across his forearms as he protected his face, and he landed hard.

Woods scrambled back to his shaking feet with gun in hand. Stars swam in his eyes. He forced his vision to focus on his iron sights, lining up the posts as Ulrich's hound roared. The dog launched like a missile through the window. Any thought of ammo conservation evaporated. He wasn't sure how many times he fired. Four, five?

Yellow, syrupy blood splattered onto the dusty wooden floor, and the dog landed as nothing but dead weight. Woods sidestepped. The planks groaned beneath the dog, and smoke sizzled as its blood ate into the wood until it finally burned through and fell beneath the floorboards.

Two to go.

He took just a moment to catch his breath. The riddle of Ulrich's return was something Woods couldn't shake. Perhaps he'd mastered genetic engineering more than they'd thought. Could the Ulrich he'd shot and thought dead have been a clone? Seemed unlikely. Each answer to the riddle seemed equally unbelievable. Occam's Razor demanded that Woods must have missed his kill shot, and the blood spatters were somehow faked.

As he stepped back outside, he spotted the third hound making a mad sprint for Cross, who crawled to his six shooter. Woods aimed, but three rapid gunshots from behind him sent him scuttling for cover.

"Stop destroying my work!" Jasper Ulrich shouted from the church.

Ulrich was a scientist not a marksman, and Woods knew the hound was the priority. As Ulrich screamed and raved something about sending him to hell, Woods lobbed one of his flash-bangs through the church's window. Ulrich would have Woods' full attention soon enough.

The soldier was back on his feet running for Cross when the stun grenade went off. Ulrich yelped in surprise. The brief reprieve in gunfire gave Woods the time he needed to close the distance and fire at the third hound. The bullet took its ear off and left a burning streak across its face. When he steadied his aim to put one between the hound's eyes his hammer fell on an empty chamber.

Shit.

The hound forgot about the cowboy, and went for the soldier. Woods didn't attempt to reload. His spare magazines hadn't been laced with Cross' venom. Would've been a waste of lead. Instead, he stared the beast down as it charged. They played the most terrifying game of chicken imaginable. If he made his move too soon, then the dog would simply tear him to shreds. Too late? The dog would simply tear him to damned shreds. There was a single moment when his plan would work.

And there it was.

Yellow spittle hissed against the ground as the hound dove through the air. Ulrich's monsters had jaws wide enough to swallow a grown man's head whole, which meant they were plenty wide to swallow a frag grenade. He dropped out of the way at the last second. The grenade went down the beast's gullet, and Woods let momentum roll him away as the internal fuse burned down.

The explosion blew the monster in half and a blast of heat buffeted Woods' back. The dog's legs and bottom half were mulched into an amber-tinted mist, its forelegs and head hurtled towards his feet.

Woods took the time to reload and look down at the muti-lated third dog.

"No…" he breathed.

It was *still* alive.

It crawled towards him leaving a yellow slug trail of its own blood behind. The dirt sizzled and burned with every miserable splatter of blood.

Cross shouted for Woods to get out of the way.

Which was when the fourth and final dog came out of nowhere. Teeth like spears sank deep into Cross' thigh. The man's scream was horrible. The blood that gushed forth and instantly soaked his pantleg down to his boot was worse. There was so much of it, and so quick, that Woods knew the cowboy had maybe seconds before he'd bleed out. Then it wasn't Cross lying there bleeding out, but Hudson from two months prior, dying all over again. Less than a minute was all it had taken, and that was from a far less vicious bite.

Woods blinked, and was Cross again, the dog whipping the cowboy about, tearing the leg to ruins. It finally threw him hard against the semi-truck and lowered its head to take another taste of his flesh. Cross was one tough son of a bitch though, because somehow, he'd held onto his gun the entire time.

"You go straight to hell!" Cross pulled the trigger and blew the top of the dog's skull off.

Woods ran over, sliding to a stop like a player stealing home plate, and used his belt to cinch a tourniquet above Cross' femoral. "You still with me?"

The cowboy answered by cracking off a shot to finish the bisected third dog. "Fit as a fiddle, Major."

Woods helped carry Cross to the side of the building catty-corner to the church.

"He in there?"

"He was a second ago when he was shooting at me."

Cross studied the church's many windows, then winced in pain and eased back to the ground. He'd lost a dangerous amount of blood. The fact the cowboy was even conscious was impressive enough.

"You're going to have to go in there alone," muttered Cross. He reloaded his revolver with surprisingly dexterous fingers, then gave Woods a wink. "Don't you worry, I'll be sure and give you some good covering fire before I keel over."

Woods readied his .45, nodding to his companion. Then he was up and running. Cross fired behind him. The windows shattered. A silhouette inside ducked away. Then Woods was crashing through the doors.

Ulrich shot at him from deep in the church, and Woods slid behind one of the pews for cover.

"I'm not going back!" Ulrich screamed. The wood of the pew chipped near Woods's head as Ulrich shot twice more.

"Don't worry." He fired blindly over his cover. "I'm not planning on bringing you in alive."

It seemed a foul deed to murder a man in church, but Woods had never been very religious. And he wasn't about to let Ulrich get away again on account of hallowed ground that hadn't been used in a hundred years. He stood, ready to finish the job with a single shot, and instead took one to the chest.

The bullet knocked the wind out of him, and he sputtered for breath as he fired wildly to send Ulrich back to cover. Woods went down to a knee, Ulrich hunkered behind an old bench.

"I've got something for you, asshole," Woods wheezed, clutching his chest.

The sound of rolling metal echoed through the church, and Ulrich looked curiously at the object sent his way: the last flashbang.

Woods squeezed his eyes shut and jammed his fingers in his ears. The flashbang went off with a deep *BOOM*, and Woods forced himself to seize the advantage. He pressed forward through the smoke, eager to line up the shot on the disoriented geneticist. Except the smoke cleared, and said geneticist had also been moving towards Woods.

They stood in the center of the church. Both caught off guard as they found themselves mere inches apart, guns pointed at each other's faces. But both had the same problem: their guns were empty.

Woods and Ulrich ejected their magazines. The span of a single heartbeat stretched for what seemed like minutes as both empties clattered to the church floor. They reached for spare magazines. Movements nearly tandem.

Jasper Ulrich was an unequaled bioweapons geneticist, but a quickdraw he was not. The fresh round slamming home into the chamber of Woods' pistol was the sweetest sound imaginable. Just as Ulrich finished reloading, Woods pulled the trigger. Ulrich let out a startled yelp as the bullet took off his thumb, causing the gun to fall to the ground. Woods fired twice more, aiming for spots that wouldn't be protected if Ulrich was wearing a bulletproof vest. A bullet each hit Ulrich's left and right shoulder and rewarded Woods with a spray of blood.

There was no anger in the way he gunned down his target. No warrior fury burning within. Instead, he was cold. Professional. Ulrich's life was nothing more than an outstanding debt in Woods' ledger, and each pull of the trigger was a precise check in the box for completion.

Another shot to the gut and Ulrich stumbled backwards. Woods walked him down, putting three more dead center. Each shot made Ulrich jerk and contort with every impact. No vest this time. The man's shirt was completely stained with blood but Woods wasn't letting up. He adjusted his aim, and put a double-tap right between Ulrich's eyes. The geneticist's neck snapped back, and his body toppled through the church window to the dirt outside.

Woods stepped out and took a long look. There were no last, desperate gasps for air. No final defiant curse flung with his dying breath. The target was down, and that was that. The bullet wounds were real. No amount of makeup could've faked the brains leaking out the back of his skull. All the same, he emptied the clip into the dead man's head and turned it into a hollowed crater of bone and red mash. No half-measures this time.

Woods let the feeling of closure wash over him, then nodded to himself. If there really were greener pastures up in the clouds, he hoped Hudson was looking down from them and nodding in approval. An obnoxious whistle ripped him from his brief moment of peace.

"Well, well, well. That there is one very dead Jasper Ulrich," said Cross with a click of his tongue. His boot spurs *chinged* as he walked closer, his gait surprisingly stable considering the bite he'd taken.

"Sorry about that," said Woods. "I know you were supposed to bring him back, but I told you what I was here for."

The old-styled bounty hunter didn't say a word. Just continued that quiet whistle of his, not unlike a tradesman busy at work. Cross knelt beside Ulrich's corpse, which was a curious thing to do, since it wouldn't take an autopsy to determine cause of death.

"If it's any consolation, you *did* kill him that night. Hope that soothes your ego, amigo."

What happened next defied all reason. Despite years of training, despite witnessing first-hand the full catalog of unbelievable, in this instance Woods could do nothing but stare.

Cross grabbed Ulrich's shadow in one hand, and lifted it up as if it were as material as a shroud. The shadow became a living thing, flailing in his grip with smoky, ethereal limbs. There was a sound like the most tortured screaming he'd ever heard, the type of scream you can only pry from a man with barbed wire and a blowtorch, but in an impossible way it was as faint as the wind grazing Woods' ears.

Cross tipped his hat at Woods like this was nothing strange at all. "I told you we could both walk away satisfied, Major. I appreciate the assist with this. Truly. The boss wasn't too pleased when this fella made off with his dogs. I'll put in the good word with him, because I'd venture to say there's a debt for a favor of sorts. You ever find yourself in a bind, I'm eager to dance another song with you."

With that, he gave a wink and flipped that shiny nickel he'd been polishing. Woods caught it in one hand, looked at it closely and found it really was nothing more than a nickel. Nothing special at all. The smell of burning tickled Woods' nose. He looked back from the coin, but he was alone.

Ethan Cross and Jasper Ulrich had vanished. A small patch of scorched dirt where the cowboy had stood was the only thing that remained. Woods couldn't make sense of it, nor was he eager to stick around any longer to try. By now the sun had gotten really low. The last thing he wanted was to be anywhere near this madness come nightfall.

On his way out of town he searched for the dogs' corpses. Black Spear would want samples. There should've been something. Bones, maybe, if that acidic blood of theirs had eaten the rest away. Instead there were patches of ash that stank of sulfur.

"To hell with this…"

Woods made good time getting back to the car. It made for faster traveling when you're throwing caution to the wind in the name of speed. It wasn't until the car door closed that Woods relaxed his trigger finger. He wasn't a religious man. And he wasn't crazy. But he was smart enough to understand that what he'd just witnessed betrayed all logic.

Once he fired the engine up, he took another long look at Cross' nickel. He thought about throwing it out the window. Maybe he should've. Woods was eager to leave this whole mission in the rearview, and rid himself of any reminder of it.

But… was it worse to be in the devil's debt, or have him in yours?

HOT BLOOD AND IRON

Sharon Gray

Everything was on fire.

The houses and barns of the Bellows' farm were a towering inferno. All the screaming coming from a group of people huddled in the middle of the yard. A ring of men surrounded them, one with a huge rack of antlers fixed to his hat. Before him was a pile of bodies, and it was only from the sparkle of firelight on her glasses that I recognized the body of Rosie Bellows, my best friend.

"Murderers," I shrieked, and the man with the antlers turned his face to me.

"Seize that human." The voice rose above the roar of the fire.

The ring of men turned towards me as one, the flames reflected in their eyes. I turned and ran. My lungs burned and my corset hugged my chest too tight. Something howled; a noise so loud and deep that it rang in my head like the church bell.

Gloved hands snatched my arms and pulled me back against a broad chest that blasted heat. When he spoke, his voice buzzed like it was composed by a thousand bees. "I have her."

I screamed again and kicked back, trying to catch his leg with the heel of my boot. My foot connected, but the flesh beneath gave like I had hit a sack of grain. A sound like a raging hornet's nest erupted against my ear, and he spun me around to face him.

It was not a man.

Under the wide brimmed hat was the skull of a cougar, with flickering balls of fire instead of eyes and winged insects crawling over ancient gray bone.

"Demon," I whimpered, trembling in its grasp.

"Human fool." It laughed. The jawbone did not move but

the bees fluttered their wings. It dragged me towards the circle where the rest of the things waited, and I could see now, they were *things*. Bodies that walked like men but topped with the skulls of animals filled with meaner creatures—a pig infested with ants, a bear brimming with squirming vipers, or a horse with rats caged within. The cougar-skulled demon brought me before their leader, whose head was the skull of a great stag, on which maggots crawled.

The remaining survivors of the farm huddled together just within sight. Most of the menfolk were dead, and it was mostly women and children. Rosie's little brother, a boy of ten, clung to his mother, who mouthed my name, Alice, as she kept his face pointed away from his sister's body.

"Is she pure?" Like the cougar, the stag demon's mouth did not move when it spoke, though its voice was endlessly deeper. Its coat was thick leather, and it carried a bronze-colored saber by its side, and a longbow across its back.

The cougar demon lowered its face to my neck. I jerked in its arms, baring my teeth. Insect wings quivered against my skin and there was a movement of hot air more like wind than breath. "There is no taint of the thing upon her."

"Why are you here, human?" the stag demon asked.

At first, I could not speak, but the cougar shook me. Maybe if I convinced them I didn't know anything, they would let me go. I managed to stutter out, "I was coming to visit a friend. I-I saw the fire and-and… I wanted to he-he-"

The stag stomped a heavy boot, and I jerked in the cat's grasp. The leader leaned forward, and the maggots raised up on its skull, reaching towards me. "Have you seen the thing your kind calls a vampire? Do you know where it dens?"

My legs buckled, and my captor had to hold me up. William. These things were looking for William. Fetch Hill's secret and shame. The monster we called our own. I couldn't just give him up. Not after what he'd done for the town, my parents, my friend.

"I-I don't know where he is." It was true. William had an office, and you could usually find him there at night, but he came and went as he pleased.

"It's probably in the town." The horse thing spoke, its rats screaming in their bone cage. "We should just raze it and be done. Almost all the humans here are tainted. It is certain to be the same there."

The pig's voice was the sound of nails scratching wood. "We do not kill needlessly. It is not what we are. Besides, if we attack straight on, the abomination may escape in the chaos. It has done so before."

"You will not bicker like humans." The stag stomped again. "We are more than that." The rest of the demons cowered. Even the cougar moved me in front of it like a shield. When the leader returned its attention to me, the stag's flaming eyes almost white-hot. "Go back to your people. Tell them if they offer the abomination and all it has infected up to us before sun-up, we will leave the town standing."

"You will warn the creature and cause it to flee!" The bear hissed like its snakes moving over dry leaves.

"Silence!" The stag bellowed like a hunting horn, and even the fire grew low, like it feared its wrath. It pointed a gloved hand at me. "Go! Tell them! And tell the abomination that if it tries to run, we will hunt it down in the day and leave it to burn in the desert sun."

I hesitated a moment. What of the rest of the people there? Mrs Bellows… The cougar demon shoved me towards the road, and I stumbled before taking up the race back to where I'd tethered my horse, Rooster. There was nothing I could do to help them. Maybe William could.

* * *

I sat with my back to the fire, not wanting to look at the flames. My clothes stank of smoke and my hands shook so bad I couldn't hold the tea my mother had made for me. I'd never missed my husband so much in my life, but he was buried back east with his family. Charlie was two years dead, and I had to stand on my own.

"Where is that damned doctor?" Papa paced across the floor, his heavy boots thumping in a quick, angry rhythm.

Uncle Simon, who'd become sheriff over the five years I'd been gone, sat in Papa's great winged chair, rubbing his thumb over the butt of his revolver. "The boy only just left to get him. He'll be here soon. What we should be doing is getting the town together to figure out what we're gonna do."

"No. I want to talk to Will first." Papa glanced at the door again, like saying his name would make him appear.

"I know you think the world of that monster, but if we're talking about him or the town—"

The door opened and my heart nearly stopped. William stepped inside, toting his black leather bag. "If it was a matter of giving my life for the town then I would do so without hesitation. Unfortunately, it is not that simple."

"And why isn't it simple?" Simon stood, running his hand over his gun. "Sounds like you're trying to save your own ass."

William remained unshaken as always. "You called me here to look at Alice. After I make sure she's fine, I need to ask her some questions. If what I believe I'm smelling on the wind tonight is correct, I may have doomed the entire town."

"What the hell—" Simon took a step forward but my father put a hand on his shoulder.

"Let him talk to her." Papa closed his eyes, face pained. "We need to know how bad things are."

My uncle resumed his seat, all the while glaring at William, who moved to crouch in front of me. "Now, Miss Alice, are you hurt?"

I shook my head. Words still didn't come easily past the taste of smoke that sat like oil on my tongue. "They didn't say who they were, but they had to be some kind of demons."

"Let me guess, men with the skulls of animals filled with beasts of pestilence?" He raised an eyebrow and I nodded. "Well, luckily for us, they aren't demons. They are ancient, powerful hunters from the old world. Fairy things. We are still in terrible danger, but at least it's not demons."

William could say they weren't demons if he liked, but I had seen the burning hellfire in their eyes. I knew what they were.

"So, what do we do about them?" Papa put a hand on my shoulder.

"More importantly, why aren't we just handing you over to them, so we can mourn the Bellows in peace?" Uncle Simon stroked his beard and sneered at William, who looked at the floor.

"Because, they are sworn to eliminate the undead and view anyone I've fed from or given my blood to as tainted by me." He stood and stared at the fire.

Simon leaped to his feet and pulled his gun. "That's most of the town!"

"You would rather I'd have let everyone die of influenza?" William glanced back, unimpressed by the pistol pointed directly at his head. "If shooting me would make you feel better, be my guest, but we both know that's the only thing you would accomplish."

"Put the gun away, Uncle Simon." I rose to my feet, my knees weak, but I moved between the two, placing my hand over his. My uncle's eyes were wide and wild, his breath ragged. There was a fine tremble in his arm that made me afraid he would accidentally shoot me.

William moved around me in a blur to seize the revolver, and pulled it from Simon's grasp. My legs buckled and the doctor caught me with his free arm.

"Damn it, give me back my gun!" Simon swiped at William, who neatly stepped around him to place me in Papa's chair before holding out the pistol, handle first.

"Gladly, now that I'm sure you won't shoot Alice." There was a calm in William's voice that befitted the dead.

Papa snatched the gun before my uncle could, and glared at his brother until the man backed away. "That's enough! I don't know what the hell your problem is, but I swear to God, if you don't cool off, I will shoot you myself. We have to figure out what we need to do now."

"We need to turn this abomination over," Simon grumbled, staring at the floor. His hands were balled so tight at his sides, they shook. "Maybe if they get him, they'll leave the rest of us alone."

"Again, if that were true, I would go to them now, willingly." William dipped his head, his eyes closed. "I think you know that isn't the case. They will purge the town of any trace of me, including your wife and son. I won't apologize for sharing my blood with them, they would have died without it, but I am sorry they are in danger because of me."

"If they die, I will stake you out to burn in the sun," Simon hissed.

William raised an eyebrow. "If that is the case, you are welcome to burn whatever bits of me you can find, because I will have fallen while defending the town."

Papa stepped forward, hands wringing around the handle of the pistol. "What do we do?"

William looked to me. "You said we have until sunrise?"

I licked my lips. "That's what they told me."

He nodded to himself, eyes focused out the window, out into the distance. Out towards the Bellows ranch. "Gather the town, especially the blacksmith. Iron is one of the few things that kill them. We can make bullets that will actually hurt them, and they will not be expecting that. Tell the pastor to get out his old army rifle. It's time to see if he's a good a shot as he always brags he is."

* *•*

We needed lots of salt. I rallied everyone who wouldn't be holding the front line to gather all the salt and sow it in the dirt, making concentric rings around the town. According to William, salt wouldn't stop the demons, but they would weaken them further with each ring they crossed.

Papa and Uncle Simon were working with the blacksmith to rig what weapons they could. They figured they could make enough iron bullets for those who would face the enemy first. Most of the older men in town had been in the war, and would be stationed towards the outer rings.

My hands had finally stopped shaking, but I kept reaching down to the cast iron pan I'd tied to one of my late husband's old belts, along with his revolver. I would not be caught unarmed while the people I loved were hurt. Not again.

My part of the circle was behind the barber shop. I dragged my boot through the dirt and threw down another handful of salt. I didn't see near enough grains of white among the brown. William had said the circle hadn't needed to be perfect, but if this first line of defense fell, it would not be for lack of my diligence. Someone cleared their throat, and I snatched the gun from its holster. It slipped from my unsteady hand and hit the ground. I hissed. At least it hadn't been cocked.

"I came to see if you were alright, but it's apparent that you're not." William walked out of the shadows, hands in his pockets. I let out a shaking breath. "Would you like something for your nerves?"

I scooped the gun out of the dirt, dusting it off. "No. I need to be sharp. I need to get this done. I need—"

"You need to stop." His voice was so harsh it made me jump and the revolver slipped out of my hands. Damn it! He caught it before it hit the ground again and held it away from me. "I will only return this if you take three deep breaths."

My cheeks grew hot at his audacity, but it wasn't anger that had brought back the tremor and it wasn't the night air that made my fingers cold. I whispered at my shaking hands, "I see their faces, those things that passed for faces, every time I close my eyes."

"They are the things of nightmares." William looked out into the desert, out towards the Bellows' ranch. "The last time I laid eyes on them was decades ago, but not a dawn comes without a thought they might come for me in my sleep. It's odd, but it's almost a relief for them to finally be here, for this to be over, one way or another. My only regret is that I have dragged the town down with me. You have all been good to me, so much better than I deserve."

"You saved half the people here." The corner of my mouth twitched. "And my uncle has been less than welcoming."

He chuckled. "Not without reason. In the past I was a bit of a villain in my own right. He senses it on some level, I'm sure."

I found some humor somewhere and laughed. My hands were still again. "You? You're probably the only man in town who hasn't spent a night in one of his cells for drunken brawling."

He sighed dramatically. "Only because I lack the ability to get drunk. Back when I was human, I woke up a fair few mornings with a splitting headache and wondering where my clothes had gone."

"That's too far for me to believe." I rolled my eyes. "You couldn't even cut loose enough to dance at the fall festival."

"And the reason for that is absolutely not because I am a horrible dancer. I move with the grace of all the undead, and deny all allegations that I have two left feet." He tilted his head up in the air, feigning haughtiness until I laughed again. The smile he gave me was small and close-lipped. He was always careful to avoid showing his fangs. "Do you feel better now?"

I looked down at the dirt, speckled with white flecks of salt. The weight that had lifted with laughter returned, but did not settle so firmly. "I do."

"Three deep breaths, and I'll return your pistol."

I did as William asked, and was pleased to find my lungs didn't hitch as they drew in the night air. Even the taste of distant smoke was easier to take. He handed back the gun and I holstered it. "Thank you."

He shook his head. "Don't thank me. I brought this trouble. Miss Alice, I'd be remiss if I didn't say something." William's voice turned almost pleading. "You could run."

"No I couldn't."

"Yes, you could." He raised a hand, like he was going to put it on my shoulder, but let it fall. "You are untainted by my blood or my bite. You could take those who are the same and flee. The hunt would not follow."

"No, I could not." I drew myself to my full height, and placed a hand over my Charlie's gun. "Both my parents took your cure. So did Uncle Simon's family. I will not leave them here alone. My husband taught me how to shoot, and I am going to defend the church with Mama and the pastor."

William sighed. "I thought as much, though that pan will do more damage than your bullets."

"Then I'll guard the door and bash the skull of any demon stupid enough to set foot in God's house." I stared him in the eye, challenging him to say otherwise.

He merely chuckled and tipped his hat. "I believe the Lord has never seen a braver warrior. I'll leave you to your work, Miss Alice. There's still much to do before dawn."

* *•*

I could hear a baby crying through the church floor, and though it was faint, it grated raw on my nerves. Maybe there was a reason Charlie and I had never been blessed with children. I laid my ear against the side door I was guarding in the back room, listening desperately for signs the battle was starting. Even though I couldn't see a window, I knew the sun was rising. Could feel it like a creeping sickness in my veins. Was this how William felt every day?

We weren't ready for this. Despite everything we had done to prepare, we were going to die. *No.* I gripped the gun on my hip. Charlie wouldn't want me to quit. My mother was by the front doors, eager to fight off hell with a fireplace poker. I untied the pan from my belt and hefted it, testing its weight. It was a strong weapon. I'd once seen my grandmother use it to crack the skull of a mad dog. It would kill these things. God help—

Howls rang out, louder and deeper than the church bell that followed. The pastor was up in the belfry with his rifle. The bell was the signal.

They were here.

My hands shook as ungodly screams and gunshots filled

the air. Now that things had begun, the waiting was worse. Something crashed into the front doors, echoing like a cannon. Someone screamed. My mother shouted for them to hold. Desperation ate at my resolve. *Mama...*

Wood splintered and I stumbled back. A hound of bone and fire launched through the door and skittered across the room, emerald flame dripping like water and catching the floor. I brought the skillet down with a roar and caught the thing in the back. Bone shattered under the strike. The impact nearly ripped the skillet from my hand. Its hind legs buckled, the surrounding fire flicked and faded to orange. It raised its head and bayed towards the sky. I screamed back, and struck its open mouth, tearing off the monster's jaw. I hit it again, and it crumpled to the floor. Again, and the head shattered. The last of the fire sizzled out, leaving only the reek of burning wood.

"They're in," I called to the others, fixing my grip on the skillet. Chaos and screams answered, and I heard the front doors break.

"Idiot human," said the cougar-headed demon as it stepped through the broken door. Its heavy boots thudded on the charred floor. Bees swarmed around it, their angry buzzing so loud, even in the cacophony. It stank of burnt sugar. "You could have run, now you'll die with the contaminated."

It reached a gloved hand towards me and met with a blur of iron. A crack like breaking sticks echoed in my ears, followed by the roar of a big cat. The bees surged forward, and I swung wildly. Insects popped and sizzled as I hit them, but there were so many. They landed on my arms and face, stingers burying into my skin, injecting burning poison.

"Alice, get down!"

I dropped to the floor, arms covering my head, my pan clattered next to me. A flash and explosion flooded the room, leaving a high-pitched whine in my ears. I raised my head to see Uncle Simon step through the doorway and rack the lever of his rifle. The cougar screamed. Its right eye was gone, and golden liquid oozed from the broken skull.

Simon lined up the shot again and as the demon lunged, my uncle fired. The bullet ripped through its chest, splattering the wall with honey, bone, and bits of wood. The cougar staggered but didn't go down, and raised its unbroken hand to grab at Uncle Simon. He racked the lever again and fired, but the gun didn't go off. With a roar, the demon tackled him, and they tumbled out the door.

"Uncle Simon!" I grabbed my skillet and scrambled to my feet.

They were rolling in the dirt outside, him trying to pull his knife while the demon pressed its broken limb against his throat. I stood above them, unable to get a clear strike. Simon rolled to his back and pushed the demon up as hard as he could.

My swing connected with the back of the cougar's head and its arm buckled. Simon drew his blade and rammed it into the demon's head. It was steel, not iron, but the demon twisted away, struggling to pull it out.

"Buy me a second to clear my gun!"

Uncle Simon's voice was more a whisper over the ringing in my ears, but I knew what to do. I raised the pan high above my head and let my knees buckle. With all of my might and the force of the fall, I smashed the cougar's face. Metal rang against metal as I hit the knife. Bone disintegrated. The demon's body spasmed, then collapsed, leaving only empty clothes. I poked the coat with the skillet, and was rewarded with a dry, wooden clack. The bees just buzzed away, like they had lost interest.

"Is it really dead?" I called to my uncle, nudging it with a pan.

"Seems to me, but we got to go. I can hear your mama, and she needs help." He took off at a run towards the front of the church. I struggled to my feet, gritting my teeth at the burn of the bee stings and the pain in my arms. My head ached and the high pitch whine in my ears wasn't leaving. I shuffled after my uncle, clinging tightly to my weapon.

Even from where we stood outside, there was chaos in the church, and bits of skeletons littered the floor. The doors were ripped from their hinges, wood shard everywhere. More towns-people had retreated inside, and the wounded fought beside everyone else. The pastor crouched behind an overturned pew, taking shots where he could.

"Foul insects!" The horse demon screeched and charged from behind the general store, swinging a short, broad sword that reflected the light back orange. "Tainted worms! Lowly—"

The crack from Uncle Simon's rifle tore through my ears as it ripped through the demon's chest. Rats squealed and dropped from its skull, skittering towards the church's defenders to bite and scratch. The horse demon rushed Simon, but my mother lunged in front of him, swinging the fireplace poker like a sword. She connected with the point of its nose, shattering it. A rat leaped from the gaping hole and attacked my mother's face. She dropped her poker and stumbled, falling to her knees clawing the rat off her and tossing it away. The horse demon charged. Another shot exploded through its chest and it staggered but kept moving.

"Aim for the head!" The pastor's voice rose above the din. My uncle cursed as his rifle jammed again. I pulled my pistol and fired. The bullet rocked the horse's head, doing no damage, but drew its attention. It hissed, and its coat heaved. A crack louder than my gun echoed through the church and the demon's jaw opened. Rats poured from its mouth in a brown flood. One skittered towards my feet and I cracked my pan down on its back, leaving it crushed, a dent in its middle.

Simon fired off another round, striking the demon between the eyes. Another bullet took it in its hanging jaw sending bone flying, and the pastor whooped. Mother seized her poker and shrieked like a banshee, smashing any rodent that got close. My uncle closed on the horse, firing another shot right into its face. It fell back, body deflating, rats scattering.

"Enough!" The word was so loud it broke through the ringing in my ears. The stag-headed demon stood at the door of the church, its remaining hounds swarming behind it. The rest of the demons ghosted to its side; the bear limped badly, and the pig was missing the front half of its skull.

"You ready to get the hell out of our town?" Uncle Simon yelled, leveling his gun at the stag.

"Give us the undead and we will go. We will leave the tainted humans be." Even the stag's great voice sounded weary.

Simon laughed. "We ain't giving you shit. Leave now, and I won't hunt you all down."

Silence hung heavy around us as they stared at each other, human eyes boring into flame. My hands shook, the air cold on my skin, but I was sweating. The world was swimming. I couldn't fall down. I *wouldn't*.

It seemed an eternity before the demon spoke. "We will go, but you will relay a message to the fiend. If he seeks to put himself under human protection here in this town, then here he shall stay. If he steps a foot over the town line we will know, and we will come to finish him."

"I'll be sure to pass it along, now get!" Simon fired a shot at their feet. The stag demon hissed, maggots dripping through its nose, then turned, stalking back down the street. Its hunt followed. None of them looked back.

In a blink, they were gone. They could have been a nightmare, but for the wounded they left behind.

I fell to my knees, the pan tumbling from my hand to clank upon the floorboards. The summer air was freezing against my skin and the world tilted. The ringing in my ears grew louder, louder, but I could hear Simon calling my name. Someone picked me up, but I couldn't will my eyes open to see who. They carried me, the motion rocking me like a boat and my stomach rolled. I was placed on something hard, and fingers pried my eyelids apart. William looked down at me. He spoke, but I couldn't follow the words. Something was pressed against my mouth and hot liquid trickled between my lips.

Copper. It tasted like copper.

The shaking subsided, the nausea eased, and the ringing in my ears faded. I took several deep breaths and sat up. My mother nearly knocked me off the table I was laying on as she flung herself at me for a hug. I was in the church basement, as was everyone who was significantly wounded. William was stumbling to each one of them, slicing his wrist open to let them drink his blood, then doing it again for the next person because the wound had already closed.

My mother didn't want to let me up, but with the blood he had fed me, I felt better than she did. Even my arms felt fresh, despite all the swinging they'd done. I helped herd the freshly healed out of the basement, up to where my father was coordinating the cleanup. Uncle Simon was out in the town, checking for survivors.

When the last of the wounded were tended, I went down to see William. He sat against the wall farthest from the stairs, looking pale and exhausted.

"I didn't know you could be awake during the day," I said, sitting next to him.

"It's an effort, but necessary today." He rubbed his hand over his face. "I will wait a little longer to see if anyone else needs tending, but then I must sleep."

"Do you normally sleep here?" A church was not an obvious place for a vampire to rest, but William was admittedly different from most of his kind.

He chuckled. "No. I chose to stay here today in the hope I could be of some little help. How are you, by the way?"

"Better than I have any right to be." I brushed a hand over where one of the stings had been. There wasn't even a mark. "Thank you."

"You were poisoned fighting off an enemy I brought to your doorstep. It is the least I could do." He bowed his head at me.

"Have you heard the conditions under which the demons left?"

William sighed, rubbing at his wrists like they ached. "I have. It's not a hardship, really, to remain forever among friends."

"Should I leave you alone for now?" I nodded towards the stairs, putting a hand on the wall to push myself up. "Give you a few moments of quiet before you sleep?"

"If you don't mind, I'd much prefer it if you stayed." He

grinned, showing fangs for the first time since I'd known him. "You could regale me with the tale of your battle."

I smiled. "Very well. Listen close, and I'll tell you how I killed a demon with a frying pan."

THE GOODNIGHT TRAIL

John Paul Fitch

New Mexico, 1868.

By the time the coyote registered the shot, a hole the size of a silver dollar had opened in its rear end. The animal pitched over and jerked in the dirt. Its legs worked into a sprint, yelping as it turned in circles, and a *whoop* carried from a rider bringing up the rear of the drive. The sun crouched behind the crest of the far-off hills, leaving a fringe of dark-orange light, and the air began to free itself from the clutches of the day's heat. Shadows slipped over the land like a shroud.

"Got him good," said Isaac as his brother hefted the smoking rifle and hollered in triumph.

"Damn straight. I ain't never missed a coyote yet." Jacob smiled and punched the air, Winchester still in his hand.

"Maybe so, but you sure as shit missed Emma Jones last Saturday at the dance. Couldn't hit a beeves ass with a banjo that night."

"Fuck you, Isaac."

"Fuck you right back." Isaac smiled at his little brother. Despite being the younger of the pair, Jacob was three inches taller and at least the same across the shoulders, with the tanned skin, blue eyes, and easy smile of their mother. He wore his youth like fancy clothing.

They were interrupted by a clanging noise. Jefferson, the cook, was banging his spare pot with a large spoon.

"Eating time."

"'Bout time too. Champ needs watering and a feedbag." Jacob patted the neck of his grey gelding and the horse huffed in return. Isaac tugged on the reins of his mare – a Pinto named

Fury – and the horse obliged him, turning quickly. Jacob did likewise.

The rest of the men circled around the head wagon where Jefferson and their father, Isaac Senior, were spooning out bowls of stew.

"Why does he always leave it so late to have a sit-down?"

"Why don't you ask him?" Isaac smiled, knowing the answer.

"I ain't asking him nothing."

"Ah, I see. You're scared he'll give you a whoopin'."

"Sure-as-shit ain't scared of the old man. Maybe when I was little but not no more. War hero or not, he's past his prime."

"Don't worry yourself, little brother. I'll go talk to him. You keep an eye out for more coyotes, or maybe ghosts or somethin' while I'm gone."

"Ain't no such thing as ghosts, Isaac. You know that."

"That's not what Achak says."

"Achak, Kajika, and Wanikiy might be Comanche, might even be the best horse men I ever seen, but our brothers don't know shit about no spirit world. Besides, I ain't never seen no phantoms."

"I ain't never seen a baby buzzard but I know they exist somewhere. I'll be back. Don't go giving yourself a heart attack or anything while I'm gone."

Isaac gave Fury a little kick on her muscled flanks, and the horse picked up the pace. He saw Jacob glance over his shoulder and heft his Winchester again. Isaac chuckled and rode forward, his horse eager to stretch its legs.

They were driving twenty-five hundred head of cattle up the Goodnight Trail from Fort Belknap, Texas, through New Mexico and all the way up towards Denver, Colorado. The smell from the beeves was horrendous at times: shit and piss and animal hide. Flies blackened the faces of the animals like a living fur. Isaac Senior had negotiated a price of forty dollars per head for the herd. If they made it all the way to Denver with minimal loss they'd be set for the year and then some.

Isaac smiled as Achak reined in near him. His adopted brother had his mother's big dark eyes and constant smile; his long dark hair pulled back in a braid.

"You getting the youngster all riled up again?" said Achak.

"Told Jake to keep an eye out for ghosts," Isaac said with a laugh.

"Out here?" His brother joined the laughter.

"I'm headed up to speak to Dad. Watch for his signal then round up any stray beeves and get the herd settled for the night."

"I'll let the others know." With that, Achak turned his horse in a tight circle and was away with a yelp.

Up ahead Isaac could make out the wagon against the horizon, and he waved as he passed the other two wranglers – Thomas and Bronson, both Africans, former soldiers in the war. They'd come south with Isaac's father after peace broke out on the promise of steady work. Thomas was a religious man, spending his down time in solitude, the good book a constant presence in his hand. Bronson preferred to spend his time carousing in town, getting into fist fights with the locals, chasing skirt. Once or twice, he may or may not have started a shootout, depends on who you heard it from, but he sure as shit always finished them. The law kept a close eye on him, as did some of the more restless men of the town, which was why Isaac Senior kept him close.

Isaac trotted to where his father was watching the herd, having left Jefferson to the sort the food.

"Pop. Suns getting low. The boys could use a decent night's rest."

Isaac Senior spat and raised his hat. "That so?"

"Yessir."

His father's still keen eyes turned back to the desert. He glanced up along the way, and Isaac followed his gaze to a dark blot on the horizon. Isaac pulled his spyglass from his saddlebag and brought it to bear on the object.

A squat building with a high wooden rampart around the perimeter was probably a mile or so away. Maybe fifty feet across with barricaded walls as high as a church steeple and ramparts running all around the top, guard posts at the junctions of each of the walls, and a sturdy gate that lay open to the elements. An abandoned military fort by the looks of it.

Isaac Senior smoothed out his bushy moustache with a leathery hand. "That there's Fort Sumner. Been abandoned since the war. Won't be much in the way of supplies there, rats probably got any grain left behind, but it could give us some shelter. Make the call. We keep on going, or we set down here for the night."

Isaac looked back along the line of beeves and could make out the other cowboys all waiting for the word. "I think we should stop here."

The old man grunted and nodded to his son, then took his hat off and waved it. His father let out a whistle, and Isaac heard Bronson and Thomas yelp in delight as they began corralling the cattle.

* * *

Isaac made short work of the generous serving of thick stew, heavy with vegetables and beef. He'd not eaten since dawn and save for a refill of his canteen he'd spent his day chasing down rogue cattle, delivered a calf from an ailing cow, and spent the rest of the day scouting for any potential threat. After a cup of coffee, followed by a refill, he leaned back on his bedspread and watched the moon rise. The wind gusted; the heat evaporated from the day. Night chilled the air, and he inched closer to the fire. Stretching the tired knots of muscle in his back, Isaac pulled his hat down over his eyes to the sounds of his brothers talking and laughing, and let sleep claim him.

A scream tugged him from slumber. He sat up, and at first wasn't sure if he was indeed still dreaming. The sound carried in the night air was uncanny, a high-pitched, drawn-out wailing. It wasn't a human sound. Isaac was accustomed to the grunts and moans of cattle. This was different.

It came again. Ice water washed through his veins. As

the sound died into the night, he sucked in a deep breath and glanced around for anyone in the vicinity, someone to reassure him that they, too, had heard the uncanny noise.

Isaac spotted his father. The old man was already on his feet, rifle held in both hands. They locked eyes for a moment. The seriousness of his father's glance washed any tendrils of sleep away and Isaac rolled over and grabbed his rifle before jumping to his feet.

Jacob stood, chambering a round. "The hell is that?" he said, wiping his eyes. Jacob followed Isaac's gaze, off towards the infernal sound, as their father moved away from the campsite. The other men organised themselves into a defensive formation, eyes sharp. Thomas muttered a prayer.

"Whatever it is, it can't be good. C'mon."

The younger sibling nodded and followed his brother into the herd. The beeves had made a wide circle around the source of the sound. They bristled and snorted at the touch of the men and bothered themselves, preparing to stampede.

Isaac and Jacob pushed between the cattle and came to a clearing at the edge of the herd where the light of the fire barely reached. The sound came again, and Isaac's attention was drawn to a heifer laying on its side. Its body jostled and jerked, and its tail flickered in the throes of death. A dark shape moved on the other side of the cow, and Isaac's senses registered several things at once: the sound of tearing, the coppery smell of blood, the sound of snapping bone. But what could take down a creature of this size out here? There weren't any mountain lions this far south, none that Isaac had seen at any measure. A rogue wolf?

Isaac saw his father take a knee and glance down his rifle sight. Isaac came up beside the old man. Jacob joined him on the other side.

"Dad."

The old man lifted a finger to his lips. The cow stopped jiggling. A vast shape emerged from behind the dead cow. At first, it was difficult to tell what the thing was, Isaac could make out silver-grey fur, hackles raised like that of an angry wolf. But this thing stood high on two legs, taller than a man. Its thin body was sparsely covered in grey fur that ran from its head and down its flanks to the tops of its legs. Its arms, long and spindly, ended in clawed hands, but it was the face that stole Isaac's breath.

It had something resembling human features, but they were pulled out of all proportion. The eyes shone silvery white, casting light of their own accord and they were wide, wider than a man's, and as large as saucers. The mouth opened, unsheathing two rows of needle-like teeth. The thing cast its eyes around and settled on the men. Pitching its head back it let out that haunting howl again. Isaac's balls tightened like they were trying to snake their way back up inside his body cavity.

Then came the return call of several other creatures.

Howls that sent chills racing down Isaac's body. He watched, frozen in place, as the creature bent low and plunged an arm deep into the cow's body cavity and pulled something free. It raised the quivering meat to its mouth and Isaac realised that it had snatched a foetus from the cow's womb. One bite cut the unborn calf in half. Blood cascaded down the creature's front. It stared at the trio of men as it chewed.

Then it was as if the world slipped suddenly, and in that instant Isaac saw the face of an ancient man, the skin almost mummified with age. Open sores on the man's cheeks wept blood, the eyes milky and blind, the mouth crooked and completely without teeth. The man pitched his head back and cackled. For a split second two beings occupied the same space. Isaac screwed his eyes closed. When he looked again, the creature was as before – a maw full of unborn calf. It regarded them as a predator would do prey.

The three men squatted in place, rapt at the sight before them. It was only when Achak and the others appeared that the spell was broken.

"My god," Achak said, and without any prompting, raised his Remington .36 calibre revolver and fired.

The creature was struck mid flank. It barely noticed the wound. Isaac, snatched from his reverie, raised his rifle and let loose, as did his father and Jacob. Wounds opened on the creature's body and blood trickled from the holes, yet it remained unfazed. Isaac steadied himself and took aim at the thing's head. The bullet tore into one of the creature's eyes.

That did it.

The thing wailed, clutching at its face. Calls returned from the distance, closer this time. Blind panic set in amongst the herd and it moved as one.

Achak grabbed Isaac by the shoulder and screamed at him. "We have to go!"

The creature stood tall once again and raised a clawed hand, pointing directly at Isaac. Behind the creature, several spots of light appeared. Isaac counted. *Six sets of eyes behind the lead creature.* And they were coming closer.

"Get to the horses." Isaac Senior opened fire as the brothers made a bolt for their mounts.

Achak and Jacob took off through the herd while Isaac retreated, still firing. A chorus of screeching cries sprang up all round. Isaac stopped to reload as his father kept firing. The one-eyed thing began to advance on the old man, absorbing the shots. Isaac Senior dropped the rifle when he ran out of ammo and drew his revolver, unleashing a hail of bullets at the creature. One-eye coiled, the muscles in its body tightened, and then it sprang forward with unnatural speed, covering the dozen or so meters between itself and his father in a blink of an eye.

It struck his father midriff, punching through his torso, the clawed hand emerging through the old man's back, gore flying. The pistol slipped from the old man's fingers. One-eye lifted Isaac's father clean off the ground, its arm still pushed through his torso. Isaac Senior gasped and clutched at the creature's arm then turned his head as best he could, his eyes streaming.

The old man took a deep breath before bellowing: "Ruuun!"

Isaac Senior contorted in pain as One-eye wrapped a large hand around his throat and, with a jerk, tore the old man's head clean off his shoulders.

Isaac screamed. Tears pricked the corners of his eyes, and

he stooped to reload his weapon as the creature cast his father's body aside. Clicking the ammo home, he bore the rifle at the creature and unleashed a volley of shots once more. With this fresh barrage of gunfire, the earth shook as a stampede began in earnest. A large heifer bore down on Isaac and its solid body knocked him from his crouched position flat onto the dirt. Hooves compacted the soil around his head, missing him by inches, punching the ground like sledgehammers.

Isaac rolled away from the cow onto his front and tried to get to his knees but another thump on his back knocked him flat again. This time the beeve almost ran right over the top of him. Dust kicked up all around him, choking Isaac as he tried to catch his breath. He scrambled away as fast as he could, crawling on hands and knees, trying to make out the fire from the camp in the darkness.

Screeching carried over the sound of the stampede, over the cries of panicked cows and the thunder of thousands of hooves on the move. Isaac struggled to his feet as another cow barrelled towards him, its eyes wide. Just before it hit him the cow veered to his left and behind it was Jacob upon Champ, the white steed unfazed by the stampede.

Jacob held the reins to Fury in his spare hand. Isaac, dusty but otherwise unharmed, leapt onto his horse. He looked out across the herd, the beeves all now moving as one organism, seething and roiling like a living sea. Isaac spotted Achak and the others a few hundred feet away, and the brothers took off towards them.

"Head for the fort!"

"Follow me," yelled Achak. He pointed ahead to the dark thick walls of Fort Sumner, its thick wooden doors and double-bricked ramparts a haven, and it was there that they fled.

Clearing the litter of cattle, Isaac and Jacob followed behind the others riding at full pelt. He heard his brother yell and turned.

Emerging from the herd came One-eye, standing a clear foot or so taller than even the biggest of the cattle, and behind One-eye were an entire pack of the creatures. The others were smaller but no less ugly and ferocious. With a screech, they gave pursuit at a pace that could not only match the horses, but Isaac feared would catch them before they could reach Fort Sumner.

The stampeding herd afforded the men some protection, a veritable wall of moving muscle that kept the beasts from catching Isaac and the others. One-eye threw its head back and screamed, and two of the creatures began attacking the cattle, picking off stragglers at first and those animals that veered too close. The others took off into the darkness away from the stampeding herd. Isaac watched as they made their way at speed up the side of a shallow incline before turning back, darting towards the middle of the stampede. Some of the cows saw and panicked; the collective broke and scattered into multiple streams of animals. It was chaos but these creatures knew what they were doing.

"They're splitting the herd. Look!"

A wide section opened as some of the cows turned and took off in the opposite direction. Isaac was reminded of his father's tales from the bible of Moses parting the Red Sea. He raised his rifle again and let off a few rounds. Digging his heels into Fury, he gripped the reins with an iron fist as the horse lurched forward – it could sense the danger as only a prey animal can. Adrenaline fuelled Fury's' burst of speed. A few hundred yards now till they reached the fort. He checked over his shoulder.

The creatures were closing on them. One-eye was only a few yards away now. If it leapt at Isaac, there was a chance it could snatch him from his saddle. If he didn't do something now to slow these things, then all was lost. It wouldn't just be him either. He'd just lost his father and did not wish to lose his brothers too.

Isaac slid the Winchester into the saddle holster and drew his Remingtons. He half turned and brought one to bear on One-eye again. He lowered the barrels and fired at the creature's legs. One bullet struck the lower leg, just enough to take One-eye out of its stride. It sprawled in the dirt, its momentum causing it to roll head over heels. With One-eye down the other creatures slowed, as if unsure of what to do. It was enough of a hesitation to allow the men to gain some distance on their pursuers.

One-eye let go a hellish scream which served to drive Fury onwards. In a heartbeat they reached Fort Sumner, tearing across the threshold like demons themselves. Isaac, last to enter, leapt from Fury's back and helped the others with the large wooden gates. Time had weathered the wood and the massive iron hinges, but with an enormous heave, they indeed moved, the iron complaining loudly. Before the gates met in the middle, Isaac shot a glance out into the night. The creatures watched the men.

As Jacob slid the bolt across and locked the doors, Isaac had the feeling that they'd made a terrible mistake.

Silence.

Save for the sound of panting men and the restlessness of the baying horses. The herd had long since run off into the distance. They were lost. Even if they survived this night the effort to locate the cattle would exceed Isaac's reach. The family would be ruined by this. They'd have to sell the ranch or face a winter of starvation on measly grain and vegetables. The fortune the family had accrued over the years since the Civil War would not last a year without further income. This was one of the final drives his father had planned on taking. Very soon the railroad would come through New Mexico and then there would be no need for the months-long, laborious trek across the vast terrain. The way of life would end in its current form. The end of the open range and the blossoming of a new industrial era.

Isaac tried to slow his hammering heart, and looked for Achak and Jacob, and found them huddled together. Achak was as white as a ghost. Kajika and Wanikiy crouched beside him talking hurriedly between themselves. Thomas and Bronson had taken up positions inside a small building Isaac assumed was an old guard house secreted into the corner of the courtyard. It had barred windows and a solid door. They had already lit the lamps inside and Isaac could see their shapes behind the barred windows, rifles at the ready.

"Is everyone okay?" he asked.

"Might need a change of long johns but yeah," said Jacob.

"Are we all here? Headcount."

Isaac counted out the men starting with himself and Jacob, then his brothers Achak, Kajika and Wanikiy. Thomas and Bronson. Seven men. With the old man dead…

"Where's Jefferson?"

Silence. No-one wanted to admit what had happened.

"Did anyone see the cook when the herd stampeded?"

Jacob shook his head. "I heard him screaming. Don't know if it was the herd that got him or something else."

"Damn it. We left him behind!"

"There's nothing we could do, Isaac. Not with those things. What the hell were they?"

Those things. The thought of them made Isaac shudder. Never in his life, on the dozen or so cattle drives he'd made with his pop had he ever seen anything like them. "I never seen anything like them. Achak? What were they?"

Achak seemed like he was reliving what he'd seen, possessed by the images of the creatures. Then his eyes darted up towards Isaac and he whispered. "The kind of thing our people don't talk about. Even saying their name out loud is bad luck."

"Achak." He looked at his brother with a mixture of concern and impatience.

Achak cast his eyes to the sky. "Comanche call them anti'jh-nii. *Skinwalkers.*"

"Skinwalkers?"

Kajika drew his blade and began to cut lines in the dirt. He spoke in a deep baritone, his eyes never leaving the pattern he was tracing. "It is a witch. It was a medicine man once but consumed the flesh of another man and became evil. Shapeshifters, sorcerers. They become any animal they choose, even other men or women."

The shape Kajika carved into the ground was like that of a wolf on hind legs.

"I don't believe in any of that horse-shit, Kajika."

Achak looked like he was about to cry. "Isaac. It was what

Kajika says. You saw it with your own eyes. I didn't even believe they existed until tonight. My mother told us stories of Sk— of *them*. I always thought it was to keep us from walking too far alone at night..."

Isaac grunted. "For a moment, just a moment, I thought... I thought I saw something else. An old man..." Isaac stopped himself. He sounded crazy and he knew it.

"Shapeshifter." Achak nodded. "It took our father, Isaac. It cut him in half. It will eat of his flesh and take his soul and with it his shape, his memories."

"Shit. Dad." Jacob's eyes glazed over, and he struggled to contain the sobs.

A wave of emotion rose in Isaac but he stamped it down hard.

Achak continued, "You saw what it can do. It's not human. It can run faster than a horse, jump higher than a man, is stronger than a bull. It is born of dark magic—"

Isaac gestured for Achak to stop talking. "There'll be time for sorrow if we survive the night. Skinwalkers, if they are what you say they are, then we're in for a hell of a time. How do we kill them?"

Achak shrugged desperately. "Maybe blades, maybe bullets if you get them good? Only another medicine man can really kill them. They hide away in daylight and come out when the moon rises..." He trailed off, lost in thought.

Isaac sucked in a deep breath. "Well, I ain't never met a living thing that can survive being shot in the face. Maybe, if we can slow them down, we'll see dawn. Jacob, if you're done crying, we got work to do." The words stung Isaac as they left his mouth. He knew it would hurt Jacob to hear his brother talk that way, but the boy needed a firm hand tonight. There would be plenty of time to mourn later.

He went on. "Fellas, we gotta do what we can to survive here. Lasting till sun-up may be our only chance."

The men regarded him then and, one by one, they slowly nodded their agreement.

He looked around the inside of the fort. On close inspection, the walls appeared solid, their foundations strong, and aside from the front gate, Isaac could see no other way in or out of the place. The guard house had a dozen lanterns, some old oil, a few rags, some rotting furniture, a moth-eaten military dress overcoat, and nothing much else. The stables were barren of any hay or grain, the barracks had several rotting bunks with musty blankets.

Isaac instructed Jacob, "We can make torches with some of this furniture and these blankets. Set them up on the ramparts and all around the square. Make it as light as possible. Thomas and Bronson found lanterns. There's oil we can dip the blankets in. Get a fire burning in the courtyard." He ruffled Jacob's hair in a brotherly gesture and the younger man pushed his sibling away, suppressing a hint of a smile.

In the centre of the courtyard stood a circular stone wall that harboured a well. The bucket and rope were intact, and Jacob scooped up water from its depths. The first few buckets were filled with silt, but soon after he pulled clean water. They watered the horses first. When the animals did not complain then the men began to drink.

Outside the confines of the fort, the plains took on the oppressive nature of a dark sea, still and cold and unwilling to give up its secrets. Isaac walked the ramparts, Jacob a few steps behind. All the while he scanned the darkness and aside from a few shadows, nothing caught his eye. The atmosphere between them had been heavy since they'd arrived, and Isaac knew he had humiliated his brother before the men. The boy had words to speak, but it would have to wait. He could say all he wanted when they made it out of here, hell, Isaac would even apologise to him.

Just as Jacob opened his mouth, Isaac shushed him. He held his breath and opened his mouth slightly to dull the rush of blood in his ears. A rustling sound, something skirting the perimeter just out of his range of vision, crept through the plains grass. He pulled the eyeglass towards the source of the rustling and, there, made out a tall shadow. He let go of the eyeglass. It thumped on the wooden deck as Isaac raised his rifle, letting off a single round. Barely aiming, firing on instinct.

A yelp, and the skittering of a wounded animal. He knew it would not hurt the creature seriously, but he took great pleasure in maiming the thing slightly.

Isaac grinned to himself. "Got you, you bastard."

It was as if the creature heard him. There in the dark he saw the opening of two points of light, like torches, sharp and piercing. The shining eyes bored right into him. Isaac turned and ran his eyes over the fort.

Most of the men had taken up defensive positions around the ramparts. Achak had been sent to gather wood and other combustible remnants to start a fire.

Isaac grabbed Jacob by the sleeve and clambered down the ladder to the earthen floor. "Achak. Get those torches fixed. Set them all around the ramparts. Jake, get a fire started in the courtyard. We need to make this place as light as possible. If one of these things get in here, we need to be able to see it."

"I'm on it." Jacob ran to the guardhouse to find some wood and oil.

Isaac counted the rounds they had left and laid them out on the ground before him as Jacob got the fire started quickly. Isaac stared at his brother, proud of how much he had grown and how adept he was at frontier life. He remembered his father teaching both him and Jacob how to strip down and clean a rifle when he was barely a teenager.

"A well cared for weapon will never let you down. Keep it clean and oiled and it won't fail you in times of need."

Isaac knew they were all well and truly in need. He fetched his rag and oil and bear grease from Fury's saddlebag and began the process of methodically stripping the weapon down and cleaning its parts individually. With that done, he oiled them with the bear grease then slid the parts together, each segment fitting in perfectly. Sliding the barrel in last, he fixed it with the bolt. Under the light of the fire, the rifle gleamed. He loaded his magazines with rounds in preparation for the coming fight.

He walked the rampart. At the north wall he stopped and scanned the perimeter. Under a full moon he would have been able to see clearly the land surrounding the fort but the moon betrayed them, hiding itself away behind a barricade of cloud, as if it knew what fate awaited them… or it was fearful of the evil magic at play. Isaac hefted his weapon. There was a reckoning coming and he sure as hell was going to be ready.

He ran his eyes over the walls and the men who guarded it. His men. Men he'd known all his life, men he'd worked with and lived with since he was a young buck. Bronson and Thomas stuck together on the east wall, Achak and Kajika on the south, Jacob and Wanikiy took up their positions on the west. With the place locked up tight, plenty of ammo, and hopefully only a few hours till sun-up, maybe they'd make it.

The men all heard the sound at the same time and knew the source. Isaac turned and shot a look over the wall. Below him, several shapes moved. One was prostrate on the ground; limbs being separated from body slowly by a sinewy figure that towered over him, its long fingers slicing his flesh like butter.

Jefferson screamed in agony. Blood gushed from his head and torso, a multitude of cuts and gashes ran up and down his flanks. He'd been stripped naked. One-eye held him up by the legs. It stared up at the gathering men on the ramparts with something approaching glee. It let go of one of Jefferson's legs and, with its free hand, reached down to the man's groin.

Jefferson's screams became screeches. He wailed like a child; a panicked, yelping cry that cut Isaac to the heart. One-eye took Jefferson's manhood in its clawed hand and pulled. The gelding took only a moment. The thing tore Jefferson's organs from their resting place, splattering his thighs with red-black blood. The space between his legs was now a gaping, wet wound. His screaming died off as shock hit. One-eye dropped the man. From the gloom, two smaller Skinwalkers emerged. They fell on Jefferson's prone body and tore at it.

Isaac willed himself to snap from his stupor. He snatched up his rifle and fired.

At the sound of Isaac's rifle report, the other men with him also began to fire upon the beasts. Bullet-holes pockmarked the creatures and almost at once they fell back. The creatures loped away into the desert with supernatural speed, and Isaac signalled for the firing to stop.

They looked down upon Jefferson's corpse. Even from this distance, the damage was terrible indeed. His flesh hung in crimson ribbons, the white rib bones stood free from the body cavity, exposed to the air. His innards had been pulled out and lay scattered around his body. Jefferson's face had been torn back from the skull and flapped down over the top of his head, held by a thread of sinew.

Before anyone could speak there came a terrible yelling from the south side. It was then Isaac knew they had been tricked. The gruesome show from One-eye had been a diversion. Achak and Kajika fired wildly. Isaac turned just as four Skinwalkers clambered over the south wall and overwhelmed the two brothers. Wanikiy cried out in a mixture of anger and terror before he took off running towards their siblings.

"Wanikiy!" Jacob lifted his weapon and drew a bead on the struggle across the courtyard. Kajika was being torn apart by two of the smaller Skinwalkers. From behind, one of the creatures speared Kajika through the back. Their brother stiffened in shock. Another Skinwalker grasped his scalp with two clawed hands and, with a flex of steely muscle, tore the skin from his face like paper. Kajika didn't even scream before they hefted him aloft and pitched his body off the rampart.

Achak tossed his empty rifle, drawing his hunting knife in one slick movement. It gleamed in the light, slicing an arc through the air. The knife embedded itself in the skull of one of the beasts, which let out an ear-piercing scream and staggered back, its momentum carrying it off the rampart and onto the dirt floor of the courtyard. Achak was left weapon-less against three Skinwalkers. Before they could close on him, Wanikiy leapt to his brother's defence, releasing a volley of shots that struck two Skinwalkers clean in the face, opening their heads up like cut melons. Wanikiy pulled his knife and sprinted at the remaining Skinwalker.

The two wounded Skinwalkers' clambered back over the ramparts and disappeared. Wanikiy lifted his blade to his shoulder and braced himself as he hit the Skinwalker mid-breast, driving the blade into the creature till the hilt hit bone. They stumbled back, careening into the wooden rampart, and with all his might Wanikiy pulled the blade straight down. The Skinwalker didn't even have time to yelp. The skin of its chest opened like petals of a flower and from within came smooth, glistening organs that fell to the deck with a wet thud. The creature looked down at its innards and stumbled to its knees. Wanikiy stepped back, pulling the blade free and lifting it above his head to strike the killing blow. In the split second it took him to raise his weapon the dying Skinwalker sliced upwards with its clawed hand, delivering an equal blow to Wanikiy as it had received.

It took Wanikiy a moment to register what had happened. Achak lifted his head as his brother turned towards him, a strange smile on his face, as his torso slipped open. Wanikiy fell face forward and was dead before he hit the deck.

Isaac glanced down at the dazed Skinwalker in the court-yard as it began to lift itself from the earthen floor. Bronson and Thomas left their places on the east wall and descended to the courtyard. They opened fire on the Skinwalker as it staggered to its feet, holes opened in its chest, but barely slowed it down. The thing swatted at the bullets as a man might do to eager flies in summertime.

It advanced on the two men as they continued to rain shots upon it. Isaac grabbed the lantern from his brother and leapt from the rampart. He landed heavily, toppling forward, and threw himself into a forward roll. He managed to stop the lantern from smashing and rolled to his feet just as the creature drew close to Bronson. It smashed Bronson in the face with a massive fist and then lunged at Thomas with open jaws.

"Thomas, move!"

Isaac's shout turned the Skinwalker towards him, and he launched the oil lamp at the creature. The glass shattered as it struck, showering it with tongues of flaming oil. Its mangy fur caught instantly, and it thrashed around, blinded by flames, screaming in agony as the fire consumed it. Thomas rolled away and wedged himself against the rampart wall as the Skinwalker took off at enormous speed straight towards the wooden gates.

"Oh, Christ." Isaac's heart dropped as the creature careened through the doors, smashing them wide open, taking one clean off the hinges. It loped into the desert and was soon out of sight.

"Bronson?"

Thomas knelt over his friend. Isaac tried to slow his hammering heart as he staggered over to the prostrated man. One side Bronson's face was a mess of shattered bone and gristle, the skull caved in. He was still breathing, gurgling through bubbles of thick blood. Thomas cupped Bronson's head, but the skull was so slick it slipped from his hands.

Isaac placed a hand on Thomas' shoulder as Jacob and Achak came up alongside him. "The doors are busted. We're sitting ducks." Isaac could see his brother was as scared as he'd ever been in his life. They'd been in plenty of fights in their time, even a couple of shootouts with rustlers, but nothing came close to this.

"How many of them are there?" Achak, the colour drained from his face, his eyes bugging out of his skull, glanced at every shadowy crevice in the fort.

"I counted seven back on the plain. Wanikiy gutted one, two took rifle shots straight to the face, one we set on fire. That's four down."

"The three that killed Jefferson." Jacob shuddered. "They're still out there."

There came the squeal of metal. Isaac turned as the lead Skinwalker tore the remaining door from its frame and tossed it to the ground with a crash. The three remaining Skinwalkers slipped into the compound.

"Not anymore," said Isaac. "Get to the guard house!"

Isaac ran to where Thomas was struggling to lift Bronson, but between them they dragged the man's dead weight towards the guard house. Jacob and Achak laid down covering fire, just enough to allow the men to get Bronson inside, and for Jacob and Achak to retreat into the room. Isaac slammed the door closed and slid the barricade plank into place, locking themselves inside.

"How long will this keep them out?" Jacob said.

"Hopefully long enough."

Thomas propped Bronson in the corner of the far wall as heavy banging filled the room. Dust shook from the rafters as the latches and hinges shook in their moorings.

"Load up the rest of your ammo, boys. We gotta make a stand here." Isaac grabbed his brother by the arm. "If this doesn't go well… I just… I mean…"

Jacob stared Isaac in the eye and held it with steely intent. "We're making it out of here."

Isaac nodded and turned, but his brother caught him in a bear hug.

Jacob whispered. "But yeah. Me too."

Isaac glanced at Achak and beckoned his brother closer. Achak joined the embrace. He looked over to Thomas who stoically nodded. Something had died inside of the ranch hand. There was a look in his eyes Isaac had never before seen.

Thomas knelt on the ground and loaded his rifle and pistols. By the time the men had broken their embrace, Thomas was on his feet, weapons ready, eyes fixed on the door. He was muttering to himself. With each infernal thud on the door, with each blow upon its frame, Thomas' voice grew in volume.

" —I will fear no evil, for thou art with me. Thy rod and thy staff comfort me!"

Thud.

" —Thou annointeth my head with oil. My cup runneth over!"

The men faced the door together as the banging reached a crescendo. As they raised their rifles there came a splintering sound from behind them.

Isaac saw a flicker of movement in the corner of his eye. While two of the creatures had been working the door, One-eye had been timing its blows on the ceiling. The rafters exploded as it landed in their midst. One-eye was a flurry of movement, its limbs striking so quickly that the air cracked like a bullwhip. Isaac caught a blow square in the chest that tossed him against the wall, knocking the stuffing from him. He hit it at an awkward angle, and the bones in his forearm snapped, a rod of fire running up his arm to his elbow. He collapsed in agony just in time to see Achak and Thomas thrown backwards by the strength of the creature.

Only Jacob remained standing. He unleashed the power of his Winchester into the Skinwalkers abdomen, blowing a gaping wound straight through the belly of the beast. There was a quiet moment as the creature regarded its wound.

Jacob turned to Isaac and smiled.

The creature reared up and its jaws opened wide with a roar. Isaac felt his eardrums rupture and the world was filled with high pitched ringing. Clutching at his head he could only watch as One-eye swooped forward, closing its jaws around Jacob's head. The teeth cut through his brother's skull like fingers into soft dough. If he could have heard anything, it would have been his brother's skull collapsing, a dull popping like crab claws being snapped. Isaac could not tell if he was screaming, but he could feel the breath leaving his trembling body and his throat felt like it had been scoured with sand.

One-eye bit the top half of Jacob's head clean off. It took his limp body in one hand and tossed him up and out of the guard house just as the other two creatures broke through the remnants of the door. In a blur they moved upon Achak and Thomas. Achak lay unconscious when the Skinwalker opened him up. Thomas, on the other hand, was very much awake. He tried to stand as the second creature advanced upon him. Even had time to draw his pistol and unload his weapon as it wrapped its enormous hand around his face and began to squeeze.

Blood spouted from between the Skinwalker's fingers and

within a few seconds the massive fist closed, and Thomas struggled no more.

Isaac, his arm shattered, spied his rifle lying a few feet to his right. One-eye towered over him, its white face and shining eyes filled his vision. His family was dead: Jacob, his father, his three native brothers, Thomas, and Bronson, all gone.

He sucked in a breath and braced himself against the wall. "You know what? Y'all are ugly bastards."

One-eye tossed its head back and its body wracked in spasms. The world slipped again and just like before Isaac could see the form beneath the Skinwalker's face, the frail body of an ancient sorcerer, his rheumy eyes, his sunken flesh. The world reset and the beast turned its gaze to Isaac once more and it moved for him.

Isaac closed his eyes and waited for the inevitable.

Yet death did not come. He opened his eyes and saw a thin beam of light cut through the dusty air in front of him. One-eye's claws hovered centimetres from his face, cut off by the light. Dawn spilled into the room. The air was filled with the smell of burning hair, a smell Isaac knew from branding season when his father had burned the family mark into the cattle hides with a red-hot poker.

The creatures began to retreat. The two lesser Skinwalkers made a beeline for the rampart walls and clambered up and over, the weak morning sun scalding their hides as they went. In a moment they were gone, screeching as they went.

One-eye backed itself into the corner beside Bronson's body. It regarded Isaac for a moment before turning towards the corpse. It huddled over the dead man and began to quiver. Isaac watched as the skin on the creature's back loosened and bubbled, as if there was a reaction going on underneath, bones rearranging themselves, shaping into a different form.

The Skinwalker latched onto Bronson, its lips forming a seal over the dead man's face. Their forms melded together, and they were, for a fleeting moment, a single thing, joined at the head, undulating, writhing. One-eye's skin began to darken to mimic Bronson's skin tone.

No. Isaac hauled himself over the floorboards as One-eye's bones cracked and snapped as it reconstituted its body shape to approximate the dead man before it. The whole transformation took barely a minute.

It turned to face Isaac; a large smile spread across the caved in face. It had mimicked Bronson exactly, down to the very wounds that killed him. Every gash, every splinter of bone. It smiled dumbly, blood bubbling out of its nose, the shattered jaw working absently.

"Sunlight can't harm you if you're human?"

One-eye smiled broadly with Bronson's smashed face and stooped to lift the large blade from Achak's body. It held it up to the sunlight, letting the light dance across the flawless metal surface. Satisfied, it advanced on Isaac, eager to finish the job it had started.

"How about bullets?" Isaac rolled onto his back. In his right hand he held his Winchester, the same one he'd loaded before the creatures burst into the room, the same one his father had given him when he first turned fifteen.

The round tore a fist-sized hole in One-eye's chest. "That's for my brothers."

Another round tore the left arm from the body just below the shoulder. "That's for my father."

One-eye slipped to its knees; a look of incredulity crossed its face.

"This one? This is for me." He raised the rifle to the creature's face, which was only a foot or so away, and pulled the trigger.

One-eye's head exploded.

• •*

Isaac swam in warm, dark waters. He was barely aware of the army of flies that roamed his face, pushing themselves up his nose and into the back of his throat. He floated for an eternity before something rough dragged him back to the world.

A large brown and white face nudged him and the rasp of a long tongue on his cheek pushed his head to the side. His swollen tongue filled his mouth, and his throat ached.

"Fury?" he croaked. "Goddamn. Ain't you a beauty."

Fury huffed and nudged Isaac again. The message was clear. It was time to go.

"Gimme a minute, will ya? There's something we have to do first."

They passed out of the gates of Fort Sumner as the last light drained from the day. The chill of evening crept upon him as they rode out onto the plains of New Mexico. He tugged Fury's reins gently and they turned to watch the fire take the wooden walls and guard towers of Fort Sumner, and for the smoke to rise like a black finger into the sky. The horse huffed, bristling at the sight of the inferno. As the fire raged and the night claimed the sky, Isaac became aware of a growing chorus of yips and yowls from the plains as coyotes emerged from their burrows, curious and eager to feed.

Smoke swirled, twisted by a sudden gust of wind, and enclosed them with an unexpected speed. Fury panicked, spooked by the fire and the noises, and turned in circles. From every direction came the yips and barks of the coyotes and for a moment, Isaac thought he heard something louder, more ferocious amidst the infernal chorus.

THE BATTLE FOR HALLOWAY PASS

Richard Beauchamp

Mine #4, Halloway Pass, Colorado, June 7th, 1879

Well shit fire, I do hear something,'" Otis Boward muttered as he approached the end of the cavern where boulders the size of his shotgun shack towered above him. It was his unlucky job to blow the plug, and after years of stripping gold from Bear Horn Mountain, this was the last bit of un-raped land left in the county. This part of the cave system had been avoided by three generations of miners as folktales and rumors of the cave being cursed travelled down the family lines. Of the pure black boulders that did not appear to come from any land remotely close to the mountain. Tales of men being driven insane by voices that could be heard if you put your head right up to the rocks and listened.

But that was all a bunch a goddamned hogwash to Otis, who'd moved to Halloway Pass on the ass end of the great gold rush and had been left scraping pebbles out of already plundered earth. He and the rest of Mine Troop 37 would go broke soon if they didn't strike a new vein, and this was all they had in terms of virgin land. Otis held the leaking dynamite for a moment, blinking as he heard the ethereal voices floating from the rock. *No way, no god damn way.* For a second, he half considered hollering at Joseph and Ken, who stood at the other end of the fuse, waiting for his signal to ignite.

The bundle of dynamite in his hand was the leftovers from their last shipment four years ago, and it sweated something fierce. He was the only sumbitch crazy enough to go near the stuff, but Otis knew how to handle the sweaty sticks. You just walked real slow, holding the sticky bundles the way you hold a sleeping child. He'd gotten all the way down the quarter mile of ever widening corridor before coming to the infamous blocked wall. The whispers grew louder, more incessant, and Otis began to feel lightheaded. How did these big black boulders get here anyway? And these walls were too smooth and round to be natural, they…

His thoughts got away from him, and his grip loosened on the five pounds of dynamite – just enough to blow a hole in the wall without bringing the whole thing down on their heads. It was already slipping from his old, leathery fingers by the time he registered he was dropping it.

Otis's fate was the most merciful. Vaporized almost instantly as the explosion roared through the cave tunnel, shaking the ground beneath the cluster of miners who waited tensely some three hundred yards away. Dust and smoke engulfed the men as a miasma of burnt flesh, excrement, and stale sweat washed over them. With the stench came an ungodly caterwauling. Joseph Whittaker, the chief engineer and the one holding the detonator, was the first to come to his wits. He turned to run just as something slammed into his back, driving his face into the stone floor.

He was aware of teeth. Vicious, sharp little teeth tearing into his shoulder, biting through his overalls like it was the skin on a well fried chicken. He raised his head to scream, and a taloned hand closed around his jugular. White-hot pain lanced across his throat. As he lay there, aspirating his own blood, modulated wails sounded over the cries and screams of his men dying. The last thing he saw was a human foot moving past his head. Except it was all wrong. The ankle was distended and hung at a wrong angle from the lanky appendage of its leg. The flesh was seared and blistered, dripping pus as it arced through the air. The toenails long and curved and filthy yellow.

Then those tiny teeth fell upon him, thousands of them. Eating the flesh from his bones with maniacal efficiency.

* * *

"Christ, you smell that?" Virgil asked the group traveling behind him. His Mustang tensed under him the closer they got to Halloway Pass, and as the stench of exposed organs and blood tickled their noses on the mountain breeze, Winrey had stopped and bucked just a bit. Ol' girl was spooked, like the rest of them.

"Smells like a killin' field to me, Mister Mayson," Johnathan Bailey said. "Mighty fresh one I might add."

Virgil heard the click as the 'retired' Texas Ranger cocked his revolver.

"We're still two miles out," said Kuruk. "Gotta be a lot of spilled blood for us to smell it from here." His Appaloosa, which was the surliest of them all but seemed to love Kuruk, whinnied in protest and flat out refused to go any further. They were in the middle of a high gorge, Ponderosas on either side of them.

"Well, the telegram did sound urgent," Andrew Gregors added from the rear, the portly Canadian trapper's face pouring sweat.

"Urgent?" Virgil said. "Shit, sounded like the ramblings of a man who lost his sanity in some poorly distilled hooch. Something about opening up the gates of hell, demons with the speed of mountain lions killing everyone. This is the first evidence I've gotten since we set out that this is a legitimate situation." Virgil dismounted, and the others followed suit. "Let's tie up here, it's clear we ain't gonna ride in. Probably best to go slow and easy, keep our eyes open."

Each of the men found a nearby tree and tied off their horses, whispering calm words of reassurance to their animals, all of them hoping their mounts didn't sense the scrotum-tightening fear in their voices. Then came the sounds of guns being primed and loaded and the clink of shells falling into ammo pouches, which was very loud in the preternaturally quiet valley. It was high summer, yet the birdsong, the rustle of squirrels and foxes running through the woods, none of that was present. Despite the sun that had followed them with malicious intent, burning their necks raw, it felt more like the dead of winter out here.

Virgil had heard that kind of silence before in the aftermath of Little Bighorn, where even the animals had to stop and gape at the sheer animosity of man's cruelty. He was one of the few Yankees that survived, because he'd ran and hid before the battle started. In the eyes of the US government, he was a deserter. Virgil wasn't the coward the WANTED posters proclaimed. He just didn't want to kill his fellow human beings. Especially those he respected. After the battle of Standridge, he began to loathe his fellow countrymen, had seen them rape and pillage first nation villages in the way they accused their enemies.

Once the great plains wars had died down, and the bounties on his head went by unheeded, he'd quietly begun work as a rogue mercenary, eventually finding men of his same demeanor —

"I don't like this," Kuruk said, nearly making Virgil piss himself with that cat-quiet way he could creep up on you.

Virgil looked into the Apache's eyes, and saw that fierce, primal intelligence he'd noted when he'd freed Kuruk from a cattle rustler turned crazed vigilante. After killing the fat rancher twice over for what the man had done to Kuruk's mother and sisters, the Apache had been the second member to join Virgil's unofficial brigade.

Out of the other three mercenaries, Virgil trusted Kuruk's instincts the most. The fact Kuruk was scared only made Virgil more tense.

"I don't like it either," Virgil said, "but we got ourselves a town in distress, and the army sure as shit ain't coming all the way out here. We gotta investigate." He shouldered his Springfield repeater and checked the sights. On his thigh was one of Johnathan's big ass hand canons, given to him as a gift after Virgil had rescued the belligerent Texan from a surly band of banditos who'd wanted his balls for busting their tequila still located in a bad part of Laredo. The damn thing was heavy and kicked like a pregnant mule, but it could blow a hole the size of a fist in anything you pointed it at, and that was good.

He checked that his men were ready. Andrew with his blunderbuss and carbine, a wicked buck knife sequestered somewhere on his person. Johnathan with his hand canons and viper quick draw. Kuruk had his war club, an intimidating piece of primal weaponry, along with four union bayonet-turned throwing blades, and the instincts of a well-honed predator. Virgil led them single file down the descending pass until they spied the small mining hamlet of Halloway Pass, sitting unassuming and idyllic, surrounded by mountains. The tallest of the peaks – Bear Mountain, the map said – was conspicuous by the gaping black maw of a cave entrance at its base and the barren absence of flora on its soil.

But as they neared, the evidence of a massacre revealed itself to them.

Crimson droplets misted out in various directions along the bare earth, blood spatters indicative of tremendous blunt force trauma. Virgil spied a single boot in front of the swinging doors of a saloon, a white, ragged stump of calf poking up from the crimson-stained leather.

A wooden signpost read: HALLOWAY PASS. PO— sat at the very mouth of the valley they'd just traversed. Virgil used the barrel of his carbine to cautiously lift away a chunk of glistening viscera to read the rest of it.

POP 203. Two hundred and three souls.

The preternatural silence that had followed them through the valley, now lay heavy and suffocating. These small glimpses of bloody violence, the shattered bar windows, torn pieces of blood-spattered clothing fluttering lazily in the foul wind, and spent shell casings that glittered in the sun, marked the beginning of all hell breaking loose.

The thing that slammed into Virgil was fast, but he managed to get an arm up just in time to block it. It was bony and foul-smelling, and Virgil's wits were temporarily slowed as he got his first glimpse of the thing. Its head was vaguely human-shaped, but the proportions were all wrong. One side bulged with a grotesque semi-translucent boil, a few strands of straw-like hair sprouted from it. Its eyes were completely white, and a diamond-shaped furrow had been gouged out where nose and mouth should be, exposing bloody cartilage and bone. The mouth transformed into some clefted monstrosity with double rows of teeth.

It inhaled deeply then unleashed a screeching wail so loud Virgil thought his eardrums would burst. He was sure they would've if Kuruk hadn't sunk his war club into the thing's skull, destroying the entire upper mass of its head as easily as one would a rotten egg. Terrible ichor tinged red and yellow exploded from all sides as the thing spasmed wildly in its death throes.

"Woo! Gonna be a shootout today boys!" Ranger Bailey said in that maniacal voice he took on when his blood was up and the lead was flying.

Virgil's aching ears rang harshly as a double boom from the crazy Texan's .357s blasted crimson and mustard yellow coronas out of the backs of two more charging creatures. Christ, yes, they were fast. They moved with animal-like efficiency, some loping on all fours like deer, others running with preternatural speed and grace despite their hideously deformed physiognomies. Each sported different corrupted forms, from long-snouted weasel-like bastards that bulged with muscle and hugged tight to the ground like a snake, to bloated corpulent forms that could withstand a shot from Andrew's elephant gun – by far the most fearsome of their weapons in caliber and damage – and still shamble forward.

Virgil snapped out of his stunned awe just in time to see something that had no flesh and glistened in the high morning sun land on him. Monstrously foul breath washed over him as crooked, blackened teeth snapped inches away from his jugular. He looked around for Kuruk, but the Apache was busy fighting for his own life.

He managed to slip his revolver free and angle it upwards into the thing, praying the back blast wouldn't blow his hand off. Virgil pulled the trigger. A muffled *whoomph* like an underwater canon blast filled his side with a searing heat, and he watched as black and purple organs arced high in the noon sun and splashed indifferently on the Colorado soil. His wrist ached like a sumbitch as he kicked the thing off him, recoiling at the long strands of goo that reluctantly snapped away as they disconnected.

THE BATTLE FOR HALLOWAY PASS

He heard a scream from somewhere to his right but didn't have time to look and see who it was. Searing pain lanced across his right bicep as something hooked came up on him from behind. Virgil rolled in the dirt, grabbing his dropped knife, and brought his left hand up in a vicious swing that saw the blade sink into hot, spurting meat. Something was grabbing at him, trying to bite through his thick leather tunic, and he stabbed four more times. Quick, savage blows that felt like he was cutting through gelatinous paper. A thing that looked the most human of them all so far stared up at him with eggshell-colored eyes and let out a gurgled moan before falling to the ground.

"Come on! We gotta find shelter!" Kuruk yelled.

When Virgil turned, Andrew had an arm draped over Kuruk, the other arm a gored mess at the shoulder. The creatures were closing in from all sides, and Virgil swallowed back the panic trying to surge up within him. His eyes roved over the humble town; run down shot-gun shacks and a few adobe buildings. Then he spotted solid walls and barred windows. Town jail. He knew from experience that the jail house of any gold mine boom town was usually built the strongest to make sure those (usually belligerently soused off shine) miners couldn't break out.

"There! The jail!" Virgil shouted, and bolted for it, dodging an incoming creature and ducking as its claws whistled inches above his head.

He got to the wooden double doors and pulled, expecting them to be barred shut. To his surprise, they swung open with a groan. He turned and kept them propped open as he shouldered his Springfield and started laying down covering fire. He picked off two creatures who were converging on Kuruk and the wounded Andrew, the two men shambling in at an excruciatingly slow pace as Kuruk did his best to support his friend. Johnathan stood his ground, feet planted wide in that cocky Texan shooter's draw of his, mowing down the creatures as fast as they appeared from around building walls and scrub brushes.

"Mister Baley, if you don't haul that skinny ass of yours into this jail, I swear I'll leave you to the buzzards!" Virgil roared as Johnathan's pistols clicked empty, and just as smooth as you please, the man holstered them and withdrew the double set of sawed-off shotguns holstered to his back. He turned to sprint, a look of sheer lunacy and elation in his eyes as he bolted for the door, a dragon plume of smoke erupting from his right hand as he shot down one of the imp things in midair without even looking at it.

As Johnathan took his time butchering, Kuruk and Andrew fell through the jailhouse doors, and it wasn't until the shotguns clicked empty that Johnathan finally decided to seek refuge. Virgil slammed the doors shut as Johnathan dove inside, and half expected the heavy oak barrier to be ripped from his hands. He waited, Johnathan bracing the door with him, but no resistance came. The abominations didn't even claw at the door. After a tense few minutes, Virgil let go.

"Guess they don't like jails," Johnathan said as he turned to survey his surroundings. "At least these demonic fuckers got a lick of sense to 'em."

"Hello?" Virgil called out. The front desk was barren, and two doors on either side of the desk led out to the jail cells. It appeared abandoned, yet all of them immediately noticed a thick, breathtaking smell of rot, a stench so powerful it had no context. Virgil bit back his gorge as he waited for a response.

"Hu... Hello?" came a voice – frail, trembling, weak.

Virgil had not expected a reply at all.

Johnathan reloaded his still smoking double-barrel and nodded toward the left entrance. "I take left, you take right, let's clear this place right quick."

Virgil nodded, his rifle held ready as he headed past Andrew and Kuruk. He tossed a quick glance at Andrew, saw the man had taken on a fish belly pallor, sweat pouring down his face. Virgil would deal with that later.

He entered a hallway that was stiflingly hot, the miasma of rot growing into a physical thing that pushed into his nasal cavities and made his eyes water. In the first jail cell he saw what looked like liquidized lasagna with a rainbow-esque oily sheen coating its surface. A horde of flies with their little legs sticking straight up to the ceiling bordered the puddle.

"What in god's name..." He croaked as he put his bandana up over his face.

"Sir...? Are you... real?"

The frail voice came from down the hall. Virgil blinked away tears and peered down the hallway. A tanned, wrinkled arm hung out from one of the cells. Virgil strode away from the abhorrent mess in the first cell and found himself looking instead at the oldest woman he'd ever seen. She wore beautifully quilted ceremonial garments, her face a ragged topography of deeply etched lines. Both eyes were milky with cataracts. She groped blindly, and Virgil put out a reassuring hand. He stared at her gray bird's nest of hair, somewhat tamed into messy rows by bone trinkets. He knew right then she was a shaman of some sort.

Her leathery hand gripped his with surprising strength, and the woman let out a cry of relief. She muttered something in Apache, Virgil thought it might've been *bless the gods* but his rudimentary understanding of the beautiful language only let him hear snatches of the words.

"You're all right now, ma'am," Virgil said as he tried to steady the tremor in his voice, trying to make it sound like his noggin wasn't tripping over itself trying to make sense of what biblical horrors he'd just experienced. "Please, can you tell me what the blazes is going on here?"

She brought his hand close to her face, sniffed. A look of confusion creased her wrinkles even deeper. "You... You are not him... The one I was told would come to fight. No white man can fix this."

"M-Ma'am?" Virgil asked, confused.

The woman began to cry, agonized wails that echoed balefully off the stone walls. Virgil held her hand and waited patiently, wondering how long she'd been cooped up in this foul furnace.

"I tried... warn them. They wouldn't... listen..." she said between sobs as she struggled to regain her composure. Her speech was heavily accented, and it was clear she spoke English like he spoke Apache.

"Kuruk!" Virgil called, and barely heard the soft patter of approaching footsteps from down the hall.

"Listen, young lady, I got a fine feller over here whose Apache himself. I want you to explain to him everything that happened here, all right? I have a friend that needs tending to, but I promise we're gonna get you out of this." Virgil squeezed her arthritic hand in both of his as Kuruk appeared like a shadow at his side.

"You should go check on Andrew, he's not doing so good," Kuruk said, a look of tense worry on his face.

"I'll do that. You lend an ear to this lady and see what she has to say." Virgil clapped him on the shoulder as he made his way out to the front reception, thankful for the lesser degree of stink out there.

When he saw his trapper friend, his stomach dropped into his boots. "How's goin', feller?" he said, gently touching Andrew on his good shoulder.

Andrew began to shiver upon the wooden bench, and looked up with something Virgil had never seen in the man's eyes before: frightened desperation.

"Not doing so good, boss. Feels like... Feels like fire through my veins... It burns so bad... Bastard bit me good..."

Virgil helped the man out of his shirt; Andrew always dressed light on account of him being from up north, poor boy never acclimated to the heat. Virgil winced when he saw the dark red lines emanating from the crescent gore of the bite wound. *Blood poisoning already?* The exposed flesh from the wound was blackening, turning gangrenous before his very eyes. *No... Not possible...*

Johnathan returned from scouting the other cells, his face pale as he stood by Andrew. "All clear except for... some kinda puddle of awful sitting in one of those— *Jesus Christ*, Andy, you look like a cat turd covered in cracker crumbs, if I'm to speak frankly." Johnathan knelt to look at the wound then nudged

Virgil. "Hey partner, let's talk in the corner real quick," he said, pulling a stunned Virgil away from Andrew.

They stood towards the left entrance, where the familiar rot grew stronger. "Listen, I seen that kind of wound before, but on men who've been on their death bed for weeks. Nothing about this makes sense, but I tell ya, we gotta chop that arm off before whatever kinda poison he got hit with, spreads," Johnathan said in a low voice, the maniacal Texan Devil side gone from him now.

"Yeah…" Virgil had been thinking the same thing. Christ, this was going downhill fast. For a minute he half considered turning tail to run, but he couldn't leave the woman behind, and there was Andrew… They'd get cut to pieces before they got halfway back to their horses.

A shuddering groan sounded from behind them, and they turned to find Andrew convulsing. His feet drummed an obscene tattoo on the floor, his whole body shook as foam erupted from his mouth, and his head slammed back against the wall.

"Shit!" Virgil ran to his friend, but in the time it took them to cross the ten feet, Andrew's convulsions stopped, and he slid off the wooden bench. Virgil shook Andrew gently, but the man was a heavy ragdoll in his arms.

Virgil knew real fear then. More than what he'd felt on the battlefield surrounded by an unending horizon of fierce whooping Cheyenne in full battle dress, the scalps and scrotums of his countrymen dangling off their war horses. What was happening here defied logic, and Virgil would've gone on staring at his dead friend, but Kuruk returned holding a strange object made of polished ebony and hair.

* *

"The Chiwa'ee…" Kuruk said, sounding stunned, and staring at the strange talisman in his hand.

Virgil recognized the word from the old woman's ramblings. "Go on, son, what'd she say?"

"I'd heard the legends… but… I thought they were just tales told by the elders to keep the children in line. But it's real…" He sat heavily on the floor, the burden of knowledge weighing him down.

Johnathan's foot tapped impatiently. "Spit it out, boy, we ain't got all day."

Kuruk looked up at them, then at Andrew's dead form, a single tear springing from his left eye. "An ancient demon. He feeds off people's worst desires. Greed, lust, rage, anger. He takes whatever poisons your soul, and manifests it physically. Turns people into the most monstrous versions of themselves once they die… and… and then you're a slave to him," Kuruk whispered, his eyes fixed gravely upon his fallen brother. "Your soul leaves your body and becomes his if you die by his hand. The things that attacked us, were once people. The people of this town, and the people of Dahteste's village long ago… they—"

"Dah what? Who is that?" Johnathan asked.

"Dahteste. It means warrior-woman. That is her name," Kuruk said, hitching a thumb back towards the jail cells. "She was one of the most respected elders in her village before the whites came and took over. They didn't kick them out like other frontiersmen did, and for a while everyone lived peacefully together until they started mining the mountain." His eyes closed as more tears threatened to spill over. "Dahteste and her people warned the white men that one must not harvest anything that comes from that specific peak, because long ago, they'd managed to trap a fierce demon within its bowels. Dahteste had called upon some of the most powerful shamans of all the First Nation people to come together and help her seal the Chiwa'ee away after he'd nearly decimated her whole village, turning loved ones into monsters, claiming everyone who died in the plains battles and corrupting their spirits."

Kuruk glanced back towards the cells as he continued. "She was one of the last survivors of her village by the time they began to mine. When they'd blown a hole into the barrier created by a most powerful magic, the townspeople began to turn into monsters, and they blamed her. Locked her up in here because they thought she cursed them. In reality though, she was trying to save them..." Kuruk's eyes turned glassy as he recounted the woman's words. "He's... real..." he said again, more to himself than the others.

"Uhm... All right..." Johnathan said, clearly dubious.

Virgil knew the Texan had grown up being taught Kuruk and his people were nothing more than savages, and it took a lot of careful sit-downs and rounds of fire water between ranger and warrior for Johnathan to take a liking to Kuruk. Still, talk of Native American esotericism was so much hogwash to Johnathan, and Virgil knew it.

"Are we sure this woman's ramblings can be trusted?" Johnathan asked.

"You have any other explanation for what the fuck is going on around here?" Virgil snapped. "How do we stop it, Kuruk?"

"He resides deep within Standing Bear Mountain, its true name. We must destroy him, or rather, *I* must destroy him. He can be damaged by mere weapons, but he cannot be killed unless the death blow is struck by someone of pure Apache blood, while wielding the Dilhil Ba'cho, Fang of The Black Wolf," he said, holding up the ornate sigil in his shaking hand. "It is to be wielded by me. She knew we were coming. That *I* was coming. We are part of this prophecy..."

At this, Virgil remembered the way she sniffed his hand, the confusion on her face, as if she were expecting someone else.

"And just what the hell is that supposed to be?" Johnathan asked, pointing at the item in Kuruk's hand, the skepticism slowly fading from his voice.

"A powerful totem, blessed with the blood and tears of Dahteste and three other shamans," Kuruk said. "It is why the demons have not attacked this building. They cannot stand to be near it. It will protect us so long as we are within its range."

Virgil and Johnathan looked at each other. Despite the fanatical nature of the tale, it all made too much sense with what was happening around them, and why the beasts didn't try to barge in here and kill them outright.

Virgil sighed, understanding what must be done. "All right, here's what's going to happen. We're hunkering down here for the night. Come sunup, we're going into that cave and we're gonna see what's what. Then, we're going to come back here and bury our friend." He nodded towards Andrew, whose skin was drooping from his face in a sickening way. "I'll see if I can find the key and let out Dahteste—"

"She wants to stay locked up," Kuruk interrupted. "They can't get to her through the bars."

"All right," Virgil said. "Go in there and give her a swig of your water skin and some hard tack. Give her the key anyway, in case she changes her mind. Poor woman's probably been stuck in there for days."

Night came and the three men huddled around the two candles they'd found in the place, all of them taking swigs off Virgil's home-brewed shine, none of them able to eat with the stench that permeated the place. Floating off on the numbing embrace of booze, Virgil let himself drift to sleep, hoping this was all some fucked-up, desert-induced fever dream.

But by morning, and in the meager rays of dawn light splicing through the barred portals, Virgil awoke to find Andrew gone. The man's clothes remained, sitting flattened in an abhorrent goo that spread in a wide puddle. Johnathan woke a few minutes later, and upon seeing the remains of his friend turned his head and vomited up his humble dinner of whiskey. The retching roused Kuruk, and, after groans and sighs, the men wordlessly grabbed their gear.

Virgil said a prayer for his fallen brother then handed Kuruk the big elephant gun and the powder bag that went with it. "Here. You're the only one without a gun. I know you hate the damn things, but just take it. He'd want you to have it."

Kuruk took the weapon without protest, strapping it to his back while Virgil and Johnathan reloaded their guns and took fortifying sips of the fire water, bracing themselves for the horrors outside.

"All right," Virgil said. "Let's see if that lady's totem is the real thing or not." With a breath, Virgil kicked open the doors of the jail.

They all winced as the bright morning sun stabbed their eyes. Kuruk went out ahead of them, the sigil thrust high into the air. Virgil squinted as his eyes adjusted; the town square was empty. Johnathan and Virgil flanked Kuruk, blinking away after images as they searched for signs of movement. They got about ten feet outside when they heard a bestial ululation to the north, in the direction of the cave. The three men turned.

The beasts came in twos and threes at first. Then more. Popping their deformed little heads over the outcropping of boulders leading up to the cave. Their pale forms scuttled and galloped down the hillside at disturbing speed. Virgil's asshole puckered and his balls retreated into the safety of his stomach cavity. Various cocking hammers clicked into place as Johnathan got ready to go to war.

"Hold..." Virgil commanded.

Kuruk now also held his war club, while Virgil and Johnathan's barrels pointed out to either side of the Apache, the three men watching as hell raced to meet them.

The beasts drew closer, the ground thudding with their approach like a stampede of wild buffalo. They closed in.

Three hundred yards, running and crawling and galloping without fear or reservation.

Two hundred yards, and Virgil could see them clearly, and the sight of their grotesque forms was made all the more terrible by the knowledge they were once people. He almost wondered if he would soon join their ranks, but quickly stomped the thought back into his subconscious.

One hundred yards.

"Boss?" Johnathan asked, his voice tight as the monsters showed no sign of stopping.

A wave of thunder and the discordant chorus of hell itself rang out over the pass as the beasts hissed and howled, hundreds of them bearing down on the men.

"Hold..." Virgil's finger rested on the trigger of his carbine, every orifice in his body clenched tight enough to crack walnuts.

Fifty yards.

The tidal wave of dust they kicked up behind them spread as far as the valley walls, their many snapping maws glinting and flinging glistening runners of drool as they ran.

Twenty-five yards.

Two more seconds and they'd be in striking distance.

"FUCK IT!" Johnathan let loose. His .357s created their own thunder to answer the monstrous roar.

Virgil lost his resolve and fired as well, aiming carefully at the front most row of corrupted flesh. The top of a beast's head exploded, and when his vision was lost to so much dust and gun smoke, he fired blindly.

He braced for the pain, the agony, to feel his flesh rend between needle teeth, to feel the breathtaking hotness of his throat being sliced open. But the pain did not come. Only mild suffocation as the tsunami of dust the beasts had kicked up in their charge came rushing past them, stinging their eyes and punching into their lungs. After an indignant bout of coughing, the dust cleared.

They were surrounded on all sides.

Virgil stared around, amazed. There was a definitive fifteen-foot circle of bare earth the creatures refused to cross. The monsters reached out with wicked claws and snapping jaws, one even tried to charge forward but made it two steps before letting out an indignant screech and staggering backwards.

"Ain't no god damn fuckin' way…" Johnathan breathed.

The three men stood frozen, all too afraid to move for fear of breaking the stand-off.

It was Kuruk who took a defiant step forward, and the creatures directly in front of him shambled out of the way with squawks and cries. Inversely, the creatures at their back scuttled forward eagerly.

"Stay close," Kuruk said, and just as he did a new type of monster stepped forward. It had a long, gangly neck almost like an ostrich, and opened a vertical slit of a mouth.

"Watch out!" Johnathan yelled as the thing made a disgusting wet, throaty noise.

THE BATTLE FOR HALLOWAY PASS

An arc of yellowish fluid shot out across the fifteen-foot gap. Kuruk ducked and sidestepped. Virgil tried to follow but the tail end of the globule caught his leather tunic, and it started to spit and sizzle, quickly eating through the fabric. It burnt through his thick long johns and down to his undershirt before the last trace of it nicked his flesh with a bright hot flash of heat. Virgil ignored the pain and focused on the bulbous undulating head that spat the venom. His carbine bucked, and the monster's skull popped like a squashed grape. The thing collapsed to the earth, smoking ichor draining from its ventilated head.

"Okay," Johnathan said, his voice cool, collected. "So it ain't gonna exactly be a stroll down the beach. That's all right. Take us forward, son. We'll cap the spitters."

* * *

The journey up to the cave entrance was arduous and tedious. They walked slowly, keeping their ranks tight as they traversed the steep terrain while keeping each other within arm's reach at all times. Occasionally, one of the spitters would pop out from behind a rock and try to tag them. One got lucky and nicked Kuruk, the stuff getting in his long black hair and sizzling it away, one side now comically short. Kuruk had dispatched that one himself, one of the bayonet throwing irons whistling through the air and planting itself firmly in the thing's forehead. A weak stream of venom shot out before it collapsed.

It took them two hours to get to the mouth of the cave, the creatures snapping and spitting on all sides the whole while. Once they arrived at the narrow plateau in front of the looming entrance, they stopped, collecting their breath and stretching muscles pulled taught by fear and physical exertion. Virgil stared at the large black maw before him. Despite the high-noon sun at their backs, sunlight seemed to wither and die when it reached into the cave. Almost like an obsidian veil covered it. He could make out absolutely nothing beyond the first fifteen feet or so, and even with the totem Kuruk held, every fiber of Virgil's being told him he should not go into that god forsaken cave.

But Kuruk, after having tied the remains of his singed hair into a horse tail, held the totem towards the cave. He spoke something then, his voice bold and imposing and resonant. The words sounded like an archaic version of the Apache tongue, with harsh consonances not typically found in the language.

In response to Kuruk's incantation, the sigil began to glow – a deep, hued red that cast away the hungry shadows of the cave. He took one step forward when they all heard it.

Virgil was reminded of the first creature he'd encountered that'd screamed in his face, but the ungodly roar that emanated from the mountain made that ear-splitting screech sound like a kitten's mewl in comparison. The roar echoed from the throat of the cave, slowly fading into a bassoon dissonance that gave Virgil a bout of vertigo before two creatures came spilling from the void.

These were the slow-moving leviathans that stumbled toward Kuruk; huge monstrosities whose skin seemed wholly comprised of boils and abscessed flesh. The Apache warrior stood his ground, thrusting the sigil before him.

One of the things extended an arm that looked cast from granite. It grabbed Kuruk's arm, desperate to destroy the totem. The leviathan's arm lit up, pustules popping like grease in a skillet, but still it kept on, driven to destroy that which its master detested. Johnathan fired four rounds into the monster in quick succession, all direct hits that did nothing to the creature. Virgil was about to raise his carbine when Kuruk dropped the totem from his trapped hand and let it fall between them.

The creature reached for it with its other hand, but Kuruk was faster, twisting and snatching it with his free hand, and driving the spiked point into the leviathan's side.

Bright, molten flowers of light blossomed all over the abomination before a blinding flash and a great inrush of air. Virgil blinked away the after image to find Kuruk standing alone, his right arm seared bright red where the thing had touched him. All that was left of the leviathan was a molten pile of slag.

The other beast stood there, unsure, glancing back towards the cave like a scared, monstrous puppy. Kuruk let out his war cry, something Virgil hadn't heard since the Apache warrior had taken retribution out on those who'd killed his family. Moving with grace and speed, the Apache warrior charged, ducking and dodging the beast's snatching arms, twisting behind it and driving the now brilliantly glowing sigil into the leviathan's shoulder. Again, another bright blast of light and a plume of ashes.

The roar came once more, but its pitch and timbre had changed.

"It's scared," Kuruk said, a coldness in his voice that Virgil had never before heard. "Good. Let's finish this." The young warrior strolled boldly into the cave, waving Virgil and Johnathan on but not looking back to see if they followed.

• •*

None of the creatures assailed them as they moved deeper into the cave. The huge, winding passageway seemed to go on forever but a distinct smell of charnel and rotting flesh grew stronger the farther they went. The sigil in Kuruk's hand grew brighter, fiercer, an ethereal red blade growing from its point. They stepped past the jagged mouth of obsidian that'd been blasted open not four days ago, vague smears on the ground that had once been men. As they moved past the threshold, their surroundings changed completely.

"Lordy," Johnathan said as they crossed into what seemed like the gates of hell itself. "I've been in ten-cent whore houses that made me feel less dirty than this."

The walls glistened black, with tribal etchings gouged deep into the stone as far as the eye could see. The symbols bled steadily with that foul yellow ichor. The passageway narrowed until the men could barely fit three abreast. A deep rumbling resounded from directly ahead, and Virgil wondered if he'd ever see his testicles again – they'd apparently taken up permanent residence in his guts. He didn't blame them for hiding. He wanted to shrink into himself, to turn and run. He knew he was about to face something that would defy every sane thing he thought he knew about the world.

But Kuruk marched forward, undaunted, his courage spurring the men behind him. Soon, the narrow corridor opened up into a vast atrium, the edges of which no human eyes could detect. Virgil had to look down at the ground, which had shrunk to a peninsula some four feet wide jutting out into the black void, and assure himself he wasn't floating in space itself. The abyssal dimensions of this place tortured one's sense of balance and spatial awareness.

Kuruk roared more of those guttural incantations. His voice carried with it the collective rage and sorrow of his people, daring this so-called demon to show itself.

And show itself it did.

From the undulating black mass that surrounded them materialized a great mouth of bone-white teeth that pulled and snapped from the pulsating mass of itself. Each tooth looked to be the size of a house. It spoke to Kuruk in that same, almost Germanic-sounding voice, its own dozens of octaves below anything that had ever spoken a phonetic language, and made Virgil's body resonate the way cannon blasts on the battlefield did – a deep vibration you felt in your chest.

Kuruk roared back, and Virgil wondered what on Earth these two could possibly have to say to each other. Man and deity. Mortal and immortal.

Then the thing let out a laugh that sounded far worse than any bestial roar. It opened its mouth wide, and creatures leapt from its maw. Many of them fell howling into that unending black mass, but several managed to cling onto the narrow peninsula of land the men stood upon. Johnathan and Virgil did what they were born and bred to do, and opened fire. Kuruk continued to hurl his prayers and incantations at the thing, totem held aloft, all the while the red glowing blade grew in size and radiance.

"Whatever you're gonna do, better do it quick, son!" Virgil yelled over the cacophony as he picked off deformed heads and watched snapping jaws explode as he emptied the last of his rounds from his Springfield.

"I'm almost dry!" Johnathan yelled as his thundering cannons soon fell silent, but the creatures kept coming.

Kuruk turned, swiping the sigil, its ruby-red blade slicing through the beasts with ease, causing them to implode. Then the young Apache warrior stood, that huge mouth looming behind him, and looked Virgil in the eyes. "Run, Virgil. This is no longer your battle."

"What? No, no way! You're my brother, Kuruk, and I don't leave—"

"You're a good man, Virgil. You too, Johnathan. You taught me that even white men can have honor. You taught me to cherish that honor and morality over vengeance, and now the time has come for me to honor my people, and show them they raised a true warrior. Destiny has brought me here!" He turned to once again face the abyssal leviathan before him, and roared.

The great disembodied mouth lowered itself towards that narrow strip of land, mouth stretched wide to devour all in its way.

"KURUK!" Virgil screamed as the young man he'd come to trust with his very life jumped impossibly high into the air, the blade of the wolf's fang erupting into a wicked ten-foot scythe and flashing brilliantly with a red light. Virgil watched helplessly as Kuruk took the holy relic in both hands, stabbing downward as he disappeared beyond those monstrous fangs, his battle cry going with him.

There came a sound of great ripping, as if the hands of God were tearing open the fabric of space and time. The ground shook. A huge flash of red light exploded from the maw of the Chiwa'ee.

"RUN!" Johnathan yelled, pulling on Virgil's shirt as the ground beneath them began to crumble away. Virgil could feel his mind beginning to fall with it, his brain had simply had too much to process these last twenty-four hours, but despite this, his primal impulse to survive got his feet moving and he followed Johnathan, sprinting through the narrow corridor, the ancient, bleeding etchings on the wall now sizzling and spitting flames as they ran past. The whole place felt like it was about to come down, and Virgil hoped it would, hoped this place collapsed in on itself so no mortal being would ever stumble upon it again.

Just as they reached the narrow aperture of obsidian, there came an explosion so deep and jarring Virgil thought the earth itself was splitting open. He turned to look back before Johnathan yanked him through the hole. The walls imploded, dust and fire racing up the passageway to consume them. Virgil stumbled out of the hole as Johnathan pulled him with all his might and, using their last reserves of strength, ran towards the mouth of the cave, which seemed miles away.

Then Virgil was being lifted off his feet on a wave of heat and rot.

* *

Virgil came to at the mouth of the cave, gentle, leathery hands touching his face and waking him. He groaned; his head felt like it'd been used as an anvil. When he looked up, it was the ancient but beautiful face of Dahteste.

"You... you did it..." she said in awe, helping Virgil to a sitting position. His body was banged-up and bruised but no fatal injuries could he feel.

"Johnathan..." Virgil groaned again, and got to his feet, his head spinning for a second before he grounded himself. He looked around at the scores of ash piles gently blowing away on the desert breeze, and finally found Johnathan propped up against a boulder, one booted foot hanging at a sickening angle. The Ranger's beloved Stetson was long gone, revealing a balding thatch of bloody hair, and a nasty gash up the side of his face.

"Looks like I... got the shit end of the... stick on our... express exit from hell..." Johnathan laughed as Virgil knelt beside him. He looked the Texan over and saw that besides the twisted ankle and his superficial gash, the crazy devil would live to fight again.

Virgil then turned and looked out over Halloway Pass.

It's peaceful and idyllic veneer now seemed a hollow, poorly disguised façade in the wake of all this hellish violence, its terrible legacy claiming his best friend. Dahteste had collapsed onto the ground, sobbing, and Virgil made his way over to her, placing a hand on her shoulder.

"You did it... You did it... You..."

"Ma'am," he said softly, his voice growing thick with grief. "Ma'am..." he repeated, getting her attention.

She looked up, her eyes rheumy and glazed over.

Virgil swallowed, despair and a sorrow so deep he almost couldn't breathe as he struggled to speak. "Wasn't me. Kuruk did it. He saved us all. Please... Can you give my friend a proper burial?" He held out the flint knife Kuruk had made by hand, the one that held an edge far better than any steel blade. "This is all I have left of him."

And so Dahteste performed a traditional Apache burial, waiting for the cleansing rays of the moon to come out and bathe them before saying several prayers from her people while burning a bundle of sage and moss she'd had in her medicine bag.

Virgil knew the words to this prayer, he'd heard Kuruk say it for his own family. So Virgil spoke the prayers with her, holding her hand, and sobbing freely. Then he turned toward the mouth of the cave, and Virgil Mayson knew he'd be leaving this place a profoundly changed man.

SIX GUNS & SORCERY

Nathan E Meyer

St Louis, gateway to the West, 1888

Tobias Quill stepped off the train and his headache returned. He massaged his temples beneath his dreadlocks; the tinctures were becoming less effective, the headaches more severe. In minutes he could be crippled with pain, but his plans were too close to fruition for him to succumb now. He'd been warned as an apprentice that power came at a price.

Pushing the pain back, Quill strode into the night. He had an appointment to keep.

Weaving his way out from the gambler's quarter towards the river docks, he mentally warded against the fecund stimulus around him. The fish stink of stagnant water, the stench of gutters and refuse piles. Like a rumor, the scent of opium competed with the puissant odor of free-flowing wine and the musk of unwashed bodies. Infused through all of this hung the aromas of a thousand exotic spices.

It was over twenty years after the War Between the States, but the peace and equality prophesied by Lincoln refused to manifest. In some areas of this city a Black man such as himself could be killed merely for being in the wrong place, and the law would do nothing.

St Louis was the gateway to the West. Here, the roads from south and east intersected on the Mississippi River and the Santa Fe Trail began. Though longtime residents pushed for pacification, the bustling city retained rougher, frontier aspects.

Arguments were still settled by a gun.

Deputy marshals moved through an almost bellicose crowd. Merchants hawked wares while cobblestone hucksters promised miracles, and street-whores did the same. A line of bald monks, shook tambourines and chanted, weaving through the throng in orange togas. Entertainers juggled, ate fire, or swallowed swords. Furtive men eyed purses while evangelists predicted the end of the world.

Quill entered a putrid alley while a desert mystic – face alive with tiny albino scorpions, the totems of some inscrutable god – finished his prayers.

He emerged onto a narrow lane fronting the wharves. The yards of river boatwrights sat among innumerable warehouses, interspersed by the occasional seedy tavern. Halfway down the cobblestone street, Quill noticed a weathered, salt-eaten, sign hung crookedly above the tavern door that showed a rooster riding the back of a black cat. Old English lettering read: *The Cock and Pussy,* in tired, lowbrow humor.

The door gaped open, but no sound came from inside. No raucous laughter, no troubadour's music or piano, no drunken shouts.

A shabbily dressed man lay in the middle of the street. The body was so still Quill thought the man dead until he noticed the swelling nose and blackened eyes. Blood dripped from the open mouth, but the man breathed. Below the burlesque-minded sign, three more men lay heaped, as broken and bloody as the first.

Hearing only silence from within the tavern, Quill entered.

Four more bodies lay scattered around the interior.

Tables were broken, chairs smashed. Someone had pulled the chain holding the wagon-wheel candelabra loose, crashing the heavy thing to the floor. A fifth man was sprawled across the bar, the chain wrapped around his neck.

At the back of the room a massive figure in a deerskin tunic sat with head bowed on a wide chest. A leather and beaded headband kept long black hair swept back. Thick arms, veined like the Mississippi delta, rested on the only table left intact in the place. Near one hand sat a whiskey bottle, on the other a bloody table leg. A warlance rested against the wall behind the figure, adorned with eagle feathers. A Colt .44 caliber Walker was shoved into the front of a beadwork belt.

Quill looked behind the bar to find a serving girl cowering behind the fat barkeep. The man obviously had no intention of confronting the quiet figure.

"I called for the deputies," he said.

Crossing the room, Quill spied yet another body under the table. The man's jaw sat at a gruesome angle; shards of his teeth scattered like dice.

The seated figure's head lifted as he approached. Quill stopped. Square-faced, raven hair, brown eyes set above an unsmiling mouth.

A woman? Quill wondered, *all this?* He decided his purveyor, Farq, had earned his fee.

"Oh, you're a pretty one, ain't ya?" she said. "These louts friends of yours?"

Her voice was a coarse mixture of accents. Sioux, maybe Cheyenne. He eyed her beadwork: definitely Cheyenne.

"No," Quill assured her. "Nor am I the law."

She continued as if he hadn't spoken. "'Cause if they are, I can arrange for you to join 'em."

"Farq sent me."

"Farq yourself. I don't know any Farq." The woman hiccupped, then burped. "Wine, damn it!"

Quill eased forward as the serving girl sprang to obey. The brawler watched Quill as he picked up an unbroken chair and set it at the table. "I have a proposition," he began.

"So did these louts, pretty boy." She pointed a finger at the terrified barkeep. "And *that* one said an *Indian* couldn't drink in here." She burped. "So take your proposition and shove off."

"Not that kind of proposition, obstreperous fool. An offer of employment."

A surly looked splashed across her face, and the brawler leaned forward. She snatched a fresh bottle of wine from the shaking girl, who promptly scurried back to the dubious safety of the bar. "Employment? Money? That's good, I can always use money."

"Don't you want to know what the job is?"

"I assume you ain't hiring me to nurse-maid your whelp. Fighting, right?"

"Yes. Against the Tongs."

She looked at him and he noticed a scar running from the line of her jaw back toward her ear. "Tongs? Chinatown?"

He hesitated then nodded. "The Street of Illuminated Temples."

She thrust out a scarred hand, beefy as a stone mason's. "Sarah Six Kills."

Just like that the bargain was struck.

* •*

Beneath a starless sky, the river harbor was fouled with the city's runoff. Gulf sturgeon, attracted by the near constant state of chum from the wharfs, cruised the oily, offal-filled water. Despite the presence of a multitude of scavengers, the town dragged corpses out of the water daily. Bodies brought hard coin from the thaumaturgists and alchemists in the Scholars' Colloquium, no questions asked.

The voodoo Houdans paid even better.

The flat bottom craft cut across the harbor, poled smoothly by Six Kills while Quill directed. They hugged the stone walls of the harbor jetty, working their way towards a line of decrepit buildings built away from the more populated market areas.

Greasy waves slapped a choppy rhythm as Six Kills navigated the boat into a stone culvert gurgling noxious sludge, and concealed from the gloom. With hushed whispers Quill guided her toward the opening.

He smoothed his dreadlocks out of his eyes and studied his surroundings. "Go into that gutter-run."

Six Kills muttered under her breath as she looked up at the pagoda-styled building, but did as Quill instructed, slipping the punt inside the crumbling aqueduct. As she poled, Quill chewed a bitter tablet of Willow Bark and small fragments of crushed Lotus against the stabbing pain in his temples.

"You're dressed nice for an evening in the sewers," Six Kills grunted.

"I'm not here to buy you dinner." Quill pointed into the gloom to where a torch burned an oily flame on a slimy wall. "Up on the left, where those stairs run down to the landing. Tie up there."

Six Kills steered the punt in. "What is this place?"

"It's where the kitchen help dumps the refuse."

Rats squeaked in indignation at the edges of the torchlight. The narrow stone landing was caked with cooking grease and stank of rotting food. Little bones lay scattered around among the scrapings of cooking pots.

"What's that symbol, burned into the door?" she asked. Dressed in her leather tunic, Six Kills coolly wrapped a studded cestus around her left hand. A round shield of buffalo hide hung strapped across her back, over her lance.

Already heading up darkly stained stairs, Quill answered over a shoulder. "That's Yen Lo Wang, the Yama King called the Hungerer. We're under his temple. It was the first thing constructed when Chinese workers arrived to build the railroad."

"You didn't tell me this job involved devil-worshipers!"

"They prefer Yen Lo Wang to be referred to as god, not devil."

"They heat up a hollow bronze idol until it is glowing red hot, and then pitch babies into its open mouth to hear them scream."

"They say their oracles are, 'interpreting the screams for purposes of divination', actually." Quill stopped before the door, checking to ensure it was locked then began tracing signs in the air.

"Sounds like devil-worship to me," Six Kills muttered, walking toward the stairs, flexing her fist around the studded leather cestus. The brass knuckles gleamed dully in the uncertain light.

"Then stealing from them shouldn't bother you, no?"

Six Kills' reply was cut short by a wretched squealing.

The pair spun to the refuse pile in the corner where a rat screeched. A rattlesnake, long as Six Kills' arm, burst out of the rotting compost and snatched up the unwary rodent in dripping fangs.

Quill and Six Kills shared a look. They had both stepped over the pile to reach the stairs. The snake coiled and shook its rattle in warning.

The bolt on the door worked and Quill turned as the heavy wooden portal swung open. The edge struck him as he tried to dodge, sending him sprawling off the grease-slicked edge. He landed hard, breath bludgeoned from him.

A squat, round, Chinese man of middle years stepped onto the landing, head shaved bald except for a topknot hanging over one ear in a tight pigtail. He held pails of slop in each hand, his mouth slack in shock as he gawked at the intruders.

The pails slipped from his hands, and spilled their odious contents over the edge in an avalanche. Quill yelped in surprise, throwing up an arm to cover himself as the slop splashed onto him.

The kitchen worker tried screaming a warning, but with agility earned on the backs of wild mustangs, Six Kills leapt. She snatched the man by one filthy ankle, and heaved his feet out from him.

The man squawked as he hit the stone steps with a sickening *smack,* making no protest as Six Kills yanked him closer, head thumping down each stair as he went.

The big warrior's brass knuckles rose and then fell with the force of a hammer. "Who's screaming now?" Six Kills snarled. She continued punching. "Divine this!"

Six Kills struck the man a final blow, changing the consistency of the kitchen worker's face to mush. Satisfied, she heaved the limp rag of the man's body up and thrust it over the lip of the landing into the filthy runoff of the city.

She watched in grim satisfaction as the foul water claimed him. "More. I liked that. More please."

"Pox," snarled Quill. "It's ruined!" He flung his befouled

suit coat from him in disgust. A Bowie knife appeared in his fist; unearthly flames circled the blade.

Six Kills hissed in surprise, then said, laughing, "I told you this isn't a church picnic. You didn't need to dress so pretty."

Quill opened his mouth to rejoin, when a shriek echoed from the doorway and the unlikely team looked up.

A second kitchen worker – a skinny, young, Tong soldier – ran back the way he had come. Six Kills pulled her lance free. The center of the straight, double-edged blade was tempered to a bluish hue.

Quill felt the subtle hum of power emanating from the blade. Six Kills started up the stairs, but Quill grabbed her arm. "Wait," he hissed. "Follow behind me, stay close, I have the path memorized, but the place will be crawling with Tong soldiers now."

"Good."

Sprinting through the open door, the shrieking peals of alarm bells rang out.

Behind them, the rattlesnake swallowed the rat.

* * *

Quill led the way into the kitchens.

Flaming Bowie knife held high, he scared off any foolishly brave servants. It wouldn't slow temple guards or Tong soldiers, zealots all, but it granted him breathing room for the moment. He counted his steps, ticking off doorways and landmarks as he moved.

'You've been inside the temple before?' Six Kills had asked.

'Yes. It took me months to find what I was looking for. I know the building well.'

'By Coyote's crotch, how did you pull that off?'

'Not all clergy are bound by laws of celibacy. I managed to become chief paramour to Chazra, head of the Cloistered Daughters of Yen Lo Wang.'

'She doesn't sound very cloistered to me. I take it your first attempt failed?'

'Yes. They caught me in the chamber of divination. It is a death sentence for all but the highest of initiates.'

'You are not dead.'

'No.' Quill's voice was so bitter it startled Six Kills. *'Chazra watched while they tortured me. Then she cursed me so each use of my power weakened me further, knowing I could never stop using my gifts.'*

'You're dying? This is why the headaches and the nosebleeds?'

'Yes. The only thing that can save me is the very thing I sought to steal to begin with. The Reliquary of the Charioteer.'

Sticking close behind Quill, Six Kills threw obstacles in the path of pursuers. She overturned chopping tables, pulled down stacked cages of chickens, kicked over cauldrons of steaming noodles and slung pots and pans. Servants, yelping and screaming, retreated. Twice, small bands rushed forward, waving meat cleavers and carving knives, yelling prayers. Both times, Six Kills and Quill cut them down, guns blazing.

Ahead of her, Quill ducked through a door, and she followed. They plunged down rickety wooden stairs lit by torches set in wall brackets. Six Kills looked back, hearing angry shouts, as a squad of Tong soldiers appeared.

"Hurry!" Quill snarled.

The pair plunged around the twisting stair, descending into the earth. Soon the torches were spread farther apart, then disappeared altogether. Obviously, those traversing under the cathedral proper were expected to provide their own illumination. The only light now was that cast by Quill's flaming blade.

"Wait," Six Kills hissed. "Douse that flame!"

Quill didn't argue. He sheathed his Bowie knife, but continued moving down the stairs as fast as he dared in the dark.

"Keep them off me!" He ordered, turning a bend in the stair.

• •*

"*'Keep them off me,'*" Six Kills mimicked in cultured falsetto. "Ungrateful jackass— Oh!"

The first of the Tong soldiers barreled around the turn of the stairs at reckless speed. Six Kills shoved her lance into the man's groin. Hot blood sprayed as she ripped it free. She lunged over the fallen Tong soldier's head and thrust upward, stabbing through the knee of the following guard. He screamed and went down, leg severed at the knee joint. Six Kills pulled back and threw herself against the curve of the wall. The shield strapped to her back slapped against the stone as a Qiang spear thrust into the space where she had been. A Tong soldier tripped over his screaming brother and bunched the group up in a chaotic tangle.

A third brought his lever action Winchester carbine around. Six Kills dropped to a knee as she drew her Walker. The .44 went off like a canon, the 240-grain slug ripping into the Chinese warrior before he could work his own trigger. The bullet cored out his heart and burst from his back in an explosion of bone shards and blood.

Turning, Six Kills scrambled down the staircase. Trailing one hand along the wall as a guide, she ran the corkscrew of the staircase, stumbling when the stair ended abruptly in the pitch-blackness of a tunnel passage.

Up ahead, light from Quill's flaming blade flickered then disappeared. Six Kills fled down the gloomy hallway, eyes locked to where she'd last seen the flame. She gained the distance, lance gripped tight, dripping gore. The blade gleamed softly, glowing like subterranean lichen, returning her to the conversation with Quill.

'*That blade reeks of power like a preacher reeks of wine,*' he had noted.

'*I don't know about any magician's tricks,*' Six Kills replied, '*but I have yet to find anything it can't cut.*'

'*Where did you find it?*'

'*In the service, riding guard in trader caravan. We were hit by a tornado out on the plains. Three days we hunkered down, helpless in the storm. The fourth morning the winds fled, and we found ourselves traveling across a scoured earth. A strange fog rose and lasted for days. We found a Sioux burial ground in the mist. Of the old style, but not of my band.*

'*Some of the whites went in, looking for loot. They found nothing but withered husks and the skeleton of a giant clutching this lance. I took it so the whites would not. It has served me well since. I care not for the taboos of the Sioux. I am a Cheyenne Dog Soldier, my medicine is greater than theirs.*'

'*There is more to you than meets the eye,*' Quill said.

'*Don't be trying any of your poet's words on me, I'm no high priestess of a death cult to be wooed into bed.*'

Quill laughed. '*No, no, I guess not.*'

Stepping over the corpses of guardsmen, Six Kills darted through the doorway behind Quill. Entering a massive, domed chamber, she halted then stepped forward, cursing.

A massive bronze idol of the demonic Yen Lo Wang rose up from a marble dais across the room. It glowed scarlet from the furnace ablaze below it, the illumination casting shadows on the ladder-like structure set next to the hollow idol.

The mouth gaped wide, and Six Kills saw, with a sickening, sinking horror, the line of empty cribs at the bottom of the ascension platform.

Quill had led her into the Chamber of Divination.

The man rushed forward down the center aisle between twenty acolytes genuflecting before the massive edifice of the Yama King, Yen Lo Wang the Hungerer. Naked but for linen loin wraps and oily with sweat, their heads were shaved except for the mark of their devotion – a single braid dangling over their left ear.

Upon the dais, a sultry woman stood before the worshipers. Dark-eyed, she was topless like the men, as oily with sweat and wearing the same white-linen loin wrap. Her braid hung from the back of her shaved head in a thick coil. Face sharp, austerely stamped with aristocratic belligerence, her nipples showed taut.

When she saw Quill, her cool aloofness shattered. She screeched in outrage, bringing the throng of devotees to their feet.

"Bastard! You dare, argh— Kill him!"

The acolytes cast about for the cause of their leader's outrage.

Quill, flaming Bowie knife in hand, plunged forward, and yelled over his shoulder at the startled Six Kills. "Bar that doorway!"

Six Kills spun to close the great doors, straining at the effort until the portals boomed closed.

Bald acolytes threw themselves at Quill, stopping him halfway before the glowing idol of Yen Lo Wang and the burning eyes of Chazra. Heedless of the flaming thaumaturgy he wielded, they rushed forward, arms wind-milling blows. The enchanted Peacemaker filled his hand and he fired from the hip.

The pistol roared and spat death. Men fell, blood spouting in gouts from wounds like scarlet blossoms. His fourth shot dashed a man's brains out of his head and splashed the acolyte next to him. Still, they charged onward.

Quill was forced to hurry his shots as they converged. The last two slugs dropped the screaming men with horrid belly wounds. With no time to reload, he holstered the Colt, and used the magic-infused blade of his Bowie knife to fight on.

He cut them down with swipes of his knife, weaving a defense of flame around himself, turning like a dancer. The burned and dying screamed their agonies and above their turmoil, Chazra's anger was a tempest.

Six Kills turned toward the heavy beam of oak that fit into the brackets of red gold set in the gigantic doors. Cursing, she realized she'd never lift the massive beams without using both hands. Dropping the lance to her feet, she knelt, setting her back against the pillar-like beam.

She grunted and strained, forearms and legs bunched dense and vibrant against her bronze skin. With a grunt, Six Kills lifted the weight and shoved one end into a bracket. Her head swam from the effort, and she gasped for breath. Sucking in a lungful of furnace-tainted air, she whirled at the slap of bare feet on the dirt.

Three acolytes charged her, eyes alight with zealotry, faces twisted in indignation and righteous anger. Six Kills lunged and slammed her cestus into the face of the first man. He went down, his speed lending power to her blow. She twisted at the waist, avoiding a clumsy swing from the second man. His inertia carried him past her, and she struck him where the spine met the skull. The acolyte's execution was instantaneous.

The third man pounced, and Six Kills caught his blow on her wrist bracer before crushing his throat with a sweeping strike. She drew her Walker Colt and fired her pistol empty into the backs of the milling monks, protecting Quill as best she could. An acolyte rushed her, and she grabbed up her lance and impaled the rushing warrior.

Six Kills left her lance sticking through the dead man and spun to the door. Without conscious thought she hefted the second side of the rude crossbeam and shoved it into place.

"This is a plan? This is a plan?" she muttered.

But she was smiling.

● ●●

Quill wove among the swarming acolytes, tendrils of flame lashing. The stench of burning flesh rose on the heated air, mingling with the hot metal smell of the bronze idol.

On the dais, Chazra glared at the struggling spell-slinger in keen hatred. Her lips, sensuous and full, formed strange syllables as she uttered vile prayers. Quill felt the weight of her stare, felt power sparking like static electricity.

Unless he stopped the escalating power of his former lover, he risked being struck down. Acolytes swarmed around him, enraged and reckless. Quill struck out, blows more frantic. This was how it had been the last time, when the monks had drug him down beneath the weight of numbers and beat him nearly to death before Chazra stopped them. Saving him for her own punishment.

Panic churned beneath his surface. Chazra's punishment had been truly horrific, he could not face it again.

A primal war cry echoed inside the chamber, and Quill sensed a maelstrom of motion behind him. Acolytes flew past him, horrible wounds rent in their bodies, hot blood spraying.

Six Kills rose up, battle mad. Beneath his armor of aloof-ness, he felt something strange: gratitude. Gratitude and pride of association. Here was a companion that stood firm in the face of danger, here was someone in this city of fanatics and thieves who had his back.

"Guard me!" Quill cried. "I must keep Chazra's cantrips from us!"

• • •

"Do it!"

Six Kills shoved her way in front of Quill. Bodies piled up at her feet, and her face would bruise where hysterical worshipers had managed to break through and strike her. Their numbers fell fast, but already she heard the shouts of reinforcements at the door.

Even as Six Kills cut them down, the faithful did not waiver or flee. Her lance stuck deep in the skull of an acolyte, then twisted from her hands as the corpse fell. Quill shouted arcane words, face agonized as drops of rich blood ran from his nose.

Chazra swept her hand up and fired a double-barreled shotgun. Shimmering buckshot spat out, hurtling toward the interlopers. Finishing his incantation, Quill slashed his blazing Bowie knife before him. A strange sigil glowed in the air.

Three acolytes went down under Chazra's blast. A dozen more disappeared into the flame-shield of Quill's sigil. Six Kills stopped the final acolyte's rush with a strong hand, grasping his throat in a vice-grip.

The stunned man gagged as she smashed the cestus into his gut, doubling him over, then brought the steel-studded leather wrap straight up into his face. Six Kills dropped him like a sack of loose meat.

For a moment there was silence.

Corpses littered the room.

Bloody, Quill gazed up at Chazra. Six Kills reached over and tore her lance free of a body. Behind them, Tong soldiers put their shoulders to the doors of the Divination Chamber in futile attempts.

"You have returned, lover," Chazra said, as she slowly backed up the platform.

"How could I stay away?" Quill replied. "The memories are too sweet. You wearing my shirt in the morning. The smell of jasmine in your hair. Your acolytes pummeling me almost to death. You cursing me... how can a man resist such charms?"

"I see my curse has not finished you... yet." Chazra smirked. "But I see how you *suffer*."

Quill wiped the blood dripping from his nose. He spat, striking the mangled corpse of an acolyte. He eased the look of pain from his handsome features, and spoke a word, stilling the flame of his blade. "You owe me for more good coats and silk shirts than I care to tally at the moment, Chazra. I have come for payment."

"Fool. Steal from the Yama King? From Yen Lo Wang?" She laughed wildly. "See how he gifts those loyal to him!"

Six Kills stepped forward, raising her lance, but Quill stopped her. Chazra retreated to the top of the platform to crouch by the looming, bronze idol.

"No," Quill said. "I'll deal with her. You do as I've instructed, before the guards break the doors down."

"Coyote's dirty buttocks!" Six Kills roared. "I'll tip the statue after gutting that baby-burning bitch!"

He shook his head again, moving forward. Six Kills snarled then started for the glowing statue as Quill reached the bottom of the platform. Chazra's shriek brought them both up short.

Six Kills started at the sound. Quill stopped mid-stride. At the platform's pinnacle, Chazra fell to her knees, her body wracked in painful contortions. The knobby protrusions of her back burst into bony spines as a third breast erupted from her chest and new joints manifested on her arms and legs.

Throwing her head back, Chazra shrieked as her nose flattened and spread across her face. From her screaming mouth a muzzle, dripping with spittle and filled with rows of wicked teeth pushed forward, distorting her face.

"Help us Father Sky," Six Kills gasped.

"*This* is new," Quill muttered.

"You bedded *her*?"

"She really let herself go."

The crouching, twisted figure, all claw and fang, scuttled down the platform. Eyes burning black under a jutting brow, her gaze never left Quill. Once supple skin was now leathery, scaled hide. Six Kills realized the monstrosity charging down on them was a mirror image of the idol dominating the room.

"Move, damn you!" Quill ordered.

Six Kills snapped from her horrified daze. She jumped past mounds of broken corpses and mounted the dais as Quill reached the foot of the riser. She looked towards the spell-slinger, but Quill stood calmly, waiting for the rushing monstrosity his former lover had become.

Something pulled at Six Kills, loyalty perhaps, she didn't want him to face that thing alone. Still, his instructions had been precise, his plan hung on razor margins.

She circled the idol. A huge brazier heaped with glowing coals sat recessed into the dais below the statue. The metal of the idol was fired a bright scarlet and the heat clung to her. At the back of the dais the idol nearly touched the chamber wall.

Coming up to the tight space, Six Kills threw her lance down, near to hand. The heat blazed, and sweat dripped from her as she squeezed into the cramped space. Her buffalo-hide shield scraped against the idol, protecting her from burns, and she cursed and snorted as she fought into position.

Six Kills pressed the soles of her boots into place and shoved back against the idol, her breath strangled. Gasping, her back bruised up hard against the lining of the shield.

The massive bronze edifice refused to budge.

For all she knew, it wouldn't. All she had was Quill's word the idol concealed the opening into the Reliquary of the Charioteer. Six Kills pushed the limits of her strength, but still the idol did not budge. She closed her eyes; trusted Quill. Six Kills shoved anew.

• ••

Quill stared up at the crouching evil. In an appalling show of faith-power, the high priestess had metamorphosed into the very image of her repulsive god.

Cold fear clawed his guts. Adrenaline sharpened, details around him magnified. Doors boomed under a dozen fists. Shouts of angry Tong soldiers. Six Kills cursing as she strained. He smelled the hot metal of the idol, the burnt flesh of the acolytes he'd killed. His vision filled with the image of Chazra crouching above him.

She commanded the higher ground. Her strength would be beyond human ken, and he was trapped within striking range. His hand went to his Bowie knife. Chazra drew back rubbery lips, revealing a triple row of needle-like teeth.

Quill saw the grotesque muscles of her multi-jointed limbs clench in anticipation. "You let your god ride you like *Legba*, Chazra. It will not end well." His words whispered clearly from directly behind Chazra.

The priestess spun on preternatural reflexes, one oversized claw swiping through empty air. She roared, spinning again. At the bottom of the platform, five mirror images of the spell-slinger stood in a semi-circle. The illusions were indecipherable from the real Quill.

Chazra leapt down among the illusionary images, hunting the true form of her former lover.

• ••

Six Kills struggled against the idol.

Her vision dimmed and a rushing sound filled her ears. Her muscles strained, starved for oxygen, and she struggled to breathe. Against her back the shield heated, the leather of her deerskin tunic steaming. Her back cramped under her effort while the muscles of her legs clenched in columns against the strain.

The rushing in Six Kills' ears became a feverish pitch, then sound evaporated and she was wrapped in a cocoon of impenetrable silence. The darkness at the edge of her vision contracted until her sight became little more than pinpricks. The searing heat of the statue scorched her flesh, the pain growing rabidly intense.

A small voice deep inside her submerging consciousness said, *you're dying.*

That's what warriors do, she thought with giddy ambivalence. Something inside her tore as she strained, and Six Kills pushed harder.

The idol began to tip.

* * *

Quill and Chazra danced.

They spun and struck, twirling and lashing out in a ferocity found only in ex-lovers. A ferocity that had marked their lovemaking, and now joined them in a different intimacy.

Chazra twisted, striking out with claws, snapping with monstrous jaws as illusionary figures pirouetted. Half-a-dozen flaming blades stabbed or cut towards her, but only one bit home. The figures shuffled like cards in the hands of a smooth gambler.

The priestess grew frustrated, but even as the figures danced, she saw agony mirrored on the faces of each Quill, saw blood dripping from the noses of each identical image. Quill fought hard; but the harder he fought the more rapidly he brought his own demise.

When the thing that had been Chazra spoke, it did so with two voices – hers and Yen Lo Wang's. One deep and guttural, the other Chazra's smoky alto.

"Lov-*Lover,* let-*let* me-*me* hel-*help* you-*you.* Sto-*stop* fight-*fighting,* let-*let* my-*my* pray-*prayers* heal-*heal* you-*you.*"

The swirling Quill forms milled around her while waves of heat from his enchanted weapon cut ribbons of fire through the stale air of the chamber. Suddenly the forms stumbled, hands raising to eyes as they cried out in unison. They went to one knee, then just for an instant, the false images flickered, and blood gushed like water from a culvert out of Quill's nose.

His concentration hiccupped and his spell blinked.

Chazra needed nothing else.

With the speed of hell, she struck.

* *•*

Six Kills felt the massive idol shift under her burning shoulders.

Roaring a strangled snarl of triumph, she shoved up against the red-hot idol all the harder. She felt the statue lose its center and begin toppling

Six Kills pulled an antler-horn knife from a boot sheath, and the brazier section of floor under the idol popped open. Glowing coals spilled out across the corpse-strewn floor. Flowing blood hissed, turning to steam where it met the insatiable heat of the coals.

In the strange elasticity of all traumatic moments, Six Kills looked up and watched the idol fall. She saw Chazra leap towards a crumpled Quill. Heard him screaming as if from the end of a long tunnel. He looked up as Chazra struck, his face a mask of streaming blood.

Then Chazra's bone-studded back blocked the kneeling man from Six Kill's sight. She cried out, lifting a useless, supplicating arm as the shadow of the falling idol fell across the struggling pair. The idol struck the floor hard enough to crack earth, and shards of stone flew.

Six Kills slid her knife under the buffalo hide straps, cutting herself free from the burning shield. She scooped up her lance and bounded around the idol, noting the opening in the floor.

She stopped. "You're alive."

Quill nodded.

"You look like dung."

Quill rose. "Yes, but I clean up well."

Six Kills looked at Chazra. The high priestess had resumed her own form. Her legs were pulped to a jelly beneath the idol, her skin boiled off her bones.

"Are you good?" Quill asked. "We're close now."

Despite the hurt low in her gut, Six Kills nodded. "I'm ready."

Quill sheathed his Bowie knife and made his way onto the dais. His eyes showed a light as feverish as any acolyte, and he approached the secret compartment beneath the idol like a supplicant approaching an altar.

Something in his obsessive triumphant bothered Six Kills. "Now that she's dead, are you cured?"

Quill snorted. "What? Kill the witch and the incantation goes away?"

"Sure."

"Does the building disappear when you kill the architect?"

"I don't know. I've never killed an architect."

Quill looked into the opening. A metal tunnel ran down into the dark. Set into the wall of the vertical tube was a ladder, also made of shiny, reflective metal. Quill frowned, holding a silk kerchief to his bleeding nose. He'd never seen metal worked in such a fashion. Spasms raked his body and he coughed; spat bloody waste out.

He looked up, meeting Six Kills' eyes. "If there's a cure for me, it's down there."

Six Kills just nodded before following him down the tunnel and into the darkness of the Reliquary. As she descended, she heard the Tong soldiers continue to pound the door to the main chamber.

* * *

Lying broken under the burning idol of her god, Chazra felt her soul slipping free of her body. Hatred seethed through her, powerful as any prayer. She put a finger in the ready ink of her spilling blood, and traced a series of symbols on the ground. The blood shone, illuminated by green fire, as she hissed fiercely with her last breaths. Incantation finished, Chazra laid her head down and died.

* *•*

I II III V VIII XIII XXI XXXIV LV

Quill looked up at the string of numbers etched with impossible precision into the metal of a strange, circular door. Set in the wall beside the door hung a cenotaph displaying numerals on small, individual slates.

Six Kills stared around the room in amazement. It was metal. What she saw was impossible: a room of seamless corners and doors without hinges. Around the chamber, colored lights flashed incomprehensible cadences in stations, reminding her of apothecary tables. She looked into what appeared to be windows set into the walls and tabletops, and pulled back, hissing.

The images in the glass were impossible. They showed the night sky, though the windows were set into the top of desks. Panoramas seen from the tops of mountains. They showed impossibilities.

"The medicine is bad in this place," she muttered darkly.

"That's why I came," Quill countered. He turned back to the string of numerals. "One. Three. Five. Eight. Thirteen. Twenty-one. Thirty-four. Fifty-five," Quill read to himself.

"Where's the treasure?"

"Behind this door. These numbers are a code, a key to letting me in."

"You don't have the key? We don't have all night!" Six Kills shot an apprehensive look back up the tunnel.

Quill ignored her just as he ignored the blood leaking onto his beard. He was dying, just as his lover had promised. His vision swam, he felt weakness, but also peace. He was simply too hurt to fear anymore. He thought of nights with Chazra.

Then shook himself from the memories and looked up, fighting to bring the numbers into focus.

Quill could make no sense of them. Sagging, he caught himself against the cold metal wall. He left a scarlet smear when he removed his hand. He spat more blood. Six Kills made no move to help him. She had redrawn her lance and was watching the entrance hatch intently.

"I heard something."

"Perpetual motion," Quill mumbled.

"What?"

"Limitless, self-sustained thaumaturgical energy. As the artifact works, it powers itself, yet produces a profusion of power for direction by esoteric means."

"Coyote's warty—!"

An acolyte dropped straight down the vertical tunnel and hit the floor. It rose, head lolling on a broken neck. As it shambled forward, three more bodies dropped like stones down the shaft to strike the chamber floor.

"Quill!" Six Kills yelled. "Open that door, damn your eyes!"

The Cheyenne leapt forward, stabbing with her lance. The force of her blow drove the blade deep into the thing's shoulder. She kicked the abomination clear then immediately began shoving her weapon into the others. Three more undead acolytes dropped down the shaft. Then three more. Six Kills stabbed wildly.

"Twenty-one. Thirty-four. Fifty-five..." Quill trailed off. "All magic is mathematics," he murmured.

Blood from Six Kills' back-swing splashed him. It splattered crimson across the walls. Quill heard the exertions behind him but ignored the struggle, too deeply hurt to help. He needed to open the door.

"Outsmarted by the Charioteer," he whispered. "Probably just one of many in a long line..." He looked up at the numbers. "A long line? A sequence perhaps?"

* * *

Six Kills gasped for breath, her fear simple, creeping revulsion. Let death come cleanly at the hands of a warrior, not dark-spawn abominations. Her arms tired in the face of the onslaught.

She chopped apart the attacking corpses. Piles of severed limbs stacked up around her. She was streaked in gore and her feet slipped in entrails. Her leather headband flew clear, leaving her so drenched in blood she looked painted.

More undead acolytes dropped into the chamber. They clambered forward, crazed, scrambling over the bodies of their brethren, mouths wide, teeth gnashing. Each of them stumbled forward with only the whites of their eyes showing, radiating cold like the darkness that birthed them.

Nails raked Six Kills' flesh, teeth tore into her exposed limbs. The sheer weight of their frantic, undying numbers surged forward, promising to carry her down. Hands mobilized by supernatural power grasped and rent. Six Kills' lance rose and fell. She screamed. Screamed her hurt and her horror, her anger and fear.

Quill did not answer.

Her lance caught in the spine of one just as the hands of two more snatched hold of her wrist. She struggled, slowed, and a zombie-acolyte leapt atop her, driving her down…

● ●●

"Sequence. Sequence!" Quill shouted, wild light burning in his eyes. "The sequence of al-Khwarzium, from his book of calculations, the *Hisab Al-Jabr wal Muqabalah.*"

A sequence of numbers arranged so that the next number was the sum total of the two numbers directly preceding it – the *Fibonacci* code of magicians.

"Thirty-four, fifty-five," Quill calculated. "Eighty-nine."

Frantically his fingers found the individual plates of the cenotaph. He did the calculations easily, instinctually punching the numeric code.

LXXXIX

The round door opened like a dilating eye.

On a cylindrical pedestal in the center of the room rested a strange device of vacuum tubes like Edison's new-fangled light bulbs, and a twisting sculpture of carved jade the size of a breadbox.

Quill lunged in a hypnotic daze, feeling the pulsing power of the relic. He understood that here was redemption and salvation and capability beyond his ability to comprehend. The power of gods. He reached out with shaking hands and grasped the artifact.

"Mine," he said, and was swept away.

Behind him Six Kills died.

* * *

Quill floated, alone in a motionless vortex.

The sense of space was infinite, eternal. It stretched in undulations of impossibility. The sensation was too physical to be purely esoteric. The unremitting timelessness suggested mathematics instead of philosophy. It spoke not to wispy, ethereal dreams, but to machinations articulating precisely.

Out of the dark, and that sense of boundless space, a streak of light rushed, hurtling towards the floating Quill. He felt no apprehension. The power of all those distant suns surged through the device he clutched.

The light formed into shape out of blinding motion and Quill beheld a giant mounted in a horseless chariot. The godling was huge compared to Quill, yet remained insignificant in the face of the teeming eternity around them. Golden skinned, he was magnificently formed. His beard reached his chest in a braided cone. He wore only a golden loincloth, folded under angular hips, and sandals strapped to the knee.

You possess my Reliquary.

"You are the Charioteer. Bastard son of Vishnu," Quill marveled. "Have you come to take this relic back from me?"

No.

Quill looked up into the eyes of the godling and beheld neither pupil nor iris but galaxies spinning. When the Charioteer spoke, his mouth revealed the same. A feeling of crushing insignificance hammered into Quill.

I have moved past such capabilities into a realm of understanding at once far more powerful than you could comprehend, but also more limited than you would believe possible in one such as myself.

"Or as obtusely cryptic?"

I may only reclaim what you choose to relinquish.

"Why do that, on the edge of my triumph?"

To save the woman.

"Six Kills? What? What of her?"

Her soul teeters on the edge of darkness, the Final Crossing imminent.

"What matters a mercenary to me? She was paid, she knew the risks." Quill's voice was hollow even to his own ears. It surprised him.

Don't lie to me, mortal, or to yourself.

"The energy of perpetual motion is surely powerful enough to reverse her condition."

The power that drives that improbable engine is much closer to that of irony than to the vigor of any locomotion. Suffice to say, upstart, you must choose: either the power of my Reliquary, or the life of your friend. Such things are the province of Godhood. You could certainly deny her death, reanimate her in the manner the Yama King has raised his acolytes. But her, *but* she, *would remain in the Outer Darkness.*

"What of my curse?" Quill demanded, avoiding the choice.

Already you are hale. Know this, Yen Lo Wang hates you now and forever, priest-slayer. But the curse of Yen Lo Wang's manikin is muted already by the power of my Reliquary.

Now, how do you choose?

Quill was silent.

He saw all the nations of man spread out under his boot in a vast tableau. He saw the wealth of empires pour into his coffers. The wisdom and power of epochs submissive beneath his fingertips. The pinnacle of white society forced to accept him.

He saw the broken body of a dead native warrior, peaceful now in her repose.

What was the scout to him? A woman he barely knew. What was loyalty to a retainer bought and paid for, compared to the greatest source of power in the world? What matter some warrior-woman he'd never bed?

This stopped Quill.

Stopped his chain of logic in some manner he could not fully decipher. Why was it important that he couldn't bed her? What juxtaposition of understanding and feeling could lead him to such questioning? She was his equal, a partner worthy of loyalty and not an emotionally disposable vessel to be forgotten.

Quill rejected the introspection needed to determine why such a theology would have been rooted in his psyche. All he knew was that Six Kills was no Chazra, and he would not betray her.

"Take back your entrails, Charioteer," Quill said. "I am a rogue. A liar and a thief. A seducer of innocents and a robber of graves. But I am not that. Save the woman."

So be it.

* * *

Quill drew the Peacekeeper and fanned the hammer, his violent incantation spinning out a scythe of force, sweeping the undead from Six Kills' prostrate body. The enchanted bullets blew them aside like chaff on the wind.

Power welled up, flowing through his hands and out into the gun, and he felt *only* the passing of that power. Whatever had poisoned him was gone, as the Charioteer had promised.

Six Kills gasped as he moved forward. She struggled to her feet, face white as linen. He stepped to her side and put a hand under her arm, steadying her. Six Kills looked at him, some strange emotion crossing her face.

She looked to the mangled bodies of the acolytes. Random jaws still snapped, and hands grasped, but the force of Quill's spell had rendered them ineffectual. Six Kills gave no indication she understood what had happened to her.

"I thought I would end up dancing with the Sky Father there."

"You almost did," Quill admitted.

"You're healed?"

"So it appears."

"Your prize?"

"It seems I have it."

"Good. Now, how the hell are we getting out of here?"

• •*

The doors to the Divination Chamber burst open and the temple guard spilled in. They came to a stop, Qiang lances raised, just beyond the entrance. To a man, the faithful stood in shock and disbelief. Eyes wide with denial, they took in the blasphemous horror. The mouth of the Tong warlord worked, but no sound emerged. His pistol trembled in his hand.

The chamber was an abattoir.

Blood lay smeared in huge stripes across the floor or stood in thick pools. But where were the dead? Here or there a limb or entrails, but the bodies were gone. The huge effigy of the great Yama King lay overturned like an empty whiskey bottle. Worst of all, the broken corpse of their priestess was pinned beneath the idol of the Hungerer.

Quill stood before them, eyes burning and blade flaming naked. His clothes were splattered with blood.

"Kill the blasphemer!" the warlord screamed.

The Tong soldiers surged forward, the instinct to obey stronger than the iconoclastic horror before them. A sound like rushing wind filled the chamber though not the slightest breeze stirred. Green lightning arched in brilliant cables from Quill's pistol.

Bolts of energy struck the group with devastating power.

Lightning burrowed deep into the guardsmen, punching

easily through flesh. Light arched back and forth to the bodies of the men nearest those struck head on and they too convulsed in agony. Once again, the stink of burning flesh filled the Divination Chamber.

Men screamed through tightly clenched teeth.

Quill dropped his hand, lowering the Peacemaker, panting as if he had sprinted a race, and the light evaporated instantly. Men dropped from the formation like stalks of wheat beneath a plow. The warlord's face looked like the side of a well-used candle and the flesh of his hand had melted into his pistol handle.

Six Kills went to work.

Leaping in from the side, her lance struck in a whirling tattoo. The blows cut from every angle as she drove into the survivors. Half were down before the cohort recognized the threat. A guard in the rear sobbed and ran.

His flight was like a dam suddenly breaking and the rest of the guardsmen followed.

Bloodlust raced through Six Kills.

She buried her lance in unguarded backs as men scrambled over each other in flight. No guard stood to provide a defense for his brothers. Here were killers, and deadly good.

The guardsmen of Yen Lo Wang ran.

"Enough, Six Kills!"

His voice broke her savage revere. She turned to the spell-slinger. Quill noted, again, the faint bluish tinge to the air around her bloody lance blade. Her face ran scarlet with the blood of her foes. Flesh clung to her blade like bits of wet parchment.

She was smiling. "Are we done then?"

"I have what I came for," Quill repeated. His voice sounded strange, even to himself.

"It's your money." Six Kills shrugged. "Can't you just throw a frog leg down and whisk us out of here?"

"I'm afraid not."

"Even with Chazra's curse gone?"

Six Kills sounded skeptical, as if she suspected Quill of loitering, aimless. "Look, you weren't complaining when I swept the dead acolytes off you, or burned the guardsmen!"

"Well, yes. You were doing *something* then."

"Of all the ungrateful...You knuckle dragging—"

"No time for pillow talk, spell-slinger," Six Kills interrupted. "Follow me."

Quill worked his mouth, nearly choking on his curses. Finally he spat. He looked back at the broken corpse of Chazra, and followed Six Kills from the chamber.

Thanks for reading *SNAFU: Dead or Alive*. We hope you've enjoyed it as much as we did putting it together.

Please consider leaving us a review if (and anywhere) you see fit. Any and all reviews are gratefully accepted.

If you have any questions, or want to quote from the book, please contact us at any time via our website contact page.

I would ask please, if you DO review online, send a link to Geoff via editor@cohesionpress.com or via our Facebook page messaging system. If you review for a magazine or paper, let us know and we'll buy it.

Thank you.

+ + +

Geoff Brown - Director, Cohesion Press.
Mayday Hills Asylum
Beechworth, Australia

Amanda J Spedding - Editor-in-chief, Cohesion Press
Sydney, Australia